The Rising
Book One of the Painted Maidens Trilogy

By Terra Harmony

A Patchwork Press Title

Copyright 2013 by Terra Harmony

www.patchwork-press.com

Editing Team: Jessica Dall, Cathy Wathen, Kellie Sheridan, and Erica Crouch

Cover design by Keary Taylor
www.indiecoverdesigns.com

Delving into the deep was not easy. I want to send a special shout out to all of my beta-readers who read the earliest version of 'The Rising', and an especially big thank you to Kellie and Erica, the wonderful ladies of Patchwork Press. Thanks for taking the plunge with me!

Chapter One

Claws skitter over loose gravel and Serena risks a glance over her shoulder. A mass of black fur stumbles over tangled hind legs, then goes sprawling into the bushes.

"I thought you were supposed to be faster than this!" Serena yells. Her laughter floats through the air like a melody, intensified by the quick thrumming of bare feet against the ground as she sprints away.

The hulking form bursts back onto the path, a spray of sharp branches and bits of leaves coming with him. Even on all fours, its head stands as tall as Serena. Red eyes lock onto her. His animalistic growl leaves no question that he is angry. Serena looks forward, digging into the ground with her feet for a faster run. The wind rips tears from the corners of her eyes. Breath comes in short bursts. Her lungs and the gills behind her ears pulsate, working to find oxygen where they can.

The trail curves ahead, and Serena teeters on the edge of the path struggling to keep from flying off herself into the bushes. When she brushes against sharp shrubbery, shallow cuts crisscross down her scaled legs like the sting of a jellyfish, etching into her skin.

Serena breaks through the tree line onto the soft sand and slows her pace. Hot breath tingles against the back of her neck; the werewolf is close. She hadn't expected the beast to be even faster on sand.

He snaps at her, his jaw almost reaching her long, inky-black hair.

The greedy thing doesn't even wait until he has a sure kill. He swipes, tearing through armored scales on her calf, forcing Serena to stumble to her knees. Behind her, the werewolf leaps. Dropping down into a roll, she barely avoids its razor-like teeth. Sand sticks to her open wounds. Claws sink into her shoulders, and the beast rolls with her, unwilling to surrender his prey. In the split second he is on top of her, Serena manages to thrust the wolf into the air with her legs, pain shooting through her calf in protest. The werewolf yelps as he spins head over tail toward the ocean. The sharp crack of a body breaking the surface of water echoes across the beach.

Rough waves topple over fur as he struggles to regain his balance. The ocean pushes and pulls, growing in strength, as if working against the wolf.

Serena forces herself to her feet and brushes sand from the midnight blue scales along her legs and waist. Although her breath is still coming in hard bursts, she cracks another smile watching the mighty creature thrown out of his element, and into hers. Further out to sea, past the werewolf struggling in the waves, she sees more of her kind. Their eyes grow wide, pinned on the beast. Finally, her teacher emerges to usher the group away. They disappear underneath the water after Serena receives one piercing glare from the teacher whose lessons she abandoned for a little fun in The Dry.

Serena's smile disappears. *I am in so much trouble.*

The werewolf drags himself out of the water gasping for breath, weighed down by his thick matted fur.

Skirting around the creature, Serena gives him a wide berth as she walks toward the ocean. Frothy waves reach out with promises of swallowing her whole. She succumbs to their grip and sinks into familiarity. Once she is bobbing up and down with the waves, she turns to look at the werewolf.

He shakes his fur, ridding himself of the salty sea water, then scans the surf. Their eyes lock, his flaring bright red again. He turns them toward the moon, lifts his snout in the air, and howls.

Chills crawl down the back of Serena's neck, goose bumps only held at bay by the warm ocean lapping at her shoulders. Serena cringes, then flicks her freshly formed fins, spraying water onto the hound. His howl ends with a sharp yelp as he stumbles back.

Serena turns, flinging her body up before plunging down again, diving into the dark water.

Chapter Two

Past the vivid pink and blood-red coral forest and over the cliff, Serena descends into her kingdom, The Deep. Moonlight shimmering along the ocean surface fades and the water grows colder. Serena sends out a series of high frequency clicks, then stops to listen for their echo. It is mating season for the sixgill shark, and they can get aggressive. The sound comes back to her. No sharks, just a large school of salmon closer to the cliff.

Another series of clicks and buzzes leads Serena to a group of her kind; a dozen Undine maidens that make up her caste. Their scaled bodies of burgundy, bright orange, deep red, and plenty of yellows and greens are as plentiful and diverse as the corals overhanging the sea cliffs.

The maidens wait in formation; two columns of six. Without their thirteenth caste mate, they look almost flawless. The group has been together since they began school, and each year the thirteen maidens move from one caste to the next. This will be their last year of school, as most have already reached their eighteenth birthday. Soon, they will enter The Choosing and be given a permanent position in Society.

Zayla, the Caste Master, swims up and down the column, her bioluminescent hair streaming out in all directions—an agitated mess. Serena takes a deep breath and emerges from the shadows—steeling herself for Zayla's inevitable wrath. Zayla rushes forward in an efficient streamline of scales and fins, stopping just in front of Serena. The deep blue strands of Zayla's braided hair slick back tight against her skull under her own will. Scowling, the corner of her lips turn down in disapproval.

Motioning the entire column forward, Zayla blocks Serena until everyone else has gone forcing her to stay in the rear for the swim home.

Serena moves forward only after the rest of the Undine pass. Most stay within their cliques, bumping into each other in the currents. They laugh, scooping up jellyfish and flinging the stinging tentacles toward one another. Cordelia, one of the more popular caste mates, sends a jellyfish to her friend, Simone. Simone laughs, her scales flashing in bright red as she dodges the creature avoiding a stinging jolt.

Serena is forced to zigzag around the tentacles as the group moves forward. Her shoulders and arms are already scarred with faint white lines from not evading some of the jellyfish during her years in the back of the formation.

Despite the obvious hazards, the back of the line isn't so bad; there are no eyes on her. If Zayla were more astute, she would dole out a real punishment like sentencing Serena to join one of the cliques clustered in groups in the Great Hall, chattering about the upcoming Choosing, or carrying on about which male Undine in the King's Guard is worth a pairing.

The entire journey home Serena works to block out the hyper, overactive vibe of her peers, instead concentrating on the world around her. The ecosystem is far more welcoming than the Undine ever were toward Serena. It does not avert its eyes whenever she walks into the room. It doesn't stop mid-conversation when Serena is near, only to resume in hushed tones once she turns her back. Though these actions were never explained nor justified to Serena, she has long since accepted her fate as an outcast, choosing instead to focus on the world that surrounds Society.

She turns her head as she swims, emitting a series of whistles and clicks. The vibrations ruffle the scales of those ahead of her. Some glance back, annoyed, but most have learned to ignore her by now. The sounds return to Serena, and the underwater world shifts from blurry, darkened forms into sharp, focused shapes.

Rockfish loiter in and out of the kelp forest along the shore while the plants move, occasionally allowing shafts of moonlight to pierce deeper into the ocean. Where the bottom shallows out and rock changes to powdery white sand, candy-striped shrimp dart among sea anemones, immune to their sting. A brown and yellow decorated warbonnet peers out with large eyes from behind pink coral. The eel-like fish retreats as the caste column passes.

The caste moves around the northern edge of Vancouver Island, Canada and into the unrelenting Pacific currents of the strait between the mainland and the islands.

Serena's caste approaches the inconspicuous caves they call home. The currents keep most scuba diving Ungainlies away, but as they grow bolder in their underwater expeditions, the Undine have been forced into subtlety. The pillars that once stood outside the caves, along with other obvious signs of inhabitance has since come crashing down or has been chipped away.

The columned line separates—each maiden drifting off to their families as the lessons conclude for the day. Only Zayla remains, gesturing for Serena to join her.

Serena bites her lip. Punishment for her adventure today will go beyond what Zayla can administer as a Caste Master. The King's Second will have to get involved. Serena sighs. This wasn't her first unauthorized trip to The Dry, but it is certainly the first time she's been caught.

After the briefest hesitation—all that Serena dares to give— she follows Zayla's golden tail flippers.

They wind through the corridors of the rocky seabed, small holes serving as windows lining the passageway. Serena never understood it. A hole in the rock, just to stare at more rock. At the age of sixteen, when orphans are allowed to leave the orphanage for their own quarters, Serena insisted that hers be an outlying cave, as far as possible from the mainstream of the rest of the Undine. It is deemed dangerous—the location is too far from the majority of Undine to be considered secure, but the worst Serena has to endure are curious eels or squids. Besides, this far out she isn't under the constant reminder that the whole of Society prefers to avoid her. Better to save everyone the trouble.

Zayla and Serena reach the center of the underwater mountain and angle their fins to travel up. The pressure in Serena's chest decreases, just as it does before she surfaces near a beach. It is deceptive; there is no escape to the surface from inside the mountain.

The highest portion of the inner mountain is not underwater during low tide and, judging from the position of the moon when she left the surface, the tide has just begun to recede. The king will have left, retiring for the night. It is said he sustained an injury so great he is unable to take his human, the Ungainly, form. He cannot walk away from the throne, he must wait until the tide comes in to carry him away. Always refusing to be carried by the King's Guard, his reign over the Great Hall is regulated with the tide.

Serena watches as Zayla's scales sink into the smooth skin of her legs, which reveal themselves as she uncrosses them. Zayla kicks the rest of the way to the surface, Serena moving aside to dodge the fizzy bubbles amidst clumsy feet.

Zayla surfaces first, her hair losing its glow. She leaves enough scales above her skin to cover herself from knee to neck. More scales equal more formality, and the pair are about to enter the King's Court. Here, everyone is almost fully scaled. Glittering, diamond-shaped armored plates reach up to their chins—and in some cases, even cover the sides of their faces.

One by one, the scales below Serena's knees quickly retract, copying Zayla's dress, as is customary when following a superior. The receding scales leave behind small trickles of watery blood on her legs. The maidens cross wet sand, then hard rock. The narrow entrance, chipped open by Society's ancestors several thousand years ago, leads them to the Great Hall; there are no doors here.

Unable to speak underwater, Serena expects a mouthful from her Caste Master as soon as they emerged from the deep into their caves. But Zayla continues to stride straight toward the Great Hall, eyes forward. Her silence is far more disconcerting than a lecture.

Walking under the arches of the cave, the Undine maiden's eyes adjust to what little light the shimmering minerals give off above them.

Zayla looks up and falters. Her hesitant steps almost cause Serena to walk straight into her back. Serena peers around Zayla's shoulders to find herself under the scrutinizing eyes of King Merrick.

The king's eyes flit from Serena to Zayla, who tenses for a brief second, then curtsies. Serena remains still. Behind the king stands Nerin, her hand resting on top of the throne chair. She holds the official title of King's Second and has been by his side since before Serena was born.

She bends to whisper into the king's ear. Both their eyes dart to Serena, scanning the fresh crisscrossed cuts on her legs. It is evidence of her jaunt in The Dry.

"Curtsy to the king!" Zayla hisses.

The king holds up his hand. His voice booms through the cave. "She is not in the wrong, Zayla. We are not holding formal court."

Zayla's back goes erect at the rebuke. Drops of salty water fall from the stalactites above; the hollow echo of the drops hitting water at the back of the cavern punctuate his point. Not even the King's Guard is present, and the only council member here is Zayla herself. Serena has been coming to the Great Hall her entire life, and she has not once seen it so empty. When every Undine is summoned, ninety-seven members of Society in all, they have to stand shoulder to shoulder in order to fit.

Crossing her arms, Serena rubs her own shoulders, then looks tentatively at the king.

"What brings our youngest Undine and her Caste Master here at this hour?" he asks.

Serena notices the dark circles under his eyes. It is a stark contrast to the pale skin on the rest of his face. She wonders if he has chosen to stay in his chair for more than just this moon.

Zayla clears her throat. "I wish to speak with Nerin, regarding the excursion with my caste."

Adjusting in his throne, the king looks at Zayla. His large tail fins drape over the chair and rest on the rocky ground, waiting for her to continue.

Zayla pulls her shoulders back, glancing at Serena. Her hesitation is costing her; every moment spent constructing an accusation in her head decreases the impact of the story.

Serena steps forward, partly blocking Zayla. "On our trip to The Dry, I disobeyed orders to stay with the caste and engaged with a werewolf."

Nerin's mouth drops open, and the king bangs his fist against his armrest. "A werewolf?"

They both turn to Zayla.

"Did you miscalculate the moons?" the king asks.

Zayla is forced to step to the side to be seen. "I most certainly did not," She says, pressing her lips together.

Serena has to stifle a smile at Zayla's wide eyes. Because the moon regulates Undine life, such an accusation is a low blow to Society's only teacher.

"Besides," says Zayla. "I cross-checked with Evandre."

The king and Nerin exchange a glance. Certainly the Head Scientist couldn't be wrong.

"But for whatever reason, the wolf was there," continues Zayla. "I saw it with my own eyes. And

Serena taunted him! She brought him straight to the group. I had to recede, leading the rest of the girls to safety."

The king's eyes snap to Zayla. "You left one of your students—one in the Temporal Caste, no less—to the claws of a werewolf?"

Temporal Caste. Serena wants to groan out loud at the phrase. Her entire life, this is what Serena and her classmates are to Society. The Temporal Caste: the final graduating class. They are the youngest Undine and none have been born since. The excursion was almost cancelled because the risk of losing one of the remaining generation was too great.

Zayla stumbles over an excuse. "I had…had to get the rest of the girls to safety. Away from The Dry and past the breaking waves, down to the coral."

Nerin finally steps forward. "Since when do werewolves go past the breakers? You should have sent those girls on and helped the one that actually needed you!"

Serena raises her hand.

Nerin's mouth snaps shut as they all turn their attention to her.

"This werewolf did go past the breakers," she says.

"He did?" The king leans forward, cheeks flushing.

"Yes, well, only because I threw him there. He didn't go willingly…" Serena trails off. The king's sharp blue eyes bore into her.

Before she can speak again, Zayla does. "I motion for a trial."

The words act as a shockwave, thundering through Serena's chest, blossoming heat up to her cheeks.

Zayla takes a step forward. She says it again, speaking louder. "A trial for Serena Moon-Shadow."

Serena shivers as her full name echoes across the cavern. It sounds odd, foreign almost. There are no other Moon-Shadows in Society. She is an orphan; the Moon-Shadow name is hardly ever spoken.

"Charges?" asks the king.

"Absconding."

The charges roar through Serena's head. Absconding; leaving the borders of Society without permission and interfering where the Undine do not belong. The crime puts all of Society at risk, and it is punishable by death in the most extreme cases.

Nerin gives a nervous laugh and licks her lips. "I hardly think—"

"I have proof of other instances," interrupts Zayla.

Serena watches the king lean back in his chair. His fingers stroke the end of his bronze armrest. The metal is etched with designs from the ancients. The same drawings, only on a much grander scale, once graced the pillars outside their caves. Swirling designs and short phrases in the ancient language depict a bustling empire of Undine life. Now the only evidence of such life rests underneath the heavy arms of the king.

No one speaks while he thinks, and it gives Serena the chance to get her own pulse under control. She slows her ragged breathing down, keeping it in time to the echoes of dripping water.

The king comes to a decision. "Charges must be announced during Assembly. In two moons, we hold another. You can bring the motion then—if you still feel you must." His words are short and clipped as he glares at Zayla.

She shrinks back. "Yes...my king." She curtsies, keeping shaking hands clasped behind her back.

Eyes wide, Serena remains still. Despite the blood thundering through her veins, she can't bring herself to move. *Absconding.* The accusation is a betrayal by her own Caste Master, the woman who has taught her since she was a young calfling.

The king waves his hand, and Zayla turns to leave. When Serena doesn't follow, Zayla puts a hand on her arm and pulls. The Caste Master's touch burns. Serena yanks her arm free, making it clear she can see herself out of the Great Hall.

"Zayla..." calls Nerin, interrupting the escalating exchange. "Serena is not to return to her caste for the time being. As you are the accuser, it would be a conflict of interest."

Zayla nods, her eyes flitting over Serena. Serena pauses a second longer, forcing herself to look away from Zayla. Instead, she looks at the king. His forehead is creased, and Serena can't tell if it is from anger or worry. His fingers no longer stroke the armrest, but he grips it tight, his knuckles white. Turning, Serena follows Zayla out the door.

Chapter Three

Turning down one of the closest corridors to the Great Hall, Zayla heads toward her cave. She won't have to go far—the higher the standing in Society, the closer to the Great Hall your cave resides. Greedy eyes watch the comings and goings of King Merrick, and are the first to hear any news.

"Twenty years, Serena. Twenty years I've taught—twelve with you—and never has a student shown such disregard for my rules, for the safety of her own caste mates, and for the well-being of the whole of Society for that matter!" Zayla does not look over her shoulder at Serena as she talks. Nor does she mention Serena's safety, or why she even did it in the first place. "Thirteen left." Zayla shakes her head. "I used to have hundreds of students, and now there are only thirteen of you."

The hallway splits. In one direction the water is ankle deep and still rising. The other direction is dry; even high tide won't touch most of it. Zayla pauses, her hands in tight fists by her side.

"Apologies, Caste Master," mumbles Serena. "I would never intend for harm to come to you or my caste mates."

"As the last and final graduating students, the Temporal Caste has proven to be difficult for me. Because of the constant attention Society gives them, they have become spoiled and bratty." Zayla's shoulders sag just a bit. It is the same action Serena has observed after classes are done each day and the caste is leaving to go home. "But not you, Serena – you were never like them."

Serena looks at Zayla, eyes wide. She has been told as much her whole life, but this is the first time it has been depicted as a good thing.

"You disappointed me today, Serena." Zayla speaks softly, but the weight of her words thunder through Serena's chest.

"As you say." Serena is barely able to squeak out the customary phrase.

The Caste Master finally turns, looking down her nose at her student. "I'll speak no more on the subject. Not until the trial, at least. Have a good night."

Watching Zayla turn down the dry, darkened corridor, Serena's nerves calm just as the glittering gold scales adorning Zayla's back blink out of sight.

Serena turns in the opposite direction and trudges through ankle deep water, following the tide to her cave. When she enters, water still covers the lower half of the room. It is so far from the Great Hall that the tide never fully recedes. In order to sleep in Ungainly form—preferable because it allows a deeper rest—Serena has to lie on a small cove carved in the wall close to the ceiling.

What few personal items she has are in a dry box, lashed down to withstand the currents that invade her space during high tide. Inside the box are several tools, a set of small knives, notebooks, a microscope, bracelets, and one necklace passed down from her mother. Serena has yet to wear any of the jewelry. As the only pieces she has left of her mom, there is no sense in risking losing them.

Serena walks past the dry box and kneels in front of a series of crab traps lining the floor at the end of the cave. Inside the traps are algae and kelp, plus a host of individual jars holding sea urchins and oysters. She bends to inspect her experiments and what little light the cave opening allows winks out.

Turning, Serena finds a dark form in the doorway. She scowls. "You're blocking my light."

The silhouette moves to the side, and a large guard with light brown scales comes into view.

"Oh, how I've missed your warm greetings," says Ervin.

Serena smiles and stands. "Hi Ervin, I'm sorry. It's been a rough day."

He scans the damaged scales on her legs and the claw marks at her shoulders. "So I see."

Serena frowns, then brings forward more scales to cover the wounds, hiding them from her former orphanage friend. Ervin was three castes ahead of her and, like Serena, he has very little to say. Their preference for each other's company grew until Ervin was selected for the King's Guard, as all males are simply due to the fact there are so few of them. Guards are on call through low tide and high, leaving very little room to participate in Society.

"What are you doing here, Ervin?" She has barely seen him since his Choosing Ceremony.

He doesn't answer, only brings his sharpened trident to attention next to his side.

"You are here to guard me?" Her eyes flash and cheeks heat.

He nods, shrugging his shoulders and relaxing his grip on his trident once again. "Nerin and the king didn't seem too happy with you."

Serena plops down next to the cages, peering in at the red and purple spiny sea urchins. "Neither was Zayla."

"Maybe not the best time to fall from their graces, right before The Choosing?" Ervin walks into the room, sitting on Serena's dry box.

She frowns. "Trust me, it wasn't very much of a fall—not when I am already viewed as so far beneath them."

Ervin stands his trident in front of him, spinning it slowly on its stem. "Tonight, with the werewolf..." he clears his throat. "Cordelia was—"

"Cordelia was safe," Serena interrupts. Her eyes snap to him. "Are you mad that I put her in danger?"

"I don't believe Zayla's accusations that the danger was imminent—for them, anyway." Ervin looks at Serena, sighing. "I'm glad you are okay, but please don't do that again."

Serena turns back to the next jar of sea urchins. This one has been exposed to elevated carbon dioxide. "I didn't know the wolves would be out tonight. The moon isn't full." She taps on the CO_2 canister, stolen from a tour group of bicyclers. Poisonous CO_2 bubbles slide from the canister into the jar.

"What are you doing?" asks Ervin.

She leans back, wrapping an arm around one knee. She points to the first jar. "This is my control group. There are plenty of eggs floating along the surface of the water."

He leans in, squinting at white specks. "Yes."

She points to the next jar. "I've elevated the CO_2 in this one. The levels are just slightly higher than that outside our caves right now."

"There are only a few eggs in that one," says Ervin.

"Exactly," says Serena. "And it's where our ecosystem is headed."

He sits up straight again, resuming the spinning of his trident. "Is this what you spend your time doing after school each day?"

She shrugs. "Sometimes I go collecting for my experiments." She turns her attention to the next set of crab traps. Oysters. "At first, it was just a hobby—something to do. But then I began to notice the coral at the outer edge of our kingdom withering away into grey skeletons. I wanted to find out why."

"And thus the hobby becomes an obsession."

Serena rolls her eyes. "We all have our obsessions, Ervin." She runs her hands down the shells of the oysters, looking for miniscule cracks or erosion, but it is difficult to tell with her naked eye. Algae growing through the square spaces in its crab trap brushes her arm, as if asking for attention. She smiles, turning to the reddish-brown plant, running her fingertip along the flat, branching arms and rounded ends. Soon she will have to select one of the trunks to expose to elevated carbon dioxide, mimicking ocean acidification. She sighs. Killing her experiments is never fun.

Ervin stands and opens the dry box, snapping Serena from her concentration. He moves aside notebooks and instruments, finally selecting a pair of tools. He turns to Serena, placing them in her open palm. "Absconding, huh?"

The word rolls around her head, crashing into and burying thoughts of her experiments. Serena turns the tools over in her hand. "The king and Nerin also weren't that happy with Zayla. Maybe they won't let her accusations go to court. Maybe they just want to dismiss Zayla's claim at the assembly in front of all of Society so no one dares bring it up again." It is a comforting thought, but the unease in the pit of her stomach doesn't lessen. It sinks like heavy rocks in soft sand.

Ervin raises an eyebrow. "In the last trial that involved absconding, the maiden was found guilty and was sentenced to death. She keeps appealing, so she is still alive, locked away in the lower caves."

"Not helpful, Ervin." Serena barely remembers the trial. It was the year of her first caste. She turns, scaling the wall to a small cove aided by a boost from Ervin. There isn't enough room to sit up, so she lays down, tools at the ready. Each night, she chisels out a little more space for her sleeping area. The monotonous work helps her process the day.

"I'll be standing guard tonight. Sleep well, Serena Moon-Shadow." Ervin turns to leave.

Serena turns on her side. "You should just talk to her, Ervin."

He pauses, shoulders almost rising up to his ears.

"Want me to talk to her for you?"

He turns, eyeing Serena over his shoulder. "Don't meddle, Serena. Leave Cordelia out of it."

She smiles, then lies flat on her back, tools at the ready. As Ervin takes his post outside her door, she begins to hammer at the rough ceiling of her cove. Bits of debris and dust fall into her space. High tide will wash them away in a few hours with help from the harsh currents that surround Vancouver Island. They not only keep the Undine safe from Ungainly divers, but they also polish and smooth the rock that cradles Serena in her sleep.

Maintaining her Ungainly legs, Serena brings forward her scales to help keep her warm through the night. She grits her teeth and the stinging sensation subsides. Like brushing against an anemone, the more she manipulates the scales, the less they hurt.

* * *

A few hours later, Serena wakes to water lapping at the wall just a few inches down from her sleeping cove. She stretches, knuckles and toes hitting solid rock. She rolls over, fingers brushing over rock to find her tools before they can float away. The unstoppable tide moves in, crawling into her cove and lifting her out of bed. Cold envelopes her legs and the smell of salt and bitter seaweed assaults her senses, waking Serena better than the prick of a stingray. She crosses her legs, melding them together tighter and tighter until fins are formed. Her gills emerge, and she dips into icy ocean water.

A flash of light brown scales outside her cave catches her attention and she remembers Ervin spent the night watching over her. Serena stows her tools back in the dry box, and swims through her cave opening. Not one, but two guards stand duty. Serena bows her head toward Ervin.

Instead of bowing to return the courtesy, Ervin brings his trident to attention. The three-horned, golden weapon catches a flare of sunlight filtered through the sea.

I see we have disposed of the pleasantries. The gills along Serena's neck flare.

The second guard member moves in front of her. Offering an apologetic smile, he lowers his trident instead of bringing it to attention. Narrowing her eyes, Serena crosses her arms. She finds it hard to trust someone who offers her a smile so readily, especially when offered by Second in Command to the King's Guard. With his lips slightly parted in that lingering smile, not to mention his ranking in Society, his time is surely better spent with any other maiden.

He cocks his head sideways then nods, motioning up to the surface. Serena follows reluctantly, rising just until the tops of her shoulders emerge.

"If only we could speak underwater," he says.

"Some creatures can," Serena says. "The intelligent ones, anyway." She wants to swallow her words as soon as they leave her mouth.

"Are you claiming the Painted Maidens to be…unintelligent, Serena Moon-Shadow?" His sea-green eyes twinkle like those of a playful seal.

She glances beneath the glass surface of the water, Ervin is choosing to stay below. "Why are you here, Kai Forest?"

"Kai will do just as well, Serena." He runs one hand through ash-blonde hair, water droplets clinging to the end of long tendrils.

"As you say," says Serena.

He flashes her a smile again. "What I *mean* to say is, there is no need to be so formal. I am to be one of your escorts." In a culture full of rigid ceremonies and proper traditions, Kai has a reputation for breaking the humorless, stone-faced bearing common in guard members. Serena was always intrigued by his antics, but from a distance. He makes the drab, elongated assembly sessions bearable by making faces in court—or performing an exaggerated swagger while on patrol just to elicit the smile of a brooding maiden.

"Escort me where, exactly?" Serena asks.

"Not to your Caste Master, for sure. The king said it was a conflict of interest. Ready?" he glances out at the open ocean, a flicker of a spark in his eye as though some great adventure awaits.

"No classes?" Serena manages to return the smile. "Escort away." It would do her and Zayla well to not have to see each other today.

Serena dips below the surface to follow Kai, and Ervin takes his place beside her. She keeps glancing at Ervin's fins as they swim. There are scars, more than she remembers during their time growing up. He was not very coordinated to begin with, his extra weight more often than not dragging him down. Orphaned Undine are fed well, of which Ervin took full advantage until his Choosing. Now, his frame is wider and muscles wrap around his arms, chest, and abdomen.

The awkward movement of his tail is still there. His swish to the left is slightly crooked and he has to compensate on the right just to maintain depth. The King's Guard can't change everything about him. Serena moves to his left side, swimming close. This way, Ervin is forced to keep his tail movement on that side narrow—and correct.

Serena looks at him sideways, a wry smile on her face, but Ervin keeps his eyes steady forward.

Circling the island to the remote western side that lays bare to the Pacific Ocean, Serena understands where they are headed.

The archives.

A cycle of bioluminescent glow bursts through her hair, and her fins turn jittery.

The history of the Undine is kept in a large cave carved underneath the western Canadian continent. Books, both recent and centuries old, stack the shelves, far out of reach from the salty clutches of high tide. Suddenly, Zayla's accusations don't seem so bad, if it means Serena gets to spend the next few days here.

In front of her, Kai angles for a deep and quick descent. The only entrance to the archives is a tight, constricted passageway, so narrow in places even the thinnest Undine have difficulty maneuvering their fins. Pure speed and brute force is the only way to get through; the passageway has been known to leave its mark on travelers.

Gesturing for Ervin to go next, Serena waits after he disappears into the murky tunnel. There is a chance he might get stuck and will need a push through from behind.

She counts to ten, then follows. Streamlining her scales, Serena uses a strong surge of the undercurrent to gain speed into the dark passageway. The passageway is dark, but Serena has long since memorized the intricacies of the corridor. Right shoulder up and back here, duck the head there, slow down for the sharp curve ahead. In one rare instance where space allows, Serena moves her hands in front of her, preparing to push Ervin's wedged body.

To complete the last section, Serena picks up speed. The dim glow of the inside cavern comes into view and she realizes Ervin is not stuck at all. She spreads her fins wide, but it does not slow her down in time. She bursts through the surface, emerging almost all the way to her tail. Water sprays, coating the walls and blurring the light. Serena struggles to maintain vertical balance as she bobs twice. Settling, she treads at the surface as seawater drips off the mirror that reflects sunlight through a small tunnel above, lighting the archive's entrance once again.

Ervin and Kai both stand on the ledge. They have already transformed, their scales gone, donning the required robes in order to enter the archives. The rough material scratches bare skin, but it helps absorb any excess water his body still might have.

Kai smiles down at Serena. "Show off."

Next to him, Ervin is frowning. Serena returns the scowl, then looks at Kai's legs, bare from the knee down. It is an uncommon sight in Society. She blushes, turning her head away.

"What's the matter?" Kai asks. "Never seen legs before?"

"Of course I have." Her words are short and clipped—harsher than she intended. "It's just...I've never seen *your* legs before."

Serena swims to the ledge, ready to pull herself out. She glances up at Kai and admires his creamy skin wrapped around his bulging calf muscle. A lone, crystal-clear drop of water slides down the side.

Serena looks up as Kai clears his throat. He raises an eyebrow.

Tightening her grip on the rocky ledge, Serena fights back the flush in her cheeks as she refocuses her eyes in front of her. She retracts her own scales; all of them, and feels the cold of the ocean seeping between her toes.

"Do you mind turning around?" she asks.

Bare legs are reserved for nights of the full moon, and only for members who are chosen for mating— something that has not been done in a very long time.

Ankles and calves can lead one's thoughts to what transformations take place higher, between the legs.

Serena shakes her head. She brings forth scales up and down her legs, then retracts them again. The slight pain helps to distract her thoughts.

Ervin tosses a robe over to Serena and it pools into folds of material on the damp floor. He and Kai turn around to slip on the padded boots provided for walking amongst the archives.

Pulling herself the rest of the way out, Serena's feet touch hard rock. She takes two long strides to the remaining robes and quickly slips on a dry one. She usually goes through these motions alone, so having company is uncomfortable. Turning, she ties the sash around her when she realizes Kai is staring. Her hands drop, and she slips on her own boots.

"I assume you are to escort me inside," she says, gesturing to the arched entrance.

Kai closes his mouth, nods, and leads the way.

Chapter Four

There are certain rules involved in entering the archives, many of which are unforgiving enough to deter most Undine from visiting—which is why the archives easily became Serena's second home.

All scales must be retracted. To accomplish this is a painful, tedious experience for most. Yet Serena visits so regularly that she shows her second skin almost without thought.

As they enter the large, underground cavern, Serena watches the pair of guards out of the corner of her eye. Kai's chin lifts to the impressive display of hard-backed books crawling up the wall, and his hands brush the thick columns etched with pictures of Undine history as he walks by. They hold up the crushing weight of earth and trees resting on top of the cave.

Serena reaches toward the etchings with her fingertips. They remind her of what the entire kingdom might of looked like a hundred years ago. She takes a deep breath in and can feel the muscles in her shoulders relax.

The Records Keeper, Mariam, is perched on top of a ladder leaning against one of the columns, fiddling with a mirror that reflects light over the catalogues—the most important source of light in the entire archives. The archives is a register of all the books in the Undine library, including the king's own personal library, which is set off in a restricted room.

Flickers of light shine against what few scales show on Mariam's arms. As far as Undine colors go, the deep brown shade of her scales is rather unremarkable—a phrase Miriam has used to describe her own coloring. To Serena, the shade comes across as wholesome and genuine as opposed to the flashy gold that Zayla flaunts as she accuses Serena of absconding.

"I'll be down in just a minute!" Mariam calls as the ladder wavers.

Ervin wraps his hands around the bottom rungs, steadying it while Kai continues to gaze at the books.

"How many times have you been in here?" Serena asks him.

Kai looks at her. "Enough. Why?"

Serena shrugs. "You seem to enjoy it—more than most, anyway."

"Our visits are required every tenth high tide, at minimum." Ervin interrupts, glancing at Serena. "During our rounds."

A screech from above draws all of their eyes up. Mariam has leaned too far out. Her body balances between the ladder and open air, her arms waving in tight circles. Another gasp, and the Records Keeper falls. Serena freezes to the spot, watching in horror as Mariam's robe flaps through the air. The sound of pulsating fabric grows louder as she descends, directly over Serena.

Pulled away, Serena twirls once then finds herself surrounded by strong arms, the side of her face pressing into Kai's broad chest. Behind her, the flapping material also comes to a sudden stop. She turns around, eyes wide, expecting the worst. Instead, she watches Ervin set Mariam carefully down on her feet.

"Thank you so much Ervin," Mariam says, her hands trembling. She pats his shoulder, then tugs down on her robes.

Serena takes in a shaky breath and Kai clears his throat. Realizing she has a white-knuckled grip on Kai's robe, Serena releases her grasp and smooths out the material.

"Sorry," she says.

He shakes his head once. The smile is gone from his face, but not his eyes—and he continues to look at Serena as if there is more to say.

Serena remembers herself. "I am grateful for your protection," she nods, bending her knees in a semi-curtsy.

The corners of his mouth turn down, disappointed by the formality.

"Everything okay?" A maiden steps out from the shelves of books.

"Sasha—I'd nearly forgotten you were back there," says Mariam. "I just had a little fall. The longer I am out of water, the clumsier I get. If Ervin hadn't been here, we'd be in need of a new Records Keeper sooner than I thought." Mariam winks at Serena.

Serena crosses her arms. *She almost fell to her death, and she is already joking about it.*

"What were you doing up there?" Sasha asks as she moves to help Ervin straighten the ladder. Recognizable by her bright orange scales, Sasha Sunbeam—along with her sister and mother— are the only maidens to sport the vibrant color.

Serena looks up, walking over to the pair. "Plants sometimes grow over the holes, blocking out the sunlight."

Ervin stares up into the ceiling. "How do you get rid of them?"

Serena and Mariam exchange a glance, eyebrows raised. Neither wanting to reveal that Serena often makes trips into The Dry just to clear out plants.

"Oh, these things usually work themselves out," says Mariam. "We'll have to endure a few days of low light." She makes a pointed glance at Serena.

Though Ervin misses the exchange, Serena isn't sure that Sasha did.

Serena will have to make another trip soon. Hopefully this time without werewolf interference or any unwanted Undine onlookers—Serena isn't sure which is worse.

"Anyway, Sasha arrived with instructions from your Caste Master." Mariam motions to a table stacked with books.

"In lieu of lessons for the day…" Sasha says, trailing off. "Sorry."

"She is giving me homework?" Serena walks over and runs her finger down the spines. This isn't the first time the hard covers have been under her touch. Werewolves. They are some of the least decorative volumes in the archives, as if the ancients were trying to disgrace the species through deprivation of jewels and elaborate etchings. "Is this my punishment?" she asks.

"Punishment for what happened at our excursion?" Sasha asks, coming up alongside Serena.

Serena looks at Sasha, one of her caste mates, out of the corner of her eye. Amidst a caste that only ever displayed indifference to Serena, at least Sasha was kind, always making sure to greet Serena before the lessons began.

"Yes," Serena mumbles. "The king was not happy."

Mariam shrugs. "I don't see how it can be a punishment. You've already read—"

"Enough to know this will take quite some time to finish." Serena cuts off Mariam, looking over her shoulder at Ervin and Kai who are inspecting the ladder. She motions to the hole of depleted sunlight, and Mariam nods back.

If Serena can sneak out without catching the attention of the guards, she can fix the hole and be back before they notice.

"In fact," Serena says in a louder voice, "this will probably take me most of the next high tide to complete."

Ervin finally catches on, his shoulders sagging. "Whose punishment is this, anyway?"

"Oh, it won't be so bad," Mariam says. She hands Serena a leather strip to bind a stack of books together. "You can brush up on the history of the King's Guard while you wait."

Serena smiles to herself as Ervin groans. She's been through those books, too—directly after Ervin was chosen for guard duty. Very dry reading, for any of the Undine.

Kai walks over to Ervin and pats his shoulder once. "Good luck with that."

"You're not staying?" Serena and Ervin ask together, both looking at Kai.

Kai looks at Serena, surprise lighting his face. "I was just tasked with making sure you got to the archives—Ervin can take it from here."

Ervin crosses his arms, leaning toward Serena as they watch Kai leave. "I told them you wouldn't cause any problems getting to the archives," Ervin says. "But it might take the entire King's Guard to get you to leave."

Serena smiles up at her friend, nudging him in the arm. "I'll take being the subject of conversation between guard members as a compliment."

"Don't flatter yourself," Ervin tilts his head toward her, his demeanor more relaxed now that the Second in Command isn't around.

"Oh trust me," says Serena. "I don't." She walks over to Mariam's table, chooses five books and lashes them together. Looking from Ervin to Mariam, Serena ties the binding around her waist.

"Some tea for Ervin?" Serena asks.

Mariam nods, trying to keep a smile off her face, and disappears to the back of the cavern. Ervin walks to the section on the King's Guard, dragging his fingertips across the book spines and pulling one out.

Serena turns her back to Ervin, scaling the wall to one of many reading coves carved into the cavern. The idea was to entice more of the Undine to the archives by making it feel like home, but the design did not have the desired effect.

Reaching her favorite spot high up on one wall, Serena shrinks back into the large space to disappear from prying eyes on the floor.

"How can I keep an eye on you if you are way up there?" Ervin shouts.

"Maybe I can help with that." Sasha's soft voice floats up to Serena. The sound of scales scratching against rock crawls closer and closer to Serena, until Sasha pokes her head over the lip of the cove. "Mind if I join you?"

"I suppose not," Serena shuffles some of her books out of the way. The coves were not meant for more than one person.

Sasha crawls all the way in, lowering her voice to a whisper. "I thought I could turn pages and make some noise, you know, if you need to…exit, for a moment."

Serena risks a glance over the ledge. "You wouldn't tell?"

Shrugging, Sasha pulls her knees up to her chest and smiles. "Who would I tell?"

The smell of jasmine and chamomile drift upward—another treasure found above seas, and another secret kept between Serena and Mariam.

"Here we are," says Mariam, walking toward Ervin with a full mug of steeping tea. "It'll keep you awake and alert."

Serena catches the half-smile on Mariam's face. In fact, it will do the opposite, as sensitive as Undine are to herbs grown in The Dry.

"The tea should put him to asleep," Serena whispers to Sasha. "But it might be helpful if you were up here making noise should he wake before I return."

The maidens hear Ervin suck in his first sip. They look at each other, pressing their lips tight to keep from giggling.

"It's pretty good. You want some up there?" Ervin asks, his loud voice echoing in the otherwise quiet archives.

Serena puts one finger over her lips, signaling Sasha not to answer.

"Oh, Serena will be too absorbed in her books by now," Mariam responds from her place at the catalogues. "Always is. And Sasha—I always thought her hard of hearing, that girl."

Serena lies down on her stomach, spreading the first book open. Sasha does the same on the other side of the book.

"We'll have to wait until the tea takes effect," whispers Serena. "Don't you have to go back to the caste?"

Wriggling into the hard rock, Sasha shrugs. "I'll just tell Zayla I got held up on a task for Mariam— which isn't a complete lie."

A small pang of jealousy runs through Serena's chest. The beloved maidens of the Sunbeam family never get in trouble.

Ignoring it because Sasha has never been anything but nice to Serena, the maidens bend their heads over the book, Serena tilting it so Sasha doesn't have to read upside down. The first chapter tells of the history between werewolves and Undine.

"I can't believe we created them," says Sasha.

Serena turns the page. "We needed the protection."

Undine must go on land during the full moon in Ungainly form to conceive and then to give birth to their young. Mostly clumsy and unused to Ungainly bodies, the Undine needed protection from creatures that patrol the forest and from humans. Though male Undine are of course required to go on land the first time, to conceive, traditionally they do not accompany their mates during labor.

"Especially on the birthing nights."

"Like the Maiden's Massacre." Right as the words finish forming on her lips, Sasha covers her hand over her mouth. "I'm sorry," she says through her fingers. "I didn't mean to bring that up."

Serena tries forcing a smile. "It's okay. It's not like I remember it."

During a birthing night, when Serena's own mother was in labor with her, the werewolves revolted. A chaotic blood bath under the full moon ensued. Serena runs her fingers over the scratchy pages in the history book.

"They say it was over quick," says Serena.

Up and down the beach, werewolves slaughtered maidens and their babies, fresh from the womb. The king himself emerged to the cries of his dying wife, along with a score of guards and Serena's own father, or so she was told. The Undine were wholly unprepared for the uprising. The king's wife passed to the afterlife in her husband's arms. Turning in rage at the werewolves, the king engaged in a fight that left him eternally debilitated. The only Undine to return alive was Serena, in the arms of the king, as he crawled back to the waves.

"They say that as the bodies of the dead were burning as an offering to the armory fires, including that of the queen and her newborn son, plus my own mother and father, I was swaddled and sleeping in my orphanage cradle." Serena doesn't bother to hide the bitter tone to her voice. "It's no wonder most maidens don't like me. It should have been the queen, or at least her son that returned—not me."

Playing with the frayed edges of the hard-backed book, Sasha leans her head against one hand. "Maybe the fact that it was you who returned in the arms of the king is what sets you apart from other maidens.

It's not that you are disliked—it's just from day one, you have been on another level."

"What do you mean?" asks Serena.

Sasha shrugs, a concentrated frown on her face. "Growing up, whenever I was talking about our caste with my mother and your name came up, she changes the subject abruptly. Based on the same reaction I get from our other caste mates when you are mentioned, their mothers did the same. Discussing you is as forbidden as discussing personal habits of the king—even though it has never been decreed."

Serena stares at Sasha, trying to process this new information. Looking intently at the words in the open book in front of them, Sasha avoids Serena's gaze.

"So why talk to me now?" asks Serena.

Sasha smiles, finally meeting her gaze. "Probably because I am not supposed to."

Sasha's smile is as bright at the sun, and it is almost impossible not to return the gesture.

"Come on," says Sasha. "Let's concentrate on more important things. Like The Choosing. I'm hoping for garden duty—what about you?"

"I don't know," Serena peeks over the ledge at Mariam. "I love being in the archives, and Mariam told the council she needs a new assistant. The match just makes sense, especially since no one else will be pining after the job."

"Yeah but the council isn't always known for making sense," says Sasha. "But what else could they possibly assign to you?"

Serena shrugs, turning the page of the book. A vivid drawing of a werewolf standing over a dead maiden in Ungainly form covers the entire page. The wolf is almost twice her size, shoulders bulking with muscle. Yellow saliva drips from the beast's fangs into an open gash in the maiden's neck. A pool of her own blood seeps onto the ground beside her, and the wolf's curved claws rest in the thick, crimson puddle.

"Well if that isn't a foretelling..." Sasha mumbles.

Serena's eyes snap to hers.

"Sorry," says Sasha.

Taking a deep breath in, Serena squeezes her eyes shut and closes the book.

A clatter below startles the maidens, and they peek over the ledge. Mariam has dropped her own mug but instead of cleaning up the mess, she is watching Ervin for signs of movement. He is already face down on his book, arms draped over the table, his breathing slow and deep. Mariam looks up at Serena and nods.

Laying her hand on Serena's shoulder, Sasha leans toward Serena. "I'll help cover, and I promise I won't tell."

Serena raises an eyebrow. Kind or not, how does she know she can trust this maiden?

"Let me do this one thing for you," Sasha whispers. "Consider it a...Choosing gift."

Relenting, Serena smiles. "Thank you, Sasha." She scales down the wall, padded boots hitting the ground with a light thud.

Mariam turns as Serena passes, mouthing the words, 'be careful'.

'Always am', Serena mouths back, with a light pat on the back of Mariam's shoulder.

Serena leaves the archives, diving back into the water to navigate the entrance tunnel. When she reaches the surface, bobbing on the west side of

Vancouver Island, the sun is sinking into the ocean. Already, she can spot the outline of the moon behind her. It is waning, and though it may look the part of a full moon there will be no werewolves tonight…hopefully. Though her history lessons have taught that werewolves can only change on a full moon, the werewolf that chased her was no mirage.

Normally, the shadows cast by seagulls skimming the waves for their dinner hides Serena as she moves in closer to shore undetected. This evening, though, the skies are as deserted as the thin strip of beach. A light rain falls and thunder cracks in the distance.

Serena disappears below the water, resurfacing down the stream. The beach, for the most part, is off the Ungainly-beaten path. Only those with a sense of adventure, or those looking for a long walk and some privacy, come here. Her eyes scan the shoreline for signs of life—Ungainly or otherwise. Werewolves aren't the only animals to inhabit these forests—grizzly bears, coyotes, and cougars all patrol the borders where Serena's world ends. But there are no creatures on the beaches tonight.

She dips down once again and appears farther up the coast. The rain falls harder now, and lightning flashes as though the sky goddess herself is giving Serena the all clear.

One powerful push and Serena is caught up in the breakers. She swims just below the whitecaps, a mirror image of a surfer gliding on a wave. One of her fins slice up, catching the feel of briny air.

All too soon, the earth below angles up to meet the sky, and the ocean disappears in a squeeze between them. Serena's smile grows wider, as it always does when she flirts with the edge of the world.

Somersaulting with the dying wave, Serena's fins brush against sand, air, sand, air. On the next flip, a cold wind scrapes against the bottom of her freshly formed feet, still raw from scales retracting in. Serena tucks her legs for one more roll then straightens them to stand. She sinks into wet sand as the remnants of a once powerful wave lick at her ankles—a desperate attempt to call her back into its clutches.

Serena moves forward, toward the moon. Another force, almost as powerful as the ocean, calls to the Undine maiden.

Chapter Five

The old-growth fir and cedar forest edges up against the ocean under a dark sky. Giant conifer and maple trees reach up from a mass of wet moss so thick the soil cannot be seen beneath it. The vivid green is reminiscent of the now extinct Palau Nephthea, or green tree coral. The delicate structure long since given into deteriorating conditions in its environment.

How long until the same happens to the forest?

Through the pools of collected rain on the ground, Serena crosses the barren beach to take cover in the trees. Pausing next to a fallen tree that still stands twice her height on its side, Serena squats, listening to make sure she is still alone and waits for the crickets to resume their symphony. One hesitant chirp sounds, beginning the chorus again. Serena runs her hand over the rough bark of the tree—dark brown amidst a backdrop of green. Compared to the diverse and complex Deep, the colors and textures here are simple. For Serena, the unadorned Dry is a much needed repose from the cacophony of Society.

Briefly, Serena considers this may be a bad idea. If she is caught, there is no doubt the king will allow a trial, and a second excursion wouldn't exactly help her case.

More chirps chime in as Serena lifts her chin to sniff the musky air, which is scented with an underlying tone of rotting vegetation. Her keen sense of smell confirms neither Ungainlies nor wet animals skulk nearby.

If I am caught and thrown in prison, thinks Serena. *I will never have the chance to help Mariam.* She can't imaging the clumsy bookkeeper wandering into The Dry herself.

Serena lifts herself up and climbs over the fallen tree. The next one is so big she has to crawl under. Picking up her pace, Serena jogs through the forest toward the hallow holes of the archives. In The Dry, her body is weighted, and the ground is wet and slippery. Running and jumping is hard work, but Serena revels in the challenge. Besides, regular visits are necessary for her sanity—shrub overgrowth or no.

When she reaches the clearing, her heart is pounding inside of her chest and the gills on her neck are in a frantic flap to suck oxygen from water that isn't there, even though she breathes through her mouth on land. The occasional teasing raindrop slicking down from the curled tresses of her black hair entice the gills to keep trying.

Undine are taught that werewolves can smell their scales. Serena is bold in retracting more of her armor, hoping to remain undetected.

Glancing up, Serena pauses to look at the small, circular break in trees directly above the archives, letting the rain wash over her face. The limitless sky above is liberating. It seems to have no boundaries, unlike the constricting borders of the Undine kingdom.

Taking a deep breath, Serena directs her attention back to the ground. Stepping around several holes, she repeats the layout to herself as though she is in a naval minefield.

"Move to the right—that one opens just above my reading cove. Leap over the hole for the coral section," she whispers.

Finally, Serena approaches the chasm above the catalogues. She squats down, feeling the overgrown fern while she keeps her eyes up. Her fingers hit fresh, loose soil. She brings a handful to her face and inhales.

Recently planted…

Her eyes grow wide and her heart stills. She fights back the scales trying to force their way forward—armor that responds to a perceived threat. Her eyes dart around, searching the tree line for signs of movement, but sheets of rain distort her view.

The sky is no longer liberating. It bears down on her, creating more pressure than the ocean deep. The stars are bright pinpoints of light, threatening to sear straight into her bones. Serena hunches her shoulders, craving the safety of her sleeping cove. Out here she is too vulnerable, too exposed.

On her left, a small branch gives way to the weight of water collecting in pools on top and falls to the ground. She expands her senses, automatically sending out the echolocation signals. They work so well underwater, but here the sound doesn't travel as far, and it bounces back full of distortion. Serena can't help but think of Ervin, her temporary guard, asleep just below her. He is so close, yet worlds away.

A bush shakes on her right. She turns her head, squinting into the dark shrubbery and twisting branches. Her heart pounds furiously against her ribcage, like driftwood caught between a strong current and the rocky shore.

Eyes steadfast on the bushes, she feels the ground for the plant that has been blocking sunlight to the archives, grabbing it by its roots. She tugs it loose, losing her balance as it springs out of the ground. Regaining her center, Serena sprints for the tree line, away from the noise. Heading for a dense grove, she jumps into thick plant life.

Is that a growl? she asks herself, straining to hear the sound again—the noise is difficult to discern amidst the thundering rain.

I know these woods better than any Undine, Serena thinks. But as she runs through the trees, sharp branches lash out at her, slowing her down. Her foot lands in a patch of thick moss, sinking in. Stumbling out of it, she grows less confident. Pushing hard for the tree ahead, Serena grits her teeth and squeezes the plant in her hands. A few feet away, she leaps, catching onto the lower branch. Her legs swing forward and she uses the momentum to kip up, pushing her upper body above the branch. She steadies herself, pulling up one leg, then the other. As her last foot scrapes against rough bark she feels a whoosh of wind just below her toes, like something is attempting to grab at her feet.

A paw?!

She wavers on the branch, feet gripping it as her arms wave in wide circles, trying to maintain her balance. A vision of the blood-covered maiden, dead under glowing, red wolf eyes assaults her as Serena hunches under the chills that brush her shoulders. Pivoting on the balls of her feet, she steadies herself, backing up against the firm trunk. She throws her arms behind her, wrapping them around the tree, and peers over the branch below.

There is nothing.

Just soggy ground.

Her eyes flutter closed.

Serena breathes hard and leans her head back against the tree. It could all be her imagination, but she doesn't want to risk crawling down out of the tree. Neither does she want to risk waiting out the night and being caught at sunrise by an Ungainly hiking through the forest. Serena squats down on the large branch and crawls forward, studying the ground. It is blurry from so high up and the dark soil blends in with the even darker shadows of plants. Harsh rain gives way to a soft dribble.

Serena closes her eyes, picturing where she is and where she needs to go. The wolfsbane flower patch is straight ahead, the ocean to the rear. Either one would mean safety if creatures are patrolling the forest tonight.

The plant she still holds is crushed, caught between her hand and the branch when she climbed up. She throws it up and away from where she stands. When it lands, there is a quick scuffle and the bushes rattle. Serena scans them for a pair of red eyes.

Silence.

Seconds pass, stretching into minutes. Serena's heart resumes a steady beat, keeping time to the crash of waves in the distance. Above, a flock of birds take flight, causing bits of leaves to flutter down from the upper canopy. A smile tugs at the corner of Serena's mouth.

Numerous branches twist and turn, providing steady footholds that guide Serena up the massive trunk, easing her higher into the sky. She seeks out a strong branch on the next tree over and leaps to it before she has a chance to talk herself out of it. The air is as fresh and crisp as when the currents surge and shift. She lands hard in the next tree, gripping the trunk so she doesn't fall.

Serena makes her way to the other side of the tree and leaps again, arching into the sky, the pull of the moon fighting against gravity to keep her airborne. The Earth wins, and Serena sails back down. This time, her feet slip and she doesn't get her arms out fast enough to catch herself. She falls to the branch below, and it cracks beneath her weight and Serena is in free fall.

Scales emerge on her back, up her neck, and even on her scalp, protecting her fragile bones from several hard hits against the tree. Finally, one branch holds and Serena has a chance to catch her footing. Realizing how close she is to the ground, Serena scrambles up the tree again, out of the reach of any potential predators lurking below. There's no use in becoming immortalized as a dead maiden between the pages of a book.

Back on track, Serena thinks, hearing the sound of the ocean growing louder. *Just a few more.*

Her hands shake knowing the next leap will be the hardest—needing enough momentum to take it with her straight into the sea. She backs up to the trunk, bends her knees slightly, and runs with sure, steady steps.

Another leap. No longer concerned with the moon or the waves, Serena's eyes lock on the landing branch. It bows under her weight, but she is already moving across it. Leap, arc, land. A flutter of feet. She can't distinguish sounds on the ground from the noise she is making in the air.

Leap and arc. This time the waves appear between the trunks of the trees. Land. One more tree to traverse. There is no arc with the next jump. She aims for a lower branch, preparing for her descent to the ground. Adrenaline pushes her across the final tree and in a flash her bare feet hit powdery sand.

Serena urges her tired body on. If there was anything in the forest tonight, she made more than enough noise to attract its attention. Scores of scales emerge along her legs, driven by sheer terror coursing through her veins. Between her thighs the scales grab onto each other forcing her legs to mold into a tail. Her stride constrained, Serena stumbles and falls forward into the shallow reach of the ocean, her body already completing the transformation, instinct overtaking necessity.

Her hands scramble, trying to pull her fins forward but only coming up with useless clumps of disintegrating sand. Out of choices, Serena opens her mouth and sings, pleading for help. The sea answers, building momentum for a strong swell. Her tail gives wild flops and her voice grows louder—more urgent. When the wave reaches her, she is all but blind with fear.

She curls into a fetal position as the water crashes over. When the ocean retreats, Serena goes with it, her fins leaving faint marks imprinted into the sand that disappear with the next wave.

Chapter Six

"Are you okay?" Mariam asks, intercepting Serena with a hug.

Closing her eyes, Serena tries concentrating on something peaceful, like pink waves at sundown. Her shaking body calms as it sheds the last of the salty ocean water, dripping from underneath her robe. "I'm fine, Mariam," Serena mumbles. "Now."

Mariam squeezes tighter and Serena's eyes wander up to the reading cove. Sasha peeks out over the edge and waves.

A chair moves, squeaking against the rough floor, sending Sasha back into the cove.

Mariam and Serena pull apart.

Standing from the table, Ervin stretches and lets out a loud yawn. He rubs sleep from his eyes, then freezes.

"I fell asleep," he announces, his voice tinged with shock.

"I'd say so," says Mariam, turning back toward her catalogues, busying herself with reorganizing the card files. "I kept an eye on Serena for you."

His eyes flit across the floor. Wet footprints leave an obvious track from the entrance.

Ervin opens his mouth to say something, but is interrupted by a messenger entering the archives.

"Word on my reassignment, I hope." Ervin crosses his arms.

"Er, no." The messenger clears his throat. "There was a distress call from The Dry."

"A call?" Ervin's arms drop to his sides. Behind him, Mariam glances at Serena. They wouldn't have heard Serena's song here in the archives.

"King Merrick has ordered assembly in the Great Hall," says the messenger.

"Two days early? Must be important." Ervin turns to Serena.

"What?" she asks.

"Why do I feel like this has something to do with you?" he asks.

Mariam clears her throat. "May I remind you she was under your watch."

"Yes, but—"

"But what?" Serena cuts off Ervin, challenging him in front of the messenger.

Ervin scratches the back of his neck. "Nothing. Come on—can't keep the king waiting."

By the time Serena, Ervin, and Mariam arrive in the main cave system, most of Society is already there, and the corridor is quickly emptying into the Great Hall. Ervin and Mariam, with Serena close behind, round a corner, almost running into another group. Kai and one other guard escort a maiden, each with a tight grasp around her upper arms.

"What happened?" Ervin asks Kai.

"She couldn't resist the call," Kai tells Ervin.

Serena glances at the maiden, who keeps her eyes downcast. "It was that alluring?" she asks.

The other guard shrugs. "She didn't even come back at the King's decree. I've never seen anyone resist his orders before. If it wasn't for Kai holding her back, she'd of been in The Dry within seconds. Werewolf fodder for sure."

Kai stares at Serena, unflinching and stone-faced. His sea-green eyes are bright, his brow furrowed.

Serena shifts on her feet. *Does he know it was my call? How could he?*

Serena looks at the maiden again, almost wanting to thank Kai for stopping her. But which is worse? Risking The Dry to answer a call, or defying the king? The penalties of Society are harsh for ignoring orders, and the punishments are always carried through without mercy. There are too few Undine left to allow anyone to jeopardize Society. Serena swallows hard as she remembers the charges that she may face, just a few moments from now.

Kai turns to Ervin. "You didn't hear the call?"

"No," Ervin snaps his heels together as he addresses his superior. His scales duplicate the pattern Kai wears down his legs, almost automatically. "We were all in the archives, where you left us..." Ervin trails off, glancing at Serena.

"As you say," Kai responds, following Ervin's gaze back to Serena.

"We mustn't keep the king waiting," Mariam says, pulling Serena toward the Great Hall. "We thank you for your service," she dismisses Kai in a formal tone.

Not one word, Mariam mouths to Serena, as they follow Ervin through the archway into the large cavern. Serena nods, stealing one last glance at the maiden being escorted to her punishment.

The trio takes a place toward the rear, backing up against the rough rock. Miriam's presence is calming, almost as much as the fact that several-hundred heads face away from Serena. Few, if any, eyes are on her.

The largest room of the kingdom is packed with the Undine. The expansive ceiling is bare, with most of the larger stalactites long since removed. Underneath it, a mob of Undine stand shoulder to shoulder. They smell as bitter as a kelp forest, the stench so thick in the air Serena could almost taste it. She watches Mariam run her tongue through her mouth in distaste.

Serena smiles to herself. Mariam loathes crowds, too.

Sasha slips through the entrance after them, her bright orange scales making it impossible for her to blend. Without looking at Serena, she joins her mother and sister in the middle of the hall. Especially when they stand together, the color of the Sunbeam family shines out like a beacon. Colors are rarely handed down from one generation to the next, though in this case orange must be a dominant shade. Serena isn't sure what coloring their father had—he was killed even before Sasha and Serena entered their first caste, in one of many battles over the years as Undine endeavor to take back their beaches.

Deep reds, pinks, silvers, golds, and occasional greens crowd the hall like corals packed onto a cliff, clamoring to reach the best nutrients. Serena's dark blue and Mariam's brown scales help them blend in to the shadows of the cliff that hangs over them. Only Ervin's scales stand out, if anything because of their modesty. They are light and dull brown, as is the same with most males, lacking the vibrant colors of Undine maidens.

In the Great Hall, bioluminescent hair of most still glows like stimulated jellyfish. The radiance smolders out as the minutes pass after they've surfaced. An almost coordinated wave of dying embers, rolling through the crowd all the way to the back. Mariam and Serena have better control over their hair than most with years of practice out of water in the hall of archives, but Ervin's hair still glows, highlighting all three of their faces.

Mariam leans forward on her toes, straining to hear the session, which has already begun. Serena doesn't have to do the same to spot Zayla, her golden scales standing out among the line of council members, waiting for her chance to call Serena to trial.

"How do we know the prints aren't from last night, when the wolf was spotted by the Temporal Caste?" Nerin stands next to King Merrick sitting on his throne, questioning a young Undine in front of them. "We know for sure tonight was not a full moon."

Her small voice doesn't reach the back of the cavern where Serena stands. Whatever she says causes the king to grimace. The council members standing off to the side whisper amongst themselves.

"Speak up, so the whole of Society can hear you," Nerin commands.

The Undine turns and Serena recognizes her as a gardening apprentice, Lilly, two castes ahead of Serena. "Part of our duty when we go to the gardens after each full moon is to record the positions of wolf prints so we can track their pack numbers and locations, then erase them before they can attract any Ungainly attention. I am sure that section of the forest was cleared of tracks."

"We'll investigate the matter and consider your request for extra guards." Nerin says, folding her hands in front of her. "Is that all?"

Lilly shakes her head then halfway turns, so all of Society may hear, remembering the last rebuke. "There was another set of footprints..." she pauses, and swallows hard. Serena can see it from all the way in the back. "Undine footprints."

A ripple of murmurs runs through the crowd. They grow to panicky whispers, murmurings of an Undine traitor and conspirator. Those who haven't mastered control of their scale pigmentation begin to involuntarily flicker new colors. Yellows and blues light up the Great Hall, as though the whole of Society seeks attention.

Serena and the friends by her side are in the shadow of a protruding cliff. Their reflective guanine crystals spaced throughout Undine skin, acting as mirrors to replicate the immediate environment, don't react, leaving them lost in one large chaotic mess of color.

Serena scans the commotion, then stops. Her eyes lock with those of the king himself. He is leaning forward in his chair, hands gripping the etched armrests, and there is no doubt he is looking at her. Almost as if she sticks out simply because she doesn't mimic the rest of Society.

Nerin breaks the impasse by stepping in front of King Merrick, arms raised to calm the crowd. When the chatter dies down, she speaks. "Are you positive? Perhaps it could have been an Ungainly."

Lilly licks her lower lip. "What little webbing remains between the toes in Ungainly form was apparent in the print."

"And do you think the print has anything to do with the call for help we heard not hours ago?"

Hidden under their cliff, Serena's eyes go wide and Ervin stands as rigid as the trident by his side. Serena tries to reign in the rush of panic flooding her veins. *No one would recognize my call—I've never done it before. And I have an alibi.* She glances at Ervin.

"I'm not sure," says Lilly, twisting her fingers together. "But I did make a caste of the print." She turns to the crowd behind her. Another maiden squeezes out, delivering a large rock into Lilly's hands. Lilly looks at the king for further instruction.

"Put it down," says the king.

When she does, there is a show of Undine popping up on their toes, peeking out from behind shoulders of those in front of them, each maiden straining to catch a glimpse.

Nerin raises her hands, and the commotion dies down. "It is a footprint, fossilized with a hardened mixture of limestone and sand," Nerin says for the benefit of those who cannot see. "The Undine webbing in between the toes is apparent."

"And how do we know these two footprints, one werewolf and one Undine, were laid side by side at the same time and not hours apart?" asks the king.

"The clovers beneath them both were just beginning to spring back up when I found them, your majesty." Lilly bows in an unnecessary curtsey.

The king clears his throat, and gestures to the footprint. "And what do you expect us to do, have every maiden measure their foot against the rock? That would take all night!"

"Apologies, your majesty. I am not expecting anything of the court."

Though it was said through meek lips and a lowered head, the king glowers at the comment.

"Well the court will certainly stand idle, if that is what you are insinuating," the king's voice bellows out at the shivering maiden.

She shakes her head, but has all but lost her voice.

"Perhaps, your majesty—I might offer a speedy solution," Zayla says, stepping out from the line of council members.

The king takes a deep breath. "As you say," he mumbles to Zayla.

Lifting her chin, Zayla steps forward again. "I call Serena Moon-Shadow. Having witnessed her return from The Dry during an unauthorized visit, I believe this footprint serves as proof of the crime of absconding."

Serena's lips tremble, and her cheeks burn.

My own teacher hates me.

"Fine," King Merrick says, his rough voice rumbling through the cave. It is a stark contrast to Zayla's smooth tone and exact articulation. "Step forward, Serena Moon-Shadow."

A murmur sweeps through Society. Heads turn, each attempting to seek out the accused. A jagged line parts down the middle of the crowd, all the way back to Serena. When she looks up, the king's stare fixes her in place, the shadows of the cliff no longer offering her protection.

He raises his hand, beckoning. Like an obedient subject, Serena steps forward. With each slow stride ahead, more murmurs die out. As she passes each Undine, scales emerge along their feet or down their arms as if they are warding off whatever ill-gotten fate Serena exudes.

The sprawling cavern closes in, pressing down on Serena's shoulders and chest, constricting her breathing. She tries imagining she is in her sleeping cove. Eyes glistening around her become the minerals of the cave walls, and solitude sets in.

Lilly and Zayla move aside as Serena steps up to the smooth, mid-platform. It raises halfway up to the king's throne, slightly higher than the rest of the ground Society stands upon.

Serena meets the eyes of the king. He seems larger than she remembers, his shoulders almost spanning the width of the throne behind him.

"If you please," Nerin nods to the rock in front of Serena.

Swallowing hard, Serena lifts her foot to the mold. The king leans forward to watch.

The ridges of the webbing between Serena's toes fall into their individual places in the mold—it is a perfect fit.

The king glances only briefly, then settles back into his throne, a smug smile on his face. "Let it be noted—"

"I object," Nerin's voice rings through the cavern.

"Oh?" says the king.

"The print is a close match, to be sure. But we cannot condemn the girl on this piece of evidence alone when there could be several other close matches among us." Nerin shoos her hand at Serena, motioning her to move away from the footprint.

Taking one step back, Serena holds her breath, holding hope that the King's Second will come to her rescue.

"And since, as the king says, it will take far too long to test every Undine, I insist we explore the only

other piece of evidence offered." Her eyes fall on
Serena. "Tonight's call."

The king breaks his composure and sighs. He rubs
at his temples.

Nerin nods, as if that is all the permission she
needs. "Serena, if you will."

The weight of a thousand eyes burn into Serena.

"Sing," Nerin commands.

Chapter Seven

Serena's stomach knots. Behind her, the audience is restless.

Why should they be anxious? It's me who has to sing.

"Will the accused please sing?" King Merrick repeats Nerin's command.

Serena licks her lips. "Why?"

A gasp and a disapproving murmur runs through the crowd. It isn't customary to question an order of the king.

He frowns, and Nerin glares at Serena.

"I apologize, your majesty. I just don't understand the importance of the call last night."

"I see." King Merrick rubs his chin. He stays silent for the count of several breakers, studying his people. When he speaks, his voice is soft. The fidgeting, hushed whispers, and other extraneous noises of a crowd subside, as everyone strains to hear.

"I think no one can deny the allure of the call that night," says the king. "Enticing as it was, several Undine gravitated toward The Dry. They would've gone right to land had I not issued a decree for an emergency assembly. Even after my order, some had trouble turning their backs to the call."

Council members nod in agreement.

King Merrick continues. "According to our Head Scientist, the surge of the surf was reportedly altered. It seems it was an extraordinary call, indeed."

Everyone leans in to hear what the king has to say.

"You can see, Serena, the power one voice can have," he gestures to the crowd. His next words are spoken much louder. "Have you had occasion to sing, Serena Moon-Shadow? Recently?"

Serena clasps her hands in front of her to keep from rubbing them along her scales. "Not really."

"What about in your caste?" asks the king.

"My caste?" Serena furrows her eyebrows.

"Oh, I don't know." The king runs a hand down his beard. "For example...your first year graduation song. Your voice was surely heard then, at least by your caste mates standing next to you."

"No, I don't think so." Serena blushes, knowing the eyes of her former Caste Master are on her. "I always stood at the back and usually just lip synched."

"Usually?" King Merrick prods.

She shifts from one foot to another. "Always, actually." Her guilt over the confession feels silly and she is sure Zayla's mouth is turned down in a disapproving frown. "I don't like the attention."

"Well," says the king. "Perhaps tonight we can take you out of the spotlight for good. But first you must walk through it." The king leans forward. "Sing."

The simple command rings throughout the Great Hall. The word keeps echoing back to Serena, each time pinning her to the spot. There is no escape from the request. Turning around to face Society, they are whispering amongst each other.

Serena sighs, resigning. She closes her eyes and opens her mouth.

The first sound to breeze past her lips is a low hum. She keeps it steady, pushing it out until she hears its echoes return. The craggy walls of the cavern come into focus behind her closed eyes. She cocks her ear. Just as with sending her echolocation signal out in the ocean, the rebound is painting a detailed picture of her surroundings. It isn't hazy and distorted like it is in The Dry, but this is a different type of signal.

Serena raises her pitch and turns her head as the next hum emerges. She puts extra breath into the notes that have to extend to reach the farthest crevices of the cavern.

What comes back is more than just sharpened features of the walls. Harmony curves around baby stalactites, so small that Undine eyes cannot yet see them. It brings back with it the scent of hardened earth, dripping with condensation. Serena feels the melody returning. She pushes it back out, adding a new layer of composition for more depth.

When she opens her eyes, Society has gone quiet and still. Many have their fingertips to their lips.

Serena lets the hum die, her eyes still scan Society. Their gazes are still glassy, as if they are expecting more.

Opening the constricting gills alongside her neck, Serena allows uninhibited air to flow. Her volume increases as she sings again, this time with a quicker beat. She adds words to the song. They are in the ancient language; Serena only understands the meaning of half of them. She knows the song from the elderly Undine, humming the tune as they string together necklaces with oyster pearls. Serena found the words in a book and spent one afternoon memorizing them.

Her song resonates throughout the Great Hall. Everything looks more beautiful with the tune. The walls shimmer with jewels and stones, accentuated by glowing Undine bioluminescent hair. Society is drawn forward by the song. Some gravitating forward, while others simply lean into the pure, sonorous ring of Serena's voice.

Serena stops singing as another sound begins to accompany her song. It is rushing water, entering the Great Hall. Within a few moments the ocean is past their ankles.

She lets the last notes die off, muted by the waves.

Silence is broken by Evandre's voice. "The tide is too early."

Serena looks at the Head Scientist, standing in the line of council members. There is no malice behind her words. It is just simple fact, and with it, Serena has been discovered. Everyone knows. The call came from Serena.

She looks behind her and sees Nerin pressing her palm to her cheek.

Beside her, the king's hands lay limp in his lap, his body gone slack. He looks up at Serena, voice cracking as he speaks. "Your mother was a great singer, too."

Nerin clears her throat.

Remembering himself, the king straightens in his chair. "Serena Moon-Shadow, you stand accused before Society, king, and council for the crime of absconding." The king's words thunder through Serena, and she has to resist taking a step back. "There are witnesses including several of your own caste mates and your Caste Master witnessing your return from The Dry. There is hard evidence of your own footprint next to the that of a werewolf, and now we have proof that your song is powerful enough to beckon Undine and tide alike. This lends to the implication that there were not one but two recent unauthorized trips to the dry."

The king's words ring through Serena's head. Gray creeps into the edges of her vision and for a moment, Serena can pretend she is in a dream.

"You have provoked the werewolves and you have put our entire civilization at risk of discovery by Ungainlies. Nerin—do you have anything to add?" asks the King, without looking at his second.

Nerin's lips purse, then she pulls them back in. "I do not."

"We will now issue a verdict without further deliberations," says the king. "Do you prefer to proceed by judge or jury?"

The question directed at her brings the scene back into sharp focus. "Jury," Serena says without hesitation.

A ripple of murmurs runs through the crowd behind her and the king's eyes grow wide. Her answer is unexpected. The council members always make up the jury, and they are never divided in their decisions. If one believes her to be guilty, and Zayla almost certainly does, they all will.

The king picks up his oversized trident, leaning against his throne, and bangs the blunt end on the ground. The crack bellows like a shockwave throughout the room and Serena takes a step back. Society goes silent.

He would condemn her anyway.

"Very well," grumbles the king. "As I appoint the jury, they will step forward with their decision. The sentencing shall be carried out directly thereafter."

Serena looks up at the king with narrowed eyes. She nods, just because there is no other way to respond.

"Zayla Star," says the king.

Serena's Caste Master, as a member of the council, is already on the mid-platform. She steps forward, curtsying to the king. Serena risks one glance at her, suddenly remembering she forgot her own curtsy. "Guilty, your majesty," she says without looking at Serena, then returns to her place in line.

The word stabs through Serena like a knife, straight into her gut. Her mouth drops open and her eyes sting.

"Murphy Air-Spirit."

The Head of the Guard and the next council member steps forward. His bow is formal, full of all the pomp and circumstance expected of the King's Guard. "Guilty, your majesty."

"Kai Forest."

The crowd parts once again, all the way to the back of the room at Kai, who has returned from delivering the first prisoner. He walks to the front, eyes on Serena the whole way. Once he is on the mid-platform, he bows. "I respectfully abstain, your majesty. I was not present as the evidence was reviewed."

"Very well, Kai Forest."

Kai glances back at Serena before taking place in the line of jurors.

"Evandre Sea-Bird," the king announces the next juror.

The Head Scientist steps forward and curtsies to the king, her scales flashing a brilliant purple. "Guilty, your majesty."

Two more join the ranks—the Head Gardener, Sarafina, and the Healer, Hailey.

Guilty.

Guilty.

Serena surveys her line of arbitrators, her knees going weak. She longs for the uplifting support of the ocean.

"Isadora Night-Shade."

Isadora hesitates, and the wait is torment.

"Just say it," Serena murmurs in a bold statement to the Undine psychic. Serena bows her head in resignation of what the verdict will be.

"Guilty," says Isadora, so soft Serena thinks she must be the only one that can hear it.

The king turns to Serena. She has been found guilty—all there is left to do is sentence her. Straightening her spine and holding her shoulders back, Serena meets the kings eyes.

His hand tightens on his trident. "I will now select an appointee to pronounce your sentencing."

In the courts of the Undine, it is usually the guilty party that selects the one who decides the punishment. It is somehow more effective this way. Friends tend to give harsher punishments lest they be seen as too lenient and suffer a mass shunning from Society. It is truly a communal justice system.

Serena speaks up, forcing her dry throat to work. "I understand that the defendant is allowed to select her own—"

The clack of his trident against rock cuts her off. His eyes are already scanning Society for his pick.

Serena's midnight blue scales flare, and this time she doesn't fight back the glow growing in her hair.

She steps forward. "I will make the selection—"

"I choose—" King Merrick tries talking over her.

Tears of anger spring to Serena's eyes. "It is my verdict, my sentencing, and I elect—"

"Nerin Thunder-Cloud," they both say in unison.

King Merrick and Serena stare at each other. His mouth twitches under his white beard, but she can't be sure why. "Very well," he manages to grumble.

All Serena can think of now is the penalty for the worst cases of absconding—death. Her heart races, and she can feel a trickle of cold seawater drip down from her hair, running in between her shoulder blades and down her spine.

But the death sentence is the very reason she chose Nerin. *Nerin the Just*, Serena has overheard many a maiden assigning the King's Second a nickname. They giggle afterward, but the title is more than true. Nerin has always been even-handed and fair.

In her heart, Serena believes her ventures into The Dry were for a good cause. She hopes Nerin does, too.

The king turns to his second, and doesn't utter a word. Stepping forward, Nerin considers Serena. She glances at the fossilized footprint and over at Zayla. Finally, she looks at the king. Whatever Nerin sees there is beyond Serena, but it seems to have made her decision.

The King's Second turns to Society, raising her voice so everyone can hear. "I decline the death penalty."

It is all Serena can do to keep from running up the five steps to the high-platform, picking Nerin up, and squeezing her until she gasps for breath. Serena peeks at Society over her shoulder. Mariam has left the cozy cove and made her way up front. She gives Serena an enthusiastic wave.

"However..." begins Nerin. Mariam's hand freezes in the air, and Serena turns back around.

"Our laws dictate that if a death penalty is declined, three separate punishments must take its place. These punishments are to be assigned and carried out within a year from now, and they will be determined by those most affected by your crime."

Serena swallows hard. *I can handle this, anything is better than the death penalty.*

"I leave one punishment to the discretion of Zayla Star," says Nerin. "For the danger you put her and your caste mates in."

Maybe not.

"You were under her charge, Serena, and disobeyed her direct orders." Nerin turns to Zayla. "May your retribution be meaningful yet stern."

It'll be stern all right. She'll either throw me in prison or exile me altogether!

Zayla nods her head, accepting the responsibility.

"As for putting the whole of Society at risk of discovery, I elect King Merrick. As our king and leader, he represents all that Serena has endangered."

King Merrick merely grunts.

"May your retribution be...objective, your majesty."

To Serena, it feels like his punishment would be exactly the opposite, so she is at least glad Nerin said it.

"And finally, I elect Isadora as one who may be able to determine the best path for Serena." The Undine psychic steps forward and nods. She is the king's sister-in-law, twin to the Queen who passed to the afterlife during the Maiden's Massacre. Her black scales glitter, giving the impression they are in constant motion, moving independently of one another.

"May your retribution be well-intentioned," says Nerin.

"As you say," Isadora nods.

Serena licks her lips. *Nothing is over yet.* They can announce their punishments at any time within the year, and the wait will be torment.

Before she can object, and before she can fully process everything that just occurred, the king speaks again. "Assembly is adjourned."

Serena feels a hand on her arm and jumps. When she looks over her shoulder, both Mariam and Ervin are standing behind her.

"Come on," Mariam whispers. "We'll accompany you home."

Serena allows them to lead her away, surprised by how quickly the rest of Society leaves the Great Hall ahead of her.

Probably before King Merrick has time to sentence anyone else, Serena thinks to herself. Though she always was proud of the fact that Society could accuse, deliberate, and sentence mostly within the span of one session, Serena is no longer impressed, and can readily point out several flaws to the system.

She allows the full length of her feet, webbing and all, to drag over the rocky ground. The passageways are empty and cold. Before the first turn, Ervin spins around on his heels, causing Serena and Mariam to stop short.

"You do realize, you aren't the only one getting in trouble for this. I was supposed to be guarding you and it was just proved in front of everyone that I shirked my duties," Ervin grumbles.

"May I remind you, guard," Mariam clips her words. "That Serena was under your charge. You are the one that fell asleep."

Ervin presses his lips together.

Mariam takes a step toward him and lowers her voice. Her scales flare a deeper brown. "Serena may not have been in the right, but neither were you."

A flash of guilt runs through Serena. Ervin did her a favor, he shouldn't be punished for it.

"I won't tell anyone, Ervin," Serena says, placing her hand on his shoulder.

Mariam narrows her eyes at Serena, her lips as tight as Ervin's.

I know she is just trying to help, but it can't be at the expense of Ervin.

Ervin shakes off Serena's hand and picks up his trident. "Come on, tide is almost in." He turns and walks away from the pair of maidens.

Serena sighs. *Somehow I've managed to piss off my only two allies just as I'm about to face my punishments.*

Chapter Eight

"Serena, wake up. Wake up!"

A rough shake at her shoulder draws Serena from her dreams. As she opens her eyes Ervin comes into focus.

"Don't you ever sleep?" Serena asks, rolling over and curling her arms into her chest.

He snorts. "Not nearly as much as you. But I guarantee no one else in your caste is sleeping right now."

"Hmm? Why?" Serena asks, pushing herself up as far as her small sleeping cove allows.

"The Choosing is today! Come on, you're going to be late."

Her eyes fly open, fully alert now. With all the absconding nonsense, she had completely forgotten about the ceremony. Once an Undine maiden reaches the age of eighteen, they are assigned a job within Society. The entire caste enters The Choosing together. Although Serena is the only one who hasn't turned eighteen, they lump her in with the caste. She wouldn't rate an entire Choosing ceremony by herself.

Serena jumps down splashing water over the recently dried walls. Ervin takes a step back.

"Are you still mad at me?" Serena asks.

Ervin shrugs. "Murphy assigned me extra rounds. I could use the extra swimming, anyway—

so we'll call it even." He glances at Serena, frowning. "You're not wearing that, are you?"

Serena looked down at her scales. They still cover her entire body, just below her neckline.

She mimics Ervin's frown. *What more is there to do?*

Serena recalls the last few Choosing ceremonies. Finally, she decides on an alteration to her scales. Dots of shiny pearl pop up, like diamonds scattered across a midnight blue sea. She lengthens the sleeves on her arms until they come to a sharp point at her middle knuckle.

Serena looks back up at Ervin with a tentative smile.

"No," he rolls his eyes. "I mean—like decorative pieces. Girls usually go all out for The Choosing."

Serena cocks her head. Hasn't he realized by now that she is unlike most girls?

Her eyes drift to her dry box. Ervin nods, encouraging her. Serena sighs and moves to the box. She opens it, rooting through her tools setting aside hammers, chisels, and screwdrivers. Next are CO_2 canisters and notebooks with two years' worth of recorded experiments. Ervin lets out an exasperated sigh when she pulls out a microscope.

"This is completely necessary for observing minuscule fissures in shells," she says. "Here," she finally announces, pulling out a small case. Two rows of white clam shells are cemented to the top. Ervin leans over her shoulder as she balances the case across her knees and releases the clasp. The contents lie flat, sliding from one side to the other.

Serena picks up the only clue to her past, her mother's bracelet and necklace, part of her personal belongings as long as she can remember. The jewelry box is far too empty for a maiden her age. Serena slips on the freshwater crystal bracelet and removes the necklace, placing the other items back in the dry box.

A large, circular jewel encased in stone hangs from a simple chain. Dark gray and black swirls make the piece appear as though it is churning in on itself—the coloring similar to Serena's scales.

"Here, let me." Ervin takes the necklace from her.

Serena stands and twists her long, black locks of hair up and out of the way so he can fasten the hook. When he steps back she lets the large jewel fall to her chest. Serena retracts a few more scales so the charm rests on smooth skin. The jewel draws attention to the cleft between her breasts. Heat crawls up her cheeks and she considers concealing herself higher again. Perhaps for the first time ever, she is self-conscience in front of Ervin.

Fidgeting with the necklace, Serena's eyes dart from his, down to the cave floor, and back again. She can feel the algae in the crab trap brush her ankles.

Say something, she thinks.

"Don't worry," he says.

She furrows her eyebrows in confusion.

He puts a hand on her shoulder and squeezes. "I mean about being in The Dry for the Choosing Ceremony. King Merrick has ordered his whole guard on the beach for protection. I'll be watching your back."

"My back?" Serena looks down at her front. It is the most effort she has ever put into her appearance.

"Yeah." Ervin smiles. "Your back." He pats her shoulder twice, hard, then turns on his heels. Behind him, Serena follows, a few more scales crawling up her chest.

* * *

Choosing ceremonies have always taken place in The Dry. Proof of one werewolf out on other than a full moon was not enough caution to postpone or change the custom. Especially this time. This Choosing is special. It is The Choosing of the Temporal Caste—the final class. Perhaps the very last Choosing of the Undine species.

Serena follows Ervin to The Choosing grounds. She doesn't swim on his left this time, allowing his awkward gait to slow him. She needs time get her nerves under control and to stop her hands from jittering.

Months ago, after a year of shadowing each of the twelve jobs Society offers, Serena and her caste mates submitted their top three choices of work. Serena's first choice was Records Keeper Assistant. She would have written it down three times if she could. Her other two choices were Orphanage Attendant and Scientist Assistant. But she was sure she would be granted her first choice, especially since Mariam has petitioned for a permanent shadow. It is a job no one else pines after.

Serena and Ervin merge with the current, letting it pull them downstream. Ever since the Maiden's Massacre, the Choosing grounds change each year for safety reasons. This year Society gathers in the traditional spot, which happens to be the same location as the Maiden's Massacre, Cliff Beach.

Ervin turns for the beach on the west side of the island, struggling for a moment to leave the current. When he does, he glances behind him as if to see if Serena caught his falter. She looks away.

When Ervin turns back around, Serena sighs, then catches up to swim on his left. Serena spots fins ahead, bobbing near the surface. There are just as many Undine here as there were at the assembly, though the population looks twice the size spread out. No one wants to miss this ceremony.

Ervin swims forward, along the edge of the crowd toward the front. When the smooth water breaks into frothy, white waves, he transforms. Scales cover his body in light-brown armor as he walks from the water with his trident to join the King's Guard.

They form a semi-circle on the beach around the Temporal Caste, facing the giant sandstone cliffs that separate one world from the next. Above them, the forest grows right to the edge of the cliff, a few trees leaning over as if they are about to be pushed off by their brethren clamoring for a spot in the sun.

Only one narrow passageway through the cliffs allows entry to the beach, and it is guarded by Murphy and Kai themselves. Kai turns slightly, catching Serena's eye. He makes a pointed glance at the moon, then gestures to his shadow stretched across the sand.

You're late, he tells her with one eyebrow raised, silently chiding her.

Serena gives an innocent shrug, then nods at Ervin. *His fault.*

Kai laughs loud enough to cause Murphy to break rank and fix his Second in Command with a hard stare. Kai salutes Murphy then turns back to the cliffs with a quick wink at Serena.

When she turns to face the ocean, she realizes the rest of her caste is standing in a line parallel to the water, scowling at her. Serena's eyes snap to the Caste

Master standing in front of them. Zayla motions with her arm, an impatient gesture for Serena to join them.

Serena takes her place at the end of the line, breathing a sigh of relief that one of her three punishments did not come before the ceremony. They could very well deny her a title, robbing her of a chance to live out the rest of her days in the archives.

Waves come and go, seeming like a lifetime before members of the crowd peel their eyes away from Serena. It's not the same as enduring the accusations of absconding at the assembly. At least there she had her back turned to the audience.

Focusing on the whale-sized boulder that juts up out of the water in the midst of the Undine congregation, everyone awaits their king. Serena herself has had enough of him. She glances at Cordelia standing beside her, who wears her revealing burgundy garb even here, at the most important ceremony of her life. Serena scans Cordelia's scales, glittering in the moonlight. She has bracelets up to each elbow, and a small tiara sits on top of a mass of blond braids. Serena brushes her hair behind one ear, wishing she'd taken the time to a least pull the strands back.

Splashing at the whale-rock draws attention and the Undine behind it move aside, making room for a large wave that is gathering momentum. The crest builds then breaks against the rock. The closest Undine resurface as the thunderous swell subsides and all eyes fall upon King Merrick. He towers above Society, one throne replaced by another.

Under the light of the waning moon, the many colors of the king's tail stand out more prominently than in the dim shadows of the caves. As the only living male Undine that has color to his scales, it is said he carries the blood of the very first Undine, and that all the colors of Undine maidens are represented in his own scales.

The king settles and Nerin pushes herself up on one of the bottom ridges of the rock. "All hail our King," she calls out.

Society answers, their voices echoing across the water. "Long live the King."

The king thrusts his trident into the sky. Moonlight glints off the sharpened tips, and dances across the surface of the water creating a shimmering ring of light around the whale rock. When he brings the trident down, the ring of light races in toward the king, culminating in a shower of sparks as the trident's stem hammers against the rock. The ceremony begins.

Chapter Nine

"May I present to Society your Temporal Caste, who stand before you, ready for your Choosing," Zayla's says, her voice echoing past the breakers.

Though the caste members themselves select their top three jobs, the final decision rests with the king and council. Serena isn't aware of any Undine who did not get one of their three choices. Very few are even forced to take their third choice.

Zayla straightens from a deep curtsy, her golden scales glittering under the moonlight. The rest of Society, including the king, bow their heads in return. Zayla turns to face the caste.

"As your Caste Master, I proclaim each of you ready and fit to serve Society. As such, you are part of an endless circle of kinship."

A skitter among the mass of Undine in the ocean causes Zayla to pause. The Undine are most certainly not 'endless' and the Temporal Caste is proof itself. The ceremonial speech, uttered year after year for the graduating caste, is now invalidated by the shrinking numbers of the Undine race.

Zayla casts a glance over her shoulder at the onlookers. Her eyelashes flutter as she is thrown out of her ceremonial reverie. Her arms drop by her sides and she turns and surveys her pupils, as if seeing them in a new light. The uncomfortable silence is drawn out and Serena glimpses at the king. He doesn't intervene, just watches. Zayla takes in a shaky breath and wipes her cheek.

Serena squints, looking closer. *Is she crying?*

Another wave comes in, made weak by the rocks and sands of the earth. A myriad of bubbles reach out, skimming over the sand. The ocean's reach is interrupted by the feet of the Temporal Caste who stand on the beach, hardened scales sliding over ankles.

"How out of place we seem," Zayla says quietly. "Standing here with a mix of scales and skin, as though we are part of neither world."

The mouths of the Temporal Caste drop open. This is definitely not part of the speech. Serena is sure the Undine behind Zayla cannot hear. But the caste mates certainly can, as well as the King's Guard.

Out of the corner of her eye, Serena watches muscles tense up and down along the line of guards. It is the only break in character they exhibit, but it is enough.

Cordelia herself looks to be on the verge of tears, though for an entirely different reason. Her arms tremble in anger, the stacks of bracelets clinking together.

"She can't," Cordelia whispers to herself, crossing her arms.

Serena looks at Cordelia, meeting her eye.

"She can't do this now, of all times, to blubber about losing her job." Cordelia looks at Serena. "This isn't about her."

"No," says Serena, taking a step closer to Cordelia. The break in spacing draws attention from the crowd. Serena grasps Cordelia's wrist so the shaking stops. "But it's not about only us, either."

Serena looks out over the Undine treading water in the ocean, then up to the moon. The cliffs behind them seem to grow larger, looming over the diminishing Undine population.

Down the line of the Temporal Caste there are hesitant footsteps as the thirteen members break the ceremonial line and move closer together. The orange maiden on the other side of Cordelia, Sasha Sunbeam, grasps Cordelia's left wrist to stop the rattling bracelets. Cordelia looks at Sasha, eyes narrowed, unsure if she should be offended or grateful. The next maiden over puts one hand on Sasha's shoulder, and another around her other neighbor's waist. One by one, the line moves closer, connecting physically in one way or another.

A new wave crashes ashore, stronger now. It reaches out, encircling the young Undine group. Where the scales of the ocean meet the skin of the land, sand and water support and empower them all at once. A flock of birds take flight from the cliffs, their silhouettes moving across the light of the moon.

Serena looks at her small group of caste mates and is greeted with hesitant, but hopeful smiles.

Zayla clears her throat, approaching the caste's smaller circle. She addresses the group as a whole. "And so you are one, the Temporal Caste. And I couldn't be more proud."

A squeeze of hands run down the line of Undine maidens.

"Are you willing and able to uphold the values and principles of Society?" Zayla asks the group.

The question is supposed to be asked of each graduating caste member individually, but they answer as one. "We are willing."

"Are you prepared to enter Society, no longer a student, but as a productive, contributing member?

"We are prepared."

"Of the ocean and of the moon..." Zayla begins the closing line.

"We are Undine," the Temporal Caste finishes for her.

Zayla smiles. "Now leave this beach and seek your king for assignment of your new roles in Society."

Someone from the crowd hollers, then another. A great whooping noise spreads across the waves as the Temporal Caste release their hold on each other and break into a charging sprint straight into the ocean. Serena turns to find Ervin, but her eyes land on Kai. The King's Guard have their tridents in the air, joining in with the maelstrom of voices. Kai winks at her again, sending her on her way.

She races to catch up to the group, taking her usual place at the rear. The shouts above sea are replaced by a new vigor under water as legs transform to fins. Those not used to the quick change take longer and fall behind. Kicking, then fluttering, everyone races toward the king.

Other members of Society slap their fins on the surface of the water. Some break free of the ocean, flipping into the air and back down again. Down below, Undine send out their signals, buzzing and tickling the Temporal Caste as they pass. The enthusiasm is infectious.

Serena picks up speed and opens up her arms. Her fingers skim the wake of water behind her caste mates. She follows as they angle up, then turn on their backs. Serena knows what is coming. It is the buildup to a line of jumps, one Undine after another, each performing some kind of acrobatics in midair. This isn't a tradition, but the maidens can't stop the rush of euphoria. They are like young Undine calflings, playing in the breakers during the high moon.

Through the fizz and bubbles, Serena can see the maiden in front of her surface, make a gentle arch through the sky, and dive back into the water. Serena smiles then streamlines, gaining even more speed. She bursts through the surface at the crest of a wave, pushing her even higher. Serena bends at the waist, wrapping her arms around the lower half of her tail. She summersaults three times before opening up her body.

Arms out, Serena hangs at the apex of her jump, suspended for a moment before the moon. The curve of her arms outline the orb, a perfect sphere albeit a sliver. Her head eclipses the bottom half, as if suspended at the solemn creature's mercy. She takes in the light it gives, then falls back to the ocean, filled with every last bit of brilliant karma the moon can deliver.

After a sleek dive, Serena resurfaces. Glowing hair drapes over her face, obscuring her vision. She flips it back, a carefree laugh escaping her lips. She settles, bobbing along the surface of the ocean near the whale-rock, when she realizes all eyes are on her. Even King Merrick, who is ready to announce The Choosing of the first Undine, stares with his mouth open.

"Sorry, I was just..." Serena's smile turns into a frown.

I was just happy, Serena finishes the sentence in her head.

She dips back below water where there aren't so many eyes and swims to the end of the line.

Thankfully, King Merrick's words command more attention than any triple pike can. Cordelia is first in line.

"Cordelia Swallow-Tail, you have been chosen to serve Society as an Orphanage Attendant."

A ripple of murmurs run through the Temporal Caste in front of Serena.

"Why Orphanage attendant?" Serena hears Sasha ask. "There are no orphans left—there are no calflings."

Another maiden elbows Sasha, gesturing to Serena behind them.

"Sorry," Sasha lifts her eyebrows at Serena. "I didn't mean…"

"It's okay," interrupts Serena.

The three maidens turn their attention back to the king and Cordelia.

"My second choice was Orphanage Attendant," Serena admits to the other maidens, her voice almost at a whisper. "Rayne wants to retire soon, and I guess someone needs to take over…just in case."

Sasha nods, looking back at the whale rock. "The orphanage was Cordelia's favorite shadow job. She's the popular one, though—I always assumed she'd end up as Council Member Assistant."

"Now, go join your kinsmen and make proud the ancients who watch over us." King Merrick waves Cordelia away. Rayne retreats with her, her deep green scales complimenting Cordelia's burgundy, escorting her to the first night on the job.

The king calls forth three more caste members, including Sasha. They approach the rock together for assignment and receive garden duty. There are more whoops and hollers as they join the gardening crew and they all leave together for their first night. In a crowd as big as theirs, much of the evening will consist of a party, welcoming the new members into their lives.

Serena turns to look at the King's Guard still standing on the beach. Each has their gaze set on the cliffs, scouting for danger. All, except one. Murphy, Head of the Guard, watches the proceedings with sad eyes. There are no males in the Temporal Caste. No one to join the King's Guard this time—and most likely never again. Ervin was the last. Serena still hears rumors of the legendary party the night of his Choosing.

It will be nothing like hers. With luck, Mariam has made her special lemongrass tea. The last time Serena drank it she was pleasantly inebriated for hours, suggesting there is more more to the mixture than just lemongrass. Mariam and Serena ended up in the entrance pool to the archives, splashing and dunking each other.

Another caste member is sent away and now there is only one Undine left in front of Serena. Serena lifts herself farther from the water, preparing to ascend the rock more confident now that fewer Society members remain. As the Undine receives her placement from the king, Serena finds Mariam. The Records Keeper is observing from a distance, the same place Serena might find herself years from now, after she inherits the archives and seeks her own assistant.

"Serena Moon-Shadow," the king calls. His voice is softer now that it does not need to reach all of Society. The only Undine that remain, apart from the king, are Nerin, Zayla, and Mariam.

Serena transforms and ascends the rock, standing on the same level as the king. He scrutinizes her with a slight smile on his face. Most of the previous formality seems to have disappeared with the rest of her caste mates.

"Seems your formal name has some merit," says the king. "Your affinity with the moon is much...stronger than I've seen with any Undine."

Serena isn't sure what he means by this, but makes a mental note to research the connection between Undine and the moon when she gets to the archives.

"Let's get on with it, shall we?" The king says, clearing his throat.

Serena smiles with one final glance at Mariam.

"Serena Moon-Shadow, you have been chosen to serve Society as Werewolf Liaison."

Chapter Ten

Serena's polite smile freezes on her face, unable to move. Surely she heard him wrong.

"I'm sorry, can you repeat that, your majesty?" She asks.

"Werewolf Liaison," he says again.

Serena's eyes snap up to his. There is no trace of humor there. She looks to Nerin and Zayla, standing below, then out to Mariam. No shock or surprise show on their faces. Zayla looks away, suddenly very interested in the water that crashes against the bottom of the whale-rock. Mariam manages to hold Serena's gaze, and the way her forehead wrinkles is heartbreaking. There is worry there, but Mariam will not do anything to prevent the assignment. If there was any special brew made, it will be used to drown away Mariam's sorrow that she will probably never get an assistant.

"I'd send you off with the formal words, to your group," the king says, "but there hasn't been a Werewolf Liaison since—"

"The Maiden Massacre," Serena finishes for him, looking back to Cliff Beach, where the last Werewolf Liaison was murdered. Blood pounds in her ears as she looks at the desolate beach. Despite the cold wind spraying droplets of icy ocean water at her back, her entire face goes hot.

"Remember, as a graduating Undine you are to remain with your chosen job through the next two nights as part of your initiation before you can return home for rest." King Merrick grows taller, lifting himself up on his tail and using his trident for help.

"My chosen job? I didn't choose this," Serena says, fighting back tears. She turns back to the king, trying to understand why the Undine hate her so much. "Is this one of punishments?"

"It is," says the king, his voice gruff.

"I'd thought yours would come last..." Serena trails off, her words catching in her throat. *And be the worst. But what could be worse than this?* She takes a deep breath.

I will not let him see me cry.

The king moves closer to Serena, looking out at Cliff Beach, where the King's Guard still stands in formation.

"Almost eighteen years ago, I watched my wife go to land with her protector to have our son. By the end of the night, both were dead, and I returned to the sea with the only survivor in my hands. A baby girl."

Serena looks at the king. His face is grim and wrinkles line the edges of his eyes. He is lost in his memories. "That night was, and will always be, a tragedy," the king's voice breaks. He takes a deep breath. "But like an underwater volcano, spewing poison and scorching the area, paths are created for new beginnings, rich with minerals. Amidst the destruction, there is hope."

Serena wipes her cheek with a shaky hand, tears finally bubbling over.

"Try not to think of this as your punishment, Serena." He puts his hand on her shoulder. It is heavy, with calloused fingers. "It is your destiny—and what you do with your calling could decide the fate of our kingdom."

The touch disconnects Serena from the increasing emotions of fear, anger, and sorrow. The king has never touched her before; she doubts he ever touches anyone. Body rigid with surprise, she glances at his large hand draped over her shoulder. He squeezes once, then lets his hand drop.

"Now, go and make proud the ancients who watch over you," says the king, gesturing to The Dry.

Serena follows his gaze to the beach, then up the cliffs to the forest and down to the ominous passageway leading to the rest of The Dry, which is shrouded in shadows.

A large wave crashes into the rock. Serena stumbles forward, almost pushed off. When she straightens and looks around her tiny island, King Merrick is gone.

Serena looks back to the beach. The guard is retreating into the water, now that the king has left. Ervin sees her still standing there and pauses, frowning. Murphy steps forward to whisper something to Ervin, who scratches his temple but continues into the water.

As the last of the guard disappear beneath the waves, sharpened spikes of a trident glisten in the moonlight in a final farewell. Then, Serena is alone. She takes a deep breath and dives into the water at the next swell. She drifts with the current, her body numb. The ceremonial words come to her, rolling around her head—unstoppable as the oscillating tide.

We are willing.

I'm not willing, thinks Serena. *At least not anymore.* Before, going to The Dry was an adventure, and an escape from Society. It doesn't hold the same allure when she is forced ashore.

We are prepared.

The picture of the bloody, dying maiden fills Serena's mind. It is one image of many in the stack of werewolf books Serena was charged with studying. What she thought was punishment for her close brush with the creatures was instead maybe actually meant to prepare her for her new role in Society.

We are Undine.

Serena snorts and saltwater rushes into her nose, burning her throat. Breaking the surface, water and foam sputter out of her mouth, nose, and gills. She crawls onto the beach, her transformation clumsy and almost as painful as her first time as a young Undine. Wave after wave forces her forward until she manages to pull herself far enough away from the unforgiving surges.

Sprawled out on the sand, she turns to look at the ocean.

Even our great mother is pushing me away, she thinks.

Serena puts her hand over her mouth, choking back a sob.

What you do with your calling will decide the fate of our kingdom.

One more deep breath and her gills settle, sealing shut against her neck. Serena rubs her face, smoothing away grimy sand, bitter seawater, and the creases in her forehead that threaten to remain permanently.

Standing up, Serena stares out at the ocean until her legs stop shaking. One small, dark cloud moves across the sky. The moon blinks out behind it, then comes back, as if it is winking at Serena.

One side of Serena's mouth tips up in a scrutinizing smile. *Fine, if one world doesn't want me, I'll make another my home.*

She turns toward the passageway. Streaks of moonlight don't stretch very far past the tops of the cliffs to help light the narrow corridor in between. Crickets call out from the shadows, beckoning for Serena to join them.

"I'm coming," she mumbles back to them.

Serena brings her scales forward, letting them crawl down her arms and cover her knuckles. One by one, they emerge past her neck and over her temples until they blend in with her hair line. At her elbows, knees, and ankles, the scales stack on top of one another, providing extra protection while still giving her room to move. The bulky weight will slow her down, but the scales give her confidence. Donning her body armor, Serena stands a little straighter, shoulders pulled back.

Serena gains control over her bioluminescent features. Her hair dims, returning to its natural dark black, perfect for blending in with the shadowed forest. She increases the strength of her reflective guanine crystals spaced throughout her plated body.

As she walks forward, the tiny mirrors match the sand at her feet, until they flair with color.

She pauses, eyes drawn to something gleaming gold standing out amidst the taupe sand—a trident. Serena walks over and bends down to pick it up, keeping her eyes on the tree line. The decorative red tassels tied around the long handle brush Serena's hand. It is Kai's weapon. The Second in Command wouldn't leave it behind by mistake.

Serena looks behind her. She has never seen a guard without his trident. *Maybe an excuse for him to come back?* Hope blooms in her chest. She scans the surface of the ocean, but it remains barren all the way to the moon.

She sighs, looking back at the trident. *No one is coming back.*

Moonlight flickers off the sharpened tips as she turns the trident in her hand. Serena grasps the heavy weapon, fumbling to get one end tucked under her arm. She walks forward again, ripping off the red tassels and leaving them behind on the sand; they won't blend as well in The Dry. Serena traverses the passageway and enters the forest, her body armor reflecting the long lines of dark browns and greens of the trees.

After a short, steady jog, she climbs atop a rock, using it to jump onto a fallen tree trunk. Sprinting, Serena follows the incline of the trunk, leaping off the end to take to the trees where the wolves won't follow.

Her fingers only graze the lowest branch, then she lands back on the ground. The trident weighs her down and renders one arm useless for catching branches. She readjusts her grip on the trident and tries again. A complete miss.

Eyes darting around her surroundings, Serena squints into the darkness. *No wolves, at least not that I can smell. But I need to get into the trees.* She looks at the trident and lets out a frustrated huff. She considers ditching it, but it is her only real weapon.

She lifts up the trident so it is parallel to the ground. Widening her stance and taking aim, Serena extends her free arm as a guide. She leans back and thrusts her arm forward. Her hips rotate at the same time and she releases the trident. A resounding thud echoes through the forest as the weapon pierces wood. Without hesitating, Serena runs, plants her feet, and jumps. Her hands grip the long stem of the trident, extended parallel just a few feet under a branch.

Wind slides across her scales as her legs swing up. When Serena can see her toes above the trident, she lets go. Her body arcs and she thuds on the branch above the trident. She bends down and tugs on her weapon. It is deep, and won't budge. Serena wraps her legs around the branch and hangs upside down in order to use both hands.

When the log releases its hold, Serena runs her hand over the three punctures already bleeding sap.

"I am sorry," she whispers to the tree. "But I would be grateful for your shelter tonight."

It is the same thing Undine say when forcing their way into thick coral in an emergency, and it feels right to say it now.

Serena pulls herself on top of the branch. She leans her head back against the bark, breathing hard. Crisp air blows through the trees, pressing against her breastplate and she is grateful for her armor. But despite the extra comfort, dark shadows move in the wind, and the trees are restless, as if they can't wait to see how Serena's night plays out.

She sits on the branch, pulling her knees into her chest—trying to ward away the vulnerability that settles there. She looks at the trident once again.

At least Kai cares.

A new resolve sets in. Serena swallows, convincing herself to suspend judgment against the king and Society, at least until she has more answers as to why this particular punishment has been given to her.

Taking a deep breath, she looks up. The branches up here are plentiful, as opposed to near the ground where they are sparse and flimsy. Serena climbs with ease, using the trident's stem as leverage when she can. She stops before she reaches the weaker branches, settling into an especially large crook where branch meets trunk. The wood is smoothed down at the fork and there is a small clearing going straight to the open sky just above it.

Serena brushes away remnants of a former nest and curls into the tree, trying to imagine she is in her sleeping cove. Her mind drifts around her cave until she can almost smell the bitter kelp that grows out of her caged experiments on the floor. She hears the tide trickling in, beating against jars and her dry box. Serena fingers the charm still hanging from her necklace, wishing she left her mother's jewelry behind.

Turning on her other side, bark grabs hold of her scales, threatening to tear them off. She shifts carefully, rolling onto her shoulder so she is facing the thick center of the tree. The moon works hard to pierce its canopy. Slivers of light run down the craggy bark and across Serena's hips and legs.

With a slender finger, Serena traces the maze of lines zigzagging throughout the tree's outer shell. Just like her own scales, the dark, reddish-brown bark is smooth when she runs the pad of her finger one way, and rough the other direction.

"We aren't so different, you and me," she whispers to the tree. "Except maybe you have more friends."

Branches from its neighbors wave at her in the wind. One side of Serena's mouth curls up in a lopsided smile, and she waves back.

Chapter Eleven

A scream echoes through the forest, sliding down Serena's spine and leaving goose bumps in its wake. She climbs out of her tree and follows the sound. Pushing aside thick shrubs, Serena steps into a clearing. The scream subsides into gurgling coughs. The smells of rotten seaweed, wet dog, and dank earth greet her. She puts her hand to her mouth, trying not to gag.

Her toes hit warm liquid and she immediately draws them back, still peering at the pool of red goo, made darker by the brown soil beneath it. Serena's eyes follow the trickle feeding the pool. Forging its own path over the ground, the stream bends around rocks, collecting in depressions and dripping off...claws.

Yellowed talons tap, causing ripples in in the pool of blood. Matted fur, stinking of the coppery liquid of a recent kill, covers the beast. Serena takes a step back.

The beast emits a growl, forceful enough that it causes spit to fly out from in between his pointy teeth and splatter at Serena's feet. Fear roots her to the spot, even as the blood crawls closer to her feet. Instead of moving past, it seems to pool there, rising higher to cover the tops of Serena's toes.

"Help me," a voice whispers.

Serena's eyes snap up. The beast shifts, leaning back onto his hind legs, ready to pounce. He growls again, its stinking breath caressing Serena's bare skin. She shivers, goose bumps now popping up on her arms. Her scales must have retracted while she was sleeping, and try as she might, she cannot convince them to re-emerge.

"Help me," the voice is louder now, more desperate.

Serena tears her eyes from the beast and looks down, at the thing it has attacked. Dark hair, almost just as matted as the beast's, cover a face. But there is no mistaking the bioluminescent glow, winking out as the Undine maiden fights for her last moments of life.

Serena swallows. The blood at her feet is up to her ankles now. The maiden stirs, angling her head back.

Eyes glued to the wolf, Serena steps to the side of the maiden, trying to see her face. The wolf counters her steps, moving off of the maiden and onto the ground, revealing midnight blue scales.

Serena takes in a sharp breath, her eyes snapping back to the Undine's face. She pushes herself up on one elbow, extending her other hand.

"Help..." The rest of her tangled hair falls away from her face.

Serena looks directly into her own eyes.

The wolf lunges, not out, but down. Finishing off his prey, he tears a wide gash in her neck. Serena screams, the sound amplified by an identical shrill shriek—but one dies out, while another grows louder.

Serena snaps her mouth shut when the wolf looks up, fresh blood coating his face and teeth—his snout caught in a flap of skin hanging open from the neck. As he snarls, his lips turn up to bare more fang.

Serena shakes her head from side to side and tries to step back. She can't. The pool of blood wraps like long tendrils around her legs, all the way up to her thighs. It bites into her skin, causing her to bleed—

mingling her own blood with it so she can't distinguish between the two.

One more growl, and the wolf leaps with his paws extended out in front of him. His mouth opens wide, aiming directly for Serena's neck.

* * *

Serena cries out, throwing her arms in front of her. Rolling to the side, her sturdy platform gives way to nothingness, and she falls. A branch clips her feet, sending her into a spin. Another one catches her midsection, stopping her, but it cannot hold under her weight. It cracks and she falls again, landing on another branch with a thud. Breath escapes her lungs under a forced wheeze and does not come back for several painful seconds.

Her eyes fly open at the sound of twigs and sticks hitting soft dirt. She is too close to the ground. Tree tops spin through the branches above her. Groaning, Serena forces herself to sit up, wrapping one leg around the branch to keep steady. One hand goes to the pounding on the side of her head, the other to the pain in her ribs. Her whole body begins to shake.

Come on, Werewolf Liaison, get up, Serena coaxes herself. She turns, peering over the branch to scan the ground. A blue jewel sparkles back at her— her mom's necklace, splayed out over the shrubs below.

"Damn," Serena says out loud.

She looks up, shielding her eyes from the harsh morning sunlight that filters down from the canopy. Leaves flutter from side to side and branches sway in the wind, helping the sun to play a nasty game of peekaboo.

Serena squints, realizing she must have slept through half the morning. From the first year in school, young Undine are taught never to be caught in daylight. It is when Ungainlies are most likely to prowl the earth and sea, harvesting what they can. Besides—the sunlight hurts. And yet, the king's words were clear; Serena is to remain with her chosen job for two nights. One down, one to go.

Her weapon remains high up in her overnight nest, but she hesitates, leaving one of her only family heirlooms exposed on the ground.

A quick hop down and quick hop up.

She squats and her fingers curl in, anticipating the jump. A foreign smell drifts past her nose, and she pauses.

Werewolf.

Serena barely has time to scoot back to the sturdy center of the branch when she hears a twig snap. Her eyes dart from one spot to another, scanning the ground, trying to pinpoint the noise. Light filtering down creates sharp glares and distorted sunspots in front of Serena's eyes, blurring out part of the landscape.

I need to see.

The sound and smell of heavy breathing below are enough to convince her to stay put. From around the base of her tree, a paw—and another. Then there is a long muzzle, followed by light brown fur.

Her heart catches in her throat. Werewolves *can* transform outside of the full moon—in broad daylight, nonetheless. The light brown fur on his muzzle also covers the rest his body, except for a crescent-shaped patch of beige hair on the side of his face. The rest of the wolf emerges into Serena's sight. He is twice the size of the average Vancouver wolf. Unnaturally bulky muscles wrap around his shoulders. His back legs are larger and more defined than those in the front, and long, yellowed claws extend from every paw.

The wolf passes over her mother's necklace, its tail swinging once to the right. When it disappears behind the tree again, the necklace is in its mouth.

"Hey!" Serena shouts. "Give that back!"

She swallows hard. There is no answer but the wind blowing through the trees. Serena turns around, balancing on the branch, looking for the wolf. "Hello?"

Another twig snaps.

Her head whips around and the wolf emerges again. This time the chain of her mother's necklace hangs out between sharp teeth. Altering his path, he steps away from the tree and sits. Head cocked to the side, he looks up at her, allowing the necklace to fall from his mouth. The charm lands with a soft thud, and the chain pools on top of it.

The wolf leans to the side, then digs his nose into one of his back legs. When he finishes, he looks back at Serena, running his long tongue over his snout. Serena wrinkles her own nose.

"So are you going to give it back?" Serena asks. She risks moving forward along the branch to see him better.

He paws at the necklace, then scoots back.

"Oh, no. You're not going to lure me out of this tree," Serena says. Besides the wolfsbane garden, it is the one safe place in the forest.

The creature emits a short whine, then scoots back even farther, and lays down on his belly. His ears twitch to the sounds around him and though he faces Serena, his eyes wander to the side.

Serena stands, studying the wolf's reaction. He barely seems to notice. She reaches above her, breaking off a stick as long as her arm. She throws it like a trident, so it sails over the distance separating them and lands nearby. The wolf looks at the stick, ears still twitching. His mouth hangs open and he pants, tongue lolling over the side. He looks more like one of the small dogs the Ungainly bring with them to the beach than a ferocious beast.

"You paint quite the deceiving picture," Serena says, hands on her hip. "But it won't work." The images of murderous werewolves in her books have made a permanent impression.

The wolf licks his nose again and snaps his mouth once, then twice. Finally he picks up the necklace and trots toward Serena's tree. Before he gets there, he turns, angling away. The wolf dips his head, then thrusts it toward Serena. The necklace flies out of his mouth, landing at the base of the tree. He looks at Serena one more time out of the corner of his eye, then disappears into the shrubbery, his wagging tail grazing over a patch of blooming purple flowers.

His steady footsteps fade in the distance, like he wants her to know exactly how far away he is. Without hesitation, Serena jumps down. In one smooth motion she grabs the necklace and leaps back to safety. Her heart rate doesn't even quicken until after she is back in the tree.

Wiping the slobber off the charm, she watches the shadows behind the bushes where the wolf disappeared. *It's not the same one that chased me the night of the excursion*, she thinks. That one had darker fur, almost black, and was much larger.

I will have to focus on this one when I come back. Serena freezes. *When I come back.* She is actually considering reliving this nightmare. She takes a deep breath and stands, replacing her mother's necklace around her neck. *Which means I'll need to be better prepared.*

She climbs the tree back to her nesting spot and picks up the trident.

I need to train.

She turns, spotting a dead branch on the next tree and aims for it. It hits wood, the trident's handle reverberating with the impact. Serena frowns, it isn't the exact spot she intended. She climbs through the trees, crossing over on the thickest branches to retrieve her spear. Spotting another dead branch, she tries again. A flock of birds take flight nearby as she misses, although her aim has improved. She switches hands often, practicing until the sun has moved across the span of the sky. She only aims for targets that won't impact the trees. She has seen too many Ungainlies scale redwood trunks with spikes in their shoes, a trail of bleeding holes left in their wake. Soon after, disease, insect infestation, and mold settle in. In many cases, the trees never recover.

By evening, both Serena's speed and accuracy are much better, even as sore and tired as she is. Still high in the trees, she retracts much of her arm and shoulder armor to rub the affected areas. She longs for the cool, healing waters of the ocean. She can hear them now, beating against the shore and calling her name.

Now you want me back? She grits her teeth. *One more night.*

Serena looks into the sky, seeking the moon. It is just now gaining its light.

"Just you and me tonight," she says out loud, touching the charm on her necklace. "Hopefully."

Chapter Twelve

The wolfsbane garden is simple enough to reach through the trees, and Serena only comes to the ground when sturdy branches become sparse. Sprinting with her trident at the ready, Serena pauses at the tree line, trying to hear past her own heavy breathing. Nothing.

Serena skirts the garden checking for footprints though she can't imagine werewolves would dare go near it. Then again, she had also believed that a werewolf couldn't transform without a full moon.

These nights, anything goes.

Serena calls upon full body armor. Scales cover every last inch of her feet, legs, torso, and hands. Her movements are slow and weighted, but it is necessary when walking amidst the poisonous flowers.

Rainfall combined with shade from the canopy above keeps the ground cool and damp. A lingering bumblebee hovers nearby.

"Go home, it's closing time," Serena whispers to it.

Though Wolfsbane is a threatened species, growing only in damp woods and high elevations, Undine gardeners have been successful in yielding longer blooming periods for the sulfur-yellow flowers.

Serena picks up an abandoned Undine basket. *I wonder if the maiden that found and reported the footprints will have enough courage to come retrieve her basket, or ever return to work, for that matter.* Gardening in The Dry is one of the more dangerous occupations for the Undine, other than Werewolf

Liaison, and maybe the King's Guard. There isn't likely to be any other visitors to the secluded patch of land tonight, though. Gardeners are only required to come above seas to tend the plants a few nights during every moon cycle. It's one of the perks that entice Undine to pick the job; they can enjoy free time the rest of the month.

Serena chooses a spot and begins filling her basket. The nectar of the flower causes severe itching and dermatitis on skin of Ungainlies, Undine, and werewolf alike. Ingesting concentrated wolfsbane sap can be fatal for any species.

Serena twirls the long stem of a flower. Yellow, bell-shaped blooms hang down the stem, overlapping each other. The ancients used the flower in the spell to create werewolves when the Undine needed protectors. Emerging only during a full moon, the wolves stood watch willingly while Undine maidens consummated and gave birth.

Slowly, Serena pokes one finger inside a flower, pushing aside petals to view the hollow spur at the apex. A drop of nectar slides onto the tip of her finger.

She gasps, dropping the flower and immediately bends to plunge her finger into the earth. The soil absorbs the nectar, cleansing her scaled extremity. *Don't be stupid*, she reminds herself.

Serena begins picking flowers more carefully this time. Once her basket is full, she sets off for her nesting tree. If the wolf is to return, this is where he would seek her. Working the next few hours, Serena labors in the painstakingly precise task of placing each stem where the flower is visible but won't be blown away from the wind.

Serena places several layers of wolfsbane surrounding the base of her tree. Moving up the trunk, she wiggles the stems in between cracks in the bark. Next are the lowest branches, where she learns to weave the stems together in a tight braid. Flowers wrap around the branches, plaited around as a living lace. She completes the ward by adorning the branches above her, just in case werewolves have learned the trick of climbing trees.

Serena settles into the crook of the tree, the same spot from which she observed the werewolf earlier. In her basket, there are only a few flowers left. Before boredom can lure her to sleep, she weaves more stems together. Scales make her fingers fat and clumsy, but she persists, slowly knitting together another tight lace of poison. This time, she loops it around the three prongs of her trident, arranging it so a large bulb hangs from each of the tips.

Finished, Serena rests her head back against the trunk, still blinking away sleep. She tries to recall what happened the last few times a wolf came to her. When she ventured above seas to remove overgrowth from the archive holes, she had sent out a call in the rain. It was her attempt at echolocation that worked so well underwater, in order to see better above. She did it again, last night. Though she heard movement before, the wolf did not show himself until after she made the call.

She sits up straight, a revelation running through her head. Maybe Undine sounds have a different purpose above water. There had to be some way they could call upon their protectors.

Serena licks her lips. *It's worth a shot*, she thinks. She sends out her signal. It comes out as a soft titter.

The last few notes are elongated and nasal. The quality of the waves that come back are distorted and hazy. She turns her head, listening for signs that it has worked.

Silence.

The forest is just lightening with the rising sun, making it harder for Serena to see. Soon she will be at a full disadvantage, with alternating light and shadow playing tricks on her eyes.

She tries again, turning her head as she sends her sounds out. It is louder this time. If the wolf is anywhere nearby, he has to hear it. Before she even stops her song, movement in the brush catches her eye. She doesn't need to peer closer to see the two, glowing red eyes staring back at her. Has she called another one?

A growl answers back, and through the dim light, she can see the gleam of sharp fangs. This isn't the docile pup she encountered last night. If it is, he is no longer in a playful mood.

Fine, thinks Serena as she grips her trident. *No more playing.*

The wolf emerges from his cover, head low to the ground, ears pinned back. He slinks forward, eyes never leaving Serena.

"I wouldn't come any closer. Not unless you want to wear that pelt permanently," she says. Further contact with wolfsbane would complete the wolf's transformation, forcing a permanent change to animal form.

Sunlight hits his fur, showing off his coloring. It is the same wolf that stole, then returned, her mother's necklace. He continues to slink forward, his crescent-shaped mark on the side of his face glinting under the moonlight. Serena will have little chance of evading his jump if he risks crossing the line of wolfsbane.

I could move higher up the tree, where he could never reach me.

Serena dismisses the thought. *I don't want another chase, I have to stand my ground.*

Before she can convince herself otherwise, Serena jumps down. Landing softly with her trident at the ready, a puff of yellow flowers float up around her like a ring of smoke. Before the last one settles on the ground, the wolf lunges. Serena fights back the instinct to turn tail and run. She steels herself and steps forward to meet him.

They each take two long strides toward the outer ring of yellow. Serena extends the trident and cries out at the top of her lungs. The wolf freezes, right at the line, with the three sharp points of her weapon centimeters from his eyes.

Serena holds the heavy, golden trident steady, willing her arms not to shake. The wolf glares at her.

"I wouldn't come any closer," Serena says again, this time in a lower, more controlled voice.

The wolf hasn't moved. Serena jerks the spear forward, intending to intimidate.

He pulls his lips back in a snarl. Serena jabs again and he returns a sharp yelp. The wolfsbane on the tip of the trident is at the wolf's nose. His nostrils flare in distaste. The forest has gone silent as the two creatures consider their next move. Layers of scales make Serena's arms heavy. Another few moments of this and her weakness will begin to show.

Finally, the werewolf takes a step back. Serena lowers her elbows, leaving the trident aimed at his face.

He raises his eyebrows at Serena; it is her turn to yield.

Serena lets the back end of her trident drop so her weapon is now parallel with her body. Drawing her shoulders back and her chin high, she clicks her heels together, keeping her toes pointed slightly to the outside. It is a stance worthy of the King's Guard.

The dog seems satisfied. He sits down, then shuffles his front paws together and puffs out his chest.

Serena peers closer. *Is he making fun of me?*

She presses her lips together and allows her shoulders to relax. "I am Serena Moon-Shadow, Werewolf Liaison of the Undine Kingdom. I propose a temporary truce, in order that we may confer."

The wolf snorts, looking away.

"But in our Ungainly forms." Serena swallows. "You retract your fangs and I'll do the same with my scales."

The wolf is still looking away, eyes following a fly buzzing too close to his face. He snaps at the fly, misses, then licks his jaws.

"And," continues Serena, tone hesitant, "I want to thank you...for returning my necklace." Her fingers touch the charm at her neck. She still doubts if he can understand speech as a werewolf. She lowers her voice even more; it is only a whisper now. "It was my mother's."

His eyes drift back to her and he nods.

He can understand.

Her eyes go wide. She clears her throat. "So please, can we talk?"

He cocks his head, as if he is considering.

"Look, I'll leave my weapon." Serena rests the trident against the trunk of the tree. "We'll keep our distance. I'll be in my tree and you stay outside of the wolfsbane."

The wolf doesn't make a move, so Serena takes her eyes from it briefly enough to jump up to a low branch. She pulls herself up, creeping forward just a bit. The tips of the trident are within reach. She could grab it and pull it up if need be.

The wolf is still sitting, but at least he appears interested.

"I only have until the next moon," Serena says, light sarcasm touching her words. The sun has just barely risen.

Serena resists a smile when the wolf snorts again.

With a long yawn, the wolf gets his hind legs under him and stands. He leans back, head dipping down and rear raising for a stretch. Then he walks.

He circles the outline of wolfsbane, occasionally stopping to sniff. He lingers where the gaps between each bloom are wider. He is searching for the weak link.

Serena shifts, glancing at her trident.

The wolf circles the tree once, tail swishing as he goes. On the second time around, he disappears into the only spot behind the tree Serena cannot follow with her eyes and he does not emerge.

Instead, Serena hears hollow popping, a rustle over the dead leaves on the ground, and then a groan.

Serena bobs her head back and forth on each side of the tree, straining to get a glimpse. She sees a tail and then nothing.

"What are you doing?" Serena asks. The words come out too quick, giving away her fear.

She opens her mouth to ask again when she hears footsteps. The wolf is circling back around. Serena grips the branch, angling closer to her trident. The ground is almost the same color as the wolf's fur, but she squints, trying to catch a glimpse of long, yellowing claws.

Instead, she finds toes. Ungainly toes. Human toes.

There are ten of them. Transfixed, Serena follows the smooth, tanned skin up. Ankles move and flex as he continues to walk. Serena blushes as she stares at his calves. Next are the knees, then...

The man drapes a cape over his shoulders and pulls the opening closed.

Serena meets his eyes. "What—?"

"I am obliging your request, mermaid," he answers.

Chapter Thirteen

Nodding his head in a semi-formal bow, the now-human wolf stands, facing Serena. Having stopped in a dim section of the forest, Serena's eyes, well-adjusted for darker waters, have an easier time seeing him.

His hair is his only feature still resembling his werewolf form. It's the same color as his light brown fur. It sits parted down the middle and hangs just past his ears with a few stray strands curling in, framing hazel eyes.

"They're not red." Serena blurts out the first thing that comes to mind.

"Huh?" he asks, eyebrows furrowed.

"Nothing. It's just..." Serena clears her throat, pausing. "We don't like to be called mermaids."

His lips turn up in a half smile.

"Well, Serena Moon-Shadow of the Undine Kingdom...what did you do wrong to deserve the title of Werewolf Liaison?" The man remains outside the wolfsbane circle, his cape made of thick material and tied close at the waist. When it billows out with the breeze, Serena can see his posture is relaxed.

Serena sits back on her branch, allowing one leg to dangle. She drops her hand on the far side of the branch, closer toward the trident as a precaution. "It is my chosen responsibility," she answers.

His forehead crinkles. "You chose this?"

Her jawline tightens as she plucks the stem of a flower from one of the braids, and twirls it in her fingers. "Not exactly."

His eyes drift, studying everything from her trident to the swing of her leg, down her arms to the flower she still twirls in her hand.

"What?" she asks.

He stands taller than the average Ungainly male. The cape is pulled tight over his upper arms and wide shoulders, revealing defined but not bulky muscles. He turns, seeking out a stump, and sits. "When were you plannin' to fulfill your part of the bargain?" He motions to her legs with a jerk of his chin.

She looks down. Her whole body is still scaled. She did promise to retract them, which poses a slight problem. Even the Undine cannot touch wolfsbane with their bare skin and escape unscathed, a secret the werewolf need not know.

Serena shifts on the branch, standing to place her feet in between the braids of poisonous flowers. Petals from the branch above graze her hair. She tries to hunch without being too obvious about it, and is all too aware of the trident, which is now out of reach.

Slowly, she retracts the scales on her feet. They disappear in a chain up to just above her knees, where she stops.

He raises one eyebrow again.

"I failed to bring my own cape," Serena explains.

He nods, and gestures with his hand for her to continue. Serena reveals the skin on her hands, wrists and arms. Next, she bares her shoulders and the upper portion of her chest. The charm slides from scales to skin.

Serena touches her necklace again; the gesture is becoming a nervous habit. She steps forward, placing her feet carefully, until the branch begins to dip under her weight. Serena lowers herself, straddling the branch.

The man shifts on his stump and opens his mouth, about to speak.

Unwilling to lose the upper hand, Serena speaks first. "Care to introduce yourself, or shall I just call you Hound?"

"We prefer werewolf," he looks at her from under thick eyebrows. "Or just weres. But you can call me Liam. Or, that is…" He stands, smoothing out his cape. "Liam of the Clan Werich."

Serena purses her lips, "No title?"

"Well, I work the night shift at the bowlin' alley."

"What does that mean?"

"It is a gamin' place, for humans." One side of his mouth curls up in a smile. "Maybe I can take you sometime."

Serena calls his bluff. "Can I bring my wolfsbane?"

Now he laughs out loud, small wrinkles appearing around his eyes.

Serena leans forward on the branch, her belly touching rough bark. She folds her arms underneath her and rests her chin in one hand.

Liam composes himself, sliding his fingers through his hair. "And as Werewolf Liaison, are you goin' to extend an invitation for me to visit you?"

"I don't think so, Liam of Clan Werich. You would not survive the games we play in the ocean." Serena wonders how a jellyfish sting would affect a werewolf.

"Of that, I have no doubt." He smiles as he turns, taking a few steps away from her.

Serena pushes up from the branch. "Where are you going?"

Tracing the outer edge of wolfsbane circle, Liam walks around to the back of the tree. "To bed. To dream of tridents and yellow flowers, and mer..." He drifts off, catching himself in time. "I mean the Great Kingdom of the Undine."

"When will we meet again?" Serena asks.

"I will listen for your call, Serena Moon-Shadow. And maybe next time you can come down from your tree, little bird," he says, disappearing from sight.

"Liam, wait!" Serena calls. "I have more questions!" Serena racks her brains for a more substantial excuse for him to stay. "And I'm going to need proof that I met you."

There is another rustle in the thick brush, and as quickly as it disappeared last time, Liam's tail reappears. Liam leaps out of the shrubbery in full werewolf form, his cape nowhere to be seen. Pausing by his stump, he leans to one side and his hind leg comes up, claws extended. He scratches himself along his ribs, hard and quick. After turning to look at Serena one last time, he trots away.

Serena listens as his footsteps recede. Once she is sure he is a fair distance away and still moving, she scales her feet and jumps down from the tree. Grabbing her trident and leaving the safety of her circle to approach the stump, Serena bends down in the grass, spotting a small mass of light brown fur.

Chapter Fourteen

When Serena returns to the kingdom, an assembly is already in session. She slips into the Great Hall, taking her place in the shadows, unnoticed. Squinting, she can see the whites of King Merrick's eyes, they are so wide with disbelief—a stark contrast to his red cheeks. "What is the purpose of littering the Great Hall with dead plants?"

The young Undine, recently given the title of Scientist Assistant at The Choosing, does not expect his temper. She steps back, half turning—on the verge of bolting.

She catches the eye of Evandre, the Head Scientist. Judging by the glare he gives, no amount of bolting would help the young Undine.

"Answer your king, please," Nerin prods.

"It's just...I didn't realize," the Undine maiden continues to stutter. "I thought maybe the court wasn't aware."

"Not aware that half my kingdom is crumbling to dust?" The king sits forward on his throne, hands so tight on the armrests that the chair itself is on the verge of crumbling. "Not aware that coral, the very lifeblood of our food source, is disappearing around the globe?"

"I'm sorry, your majesty." The Undine bends in an unsure curtsey. Now she is the one with the flushed cheeks. "I've just never been so far from the Great Hall and...was shocked at the dead coral fields."

The king leans back, rubbing his eyes. "Maybe I should mandate Society borders just so my time isn't wasted whenever a new Undine discovers the coral fields," he mumbles, glancing at Evandre.

"It wouldn't matter," Serena's voice booms from the back of the room. All eyes in the court turn to her. Bracing herself for an onslaught of attention, she walks forward, releasing many of her scales that armored her body above seas. One hand holds Kai's trident, the other is balled into a fist, scales protecting the fur inside.

The back of her neck itches as maidens watch her walk the path to the front. *If I can sing in front of everyone, if I can face a werewolf, then I can do this.*

The king sits back in his throne. "Why?" he huffs. "Because you would cross the closed border anyway?"

"No." Serena approaches the assembly at the front of the Great Hall. "Because even the corals that decorate our own mountain are beginning to show signs of decline."

The king grimaces. From behind the table Evandre holds up a finger. Before either can speak, a flash of metal catches their attention.

Serena twirls the trident so the handle faces out. She takes aim and tosses it toward Kai. The Second in Command has only to extend a hand to catch it. In one smooth motion, he brings it upright to the position of attention against his body.

"I thank you for your protection," Serena tells him.

Kai nods, a slight, almost indistinguishable bob of his head. He stands rigid at attention next to Murphy, but his eyes go soft, lingering too long on her face.

Heat blossoms in Serena's abdomen, and she doesn't know why. It rises to her chest, and she has to look away before it reaches her cheeks.

"I have a request," Serena turns back to the king. His cold eyes bore into her, and she has to quell the urge to hunch her shoulders, or run from the room completely. "For my own trident and possibly other weapons. And training."

Nerin answers, "The King's Guard couldn't possibly have time—"

"As you say," interrupts King Merrick. "Anything more?"

Serena clears her throat, forcing her hands back to her sides. "I have come to speak of my chosen..." she drifts off, deciding to change the wording. "My given position."

"You cannot be reassigned." The king sighs, leaning back in his throne and rubbing his temples. First the corals, then this. The Temporal Caste is not taking to their assigned Choosings easily.

Nerin places her hand on the armrest of the throne. She looks natural there, her presence to the left of the king reminding Serena of the symbiotic relationship of a spotted goby and hard-nosed shrimp. Serena scrutinizes the pair at the throne. She wonders which is the protective goby and which is the domestic shrimp.

Folding her hands in front of her, Serena tries to exude patience, and confidence. "Had I wanted reassignment, I wouldn't need weapons—nor the training for them."

Nerin shakes her head once. Even if the king is in the wrong, it is bad etiquette to make it obvious.

Serena takes a deep breath. "I came to find out my purpose of the assignment."

"Your purpose?" asks the king.

"The title 'liaison' suggests cooperative contact. Though, maybe that is just upholding the old name. If I'm meant to look for weaknesses, or perform as a spy because you intend to attack, please tell me. I need to know where to focus my efforts."

The Great Hall goes quiet as the king rubs his upper lip. "Suppose I consider the point moot?"

"Why?" asks Serena.

"Well," the king leans back in his chair, his fins give a casual flip. "Maybe it is best to wait and see if you can actually make contact. It may take months, possibly years, for each of our species to earn trust and open up a conversation with—"

Serena extends her hand in front of her. It is still balled in a fist, covered in scales. She slowly retracts the scales to reveal thin, tight fingers. When she is sure every pair of eyes in the Great Hall is on her fist, she opens it. Brown, wiry hairs float to the ground in front of her.

The council members lean forward.

Nerin is the first to speak. "They could be from anything. One of us, even."

"Do you see them glowing?" Serena asks. Everyone knows what happens to fresh cut Undine hair.

No one moves, almost as if they are afraid to approach the beast's fur.

Serena rolls her eyes. "Smell it."

Nerin glances at the king. He, too, is leaning forward in his chair. He nods to her. Nerin steps forward and bends down to pick up one strand. With a shaky hand, she brings it to her nose.

"So again I ask, are they enemies or allies?" Serena meets the king's eyes, demanding the answer.

The king does not speak right away. Finally, after a long pause, he asks for everyone to leave. The council exchanges confused looks.

"I said go!" the king's voice booms through the cave.

Everyone jumps at King Merrick's bellow, including Serena. The room moves to action as the council and the audience shuffles to the exit. Serena half turns, expecting to be told to join them. She looks back at Nerin, who hasn't moved from the king's side. Nerin pins Serena to the spot with her stare. So they are both to stay, then.

When the cavern has cleared, Serena swears she can still hear the king's shout bouncing off the walls. A small drop of sweat trickles from the hairline at her neck down her back. The confidence she walked in with is quickly draining.

"I apologize for my gruff manner," says the king. "It's been a long few..." He glances at Nerin. "Years."

Serena peers closer at the wrinkles around his eyes. She's never noticed them before.

"Our world is changing, Serena Moon-Shadow. The werewolf packs in The Dry are no longer our biggest threat."

Serena glances down at the line of dead corals at her toes.

The king continues, "Though some in our council will still have me believe that."

Who? wonders Serena. *The King's Guard? Kai did leave me the trident.*

Serena realizes the king is looking down at his tail. It spirals into an unnatural twist at the bottom toward the fins. A long, white scar follows the spiral. Scales on either side of the scar are lumped on top of each other, like they have reached a border they cannot cross, yet they insist on trying.

It is because of the werewolves that he cannot take his Ungainly form. They have scarred him for life. For more than a decade, werewolves have chased Undine back into the sea. They killed his wife and son, and have prevented any maiden from conceiving since.

The king finally speaks. "Our situation is becoming desperate. We have tried hiding from the wolves, and we have tried fighting—losing most of our male population in the process. We need to take back our beaches. I implore you to seek an amenable relationship with the clan. However, if that cannot be done, find a time when their defenses are weak, so we can mate on the beaches." The king leans forward, fixing Serena with a hard stare. "Do not let your guard down in The Dry for one second. They are not to be trusted."

Nerin lays her hand on the king's shoulder. The intimate move shocks Serena more than the king's words. Nerin looks away, but her hand remains—her thumb rubbing back and forth over the material of the king's tunic.

The king straightens and takes a deep breath. "So there you have it. Be safe and be smart. Do what you do best and observe. Get to know them, and report everything back to us."

Serena rubs her temples. *Easier said than done. I'm going to need more wolfsbane.*

"Anything more?" asks the king for a second time.

Serena's hands drop to her sides. "Yes, there is," she says.

The king raises one eyebrow.

"I request permission to access the King's Library." Serena holds her breath. Very few are given access to the restricted library, but it contains information regarding werewolf origins. *Maybe something from their past can help me figure out how to move forward.*

The king and Nerin exchange another glance.

"For what purpose?" asks Nerin.

"In order to fulfill my duties as Werewolf Liaison," says Serena.

The king leans forward, his bright blue eyes boring through Serena. "Request denied."

Chapter Fifteen

"Ugh!" Serena shouts out, banging her first on the wall inside her cave. "Waste of time." One sole echo repeats her words back to her, a reminder of how empty her cave is.

Bending to her experiments, Serena peers into a jar of sea urchins, attempting to distract herself. The few eggs skimming the surface are no longer white. Edges drooping, they have gone flat and are pale yellow. They are all dead.

"This is what is going to happen to us." Serena stands and turns away, her feet splashing around in ankle-deep water.

We should be protecting our home, not romping around with werewolves.

Rage bubbles up inside. Her arms shake and her cheeks grow hot. Without thinking, she rips the charm from her neck and throws it. The necklace clinks against the unforgiving cave wall, then drops to the floor. The outer casing splits in two and the charm slips from its barred prison.

Shocked out of her anger, Serena drops to her knees near the charm, picking it up to wipe grime from its smooth surface. Tears begin to flow as unrestrained and unrelenting as the North Pacific Current. Her body shakes with sobs until she feels a warm hand enfolding her entire shoulder.

She looks up. Kai is looking down on her, eyebrows furrowed.

Serena stands and takes a step back, embarrassed to be caught in a moment of weakness. "What are you doing here?" she asks.

"I was sent to watch after you," he says.

Serena wipes her hand across her nose, trying to stifle the hiccups that insist on replacing her sobs.

Kai steps forward. "I thought it was to make sure you didn't make another unauthorized trip to The Dry…"

Arms hanging limp at her sides, Serena looks at him. "You have babysitting duty."

"I volunteered. And it looks like you need some company anyway."

Serena almost laughs out loud. "I need much more than that." *A mother, a new job, more wolfsbane.*

When Kai steps forward once again, the walls of her cave press in until it seems as though his wide shoulders touch each side of the room. She folds her arms across her midsection; the heat is back.

Kai extends a hand, palm open.

Looking up at him, her lips part. "What?" she breathes.

"Let me see."

"Oh," she looks down at her hands and opens them to reveal the charm inside. "It was my mother's."

Kai takes the charm from her, rubbing the rest of the grime away. "Come on," he says, smiling. "I know what we can do with this."

He steps back and Serena finds herself moving toward him like a magnet.

"What?"

"Just trust me," he winks at her.

Serena looks at him. It would be better not to get too close, she needs to concentrate on her job. Serena follows his sure footsteps down the halls. He keeps looking over his shoulder at her.

"It's quiet out here," Kai says, breaking her concentration.

Serena moves up to walk next to him. "No one has occupied these caves for a long time."

"Except you," Kai says. "Why is that?"

Serena pauses for a brief second before taking her next step.

"What?" asks Kai.

"Nothing," says Serena. "It's just that...you are the first person to ever ask me that."

"Well?" Kai prods for the answer.

"Well..." Serena stops walking and crosses her arms, turning to Kai. "Out here, I feel like I am closer to home."

He keeps looking at her, as though he expects further explanation.

"I can show you," Serena says. "That is...if you want to see?"

Kai leans against the wall, rubbing at his chin with one hand as he looks at Serena. Her eyes fall to her feet.

Finally, Kai pushes himself off the wall. "I'm up for anything you want to show me."

"Okay," Serena stammers, tucking strands of her hair behind her ear. "Come on." She leads the way toward the open ocean. Once they reach the ledge, right where water trickles in for high tide, she turns to Kai. "Ready?"

"Ready for what?" he asks, frowning and peering out into the darkness.

Serena smiles to herself. "To see what is really worth saving—even if it is beyond the borders of our kingdom."

Serena dives, forming fins and heading for the open ocean. Though coral still grows throughout the main paths of the Undine territory, it doesn't thrive and there aren't as many species that choose to dwell there. Undine seldom visit the backside of the mountain, except of course, the King's Guard during their rounds. Here, right outside of Serena's doorstep, the ecosystem is flooded with life displayed in vibrant colors and in varying textures and shapes.

Serena stops by a pile of rocks with a hole the size of her fist in between them. She peers in and sees movement. Smiling, she beckons Kai closer. She picks up a purple, spiny sea urchin and waves it in front of the hole.

A wolf eel appears, its grey lips opening in anticipation of a meal. His needle-like teeth gleam. Kai starts to back away, but Serena shakes her head at him. Serena releases the sea urchin and the wolf eel consumes it in one swallow. Kai touches his stomach, groaning. Serena doesn't blame him, thankful the Undine aren't yet reduced to have to digest such spiky things.

Before the wolf eel can retreat to its cave, Serena scratches it under the chin. It pauses, momentarily cautious, then leans into her touch. The fish runs the length of its sleek body down the back of her palm, then turns for more. For as ferocious as the creature looks, the wolf-eel is gentle and can be docile.

Wondering if the same could be learned from the werewolves, Serena gestures for Kai to hold his hand out. He does so, not taking his eyes off its teeth. The wolf-eel moves closer to Kai, rubbing against a rock. Kai glances at Serena, then back down at the fish. It touches Kai's knuckles, tentatively shrinking back;

neither one moves. Finally, the fish caresses Kai's hand with the side of his head.

Kai smiles down, mouth open in awe at the unique animal, then smiles at Serena. She smiles back, but grabs his hand to lead him away. They don't want to overstay their welcome with the temperamental fish.

Serena scans the wall of coral. Kai is sticking closer to her, stopping a moment longer than necessary next to each dark crevice, peering inside.

It is amazing, thinks Serena. *How many times has he passed over these very corals, never stopping to appreciate the life systems they support?* She smiles to herself. *I'll show him something that will put some life into his patrols.*

Farther along the reef, Serena spots what she is looking for—a dark pinkish-red octopus, spread out among the rocks. Serena motions for Kai to hang back while she swims closer, at first putting her back to the creature. He curls up his tentacles so at the end they each look like a spiral shell.

Serena puts one hand behind her, still backing up, until she reaches the octopus. It responds to her touch by reaching out himself. Serena feels the bright white suction cups slide across the palm of her hand. It tickles.

She leans back and allows the octopus to move over her. A school of fish soaring overhead is blocked out by row after row of the suction cups.

The beak between the eight legs on the underside pecks at her cheek, but it does not hurt. Its tentacles squeeze, the white cups sticking to skin and scale alike. It is the tightest hug Serena has ever received.

Suddenly, the octopus jets away, expelling ink as it goes. Serena turns around to find Kai standing there with a large rock raised over his head, trying to come to her rescue. He still doesn't understand—it's not her that needs the rescuing.

Let me try one more time, she thinks. *He has to find the beauty in this place somehow.*

She crawls along the ocean floor in the opposite the direction of the octopus, pushing herself forward with short flicks of her tail. Pausing at the bottom of a steep but short incline, Serena waits for Kai to join her. When he moves up alongside her, his eyebrow is raised in question. A devious smile slides across her face, and she gestures to just over the hill with her head. He glances up, then slowly wriggles forward.

Serena hangs back, watching his face as he displays his true inner guard. A strong but cautious thrust forward puts him at the crest of the hill, body tense and alert, eyes scanning the shallow gully below him. Finally, his gaze fixes on the deepest part of the depression in front of him, where three dozen nurse sharks lay resting after a night of hunting. His eyes fly open while he stares. Serena laughs, releasing a myriad of bubbles that float up, surrounding Kai.

Jolting away from the bubbles, Kai bats at them as if the bubbles are the threat and not the nest of nurse sharks. Serena is still laughing, having a hard time of not sucking salt water down her throat. When she rises to meet Kai, he glances at the sharks. They are beginning to stir. Panic overtaking him again, he pushes her back down the hill, covering her body with his.

Serena goes still, trying to memorize the sensation of his large body pressing into hers. His tail pins hers to the rocky seafloor, but his hand is behind her head, protecting her from the jagged stones. Soft ripples from the current rock Kai back and forth. Serena conforms to the movement, tentatively placing the palm of her hand on his chest. It swells with each breath he takes, reminding Serena of the rhythmic hum emitted by the hardened, steel engines of passing ships.

She looks up at him, and her shoulders sag. Kai is not reveling in the experience like she is. His eyes dart around as the bubbles clear, and his hands reach for a trident that isn't there.

Serena rolls her eyes, pushing him off. Before he can grab her again, she darts up and over the hill. She pauses, amidst the nest of sleeping sharks, looking over her shoulder to ensure Kai is watching. He shakes his head, from side to side, signaling very clearly to not do what she is about to do.

With a sly smile, Serena reaches for the tail of one of the sharks. Out of the corner of her eye, she sees Kai's head shake faster. A few more bubbles escape as she tries to hold back more laughter. In one, quick motion, Serena grabs a grey, sleek fin and pulls.

The shark bolts, rousing the rest of the nest. Serena feels a pair of hands under her arms, jerking her up and away from the sharks.

They crest the surface, surrounded by ocean, spitting saltwater from their lungs to breathe air.

"Why do you do that?" Kai asks.

"Do what?" Serena pushes her hair away from her face, struggling to get the glow under control after the excitement of seeing the pod of sharks.

"Put yourself in danger like that!"

"They were nurse sharks, Kai. Bottom feeders. When have you known them to attack the Undine?"

The smile disappears from her face when he frowns.

"I don't do it for the thrill," Serena explains. "I do it because it's beautiful. They're beautiful."

Kai looks at her, then stares back at the empty surface of the ocean.

"It's our home," she continues. "And it's dying. And no one is doing anything about it. Not the king, not the council, not the King's Guard..." Serena trails off as the second-in-command arches his eyebrow at her.

"There are more pressing matters," he says, lips turned down in a frown. "As one of the Temporal Caste, you should know that better than most."

She huffs, blowing a small strand of hair from her forehead. His reminder that she is the youngest Undine stings, like she is not old enough or experienced enough compared to him. "Soon there will be nothing to feed calflings, even if we had another pairing. Our own apathy has brought our ecosystem beyond a turning point."

The couple bob up and down at the surface, thrust into an awkward silence at the mention of a pairing—the Undine mating ritual. The ocean is so calm tonight, pinpoints of each star reflect on top of the water. The horizon blends with the sky, and for a moment, it seems Serena is weightless, floating in the heavens with Kai.

Serena bites the inside of her cheek, trying to bring herself back to reality. She skims her hand over the water, scattering bits of light along with the illusion.

"Where is your trident anyway?" She looks up at Kai. "You look...naked without it." The sentence came out harsher than she intends.

Kai blinks, then smiles. "My turn to show you something." He pikes his body, then dives under.

Serena shakes her head. *Don't follow him yet, you don't want to look too eager.*

She looks toward the forest, squinting her eyes at a looming cliff. There is movement—a tail, possibly. It disappears into the trees.

"Are you coming?" Kai asks. He has resurfaces and flicks a splash of water toward Serena with his tail. "Or are you just going to search for Ungainlies all night long?"

Serena sighs, wipes her face, and treads toward Kai. "It's not the Ungainlies I'm looking for."

"What then?" Kai is back to a playful mood, a smile on his face.

It's been a long time, but Serena remembers how to play, too. She smiles back, a devious spark in her eyes. "It is something...very dangerous." She says, lowering her voice and moving closer as she speaks. "Something with large red eyes, and long sharp teeth. Its fur stinks of Undine blood and its claws...ARGHH!"

Serena jumps at Kai, hands extended. His eyes go wider than they had at the nurse sharks, and she laughs as she reaches him, dunking him just below the surface. Returning to the surface with a powerful thrust, Kai heaves Serena backward. She splashes into the ocean, sunk under with more water Kai sends her way.

Sputtering and laughing together, the current pushes them into one another.

An ear-piercing howl cuts off their fun. They both turn to the cliffs. Scales along Kai's shoulders, arms, and neck pop out as quickly as the goose bumps on Serena.

"Is that the one you saw?" Kai asks.

Serena cocks her head. "The howl is familiar."

"Really?" asks Kai. "They all sound the same to me."

"I don't know," she says. "Come on, let's go."

She turns, disappearing below the waves. Kai follows a split second later, still armored in scales.

Chapter Sixteen

Serena follows Kai's lead, swimming beside him. They haven't strayed far from the kingdom, and soon they emerge into the caves, walking the corridors just below Vancouver Island. Serena breathes in the smell of wood smoke before she sees it, and knows where they are headed. The armory.

They walk in, greeted by the loud banging of hammer against metal. Ronan, the armorer, barely glances up at their entrance. The rest of the room, as crowded as it is, falls silent. Most of the guard hovers behind Murphy, who stands closest to Ronan, overseeing his work.

As withered and knobby as Ronan's hands are, they maneuver the metal on his workbench with skill and strength. Ronan is mated to the orphanage keeper, Rayne. The couple is as close as a mother and father to Serena than she ever had. Though Ronan always spent long days in the armory, he would often eat dinner with the calflings, saying very little. For that reason, Serena always tried to sit close to him. For the quiet and for the smell of wood smoke.

Serena looks at the fire, contemplating if Armorer Assistant would be a better job than Werewolf Liaison. Ronan's blackened scales represent long days that grew into years and then decades working over the fire. Most of his body is covered, as scales are better protection around the searing heat required for melting metal. Some have experienced so much exposure they are curling up. He looks as spiky as a sea urchin.

But each job inflicts its own scars. Serena looks down at her scratched legs and arms, surveying the gashes left by her most recent trip to The Dry. When she looks back up, she catches Ronan watching her. He grunts, a monotone, disinterested noise. Serena has learned he uses it for many emotions—anger, dissatisfaction, approval, humor.

"I have something for you," Kai says as he steps toward Ronan. Holding out his fist, Kai retracts his scales and peels his fingers open, displaying the charm of her mother's necklace. "Can you incorporate it somehow?"

Ronan looks down at the piece of metal on his workbench.

Serena rises on her tiptoes to try to catch a glance of what is there, but it is obscured by a myriad of tools cluttering the edge of the high table.

"Not here," says Ronan. "The metal is too far set to hold the piece in place." He rises from his seat, slowly. "But..." Ambling over to a series of weapons hanging on the wall, Ronan is slow and walks with a limp.

Serena scans the wall before he gets there. Broken and rusted tridents hang from hooks. Old knives, weakened by their time exposed to water lie in wait for melting into stronger metals. There is one weapon that stands whole and gleaming amidst a boneyard of armaments: a bow and arrow set.

The arrows are splayed out on the wall, the metal of the spearheads so clear Serena can see her own image as she nears. Next to them is a long, thin bag— their case fashioned to the back of an armored breastplate. Serena frowns. The breastplate is short and would cover little more than half a guard's torso.

The bow itself, a thin crescent, looks fragile. Serena approaches and flicks the string looped from one end to another. It is so tight it barely gives. The bow holds it strong, not bending to the pressure. The bottom edge of the bow bears Ronan's mark, a curved wave giving into flame— Ronan Sea-Fire.

Ronan holds the charm up to the center of the breastplate. "I'll have to make some adjustments to ensure it stays, but I think I can do it."

"Wait, that was my mother's!" Serena protests.

Ronan turns to look at Serena and grunts.

"The bow and arrow is for you," Kai says, standing behind Serena's shoulder.

Serena looks from Kai to Ronan.

Murphy crosses his arms. "We'll begin training tomorrow. You aren't to go to The Dry again without knowing how to use a weapon."

"But…" She looks from Murphy to Ronan. "I wouldn't know how to repay you."

Ronan's lips part. Serena thinks it is his version of a smile, but she can't be sure.

"You don't have to repay me. You were always my favorite." He holds the charm up to the fire to inspect the light that shines through.

"Your favorite?" Serena frowns, trying to remember if they've spoken two words together, until now.

Ronan flips the charm up, catching it in a solid grip. He looks at Serena and grunts.

As he walks back to his workbench, Serena tilts her chin down, hiding her smile. Ronan returns to banging away on his workbench. The guards avoid her gaze, wiping smudges from their own weapons.

Serena searches for something to distract from the suddenly awkward atmosphere.

"By the way, thank you for leaving your trident, Kai. It came in handy," she says.

"Did it?" he asks.

"It took some getting used to. Those things are heavy," says Serena. She eyes the group of King's Guard behind him. Some smile at her comment. "But my trip to The Dry would've gone very differently had I not had it with me."

"So you did see one?" Murphy asks. "A werewolf?" He stares, tensing for her answer.

Serena pauses, considering the looks from the men in the room. Usually she can decipher moods, but the King's Guard is a different story.

She nods. Murphy tenses more, if that is even possible.

"One was out there tonight." Kai says, almost under his breath.

All heads turn to look at him.

"Are you certain? It isn't a full moon tonight." Murphy says.

Kai nods. "I was at the surface myself and we heard the howl." His hand twitches, as if moving for a trident that still isn't there.

"Then how can you be sure the howl, and what you saw…" Murphy says, glancing at Serena. "Wasn't a regular wolf?"

"Same as you can tell the difference between the ocean and the sky, Murphy Air-Spirit," Serena chides him.

Murphy takes a deep breath and looks at Serena. His spine going rigid, and he seems to grow a foot taller and his shoulders a foot wider. Serena stands fast, refusing to cower for whatever rebuke is coming. Belittling the head of the King's Guard in front of his own men is as bad as stepping on the kings toes—if he were actually able to transform them.

The entire room grows silent, except for the crackling fire. Finally, Ronan's hammer resumes its steady banging. Like continual air bubbles floating up from the Earth's crust, diffusing pressure, the hammer beats the tension out of the room. Murphy's eyes flit to Ronan, and he takes a cue from the older man to move on.

"So they've found a way then," says Murphy. "To take form without the full moon." He shakes his head, looking down at his feet. "If only we could've found a way to birth our young without the full moon, or the beaches."

Behind the workbench, Ronan grunts.

Serena scratches the back of her neck, still eyeing Murphy. Kai pats Murphy's shoulder twice, hard. Murphy seems to have let Serena's remark go. She is just glad he didn't pull out his trident. Her eyes flit from Murphy to Kai, then to Ervin standing behind them. None of the three have their weapons though several others do.

"Where are your tridents?"

Their eyes snap to her, then over to Ronan. Behind her, Serena hears one last clank of the hammer at the workbench. Then a ring of metal on metal, its echo resonating around the room. Serena turns toward the bench.

As she nears, Ronan steps away. She walks around to where Ronan stands. Pushing an overturned bucket closer to the table, she steps up onto it. This side of the table is clear of tools, and the object Ronan has crafted comes into view.

A new trident, freshly sharpened and gleaming under the light of the fire, sits on the table. Serena has not seen this one before. The three tips do not contain the barb extending backward from the point. It will be easier to remove the trident from trees—or from anything—this way. The curve on the outer two prongs is deeper, and the center prong is the longest of the trio. Instead of a smooth single pole as the stem, the trident twists, convenient for a sure hold. It separates into two spiraling rods, which merge back together at the bottom.

The trident is almost the same height as her, by far the smallest of its kind to have ever existed. This trident is for Serena.

Her breath steals away, as sharply as when she fell from the tree. She recognizes the coloring. The gold of the King's Guard is mixed with magnesium alloy, a rare metal extracted straight from seawater that takes a lifetime to collect. The material is lighter than aluminum itself and is solely used to render tridents for the King's Guard.

At the stem of the weapon is a mark. It isn't Ronan's, though by all rights the sea-fire mark should be there. Instead, there is a double circle; the shape above smooth and whole, the shape below choppy. A full moon and its shadow falling upon the ocean. Moon-Shadow.

Her breath comes back, accompanied by a lump in her throat. Aside from the dolls she received from Rayne every year on her birthday, all of which had almost always been destroyed within a week by the other orphans, this is the first real gift anyone has given her. And never has she received anything so beautiful, so meaningful, and so…personal.

She reaches out, tentatively, toward the Moon-Shadow etching, her heart thudding in her chest.

"Don't touch it. Not yet." Ronan stops her hand with his own. "The metal will need to set overnight." He pats her hand. His fingers feel rough and leathery, but warm.

Serena turns her hand and grasps, pulling Ronan into a full hug, for which she receives only a grunt in response. Her body shakes as she struggles to keep silent sobs from surfacing. She keeps her face buried in Ronan's shoulder, hidden from the King's Guard. She feels Ronan's hand move to the back of her head and stroke her hair.

"You'll be just fine calfling. Just fine…" Ronan says under his breath. Though Rayne used the term of endearment for all the children in her care, never once has Serena heard Ronan use it before.

Serena takes a deep breath and steps away. Ronan smiles down at her, then turns back to his bench, cleaning his tools for the night.

As the heat in her cheeks ebb and the lump in her throat subsides, she turns to face the rest of the men. The few that were sitting stand up, and the rest turn toward her. They are large with sinewy muscle, wide shoulders, and powerful legs. They are a dream for many Undine maidens, the true fantasy of a paired partner. But Serena doesn't see that now. She sees brothers, a family she never knew she had.

And three of the elite warriors of the Undine kingdom have just watched their revered tridents be melted down and combined into a weapon for her.

"It took three of them to make mine?" she asks, looking from Ervin to Murphy.

"There was some trial and error," Murphy says.

Behind Serena, Ronan clears his throat.

"We needed it to be perfect," explains Murphy, covering for Ronan.

Her gaze falls on Kai. Ervin is Serena's best friend, and Murphy would be expected to give his weapon before he asks any other, but what motivation does Kai have?

"They were all given willingly, Serena—and for good reason. We do not see the sacrifice as a loss," Kai says. "The Werewolf Liaison is ultimately charged with saving our race, and we will do anything we can to help you, if it is you that must be out there."

Serena's chest wells with the mixed emotions of guilt, gratitude, sorrow, and pride.

One of the many guards standing behind him clutches his own trident tighter. "We tried offering ours, so the Head of the Guard, The Second, and our youngest member don't have to be—"

"And I said we will not hear of it again," Murphy turns to bark at the guard.

"As you say," the guard mumbles, dipping his head.

She smiles, stepping toward Murphy. He breathes out, and his shoulders lower as he watches Serena come closer. He holds up one hand, stopping her in her tracks and declining the hug Ronan endured. Instead, he takes his hand and lays it across Serena's shoulder, diagonal to him. This is the warrior's salute, performed before each changing of the guard when one is relieved of duty and the other assumes command.

Serena returns the salute, extending her own hand toward his shoulder. It falls short, laying to rest on his bicep. Murphy's large hand covering her entire shoulder and draping down the side is a sharp contrast to her thin wrist and wiry fingers that lay across his massive arm. They both look down. Serena laughs and Murphy cracks a smile.

Finally, Murphy pats her shoulder. "You need to get some rest for tomorrow. Ervin will take you home."

Serena nods, releasing her salute. She turns, finding herself face to face with Kai.

He doesn't give her a salute. Instead, he nods his head, that playful smile still on his face. "Thanks for showing me what is worth saving," he says.

She returns the smile. "And me," she says.

Ervin takes Serena by the arm, leading her out of the armory. A quick glance back before she turns the corner reveals Murphy and the rest of the King's Guard behind him, staring at the fires, mouths tight and grim. Kai is still watching her.

Guilt that her mind is on Kai when she should be showing more gratitude over the sacrificed weapons, overcomes Serena and she leans into Ervin. When she finally looks up, she realizes they are headed in the opposite direction of Serena's cave.

She looks at Ervin. "Home?" she asks.

They turn down the corridor that used to be filled with the chatter of a dozen Undine orphans. Now it is ghostly silent.

Ervin nods. "Home."

Chapter Seventeen

Awakening to the swish-swish-swish of a broom on floor, Serena cracks her eyes open to find Cordelia stealing glances over her shoulder as she works. Serena does not move. Instead, she surveys the otherwise empty room. It still holds cribs, toys, and swaddling blankets—objects that have been waiting for almost seventeen years to be used by a newborn Undine.

Next to the cleaning supplies is a bin of dolls. Cordelia works her way toward it, sweeping as she goes. When she pauses, Serena closes her eyes quickly, feigning sleep.

"Serena?" Cordelia whispers.

Serena doesn't answer.

Satisfied she has privacy, Cordelia picks up a baby Undine doll. She wraps the shiny pink tail in a swaddling blanket and paces back and forth across the room while she rocks the doll in her arms as steady and as soothing as a gentle summer tide.

Cordelia opens her mouth, and begins to sing to the doll. The tune is barely audible but Serena recognizes the rhythm, and the words come to her:

Hush little calfling, don't say a word,
the sting is short when scales are conjured.

Soon you will be swimming in the seas,
among Undine and anemones.

It is a tune stolen from the Ungainly song *Mockingbird*, modified to fit Society. Serena wonders which ancestor overheard the song, and if they were ever punished for absconding.

Cordelia kisses the doll on the nose and continues singing:

When you come of age your hair will shine,
No longer will you be a calfling o' mine

Grow your legs to walk ashore one day,
find a mate to take where the moon holds sway.

Cordelia pauses, swallows, and lowers her voice even further:

Even if no newborns can be found,
you'll still be the sweetest calfling in town.

Cordelia continues to rock the doll for a minute more. When she hears footsteps down the hallway, she returns the doll to the bin and the blanket to the folded pile. She leaves the room, and Serena hears a hushed conversation float in from the corridor.

Turning over in her cot, Serena's chest feels more hollow than ever. She isn't allowed to wallow in her species' misery for long. A few minutes later Rayne walks in, humming a brighter tune.

"Serenita…" she croons. "Time to wake uuuup."

Serena smiles, rubbing a palm down her face. She turns and mumbles, voice still heavy with sleep, "Morning, Mother Rayne."

"Oh, don't Mother Rayne me. Get out of bed, sleepy head." Rayne pulls the sheet off Serena with one swift motion. "You are far too old for cots and blankets."

Serena stands slowly, stretching out her back. "I don't remember them being so uncomfortable and itchy." Even still, the familiar smells and nostalgia of her childhood home helped her sleep.

"Well you are welcome to sleep here anytime," Rayne says, gathering up all the bedding for washing. "But next time try the nanny's cove."

Serena glances at the small nook carved out in the wall for the nighttime nanny, about the same size as the sleeping cove in her own cave.

"I'd forgotten about that." She looks around the room, empty save for her and Rayne. "Not that I am ungrateful, but why did Ervin bring me here?"

Rayne smiles. "Because I asked him to. You've been through enough and I thought it might help to check in at home."

Home. A small flower of warmth blooms in Serena's belly at the word.

"They've already summoned you to the Great Hall today," Rayne continues, a frown tugging at the corners of her lips.

Almost immediately the flower inside Serena shrivels.

"But first—food. Breakfast is ready, and growing cold." Rayne shuffles Serena out of the room and into the dining area next to the kitchen.

There is a long, rectangular table with benches running down the sides. Old stains spot the worn wood, and the table is pockmarked with divots and cracks, scarred from years and years serving calflings.

Bowls of food sit at one end. There is dried and shredded red seaweed, a giant bowl of noodled kelp, and nori, roasted in small sheets. A wide variety of fish and crustaceans, some raw and some freshly cooked over dried driftwood fires, are spread across the table.

It is a feast, and not just by orphan standards. The last time Serena can remember Rayne making this much food was just before a final exam. It reminds Serena what she has to look forward to today—*another punishment?* Serena slumps into her seat, her appetite gone.

But Rayne is standing over her, piling different colored sea vegetables on Serena's plate. Sliding the full plate in front of Serena, Rayne sits down across from her, then pushes a bowl of filleted salmon toward Serena. Serena crinkles her nose and shakes her head.

"You always were a picky eater." Rayne sighs. "You can't keep up your strength eating plants all day long."

"My diet contains plenty of nutrients," says Serena, her voice sour as she pushes away the salmon with her fork. Sea vegetables spend their entire lives luxuriating in the world's largest, oldest, most complete mineral bath. They soak it up and are among the richest sources of calcium, iron, zinc, and potassium, as well as fifty-three other minerals.

"Your diet has given me cause for concern over the years. Not to mention having to make sure there was something on the table you actually would eat," Rayne said, waving her hands as she talked. She always had a way of making up for Ronan's silence. "As if procuring enough food for twenty Undine at once wasn't enough."

Rayne pauses, glancing down the long, empty table. Serena remembered the chaos of mealtime. As every caste before Serena entered The Choosing, the table became less and less crowded and mealtime grew more and more quiet.

"Spent all my time in the kitchen, I did," says Rayne. It is almost a whisper as she stares at her open hands, idle with the lack of orphans.

Serena picks up her fork, digging into the seaweed. "I miss your cooking," she says, swallowing her first bite and going for more. "Now I mostly eat as I swim, picking at raw plants. There is something to be said for a warm meal." Driftwood is not easy to come by and it takes forever to dry out enough for a fire in the damp caves.

Rayne brightens with a smile. Her hands brush the table, as if they've suddenly found use.

"What's this?" Serena asks, poking at a pile of deep-green plants. "Something new?"

"Wakame. I seasoned it with salt."

Serena tries it, letting the flavors roll around in her mouth. Her eyebrows lift. "It's good."

"Thank you," says Rayne.

"No—I mean really, really good." Serena takes another bite, talking through a full mouth. "Good enough for any Undine." Serena pauses, arching one eyebrow at Rayne. "Good enough for a king."

Color creeps up Rayne's cheeks and her scales flare a deep green. "Oh, I don't think the king—"

"Trust me," Serena mumbles. "There is a lot we don't know about the king."

Rayne looks at Serena, patting her on the shoulder. "You'll be just fine."

Serena puts her fork down. "Why does everyone keep saying that?"

"Maybe," Rayne stands with new vigor, "because there is some truth to it, Serenita." She winks.

Serena grunts, sounding an awful lot like Ronan, even to herself.

"Morning, Cordelia," Rayne sings out to the new occupant of the dining room. "Want some breakfast?"

"I already ate," Cordelia says in a flat tone, glancing at Serena.

"Well, then." Rayne nods once. "If you're done with the sweeping, I suppose that's all I need for today."

The room grows silent except for the sound of Serena's fork pushing food around her plate. She can feel Cordelia staring. An itch grows on her back between her shoulder blades.

Rayne clears her throat. "Don't you have an assembly to attend today, anyhow?"

"As you say," says Cordelia.

Serena can hear her old caste mate turn and leave the room.

"As do you," Rayne says, glancing at Serena. "As do we all. If you get nervous, just look for me in the crowd. And think of...of..."

"I'll think of your wakame," Serena says. "In fact, maybe we all will. Let's pack up the leftovers."

Chapter Eighteen

"Go!" Serena pushes Rayne into the room, then steps back, hiding from the crowd.

From the quick glimpse, Serena knows most, if not all, of Society is here. There is barely room to stand in the large cavern.

"Excuse me—coming through. Can I just squeeze by?"

Rayne make her way through the crowd, bundled food in hand. The low murmur of voices grow silent and Serena risks another glance around the corner.

Rayne has only made it halfway to the front when the king's voice booms through the cavern. "What's this?"

Rayne actually takes a step back. Serena knows the feeling, but she silently wills Rayne forward. Rayne obliges, closing the distance to the throne with a hesitant stride. "Food, your majesty. For the court."

The king, and Nerin by his side, glance at each other.

"Very well," he nods, waving it toward a table on the side by the members of the council.

Rayne bobs her head, then bustles to the table.

Standing on her tiptoes, Serena's eyes come on the objects sitting on the table. They are the experiments from her cave, still sitting in crab traps and jars. Next to them is her dry box. Together, they represent every last personal object she owns, except her necklace. Serena's hand goes to the base of her neck where the jewel hung until she remembers she left it with Ronan to be incorporated into her armor.

Only a small corner of the table is uncluttered, and it isn't large enough for Rayne's food. Stacks of books, as well as Serena's personal belongings, are squeezed on the flat surface. Rayne sets the package of food on the floor, then brings her hands to the sea urchin jar, one of Serena's experiments.

"Don't touch the evidence," Zayla speaks up from behind the table. She uses her Caste-Master voice, shrill and clipped.

Heat creeps up Serena's neck and her fists clench. *That was uncalled for.* But before Serena can speak, Kai comes around the table.

"Let me," he says, laying a hand on Rayne's shoulder. Her hair has begun to glow.

He picks up the jar of sea urchins, thrusting it at Zayla. "Here, find a place for this."

She takes the jar, mouth open. She wouldn't dare challenge him, her position well below his. Still, it doesn't do for members of the council to appear divided, whether it is over sea urchins or not. They always present themselves in unity in front of Society, which is why every one of them pronounced Serena guilty. Except of course for Kai's wish to abstain.

Serena smiles when the glow leaves Rayne's locks just as Zayla's light up. Zayla leaves to set the jar on the other end of the table, forced to pile books higher for more room. A stack of them fall, toppling off the table. The noise of the accident echoes around the room and Serena overhears snickers.

Mariam bustles forward from the crowd. "Oh, good grief," she exclaims. She shoos Zayla away and picks up each book herself, inspecting them for damage as if they were her own children.

Rayne and Kai finish squeezing in each of Rayne's dishes, nudging Zayla clear of the table. With her cheeks thoroughly flushed, Zayla glares at the plate of noodled kelp.

Kai lays a reassuring hand on Rayne's shoulder. "Thank you."

Serena touches her fingertips to her lips. Kai's small actions toward Rayne mean more to Serena than a thousand golden tridents.

When Serena looks back at the throne, both the king and Nerin are staring at her.

"Serena Moon-Shadow." A voice calls out. It is Nerin's, not the king's. "You may now approach."

Serena licks her lips, trying to slow her breathing back to normal. She looks down and makes small adjustments to her scales, bringing enough out so as to be deemed appropriate for court.

Smoothing her hair, Serena glances at the end of the tresses to ensure she has her glow under control. When she walks forward, all faces are turned her way. The small path Rayne forged grows wider as Serena approaches. She tries not to concentrate on the faces, afraid of what they may exhibit. Disdain, pity, fear—each person unknowingly dousing Serena with their own form of punishment.

Instead, Serena focuses on the king's long tail, draped over the throne and extending down the steps leading up to his platform. It feels uncomfortable to stare, but it helps remind Serena even the king is not without his imperfections. Knowing this, she is able to hold her chin a little higher.

The king's flippers twitch, as if they know they're under scrutiny. Serena breaks her eyes away to survey the council, now that she is close enough. They stand as one in a line behind the table of her belongings and Rayne's food. As unified as they may appear, Serena spots a subtle difference in their attitudes.

Murphy and Kai stand tall and proud, eyes scanning the crowd. Serena catches the twitch of Murphy's right hand, the one that usually holds the trident.

Evandre, along with Sarafina, the Head Gardener, have their heads bent together, whispering and pointing to the jar of Serena's algae.

Zayla leans away from the rest of them all, arms crossed. Rayne and Mariam leave the platform together, taking their position in the front row. As Serena emerges from the crowd, she glances at them. Mariam pushes her shoulders back, encouraging Serena to do the same. Rayne winks and gives Serena a small smile. *Be brave, and we are here for you.* The messages her mentor and mother send are perfectly clear. Their colors, paired together, suddenly strike Serena as odd. Deep brown and dark green—the colors of the forest.

Serena steps up to the mid-platform, clasping her hands behind her back. She holds her breath and waits for the king to speak.

"Shall we begin?" he asks, his voice low.

Serena can imagine all of Society behind her leaning in to hear his words. "Yes, your majesty." She risks a glance behind her at Mariam and Rayne. They both shoo at her with their hands, urging her to turn back around and pay attention.

"Isadora," the king calls.

Scales glittering like black gold, the Undine psychic approaches the king to stand next to Serena. Rumor is that he has avoided her as much as possible since his wife's death. She is no doubt a painful reminder.

A few inches taller, Isadora moves so close to Serena that they brush shoulders. The psychic gives a slight nod, acknowledging Serena. Unable to return the gesture, Serena stares with wide eyes. Suddenly the audience watching her back isn't nearly so unsettling as the one maiden by her side.

"You have decided on your punishment?" the king asks.

"I have, your majesty." Isadora responds.

The king leans forward, placing his elbows on the armrests and his chin in his hands.

Forcing her eyes from Isadora, Serena doesn't wish to see her expression as she announces the next punishment.

At least we are getting through them quickly instead of dragging it out for a year.

"At first, I had a lot of trouble deciding on an appropriate punishment, one that would serve justice as well as benefit Society."

The only part of Isadora Serena can see out of the corner of her eye is her long, thin nose.

"Her past is very clouded," says Isadora. "Which doesn't lend to a clear future in my premonitions."

Serena shifts from one foot to another. *Grace Poseidon, just announce the punishment already. Even the king didn't draw it out this much. Werewolf Liaison. Boom. Done.*

"Which is why I had all of Serena's things brought to the Great Hall. Personal possessions can be as revealing as a maiden's dreams." Isadora pauses, taking a long moment to look at Serena.

Leaning back in his throne, the king begins tapping two fingers on the armrest.

Taking her cue, Isadora continues. "As you can see," she says, walking toward the table crowded with Serena's things and Rayne's food. "Much of Serena's possessions come from The Dry. In fact, I hardly see anything made right here in our own kingdom."

Serena's heartbeat flutters. She turns to watch Isadora and most of the Undine maidens in the audience come into view. There are plenty of narrowed eyes and arms crossed. Her hand goes to her flipping stomach. Squeezing her eyes shut, she pictures Liam in werewolf form. His long snout with the half-moon mark takes the place of pursed lips, and it is somehow better.

Isadora moves around the table of evidence, approaching one of Serena's jarred sea urchins. She reaches around to the back of the jar and tugs on something. It won't come loose. Tugging again, Isadora shakes the entire jar. Serena can see her sea urchins bouncing around, jostled off their rocks.

She tenses, ready to step forward. In front of her, Nerin clears her throat, then shakes her head.

Finally, an audible pop and the shaking stops. Isadora turns, and she holds in front of her a shiny, silver CO_2 bottle like a prized jewel. It stands out against her black scales. The hose still dangles from an opening.

"A prime example," she declares, thrusting the bottle into the air. The maidens closest to her lean back. She walks the length of the mid-platform, making sure all can see. When she reaches the end, she turns a knob on the bottle, releasing the contents at full throttle. She walks it in front of the assembly again, this time with CO_2 spewing out of the hose. A wave of Undine lean away as it oscillates down the crowd.

The hose makes a shrill whistle, and draws circles in the air. Isadora turns to Serena.

"You just wasted my last CO_2 canister," Serena says before Isadora has a chance to speak. "It is an Ungainly apparatus, extremely hard to come by." If the truth of the full extent of her absconding will come out, Serena will speak it first.

Isadora opens and closes her mouth, at a loss for words. The canister's whistle sputters out, the hose hanging limp with the last of the air gone. Isadora licks her lips. "So you do not deny it?"

"What?" Serena asks.

"That this was in your possession, taken from the Ungainly?"

"I very well can't deny it now, having just stated it." Serena points out the obvious, tapping her foot in time to the king's own tapping on his armrest.

A quick glow runs down the inside of the Isadora's hairline. "Then how, exactly, did you come by it?" she asks.

The event is so clear in Serena's mind, it would be difficult to fabricate a lie. Holding back her shoulders, Serena turns to the king and answers. "I entered an Ungainly camp at night, stealing four of those canisters. They were strapped to those wheeled contraptions Ungainlies sometimes pedal through the paths of the forest. No one saw me."

"And the purpose?" asks Isadora, replacing the canister back on the table.

Serena is still addressing the king. At least in this direction, she doesn't need to imagine dozens of werewolf snouts. "I need the canisters to emulate rising acidity levels in the ocean." She glances at the table of her experiments, the results speaking for themselves. "My control groups thrive with life while the CO_2 groups are in obvious decline, if not all together dead. If I may, your majesty, this is the problem Society needs to focus on, not my punishments."

"You may not," The king leans forward in his throne. "We are here to administer the second of your punishments, not to solve the acidity problems in our ocean."

Isadora takes her place by Serena's side again. "Serena Moon-Shadow has undoubtedly made unauthorized visits to The Dry," she says. "As she just stated herself, she is stealthy enough to sneak into Ungainly camps and return with their instruments without getting caught."

Serena narrows her eyes. *Where is she going with this?*

"If the king pleases, for Serena's second punishment, I task her with observing the werewolf camp and reporting her findings."

Serena's gasp echoes with that of the crowd behind her.

Chapter Nineteen

"Surely she is capable," Isadora speaks over the protests of the crowd. "After all, I'm not asking her to sneak in and steal something."

Unable to speak, Serena's hand goes to her fluttering stomach. Underneath the fear that courses through her body at the prospect of approaching the entire wolf clan's camp, Serena has to admit there is a small twinge of excitement.

"They'll smell her from a mile away!"

Serena isn't sure but she thinks it is Mariam's voice shouting out from the crowd.

The king still hasn't spoken and in his silence, Isadora feels the need to continue to justify the punishment. "It seems a fitting duty as an extension of her assignment as Werewolf Liaison. She can bring back valuable intelligence—information we can use to solve the problems of our kingdom."

The king's eyes flit away from Isadora, who continues to ramble, and come to rest on Serena.

Noises from the crowd along with Isadora's speech blend together and become a dull roar in the background while the king's bright blue eyes come into sharp focus. The corner of his mouth twitches, pulling at the long white beard that hangs from his chin.

Serena gives the slightest of nods. *I can do this.*

"Very well," says the king. "The second punishment has been assigned."

The Great Hall goes quiet—the decision is made.

"But our Werewolf Liaison will not go on the mission without some basic knowledge on how to defend herself," he says.

Murphy and Kai step forward from the line of the King's Guard at the same time, almost as if it was rehearsed. Serena turns to leave with them, still stunned—and not for the first time—at the decisions coming from the Great Hall. She is stopped short with a cold hand on her arm.

"Look for the one called Alaric," hisses Isadora. "I must know about him. Every detail."

Jerking her elbow from the council member's grasp, Serena returns a harsh gaze and doesn't answer. She is sure Isadora has her own reasons for this particular punishment, but Serena can't decide what they are.

Once in the corridor, Murphy motions to Kai who hands Serena her bow and arrow set, complete with breastplate armor. She runs the pad of her thumb over the her mother's charm, now inlaid into the center of the chest. She smiles up at Kai, but he is already following Murphy down the hall.

Serena trots to catch up, struggling to put on her new armor while she moves. The King's Guard walk so fast. Arms through, arrow carrying case adjusted on her back, straps cinched in on the sides. Just as she finishes with the last strap, Murphy and Kai dive into the receding tide. Their legs transform into fins before they even hit water.

Serena pauses for a moment, astonished. She has always prided herself on how often she transforms, and how little pain it causes compared to others. It didn't ever occur to her to practice with speed.

Though, in The Dry, it would absolutely come in handy.

She trudges into the water, her entrance clumsy compared to those before her. Calling forth her own natural body armor, her scales bump against the inside of her breastplate. It moves and shifts, then settles over a new type of skin.

In the water the bow, the arrows, and the rest of the contraption create a drag Serena is not used to. Serena follows the wake of the guards in front of her, their fins almost already out of view. She looks down, trying to adjust straps as she swims. She should have had all the scales out before she put on the armor.

When Serena looks up, Murphy and Kai are gone, and so is their wake. She opens her throat and pushes out whistles and clicks, then waits for the echo. Sound comes back to her, clarifying and expanding her vision farther than her eyes allow. She turns, completing a full circle. When she stops, Murphy is there treading water. She almost does a double-take. Kai is behind him, keeping his distance.

Murphy raises a questioning eyebrow at Serena. Then he sends out his own signal. It is loud and obnoxious, pushing her back several feet in the water.

Her vision goes wonky and she has to shake her head to rid herself of the sound. When it clears, Murphy is still there, looking at her. He buzzes again.

She tries holding up her hands, warding off the sound, to no effect. Serena is pushed back even farther. The noise is jarring and she can feel her hair begin to glow in anger.

She swims back to her original spot, letting out her own signal again. *Back off.*

The Head of the Guard cocks his head, almost as if he is studying her beacon. Then he listens to the echo that comes back to them. He turns to look over his shoulder at Kai who glances at his leader, then back to Serena. Serena doesn't understand the exchange at all.

When he turns back around, Murphy reaches out to her. As an instinct, Serena swats away his hand.

His eyes open in surprise and his mouth tips up in a smile. He points to one of her buckles that has come undone.

Serena lifts her arm, realizing he is only trying to help. His buzzing still has her on edge. She nods, allowing him to make adjustments. He moves to her side, redoing the straps and cinching them tighter. Serena's body jerks with each tug.

Now behind her, Murphy twists the arrow case. She hadn't realized it did that. The opening now faces her fins, but the arrows are strapped so they do not fall out. The pointed bottom of the case sits close to the base of her neck, and each side follows the curve of her back.

Murphy moves in front of Serena again and turns the bow in her hand so the lower limb lies against her arm. He flashes a smile and swims away. Serena follows, keeping her distance. She still expects him to turn and buzz any second. She'll do anything he wants so long as he doesn't do that again.

Ahead, Serena has to move to the side to avoid a clump of jellyfish. She realizes her arrow case and armor no longer create drag. In fact, she barely notices she has them. She speeds up, moving from side to side, then up and down, imitating waves. Still no drag. Ronan's invention is brilliant.

Murphy and Kai are almost gone again, but by now, Serena recognizes exactly where they are headed. The archives.

She angles down, then speeds up to enter the tight passageway. Fizzy bubbles from Murphy's and Kai's trails emerge from the tunnel. The usual routine follows. *Fins streamline, scales and hair slick back.* The undercurrent helps her gain speed.

Right shoulder up and back. Serena's arrow case bumps against the tunnel wall. She frowns. She hasn't bumped these walls since she was a calfling. She ducks her head. The tip of the backward arrow case nicks the ceiling. Serena can feel the buckles strain at the change in pressure.

Slowing down for the curve ahead, Serena compensates for the extra bulge at her back. Her breastplate scratches against the wall. She gasps, placing a hand over her mother's charm to protect it. In return, her knuckles scrape against rock.

She picks up speed in the last section, counting on brute force to get her through, unscathed or not. Twisting to conform as best as she can to the crooked tunnel, Serena scrapes against the wall again and feels a buckle come undone. She holds the entire contraption in place, swimming even faster. It feels like she is learning the tunnel all over again.

She is going so fast that when she breaches the surface of the archives entrance pool she comes completely out of the water, adapting from fins to feet and landing steady on the rocky ledge.

Murphy and Kai, already wearing their robes, turn in surprise. Serena refuses to look at them, keeping her chin high and her gaze well away from their ankles.

"Have you always been able to transform that fast?" asks Kai.

Serena reaches the robes hanging on the hooks. She removes her arrows and armor, setting them and the bow on the ground. She glances at Kai. "I learned from the best."

Just a few minutes ago, in fact.

She puts on a robe and picks up her weapons. "Shall we?"

Murphy nods, and Serena leads the way into the archives. Serena sets her weapons down on a table, which is still littered with werewolf books.

"What was that all about?" She turns to Murphy, arms crossed.

"What?" he asks.

"That...that...buzzing!" She almost shivers at the memory.

"Effective, isn't it?" He smiles. "And necessary. Something has to keep the King's Guard in line." He moves into the archives at a slow pace, craning his neck to follow the books straight up the ceiling of the large cavern. "You also have a very distinct call. Almost like..." Murphy trails off.

"Almost like what?" asks Serena.

"It's hard to describe." Murphy glances at Kai, who is quick to jump in.

"You know how the moon holds sway over the ocean, and to an extent, us? Its call isn't as strong as the ocean, but no one can deny it is there," he says.

Serena nods.

"Well, your call is like that."

"My call is like the moon?" Serena doesn't get it, but a flickering memory of the maiden girl led away for punishment because she couldn't resist Serena's call over the king's crosses her mind.

"Something like that," Murphy is looking at Kai, eyebrows knitted together. "Never mind," he says. "Let's get started."

He motions to several training tridents leaning against the wall. They are simple in design, and obviously well-used by the guard. "We'll start with the bow and arrow, then move on to tridents."

Serena follows him to the center of the archives. "Why in here? Why not practice in The Dry? Or in one of your training rooms?"

Murphy reaches behind Serena to turn her arrow pouch back over, clicking it into place. He removes an arrow, studying its bend.

"We don't want to practice in The Dry and give your enemies a chance to watch. Your abilities should be a surprise to them. And the King's Guard training room is for the King's Guard," he says, crossing his arms.

"Oh." She shifts the armor on her front, as though it will protect her from the sting of his comment.

"Besides." His thumb traces the sharp edges at the tip of the arrow. "What better place to perfect your aim, than in your beloved archives?"

"Oh," Serena says again, louder and more drawn out this time. Her eyes wander up the shelves as she turns in a full circle, imagining all her stray arrows sticking out of ancient books.

Mariam would be so upset.

Chapter Twenty

When Serena, Murphy, and Kai return to corridors of Society, it is nearly empty. Serena is beaming—the archery training was successful. Not that she hit any of her marks, but in that she avoided all the books.

The trident training was much more difficult. Her wrist is sore from the numerous amount of times Kai made her catch the three-pronged spear and rotate the full weight of it around until it comes to rest, straight up and down at her side. She doubted many werewolves would be throwing tridents at her in The Dry, but didn't say as much. She was working to impress Kai more than anything else.

After Murphy excuses himself, Kai turns to Serena. "Shall I escort you home?" he asks.

"To the orphanage," she answers. With all her things still on display in the Great Hall, her cave will be more barren and uninviting than ever.

"As you say," he winks, slipping his hand under the crook of her elbow.

She looks down, heat crawling up her cheeks.

"What?" he asks.

"Nothing," she glances at him. "It just feels like we are on our way to a formal dance."

"Well if we were, you'd be the belle of the ball, for sure."

"I don't think so," says Serena. "I'm no good on my short-webbed toes." She brushes them across the rough cave floor as they walk.

"Just for the record," he squeezes her arm. "I like your webbing. It's not long, almost extending to the end of your toes like Isadora's, or that old oyster gardener that likes following me around."

"That's an age thing," Serena says.

"What?" Kai frowns.

"The older generations have longer webbing while the middle-aged maidens have webbing that extends only to the second knuckle. Then there are the maidens my age—we all have shorter webbing, it is barely even there." Serena stops for a second, willing herself to shut-up. It's as if she is encouraging Kai to check out other maidens—or at least their feet. "I suppose if you took exact measurements, you'd find the Temporal Caste breaks all sorts of records when it comes to webbing length."

"And why do you suppose this is?" asks Kai.

Serena pauses in the corridor, waiting for a pair of maidens to pass. She can't help but notice Kai does not even glance at their feet. After they are well out of earshot, she looks up at Kai. "It is because the Undine are evolving. Nature is preparing us for life in The Dry."

Never having spoken those words aloud before, not even to Mariam or Rayne, Serena holds her breath waiting for Kai's response.

"Don't mention that to the old crones," he smiles. "Can you imagine their response?" His voice goes up a notch, imitating that of an elderly maiden. "These are my grandmother's grandmother's hands. They have not changed. Evolution? Not for the Undine."

Serena laughs. By the time it dies out, they are alone in the corridor.

"So…this is what you do in your spare time," Kai raises an eyebrow at Serena. "Have you discussed your theories with anyone?"

"I sort of tried to tonight, with the king. But he has other things on his mind."

"You're not lying about that," Kai says, taking her hand.

Serena allows it, and they hold hands the rest of the walk. It feels like guppies are fluttering around in her stomach, and she prays to Poseidon that she doesn't trip and fall. When they turn the corner, sounds from the orphanage assault them. It is loud, and not just the calfling kind of loud—things breaking, squawks and cries, fighting. These rooms haven't emitted those sounds in years. This time there are pots and pans clinking, teapots whistling, Rayne shouting orders, and others responding.

Serena and Kai slow their pace. Neither want any part of those sounds. Serena squeezes Kai's hands.

"Get another pot boiling!" Rayne's voice rings out from the kitchen.

Serena and Kai stand back from the door, leaning only slightly to look in. They don't want to attract any more attention than they must.

Zayla, one of three helpers there, is rooting through the cupboards. "There are no more."

"Well, we can't let the skies fall because of that." Rayne has her hand on her hip, sauce dripping from a spoon in her other hand. "Fetch a dirty one from the sink."

Zayla shrugs, retrieving a pot, pockmarked with dried stains from the previous sauce.

"You'll have to wash it, of course," shoots Rayne over her shoulder.

Zayla freezes at the jab, shoulders tight and bunched up around her neck. But she picks up the soap from the counter.

"Assembly is over?" Rayne turns her attention to Kai and Serena.

Kai nods and Serena shifts on her feet. She realizes they are still holding hands and she blushes, unlacing their fingers from each other so she can cross her arms over her mid-section.

"Good," says Rayne. "You can help with the food for assembly tomorrow."

Kai doesn't hesitate, taking three long strides toward Rayne and bowing before her. "I must return to my rounds, but I thank you for your sustenance today at assembly. It was delicious."

After Rayne accepts his thanks, Kai turns on his heel and walks out. As he passes Serena, he whispers. "I won't be far."

"What about you? You gonna find some excuse to skip out?" Rayne flicks her spoon at Serena.

Serena licks her lips, glancing around the room. Four other faces tell her she'd better not, which is exactly why she does. "Sleep," she announces.

Rayne smiles. "Well—can't argue with that, can we now? A girl needs her sleep."

Serena nods once in appreciation, and keeps her eyes down. She doesn't need to see the angry faces of the rest—the goose bumps down her back give her an accurate image.

The noises in the kitchen resume under Rayne's steady guidance and Serena smiles. After several years of an empty orphanage, it finally has purpose again making food for assembly. With Rayne at the helm, everything will fall into place just right.

Serena returns to the newborn room, this time ignoring the itchy cot and blankets, and hops up to the nanny crook. She curls into the hard rock of the foreign sleeping cove, wishing she had her hammer and chisel to work while she settled her mind. But, much like herself, they are hostages of the king and council. At least her mother's charm was spared, tucked safely away in a bodice of armor, held by Murphy for now.

Serena tosses and turns, counting out at least one hundred breakers in her head. Sleep doesn't come. Her mind is on her upcoming punishment—the visit to the werewolf camp. Serena hops down from the nook. Tiptoeing down the hall, Serena sneaks past the noisy kitchen and out the front entrance. She runs directly into Kai.

"Oomph!" he says as they both bounce back from each other.

"You again?" Her tone is sharper than Serena intended. She takes a deep breath, looking at Kai. "I didn't mean it like that. It's just—don't you ever sleep?"

"Don't you?"

Serena looks back to make sure no one sees them, then she kicks at the rocks by her feet. Kai has a point. "I just want to get my punishment over with."

"The king said you weren't to go until you've had training," Kai crosses his arms.

"Right," says Serena. "I believe the training we've had so far is sufficient enough to return to The Dry." *And I need to get out of here. Please understand*, she thinks. *I need someone to understand.*

Kai's face softens. His lips part, just slightly, and he scratches the back of his neck.

"Wait here," says Kai. "I have to get permission from the king, and…something else."

"What?"

"Your armor." He looks at Serena. "Just, wait. Promise?"

"Promise," says Serena, huffing. He'd better be quick, before Rayne finds her out here and puts her to work in the kitchen.

Kai disappears around the corner. Serena keeps an ear out for Mother Rayne.

"Psst, Serena—come on!" Kai beckons her to join him. He hands her the bow and arrow set as she does.

"That was fast..." she trails off as the rest of the King's Guard greet her in low voices. "What is this?" she asks, narrowing her eyes at Kai. She shrugs on her breastplate.

"It's your armor," replies Kai, tugging at one of her straps.

She can't tell if he is referring to the King's Guard or the breastplate.

The guards shift as they prepare themselves, and Serena spots the king, waiting in the water where the tide creeps in, arms crossed.

"What is he doing here?" she whispers.

Kai leans over, whispering back, "Murphy wants the entire King's Guard to escort you."

"So?" asks Serena.

"So?" Kai blanches, no longer whispering. "We can't leave the king unprotected. If all of us are with you, he has to be with you, too."

Serena bites her bottom lip. *Maybe this was a bad idea.*

The king is going to tag along. She looks around Kai toward his majesty. Does he resent having to do this? Or was it his idea? His demeanor gives no clue; he always looks angry.

Murphy steps forward. "Where are we headed?"

Serena looks from the king, to Kai, and finally to Murphy. "Forest Beach," she says.

Murphy looks over his shoulder at the king. King Merrick nods. He is definitely still running the show.

"Very well," says Murphy. "Lead on, we will follow. But take the long way."

"The long way?" Serena asks. She isn't aware there are two separate paths—the beach is a straight shot from here.

"Go north, out of the caves, then circle around the island to come back to the beach."

Serena frowns. That route leads over the most populated spots in the kingdom.

Murphy gestures with his arm. "Maybe sometime before the moon sinks?"

"As you say," Serena mumbles, heading toward the water.

Scales push forward, covering her body as she enters. She tells herself to look straight ahead, and not glance at the king. Once the water hits her knees, she pauses, waiting for a surge in the current. When it comes, she jumps, pikes her body, and dives. By the time she has to arch her back to keep from hitting the ground, her legs have transformed into fins.

She doesn't wait or even turn back to see if the rest of the guard follows, preferring to leave the lot behind. When the entrance corridors leading to the Great Hall come into view, there are dozens of Undine flowing in and out of the caves.

Doesn't anyone ever sleep? Perhaps she isn't as different from everyone else as she thinks; or as they think.

As Serena nears, they slow to watch her pass, eyebrows raised. They aren't smirking and they aren't backing away.

Serena glances over her shoulder and the entire King's Guard comes into view. They have organized themselves into an inverted v-formation behind her, with Murphy at Serena's left and Kai on her right. Her position, at the apex of the formation, is where the king usually resides when traveling…anywhere. Now, the king is perched in the middle of the group. He swims several spans higher where he is impossible to miss.

Buzzes and flutters arch through the ocean—the underwater chatter of Society, spreading news of an abnormality. The column moves past the entrance corridors just as a surge of Undine emerge. They scan the landscape, already aware of the excitement, then point up at the procession.

Just as before, too many eyes cause goose bumps to pop up along the back of Serena's neck. It seems that every gawking Undine brings ten more bumps with them. Serena forces her eyes ahead, keeping her chin high.

None of this was my choice, she tells herself. *They can think what they want.*

She fingers her mother's charm fixed to her breastplate.

They leave behind the crowd at the cave entrances, drifting over the oyster gardens. More Undine watch, eyes widening in surprise at the procession behind her. Serena forces her gaze to the cages of oysters lining the bottom of the ocean. They serve to filter the water, removing algae as they feed.

She relaxes a little more, the crowd of Undine isn't preferable, but it is no longer torture.

The column circles the island, and Serena leads the way back to Forest Beach, picking up speed. She is anxious to get this over with.

Angling her nose up and her fins down, Serena crests the surface in no time. She won't take her usual precautions, surveying the empty beach from upstream then down. In fact, she isn't sure how far the procession intends to follow. Their presence alone would undo any stealthy measures Serena performs.

The sound of sputtering announce breaching Undine as they force their lungs to transform for a dry intake of air.

She looks over her shoulder, annoyed. Perhaps the King's Guard patrol route needs to include at least one stop in The Dry. That is, after all, where their enemies reside.

After all the sputtering ceases, Serena moves forward, hoping the waves breaking against the shore mask the sounds of the large group. To their credit, she does not detect one whimper when they transform fins to legs.

She steps forward, her deformed Undine webbing leaving pristine prints in the wet sand. The king, of course, stays behind in the water.

Once wet sand turns to dry, Serena stops. The column, still in formation, follows suit. The forest is loud with crickets, birds, and wind snaking through the trees, ruffling the leaves like feathers.

"What will you do?" asks Murphy, leaning forward into her ear so she can hear his whisper.

"Find my werewolf," says Serena. "I think he will help me get to the camp."

"And then what?" asks Murphy.

"I   don't   know."   Serena   shrugs.
"Maybe…bowling."

"What's…bowling?"

Serena shakes her head. "I have no idea."

Murphy sighs. "I wish you'd wait until your
trident is done. Or at least until you can hit a mark
with one of your arrows." He flicks at a shaft, sticking
up out of the case on her back.

Serena turns, looking at him, trusting the rest of
the guard to watch their backs. "I'm getting the
feeling there isn't much time left, Murphy." She looks
down at her feet, wiggling her stunted webbing into
the sand.

Murphy smiles. "Okay, Serena Moon-Shadow.
Off with you then."

She nods, turning back around. One deep breath,
then a step toward the tree line.

Behind her, Serena hears the brush of armored
scales coming together as the column of guards snaps
to attention. Feet shuffling in sand tells her they are
moving forward.

A loud thud from the ocean causes them all to
turn. It is the thump of fins on water, a warning
straight from the king. He pushes the majority of his
torso out of the water, crossing his arms and staring
Murphy down. The King's Guard is not to go any
farther.

"It's okay." Serena puts a hand on Murphy's tense
arm. "I've got this."

Chapter Twenty-One

Serena steps forward, unaccompanied. There is only silence behind her. Her stomach drops more with every stride, though she keeps her chin high.

Show them you aren't scared, she tells herself. The problem is, Serena doesn't know if she is trying to impress the Undine behind her or the werewolves that may lie in wait in front of her.

Pushing aside shrubs, Serena enters the tree line. Branches and leaves close in behind her as she passes, obscuring the Undine guards from view and blocking out the sounds of the ocean. Her eyes flit to the branches above, craving their safety, but she remains on the ground. If she is to be the link between Society and The Dry then she very well can't stay hidden in the trees like a scampering squirrel. Her footprints leave a long, obvious trail from sea to trees.

The wind picks up, catching a yellow flower. The bell-shaped bloom skips along the ground, turning end over end. As it passes Serena, scales emerge over her ankles and up her legs—a precaution. She pauses, watching it float by. Even the shrubs on the ground seem to lean away from it.

Serena takes a deep breath, waiting for the rest of her scales to emerge. It stings worse when she is in The Dry. When she steps forward, parting the bushes, her tree comes into view. Only some of the wolfsbane scattered on the ground has succumbed to the wind. Most of it remains, along with the braided wolfsbane ropes wrapped around the tree. The end of the ropes have unraveled, and swing loose in the breeze, just like the kelp forest outside of her cave. It feels like home.

Drawing closer, her eyes drop to the ground and she freezes. Just outside of the wolfsbane flowers rests a steady stream of wolf prints. In places, the prints are so thick they overlap each other so there is no way to establish where one ends and the other begins. There is one long, circular path—a border created between her tree and the rest of The Dry. It smells like wet dog.

She bends down, tracing the outline of one of the prints. The tip of her scaled finger pushes through dirt, wet granules sliding across and resettling alongside the impression. Serena moves to another print, doing the same. They are all the same length and width, and each has a deeper groove toward the right side of every other print.

A werewolf spent a significant amount of time here, walking circle after circle, creating a boundary line.

Her neck prickles; she turns, surveying the tree line, but there is nothing.

She grits her teeth together. *If I can't take a single tree, how can the Undine expect to take back the beaches? This is my tree. MINE.* She won't be made to feel terrified in her own home. Or at least her home away from home. Serena walks into the wolfsbane, untying the basket she left tethered to the tree.

After a quick trip to the wolfsbane gardens, she returns with a full basket. Dropping to her hands and knees, she works as the moon moves across the sky, replacing what flowers blew away and then some. Serena extends the circle, covering each footprint with at least five flowers. After the yellow petals cover a large span past the wolf-made border, she pauses, looking at the tree stump. It is the stump where the wolf sat as he introduced himself.

"Liam of Clan Werich," Serena says to herself, out loud. She is surprised she could remember the foreign words. "Well, Liam—I suppose I can allow you some entrance into my court."

The wolfsbane has just reached the stump. Here, Serena extends it farther, elongating one side so her perfect circle has become a lopsided oval. Then, she removes enough petals to clear a narrow path from the outside to the stump.

A grand entrance, she thinks. *Or grand enough for a hound, anyway.*

She smiles and turns, surveying the tree. Now— time to do something with these swinging ropes.

Serena decides to go with the kelp effect and gets to work tightening the existing ropes and constructing new braids. When the first is done, she removes an arrow from her quiver and ties the braid of flowers to the shaft.

She looks around, Murphy's words nagging her. *We don't want to give your enemies a chance to observe you.* Serena shrugs. This isn't exactly target practice.

She nocks her arrow, then raises her hands, aiming into the sky. The string is tight, but she manages to pull it back to the corner of her mouth. *Easy...easy.* Relaxing the fingers of her string had, she releases the arrow. Serena watches it take flight, dragging the braided line of wolfsbane behind it. It arches up, and at its apex, a thin, silvery line slices through the silhouette of the moon.

The rope catches over one of the higher branches and the line goes taut, the arrow jerking back. It bounces a couple times before settling into a futile swing back and forth in the wind.

Perfect, Serena smiles.

She climbs two branches to retrieve the arrow, then she does it all over again with another line of flowers. By the time the moon sinks into the ocean, and the sun rises to take its place, the tree is adorned in dozens of yellow tendrils, swaying aimless in the wind.

Serena retrieves her arrow from the last strand of wolfsbane, and replaces it in her quiver. Standing on a low branch with one foot slightly in front of the other, she raises her chin. Her strong stance is interrupted by the slow-moving strings of poison blowing in the breeze as she leans around them. Even though she is fully scaled, she doesn't want to take any chances.

"Where are you, Liam of Clan Werich?" she asks aloud.

I will listen for your call. Serena remembers what Liam told her. Then there was Murphy's piece of information. *You have a very distinct call.*

Serena didn't think there was anything unique about her clicks and whistles, but then again, she never had to use them much. There just wasn't anyone to call.

She opens up her gills along her neck, sucking in cool air and expending it through her mouth. The sound starts as a low hum in her throat, then breezes past her lips in a whistle. Her throat rhythmically closes and opens, adding clipped clicks to the song.

She stops, listening for the echo. The birds and insects of the forest have gone silent, as if they are listening, too. It comes back to her, distorted and murky, as usual in The Dry.

Serena readjusts her breastplate and quiver, waiting. She counts out the span of fifty breakers, then tries again. The birds and insects do not resume their noisy, early-morning chatter. Instead, Serena hears footsteps. She can imagine Liam, in his wolf form, leaning harder to his right side than his left as his prints showed her. Like Ervin—only opposite.

He noses his way through the bushes and Serena stands taller, watching his every movement. He doesn't seem as big this time, and the teeth hanging through his lips not nearly so long. But it is definitely Liam, his crescent moon-shaped marking bright among the rest of his facial fur.

The wolf approaches the wolfsbane, pausing every few feet to sniff at the circle, cringe, and look up at Serena. Around the side of the tree, his path wavers as he moves in and out, as if the circle might retract when he comes closer. This time when he disappears behind the tree, Serena does not strain to look.

She hears popping and groaning, and the rustling of leaves—then Ungainly footsteps. When he comes back into sight, Serena looks at her nails, pretending to pick at them. It is useless because her fingers are covered in scales.

"Bringin' your home to work with you?"

She purses her lips. "What?" Serena finally looks at him and sees he is wrapped in his cape again.

Where does he hide that thing?

"You made your point with the wolfsbane." He moves to kick at one of the flowers sticking up out of the ground, then thinks better of it. "But did you really have to turn your tree into a giant jellyfish?"

Serena smiles, her eyes lighting up as she looks around. He's right. With the umbrella-shaped canopy pulsating in the wind, and the trailing tentacles that come complete with their own sting, she brought the oldest multi-organ sea animal with her to The Dry.

She looks back at the wolf. "Happy birthday."

There is a split second, where his eyes widen, almost with shock, and his face splits open in a grin— then laughter.

Serena doesn't understand the humor; it was meant as sarcasm. She's been witness to more than one Ungainly birthday, celebrated on the beach, always with gifts and games. It struck her as odd, more than once, how many of them prefer to be close to water when commemorating their birth event.

His laughter trails off as Serena shifts on her branch. The bow still feels awkward in her hands.

I wish I still had Kai's trident.

The wolf readjusts his cape, then saunters over to the tree branch. He makes a show of sucking in to attempt the narrow path to his stump. When he reaches it, he has to back his heels up against it to keep his toes from hitting wolfsbane.

"I guess you didn't realize just how big my feet are," he says, with a nervous laugh.

"Hmm." Serena grunts, channeling Ronan. She at least knows exactly how big his wolf prints are— she'd spent almost the entire night filling in his prints with wolfsbane.

He finally sits, knees up into his chest to avoid flowers. "So, Serena Moon-Shadow. What would you like to discuss?"

"Discuss?" Serena asks.

The wolf puts one hand over his heart, and holds the other in the air. "I propose a temporary truce, in order that we may confer." His voice is high and nasally, mocking her.

Serena steps forward. "I wouldn't call forcing a border between my tree and the rest of your lands a truce, exactly."

His eyes narrow. "And I wouldn't call shovin' a wolfsbane-laced trident in my face a truce, exactly."

Serena presses her lips together. "I was protecting myself. I didn't know your intentions—I still don't."

"And I don't know yours."

She crosses her arms, resisting the urge to stamp in frustration.

"Maybe," the wolf taps his chin, "we can just start by asking each other questions."

Serena shrugs. "Okay, I'll start—since you must still be recovering from that trident that nearly touched your face what…two moons ago?"

The wolf's face goes blank. He is masking an emotion, and Serena doubts it is more humor.

"Where do you hide your cape?" she asks.

He furrows his eyebrows. Thick, they almost touch each other in the center. "That is what you want to know?"

Serena sits down on her branch, legs hanging down from either side. "I thought we'd start simple."

"The answer…is not exactly simple. In fact, I'll take a pass on that question."

Serena crosses her arms. "We are not getting off to a good start here."

He plays with a frayed edge of his cape. "Shall I—?"

"I get another question," Serena interrupts. "Two, in fact. For every one that you don't answer."

He sighs, readjusting the placement of his feet, trying to keep them as far from the wolfsbane as possible.

"You can shift anytime, not only under the full moon?" she asks. The answer is obvious, given the form he arrived in. But right now Serena just wants to get him talking.

Liam looks up into the sky. The moon is a solid crescent tonight, the shape of the birthmark on his face. "Yes," he says.

"Is it the same with all werewolves?"

He pauses for a moment, debating how to answer. "No."

His hesitation was enough; Serena can't fully trust his answer.

The wind picks up and a braided rope swings precariously close to Serena. She leans out of the way.

"Is wolfsbane poisonous to mermaids, too?" Liam asks.

"It's Undine, and is that your question?"

He pauses for a moment. "Yes."

Serena leans away as the braided rope swings back through. She frowns, not wanting to reveal wolfsbane is harmful to Undine, too. They could find a way to use it against her people. This little game is getting more complicated than she expected.

"Two questions for every one you don't answer," taunts Liam.

It is Serena's turn to sigh. "This isn't going to work."

"Ah, and so the tables have turned."

Serena frowns at his statement, looking around. There are no tables, and the only thing turning is the earth they stand on.

Liam stands, brushing off his cape. "We need to start with somethin' a little less damnin'."

Some of his vocabulary can be confusing. She rubs her temples and feels warm light hit her back. The sun has crested the treetops. She doesn't have much time left. Dry sun is harsh on Undine skin and scales, plus it brings out the Ungainlies. "How about we start with a favor?"

Pausing, Liam looks up at Serena. "What kind of favor?"

"Show me your camp." Holding her breath, Serena holds his gaze, trying to put off an air of composure.

"Why?" he asks.

Serena blinks. *Oh no—I don't answer this question very well*, she thinks of the denial to visit the King's Library after the king himself asked 'why'. She tugs at the bottom of her breastplate, stalling. She could go with the truth, that it is a task assigned to her as a punishment or that Society wants to learn everything they can about the werewolves, but neither of those sit well even with Serena.

"Well," she starts. "The Undine created werewolves. During caste lessons we learned that maidens watched over you, just as you watched over us—in the beginning, at least."

So far so good, Serena judges Liam's reaction. His eyes seemed to have softened a bit.

"I know things have gone terribly wrong, but I believe there is a general feeling from each side that we want to fix this." Serena doesn't know that to be true, but she hopes it is. If the ocean is delivering the Undine ashore in order for their species to survive, it needs to be in the hands of allies, not enemies.

"The maidens are...concerned." Serena remembers Isadora and her request. Now that she thinks about it, was that desperation lining Isadora's eyes as she asked about Alaric? She looks back at Liam, resolve in her voice. "They want to know the werewolves are alive and well." Serena either believes her own lie, or it is no lie at all.

After a long pause, Liam stands up from his stump. He makes his way out of the wolfsbane path, then turns with a flourish. "I swear by my life, all of Clan Werich is alive and well."

Serena shakes her head. "I must see it for myself."

Running a hand through his hair, Liam huffs. He paces back and forth, constantly looking at Serena as if her true intentions might be written on her face.

He needs more convincing.

"I will be in the unique situation of being the only Undine to view the werewolf camp, at least so far as I know. I will pass on only as much information is as needed to convince my king and council to take the peaceful path," Serena says. "That's what you want, isn't it?"

He huffs again but stops pacing. "Okay, I'll take you. But you must stay hidden, and your arrows stay here."

Serena stands, frozen to the tree branch, momentarily stunned by her victory. She has convinced him to trust her, but she still isn't sure if she can trust a werewolf. *This is the very species that killed my parents*, Serena reminds herself.

"Well, little bird?" Liam taps his foot on the ground. "Are you going to fly down?"

His nickname for her makes her feel vulnerable, and leaving her only weapons behind isn't going to help that. But he is giving her an ultimate sign of trust by showing her the camp, she can at least return the favor.

Serena drops her bow and arrow set on the tree branch and jumps down. A puff of yellow petals rise up at her landing. They float back to the ground like sand after it is picked up by a tumultuous wave.

Bending down, Serena plucks a wolfsbane flower out of the ground by its stem. She twirls it in between her thumb and forefinger, bringing it up to her nose. From over the top of the petals she looks over at Liam, her mind made up.

"Okay. Show me Camp Werich."

Chapter Twenty-Two

"After you." Serena gestures toward Liam. They stand across from each other, one surrounded in yellow—the other, not so much.

He strolls, circling the border of flowers. Stopping at the end closest the ocean, he holds out the crook of his elbow for Serena to take his arm.

"I don't think so," says Serena. "I'll walk behind you."

Liam turns his head before shrugging in defeat and sauntering away from the sound of crashing waves.

Serena follows, pausing at the edge of the flowers. The gravity of The Dry is pulling down on her and everything seems too heavy. She can't bring herself to cross into unprotected land with Liam right in front of her.

"It's called trust, Werewolf Liaison." Liam pauses several spans ahead and looks over his shoulder. "You can't do your job if you don't trust me."

Why not?

As she steps out of the circle the wind picks up— a rush of musty forest and wolf scent. Serena cringes, expecting a flurry of claws and fangs to follow. Nothing happens.

One eye opens, and then another. The wolf is still in front of her, walking away. The wolfsbane flower remains clutched to Serena's chest, as she tentatively takes another step to follow.

The wolf's steps are light, barely making a sound through the forest. He knows which places to avoid, and where he can put his full weight.

"Would it help if I were in my animal form?" Liam's voice is distant as he faces forward. "It could be like the old days, a mermaid with her werewolf protector."

"The old days are long gone—your clan made sure of that."

Liam pauses, arching his shoulders together like Serena has stabbed him in the back. He whips around to face her.

Like muscle memory, Serena reaches for an arrow. It isn't there.

"Our clan had its reasons for that night," Liam narrows his eyes. Serena thinks she sees a flare of red in them, though it could be a trick of the sunlight.

"What reason did they have for killing my mother? Or what about my father?" Anger heats her cheeks.

Liam drops his arms to his sides. "Both your parents?"

"Among others," Serena answers, raising her chin. She swallows the hard lump that forms in her throat, refusing to the let the wolf revel in the pain his clan has caused her.

The wolf shakes his head. "You don't know the whole story, for what it truly is, Serena Moon-Shadow."

"And you do?"

He nods. "More than you, I'm sure."

Could he have even been there?

"How old are you, wolf?"

He smiles. "No older than you."

Serena takes a breath, willing her temper to calm. A cool wind carrying the smell of salt and seaweed tickles the back of her neck. "At least now we are getting some questions answered. Kind of." She looks down at her wolfsbane flower in her hand. "Tell me your story of that night."

He moves toward her, stepping into a swath of light filtering through the canopy. "If you return to me, I'll tell you as much as I'm allowed." He bows, then turns with a flourish of his cape, cutting off her chance to press him further.

They continue the walk in silence, Serena maintaining distance behind him. She rubs at the charm on her breastplate trying to memorize and categorize important pieces of their conversation, filing them away like books in the archives.

The terrain tilts up, gradually becoming steeper. After awhile Serena is leaning forward for more momentum, her breath labored. Just as she is about to request a break, Liam stops by an especially large tree and disappears around the back of it.

"What are you doing?" Serena asks, taking a step back. She glances behind her, suspecting some sort of trap. "Liam?"

A cape flies out from behind the tree, directly at her. Unfurling as it makes an arch in the air, Serena throws one hand in front of her face. The cape wraps around her arm, smelling of stale earth and wet dog.

"We are almost there, and I don't want to risk them smellin' you," says Liam.

Shaking out the cape, Serena allows the rest of it to unfold. "Gross," she says, as bits of dirt and shaggy hair tumble off. But she wraps the cape around her shoulders, tying it off under her chin as Liam's is. It settles over her scales, itchy and uncomfortable like the blankets in the orphanage.

"Just keep it closed in the front as best you can. And pull the hood up," Liam begins walking again. No longer on a path, they are pushing their way through thick shrubbery.

Serena obliges, lifting a hood that hangs off the back of the cape over her head. It almost hangs past her eyes. She turns her head to sniff. "Exactly how many wolves have worn this before me?" she asks.

"Shh," Liam hushes her. "No more talking." All at once his movements become slow and deliberate. Every move forward is calculated and he emits no sound at all.

Standing behind him, Serena stares at his wide shoulders working to push aside leafy branches. He turns, motioning her forward.

Serena steps through to a small clearing. She stands in the shadows of two shorter trees that have grown toward each other. Their limbs intertwine just above Liam's head, so it feels as though they are in a small cave.

"Stay in the shadows," Liam leans close to whisper in her ear. "And they won't see you."

Barely noticing his breath on her cheek, Serena's gaze is transfixed on the scene before her. On flat ground following a steep cliff beneath her, there are as many as thirty trailer homes, in varying degrees of quality but for the most part unkempt and shabby.

Still early in the morning, the camp is quiet and still. On the far right end, a trailer door swings open and the man that walks out automatically raises his hand to shield his eyes from the bright sun. Staggering toward a truck he reaches inside for a small rectangular package. He coughs as he pulls a slender object from the package and lights it from a small flame he holds in his hand.

Serena raises a questioning eyebrow at Liam.

"Cigarettes…it's…I'll explain later."

When he steps alongside her, Serena moves the wolfsbane from one hand to the other so it remains between them.

She turns her attention back to the camp. Draped on a thin line tied from one trailer to another is several capes, along with various other Ungainly-like clothing. "So you *do* wash them," whispers Serena.

Liam smiles, glancing at the cape on her shoulders. "Some of them."

"Do all of the werewolves live here?" she asks, counting the trailers.

Liam nods. "Most trailers have two pack members."

"So there are—"

"Fifty two of us," says Liam.

"The Undine…*made* that many?" Serena asks.

"Yes—made them," Liam's fingers bend in air quotes as he says the phrase. "Then dumped them on the beach to be delivered and raised here."

His tone has grown tense, and Serena isn't sure she should continue with her line of questioning, especially not this far away from safety, but she can't let the opportunity pass by.

She clears her throat and clutches at the stem of the flower. "Do you know how we made them?"

Shadows of the leaves overhead dance across his features, but Liam remains stock still, staring at Serena. Several moments pass, and Serena debates holding her hand up to his mouth to check his breath.

"You don't know?" he finally asks.

"No," Serena scowls in annoyance—mostly because she is choosing to ask a werewolf about Undine history instead of her own kind.

Knitting his brows together, Liam answers carefully. "I think that is something to ask your mother—" Liam cuts himself off, remembering too late that Serena is an orphan. "Oh, ah— sorry." He shakes his head, cheeks turning red. He kicks at the pebbles in their small clearing.

"Never mind," mumbles Serena. "I guess what I want to know is, have the werewolves had much luck mating?"

Now Liam's cheeks turn crimson, and he gives a strangled sort of cough. Before he can string together any intelligible words, several high-pitched yelps of delight catch their attention.

Serena and Liam look down in time to see kids running out of one of the trailers.

"You have!" Serena steps forward, eyes glued to the three small boys.

In no time each of the boys have found a long stick. They thrust at each other as they run around the trailer, the clacking noise of the sticks ringing across camp. "Unless they are Ungainly?" She raises her nose to the air and sniffs. "I can't tell—the air is much too saturated here."

"Half werewolf, half Ungainly," answers Liam.

"It doesn't matter," says Serena. "You found a way." She feels a lump forming in her throat and drops her wolfsbane flower, the revelation of new life blasting through fabricated barriers.

"Boys!" a woman emerges from the trailer. "It's too early, you'll wake everyone up. Inside to eat your breakfast—now!"

Liam gestures to her. "Their mother is human, the only one at camp. She married a werewolf and they had three boys. They are the only ones we know of that possess the ability to transform—all the others just come out as humans without a shred of wolf to them."

"Are they here too?" Serena asks. "You said she is the only Ungainly at camp."

"Alaric doesn't let them stay—they are sent packin' with their human mothers. Alaric agreed to let this human stay because she gave birth to the wolves, but also because she is a nurse. She is the only medical care we get." Liam's cheek color has finally returned to normal.

Serena nods, squinting at the other trailers. "Alaric," she repeats the name Isadora uttered. "Where is he?"

A howl bursts through the trees from behind Serena and Liam, blowing past them and down into the valley of trailers. The echo bounces back, followed by the sound of several tin metal doors slamming open. Six large men don't hesitate to race out of their houses at the howl.

"What is that?" asks Serena, the scales on the back of her neck standing up.

"That is your Alaric," says Liam. "If you've had your fill of the camp, we can go see him."

Serena watches the men shift into wolves as they run. They disappear into the tree line, a trail of shredded clothes in their wake.

"Your head is glowing," Liam observes.

"Yeah, that happens." Serena isn't sure she wants to seek Alaric. Something tells her she is better off facing the entire werewolf camp instead.

She follows Liam back through the forest, away from the camp. Although they are walking downhill, her legs feel like lead. With every step, Serena clutches the werewolf cape tighter and tighter around herself. The only reassurance is the sound of crashing waves in the distance that seems to be getting louder.

Finally, they are back on terrain she knows—flat ground and towering trees. Pushing their way through trees, the sun filters down through thick foliage piercing Serena even through the cape and her scales beneath.

"Here," Liam whispers, ducking behind a falling log.

Serena drops to her knees next to him and squints, focusing her eyes through the shrubs and onto the brightening shoreline. The entire King's Guard stands in a line on the beach, with King Merrick still in the water behind them. They are tense, holding their tridents at the ready, heads turning slowly and in unison.

Serena's gaze floats to where they stare. A large, hulking man paces the beach, just out of the tree line in front of them. Six wolves stroll the beach around him, casting wary glances at the Undine.

"Our agreement?" The man shouts out to King Merrick in the waves. His voice is thick and gravelly.

The King moves closer, raising his upper body out of the ocean. He points his trident at the man. "Has not yet run its course."

"Time is almost up, Merrick. My clan is anxious to know—will you follow through with your promise?" The man has long, black hair that hangs wild and loose past his shoulders, blending in with the cape on his back.

"What promise?" Serena whispers to Liam.

He shrugs. "I don't know."

King Merrick is pacing in the breakers, swimming back and forth, almost a mirror image to the man on the beach. They are both agitated. Finally, the king stops, and raises himself up again. "And if I've changed my mind?"

Lips curling up in a snarl, the man on the beach growls. "Only one other sacrifice will satisfy the debt, Merrick."

Slinking back down into the water, the king's words aren't audible to Serena over the sound of the breakers, but he is nodding his head. He turns away, then looks over his shoulder. "You will have your answer soon, Alaric."

"What sacrifice?" Serena hisses at Liam. "Me?"

"Why would he sacrifice you?" Liam looks at her, eyes narrowed.

"I don't know," says Serena. "But it would certainly explain why I am the freaking Werewolf Liaison!"

"Calm down," he says reaching toward her.

Serena falls on her backside, scrambling away from his outstretched hand. "Keep away!"

Liam nervously glances out at the guards. He pulls his hand back, and raises them both in the air. "Okay, okay. Just—shh. At least until Alaric leaves."

"Who is Alaric to you?" Serena asks, freezing in her awkward, crab-walk stance.

Liam grimaces. "My father—kind of."

"Kind of?" she asks, getting back to her feet, brushing dirt from her scaled legs. She tries to hide the fact that her arms are shaking with fear. After all,

Liam showed her the camp, and returned her to the beach.

"At least, the closest I have to a father," Liam picks dead bark off the log in front of them.

Serena thinks of Ronan. "I know what you mean…kind of," she says.

This elicits a small smile from Liam. He stands, sniffing the air. "Okay, he's gone."

Serena watches the king disappear below water, followed by a column of guard members. "I need to find out what that was all about," she says.

"I'll ask around, too—let you know what I find out next time we meet."

"Why?" Serena asks.

He looks at her, confused.

"I mean, why would you do that for me?" she clarifies.

"What he's doin' is just plain wrong." He nods to the beach where Alaric stood. "Alaric feels betrayed, and he is hell-bent on revenge."

"*He* feels betrayed?" Serena asks, mouth dropping open.

"Yes," Liam frowns. "And he is experimentin' with the pack, trying to make them stronger." Liam extends a hand and pulls back his cape, exposing the soft skin on the inside of his arm. There are dozens of small pinprick marks. "It is how more and more of us can shift without the full moon."

"And you let him?" Serena steps forward, extending a finger to his wounds.

"He runs the show," Liam shrugs. "We haven't had much choice until now. But then those boys came and…" Liam trails off, swallowing hard.

"And you can't let the same thing happen to them," Serena finishes for him, dropping her hand to her side. "So you are finally ready to fight for your future." Her voice drops as a frown creases her face.

"What?" asks Liam.

Serena takes a deep breath. "The problem is, so are we."

The pair stare at each other, an unspoken truce binding them together as they realize they might just have an ally in facing their obstacles.

Serena doesn't have a chance to ask further questions. The tips of a trident pierce through the shrubs, directly in between her and Liam. It swings wide, then comes back, pulling Liam with it. Caught in the chest, just underneath the arms, Liam disappears through the bush.

Chapter Twenty-Three

"Halt!" Serena hears through the bushes. It is Ervin's voice, deeper than usual, and loud.

Oh no.

Serena pushes her way through, rogue branches grabbing at her hair and scraping down her scales. When she stumbles onto the beach, her eyes go wide and her breath catches in her throat.

Ervin pins Liam to the ground with one foot on his chest, and another guard has his trident at Liam's throat.

"Pull back your trident!" Serena yells at the guard. She turns to Ervin. "Release him."

Liam scrambles back, getting on his feet as the two guards loosen their hold.

"Back off, just stand down," Serena hisses at Ervin and two other guards. The rest must have left with the king.

Glancing at Liam, Serena can see short, stiff hairs pop out, bristling along his neck. She steps toward him. "I'll take care of this. Just—trust me."

Serena crosses in between Liam and the armed Undine to stand at Ervin's side.

"Is this one of them?" Ervin asks through gritted teeth. "He smells like dog."

Liam sniffs. "You smell like fish. There no denying the mermaid, or...mer...man?"

"Undine!" Serena and Ervin say together.

Ervin steps forward, gills flaring.

"No." Serena puts her hand on Ervin's arm. "Let him go."

Ervin tenses even more, and the men behind him do the same.

"Show him mercy? Like he did the night of the maiden massacre?" Ervin isn't backing down.

"Look at him, Ervin. He isn't even old enough to have been there. Killing him would only spark a war. One for which we aren't prepared." Serena looks at Ervin. "Let me do my job."

Ervin shakes his head. "No, I'd rather see his pelt on the end of my trident."

"What shall I tell the king, then?" Serena asks, glancing at Ervin out of the corner of her eye, then returning her gaze to Liam. "That you interfered with the Werewolf Liaison's duty? That you willingly sabotaged a direct order from the king himself?"

Ervin stops moving forward, but refuses to break his gaze from his enemy.

"Besides," Serena says. "You no longer have a trident. Remember?"

Ervin flinches and turns, eyes full of fury. At least if his anger is directed toward her, Liam will be left alone.

After a short stare-down, Ervin brushes past her, toward the water. He shoulders her in the process, causing Serena to stumble back a few steps. Ervin splashes, very Ungainly-like, into the ocean. The two others back up from Liam, only turning when their feet hit the waves.

Serena lets out a shaky breath. With a quick glance at Liam who is still standing at the tree line with his hands hanging at his sides, Serena turns away, following Ervin.

She waits until she is fully submerged to cross her legs, transforming them back into fins. She can feel

Liam's eyes on her, and his words are still ringing in her head—*You smell like fish*. The slight stings worse than scales poking through her skin.

Ervin swims fast, taking sharp turns and occasionally glaring back at her. Her best friend is angry, but that she can handle. It is better than having Liam upset with her. He could tear her to bits. Shredded, bloody, fish bits.

Serena swats a lone jellyfish out of the way as she swims, trying to keep up with Ervin. He is going straight to the Great Hall—Serena won't have a chance to ask the king about his conversation with Alaric right away.

Besides the four of them, there isn't a single Undine spotted on the way to the Great Hall.

No, Serena thinks, *they are all already in it, ready to watch me take center stage.* She'll have to report her findings to the council.

Ervin reaches the steps first, fins transforming back into feet. He does so slowly, as if he is waiting for Serena to catch up. When Serena does, moving to stand beside him, she glances at his heaving shoulders.

The quick swim, strong as he has become, still takes a toll on him. He isn't meant for the King's Guard.

Oyster farmer, Serena thinks. She remembers how excited he was, returning from the oyster farms on the trip with his caste. The usefulness of oyster farming, the productivity. Serena wonders how productive he finds guard duty, doing the same rounds day after day.

When she looks at him, Ervin doesn't return the favor.

"Come on," he says. "You're late."

Not my fault, Serena aches to argue. But it would just come off as petty, so she stays quiet.

A few strides of bitter silence, and breathes out through clenched teeth. "You didn't have to belittle me in front of him."

"How did I belittle you? I was standing *with* you," she said.

"You pointed out that I didn't have my trident—like I lost it."

"So?" She brushes back a wet strand of hair plastered to the side of her face.

"So?" Ervin makes a fist, slamming it into the side of one of the corridor walls. "I looked like a fool. No King's Guard is ever caught in front of the enemy without his trident."

"For Poseidon's sake, Ervin—he doesn't know that."

"Doesn't he?" Ervin stops walking, the entrance to the Great Hall just ahead. The other two guards pause as well, but give Serena and Ervin their space. Ervin crosses his arms and turns to Serena, lowering his voice. "I think there is too much that *you* don't know. You are going to put yourself in unnecessary danger."

"This *job* is an unnecessary danger," Serena hisses back at him. "And you heard the king, conferring with the wolf himself. Why does he even need me?"

Unless I am the sacrifice…

Serena turns back to Ervin, distracted. "If there is something you think I should know, tell me now. Because neither you, nor any of the King's Guard," Serena makes a pointed look at the other two, keeping their distance, "will be accompanying me to the beach again."

Ervin uncrosses his arms, hands squeezing open then closed, and finally rubbing the back of his neck. Serena rolls her eyes. *He honestly has no idea what to do without his trident.*

"Well?" she asks.

Ervin sighs. "Has it ever occurred to you to ask for permission to the King's Library?"

"Of course," Serena says. "Mariam always denies it."

"Because you need express permission from the king."

"The king has also denied permission." Serena narrows her eyes at him. "Why would his library help me anyway? Have you been in there?"

Ervin shrugs. "Part of the training. We have to know every nook and cranny of the kingdom. We were allowed in once under the watchful eyes of Mariam. There is a whole section on werewolves."

Beside him, the other two are nodding their heads. "A section on Ungainlies, too," one says.

"And mating and birthing," offers the other.

Serena widens his eyes.

"Excuse me, gentlemen?"

Everyone turns, snapping to attention at Nerin's voice. She stands at the arched entrance, chin high, hands clasped in front of her.

"We have been waiting for the presence of the Werewolf Liaison to report her findings. So if you are finished with your discussion about mating and birthing..." She gestures to the entrance. "You may escort Serena in."

Each guard offers a short bow to the King's Second, then shuffles into the Great Hall with red cheeks. Serena follows.

Chapter Twenty-Four

The Great Hall is packed shoulder to shoulder with Undine once more. A path clears, making way for the three guards that enter, then an even wider berth for Serena.

"They have come to see that my punishment was fulfilled?" Serena asks Nerin with a grimace on her face.

"The king has ordered that all Undine be present," Nerin whispers back. "He even took roll." She doesn't give Serena a chance to think about the dozens of maidens staring at them. "Back straight, shoulders relaxed," Nerin instructs. "And keep your eyes forward. On the king, if you must."

Serena obliges. The faces grey out in her peripheral vision as she focuses on the king. After the werewolf camp, Alaric, and fighting with her best friend, the king is easy.

Serena and Nerin step up to the mid-platform, and curtsy in unison. On one side of them is the line of council members, on the other side is the line of guards, with Kai and Murphy flanking the ends.

"You're late," says the king. He reminds Serena of Ervin. No one is in a good mood.

"I was not able to inform the Werewolf Liaison when she should return to assembly, your majesty. She left for her mission too quickly."

Serena is thankful Nerin didn't say 'punishment'. Especially since Kai is standing right there.

"As you say." The king sits up in his chair, looking at Serena. "Let's begin. You carried out your punishment?"

Serena's shoulders sag. A sharp elbow from Nerin reminds her to stand up straight.

"Yes, your majesty," Serena glances at the council.

He continues looking at Serena, leaning forward in his chair.

"I was led to the camp by a werewolf ally—or, at least I think he is an ally..." Serena trails off.

"Alaric?" Isadora leans forward from the line of council members to ask.

"No," Serena answers. She almost has to choke back a snicker at the thought of her and Alaric huddled together in the shadows of the trees, spying on the werewolf camp. She clears her throat. "Though I did see Alaric."

"And?" Isadora stands on the balls of her feet.

"And," answers Serena, lifting her chin to King Merrick. "I believe the king himself knows enough of Alaric's well-being."

Isadora's eyes flit to the throne, red crawling up her cheeks until she looks like a black mountain, spewing hot lava out the top.

"I will consult with you later on the topic, Isadora," says the king, dismissing her with a flippant wave of his hand.

These two definitely have in-law issues.

"What I want to know," says the king. "Are the werewolf numbers. And how are they surviving? Where do they get their food? Why do they stay here, if they are so easily integrated into Ungainly life? Why haven't they moved away—or maybe half of them have?" With each question, the king leans further forward until Serena is sure he is going to attempt to stand up on his tail. "Do they have offspring?"

"Yes," says Serena, squeezing in at least one answer. "There are little ones."

The entire room goes so quiet, Serena can hear her own heart thumping in her chest.

"Younger than you?" Nerin asks by her side. It is practically a whisper. "And they are definitely werewolves?"

"Kind of," Serena breaks decorum to brush a stray strand of hair behind her ear. "As we know, there are no female werewolves, so some of the wolves have mated with Ungainly women. Mostly the offspring born are just more Ungainlies, and they are sent away. But one Ungainly gave birth to three male wolves; and the clan keeps the boys and their mother with them."

"This Ungainly," asks the king. "Is she special in some way?"

"I don't know—I just saw her from a distance."

"Well there has to be some potion," the king turns to his council members, raising his eyebrow at the healer. "Or some divine guidance?" Now he pins Isadora with his stare.

They all lift their shoulders or return blank looks.

"A scientific explanation, then. Do they mate on the full moon? Does their diet make them more virile?

"Your majesty," Serena interrupts. "I apologize, but the few discussions I've had with my werewolf confidante do not broach those subjects."

"Well why not?" It is the same booming voice, but complaining edges his tone.

Before she can stop herself, Serena glances at Kai. He is standing so stiff and straight, he could school Nerin in the art. She frowns, but doesn't answer the king's question. Everyone in the Great Hall seem to be waiting for the king to calm down.

After a few moments, he takes a deep breath. "How many are there?"

"My escort reported there are fifty-two of them, your majesty," says Serena.

"Forty-nine, plus the three young ones," the king exchanges a glance with Nerin. "None have left."

"They are half our numbers," says Murphy, speaking up from the line of guards.

"But each are twice our size," comments Nerin. "At least in their werewolf form."

"Did you see any weapons?" Murphy asks Serena.

She glances from Murphy to the king, and back again. "Why? Are we going to attack?"

"We are only concerned with protecting our own interests," says Nerin.

The king huffs, his long beard vibrating with the motion.

Shifting on her feet, Serena suddenly remembers she left her bow and arrow up in her tree. Her hand twitches, itching to leave the court and retrieve her property.

It's safe, she tells herself. *It is surrounded by wolfsbane.*

"Has my punishment been fulfilled?" asks Serena.

Without even glancing at Isadora, the king nods. "We will have more questions later, and expect them to be answered in detail," he raises his eyebrow. "But you have done well, Werewolf Liaison."

Serena curtseys, accepting his praise.

"I have something for you," he says.

Straightening in surprise, Serena folds her hands together. "For me?"

The third punishment is to come from Zayla, Serena thinks. Nonetheless, she sucks in a breath, waiting to hear what further penance she must pay.

"It comes from myself, my second…"

Nerin makes a small bow of her head in acknowledgement.

This is going to be bad.

"My council…"

They bow too, Zayla's much slighter than everyone else's, and Isadora's non-existent.

"My council," the king repeats, looking directly at Isadora.

She bows.

He nods, satisfied they all acknowledge this is a gift from them to Serena. "And the King's Guard."

A ripple of murmurs run through the crowd.

This is going to be really bad.

The King's Guard moves to attention in unison at Murphy's call. In one smooth movement, they each place a closed fist over their heart, bow their head, then return to parade rest, hands clasped behind their backs.

When Serena, Nerin, and all of Society behind them look back at the king, he is holding a new trident. He brings it up to balance in the palm of his hand. His fist closes around it, and he throws his arm forward, releasing the weapon.

The trident sails toward Serena, pointy end first. Nerin leaps to the side, and Serena hears the crowd gasp behind her. There is a shuffle, a mad scuffle of hands and feet scrambling to get out of the way.

Serena remains steady. Her hand shoots up, muscle memory. As many times as Kai has made her catch the training tridents during her one session, she now knows why.

As soon as her hand grasps one of the two twisted stems, she rotates her wrist. She doesn't fight the momentum, and her arm falls back. Her shoulder strains under the force; the king has a good arm. Three sharp tips scrape the cave floor. The high-pitched zing echoes in the cavern as Serena completes the rotation in front of her. It is one full spin, then a switch of hands. She comes to attention, settling the trident by her side, pointy end up.

Prongs, she can hear Kai chastising as he did during their lesson. *Not pointy end.*

Serena smiles.

Behind her, all movement has stopped. Only the dying echo of the ringing prongs can be heard reverberating against the walls.

The king smiles, too. "Well done, Werewolf Liaison."

"I'll say." Nerin tries to compose herself next to Serena, wiping cave debris off of her. Her leap must have ended poorly. "Though you might warn us next time, your majesty?" Nerin keeps her distance from the trident. She turns her head toward Serena, but doesn't look at her. "And in your next training session, you might learn to not leave a permanent mark every time you wield your weapon in the Great Hall?"

Serena looks down, spotting three deep gashes in the otherwise smooth floor. Though the rest of the ground is naturally rough, here on the mid-platform, the surface has been sanded smooth; until now.

Serena runs her bared toes over the incisions, then looks at the prongs. Not a scratch on them.

Her smile grows bigger. She catches Kai's eye. He winks at her.

"If we can conclude assembly?" asks Nerin. "I think we've had enough excitement for today, and Serena will need time…" Nerin glances at the trident. "To practice with her new weapon—far away from the Great Hall." *And me.*

Serena can see the last two words on Nerin's lips, though she doesn't speak them out loud.

"Very well," nods the king.

Serena puts up her finger.

"Do you have something to add, Serena Moon-Shadow?"

"Just one request, your majesty."

He raises an eyebrow.

"Your permission to access the King's Library."

"Why?" asks the king.

Serena's grip on her new trident tightens. Like last time she asked, she does not expect a question; just permission. "To do my job," she says, confused.

The king sighs, as if disappointed. "Request denied."

Chapter Twenty-Five

Nerin escorts Serena directly to Kai, who then shuffles Serena out of the Great Hall, without giving her a chance to ask the king any more questions. There is no need to push anyone in the crowd aside, they are edging away from Serena's trident already.

"No Murphy this time?" Serena asks.

"Nope," he says.

"Where are we going?"

"To train with your newest weapon." He slows as they wade into an entrance pool leading to the open ocean. "Speaking of," he turns to look at her. She is so close she almost takes a step back. "Where is your bow and arrow set?"

"I left them in The Dry," Serena suddenly can't look him in the eye. "But they are safe—surrounded by wolfsbane. And Liam would never—"

Kai interrupts by lifting her chin so she is forced to meet his eyes.

Warmth floods her lower belly. She puts her hand to her abdomen, but can't tear her eyes away from Kai. "Hmm?" she asks.

"Don't get too close to him, okay?"

The moment passes, and all of the heat that flooded Serena's system drifts away, leaving only cold in its wake.

"I know what I'm doing out there, Kai."

"I know." He steps back, dropping his hand to polish a spot on her trident with the pad of his thumb. "I mean don't get too attached."

Serena furrows her eyebrows. "He is the only friend I have out there right now. And I trust him."

Kai considers her for a moment, then nods. "Come on, let's get to those archives so we can continue to not stick holes in all those books." The playful look is back on his face.

"Can't wait." Serena dives in after Kai.

Once they are booted, robed, and in the archives, Kai motions to her trident. "Let's get started. Show me what you know."

Serena looks at her new gift, testing its weight in her hands. It is much lighter than the training tridents. Rotating the weapon as she switches hands, the prongs make wide loops in the air.

Finally, Serena takes aim and throws. The trident sails through the air, prongs first. Shooting straight through a group of training dummies that have been set up, it sticks into a wall. The entire stem quivers at the impact.

"You missed," says Kai.

Hardly," she says, walking to the trident and pulling it out of the wall. The three holes left behind underscore a plaque that reads, 'Restricted'.

"Tell me what you know about the King's Library," she says.

"Why would you think I know something?"

"I'm assuming you know more than me, since you've been in there and I haven't."

Kai crosses the floor to the wall, brushing past Serena. He is shorter than both Murphy and Ervin, but still a head taller than Serena. He isn't very wide, either, but he is quick. His fingertips touch one of the holes.

He clicks his tongue, looking at Serena. "Mariam will not be happy."

Serena turns away from his gaze. "I'm sure Mariam isn't happy about any of this." Walking toward the dummy, Serena wraps her arm around the shoulders. "Then again, there are more occupants in the archives than she's had in a long time."

Kai laughs. One of his feet lifts up and moves back, toeing the line between the forbidden restricted section and the rest of the archives. There is no door; not even here.

*Is he teasing me? Or...*Serena's gaze travels up his foot to his ankle and calf. The robe is hiked up a bit.

Before her cheeks have a chance to flush, she clears her throat. "Are you going in now? I mean, you still need permission, right? Even Mariam needs permission."

His laugh has melted into a sly smile. "I have managed to get that permission from the king in the past, for other reasons than my guard rounds." He brings his toe away.

"How?" she asks, a frustrated lump forming in her throat.

Kai doesn't answer. Instead, he walks toward Serena holding out his hand. "May I?"

Her empty hand twitches by her side, ready to submit. Just in time she realizes he wants her trident. She hands it over, biting her lip.

"You shouldn't give your weapon up so easily," Kai says, raising an eyebrow. He turns his attention to the trident, running his fingers down the middle prong and over the twisted double stem. His hand moves back, touching the weld where the crescent-moon shape holds the prongs. "I think this here was my trident. It was condensed down—it has to be the strongest part."

"How did you get permission to visit the king's library?" Serena asks again. She feels awkward, too aware of herself. "And why did you want it in the first place?"

"Because," he looks at her, the smile gone from his face, but not his eyes, "I wanted to be Werewolf Liaison." He turns, takes quick aim at the dummy, and throws. The trident flies through the neck, ripping the lifeless head clean off.

Serena gasps. "Be careful!" she says. "You almost hit the coral encyclopedias!"

She retrieves the trident, which is wedged in the side of a table. She pulls it loose, almost tripping over the dummy head in the process.

Still standing in place, the grin is back on Kai's face.

Serena bends to pick up the head.

"Leave it," says Kai. "Mariam will think you did it, and maybe word will spread. Perception is a powerful thing."

Serena straightens, sighing. "Not if Society already has their own opinions of me."

"I think the tide is turning..." he trails off, an eyebrow raised at Serena. "Anyway, the king let me study up on werewolf history, or more importantly, Undine history with them."

"Then what?" asks Serena.

"Then he simply said no. I was to remain with the guard."

"And you were okay with that?" Serena walks closer to him.

"Not at first, but he's the king, ya know?" Kai says.

"Yeah." Serena snorts. "I know."

"Besides," says Kai. "That was when he made me Murphy's second. Said I had the initiative no one else had shown. After that, I was always too busy to dwell on it. In fact, I hadn't really thought more about it until the night of your Choosing."

Kai has mastered the art of hiding expressions as well as any of the King's Guard. Serena can't tell if he's jealous of her job, intrigued, or outright supportive.

"What did you learn?" Serena gestures to the King's Library, changing the course of the conversation.

"Nothing I can repeat."

Serena puts her hands to her temples.

"But I should tell you," Kai continues, "that you definitely need to get in there. You wouldn't be able to do your job properly otherwise."

Serena rolls her eyes. "Now you are starting to sound like Nerin." She studies the darkened entryway that leads to the forbidden books, tapping her foot. "Why won't the king give me permission, then?"

"Because you aren't answering the question correctly." Kai leans in, his voice almost at a whisper. "When he asks why you want access."

Chills prickle her neck where his breath touches.

"What is the right answer?" Serena whispers back.

"I can give you many things, Serena Moon-Shadow," he steps back, placing a hand on her shoulder. "But not that. The reasons are your own."

"Fine—then give me another answer, Kai." She looks up at him from under her long lashes.

He waits.

"What deadline was the king talking about tonight with the wolf?"

Kai's hand drops from her shoulder. "You heard?"

Serena nods her head, crossing her arms.

"Because you weren't supposed to hear that," he says.

She crosses her arms, staring him down.

Kai sighs, rubbing the back of his neck. "During the Maiden's Massacre, the king made some sort of agreement with the wolves."

"Why?" asks Serena.

"I don't know the specifics," says Kai. "But once the bargain is upheld, the wolves will let the Undine mate again. That is what the deadline is all about."

"When is the deadline?"

Kai shrugs. "Soon, Serena—which is why we are all on edge."

Serena doesn't have time to dwell on what it means. Kai switches moods faster than a mackerel.

"That is enough talk," he says. "Back to training. I'm going to show you how useful the stem can be as a weapon." Kai reaches for the trident again.

Serena switches hands, holding it out of his reach.

Kai smiles. "See? Learning already."

Chapter Twenty-Six

"You got a new trident," Liam remarks. "It's smaller."

"It's stronger," replies Serena.

They stand at her tree—both are on the ground, one inside the yellow and one outside.

Serena has already retrieved her bow and arrow set, which remained untouched.

Liam nods to the trident. "You know how to use it?"

Serena spins it once in her hand. "I'm learning."

She spent the better half from one high tide to the next training with Kai. By the time they were through, they were both breathing hard, sweaty, and exhausted—just in time for Serena to make it to The Dry to scout for traps and fix her wolfsbane protection before Liam's appearance.

Up above, two squirrels scamper across the canopy, causing dead leaves to flutter down as the sky makes the transition from dark to light.

Serena moves into position, balancing the trident in the palm of her hand and holding it steady just above her shoulder. She leans back, then twists forward and releases. The trident sails through the sky. It catches a leaf mid-air, spearing it through the center and pinning it to a dead tree.

Before the trident stops quivering, Serena runs to retrieve it. She pulls, applying pressure at the most effective angle like Kai taught her. The weapon pops loose.

Serena looks at Liam.

"You're a fast study," he says.

Serena starts to smile, until she realizes how far out of the wolfsbane circle she has come. Gripping her trident tight, she moves toward it, giving Liam a wide berth.

He stands stark still, watching her the whole way. "You still don't trust me?" he says once she is back in her field of fatal flowers. "Even after last night?"

"A girl can still be cautious, can't she?"

He grunts. "Okay, Serena Moon-Shadow. What do I have to do to prove myself to you?"

"For starters, you can tell me about your capes."

He frowns. "Why are the capes so important to you?"

"It wasn't," she shrugs, "until you refused to answer the question."

"Well, where do you think I keep the cape?" he asks.

Serena toys with a tip of her trident. "I think it is your wolf skin, and you wouldn't be able to transform without it."

Liam throws his head back in laughter. "What, like a selkie?" His laugh moves into deep guffaws, and for a moment, Serena thinks he is choking.

She crosses her arms, surprised he has even heard of the mythical creature. Seals that can transform into humans and back again, as long as they have their pelts, have been the center of many Undine calfling stories.

Finally, Liam's laughter dies down to a snicker. He unties the string at his neck, then those down his body that hold the cape closed. "You need to get your head out of The Deep, Werewolf Liaison."

"What are you—" Serena cuts her own sentence off with a gasp. She turns her back, just as the cape goes sailing over her head. It settles into a pile of material amidst the flowers. "Liam?"

"Just turn around, Serena." There is still a twinge of laughter in his voice.

"No."

"Do it, and you'll get your answer." There is a shuffle of feet.

Serena sees movement out of the corner of her eye, and turns away again. "No way. And this doesn't count as answering your question."

"Oh, come on."

Refusing to play, she holds her hands up on either side of her eyes, shielding herself from the sight of his nude Ungainly body. *How would I ever report this progression to the king? Is it even progression?*

Suddenly, the forest goes quiet.

"Liam?"

There is no answer.

"Hey, wolf-boy!" she yells out, dropping her hands to her sides.

Only the crickets respond, their chirping as steady as the tide. She turns, gritting her teeth, ready to shout his name again. Instead, she meets his steady gaze. And he is fully clothed.

"You jerk!"

He laughs again. He is doing that entirely too much tonight. She kicks out and a plume of yellow flowers puff out toward him. A sharp sting from the flowers pierces her toe.

"Hey now." He puts his hands out, jumping back in case any of them should make it that far. "That was not cool."

"Why are you dressed tonight?" Serena puts her hand on her hip, hoping he hasn't noticed she is sticking her toe into the dirt—her feet aren't scaled and she worries she might have touched the poisonous center of the flower.

"I came straight from work, didn't have time to romp around as a wolf. But I thought I'd put on the cape anyway—you know, to keep up appearances." Liam keeps his gaze level with hers. "We hide capes throughout the forest. Any wolf is free to use them when needed; transformation can rip our clothes to shreds."

Serena picks up the discarded cape with the end of her trident. She brings it close to her nose and sniffs. It is covered in wolf scent. Recoiling, she thrusts the cape away from her. It dangles from the ends of her trident. A peace offering.

He shakes his head. "Can't take it now. It's covered in wolfsbane."

"A souvenir for me, then." She retracts it, then folds and drapes it over the quiver on her back, careful not to impede a quick withdrawal of arrows, if need be.

"Now it is your turn for an answer," Liam says. "Are Undine immune to wolfsbane?"

Serena freezes, her toes still web-deep in the dirt. She clears her throat, retracting her foot from the ground.

I suppose a little truth won't hurt.

"A touch of its nectar will not turn us hairy," Serena tells Liam. "But it can be harmful, especially if ingested, or if the nectar makes its way into our bloodstream. The Undine tend to be more sensitive to herbs and flowers than Ungainly." Her eyes shoot to Liam—she should not have said that much.

Maybe I shouldn't have said any of it.

He holds up his hands. "Information I will keep to myself."

He winks at her and she narrows her eyes.

"At least we're finally communicating. You ask me another question," Liam says.

"What did you find out about the conversation we overheard last night?"

"Oh," he says. "And here I thought we were on a roll. I didn't find out much."

"No?"

Liam shakes his head. "Alaric and I haven't been seein' eye to eye lately. He isn't sharin' his plans with anyone, and I couldn't exactly tell him what I saw."

"Why not?" asks Serena.

"I'm not supposed to be out here, at least not unless I am on patrol."

"But you do it anyway?" Serena smiles.

"Something like that," Liam smiles back. "It's why I come out after my shift at the bowlin' alley ends. The rest of the patrollers have usually grown tired and gone home by then. There is no excitement anymore—you guys have been slackin'."

Serena turns her face up to the sky, the morning dawn beating against her skin and drying out her scales. "In a few days, the full moon will rise."

"So it will," says Liam, almost under his breath.

"Without Undine to call on the wolves for protection, what do you do on those nights?"

Liam laughs, but it is nervous. He scratches the back of his neck and his cheeks flush.

"What?" asks Serena.

"Well, we...we..."

Serena furrows her eyebrows. *What could be so difficult to say?*

"We mate."

Serena's mouth drops open, then snaps shut. "Oh."

"What?" says Liam. "It is the same thing you are doin'."

Serena shakes her head. "Not me."

"Your kind, anyway."

Serena folds one arm across her midsection. "Why on the nights of the full moon? Can't you do it anytime? I mean, you have all the… "

"Parts?" Liam offers.

"Yes," Serena snaps back. "You have all the parts needed in either form, wolf or Ungainly."

He smiles. "Yes but we can't reproduce more werewolves unless it occurs under the full moon. Any other time, only humans pop out—and Lord knows there are enough of those runnin' around."

"So, if before—when werewolves were called upon to protect Undine during the full moon— did you even have a chance to do it? I read that werewolves were bound to patrol the beaches from sun down to sun up."

"That…is one question too many," says Liam.

Serena narrows her eyes. "Other than the full moon, are there any other tricks or secrets to bearing healthy werewolves?"

"Two questions too many." Liam crosses his arms.

Serena feels her toe begin to tingle at the wolfsbane cut. She shifts her weight from one side to another. "Yeah, maybe. Look—I need to go before the sun makes fish fry out of me."

Liam frowns, finally glancing down at her foot. "Why the rush? You've been in the sun before."

Serena shrugs, turning. "Seems like I got all the answers I'm going to get out of you. So..." she trails off as she turns away, glancing over her shoulder.

"Fine." He rolls his eyes.

Serena stops and turns back around, waiting.

"We have found that there are certain...bloodlines that lend to more control over the wolf."

Serena crosses her arms. "More control?"

"For example, better success at yielding wolves instead of humans—or transforming at will, even without the full moon."

"So your bloodline is one of them?"

"It is," Liam says, rolling down the sleeves of his shirt until they touch his wrists. "And it is not somethin' I like to discuss."

Uninterested in watching him grow angry, Serena looks away. "It's funny, how desperate some of us want to spawn and have little miniatures of ourselves running around," Serena says, voice low.

"Or swimming around," says Liam, the edge leaving his voice.

"Or howling," says Serena.

They are both smiling now, but the moment grows awkward.

"There is this maiden..." Serena trails off, remembering Cordelia's nursery song.

Even if no newborns can be found,
you'll still be the sweetest calfling in town.

"What?" asks Liam.

She can't continue with the story. It almost feels like a slight to Cordelia, putting her pain out there to the very creatures that caused it. "Never mind." Serena crosses her arms, glancing to the sky again.

Liam sighs. "Look, the night of the full moon for werewolves—if that's what you want to know—is…busy. We no longer spend it chasing mermaids back into the water, especially since you all seem to have given up on it. We have just a few on patrol, that can send out an alarm if need be."

"So if we wanted to…" Serena trails off, unsure of how to put the question in words.

"I still wouldn't risk it," Liam grinds the toe of his boot into the ground, making a small divot in the dirt. He glances up at Serena. "Unless…"

"Unless what?" she narrows her eyes.

"I could volunteer for patrol alone."

"Would that work?" Serena asks, still skeptical.

He nods his head. "Yes, I think I could make it work. Alaric brings in a bunch of—well, let's just say no one wants to miss the full moon events. Only those being punished have to patrol."

"I know how that goes," Serena mumbles. She looks at Liam. "I'm not sure—it's still too risky."

"Let me try. Let me prove that not all werewolves are bad." Liam steps forward and tentatively extends his hand to Serena. "The full moon is in three nights. Come back in two, and I'll let you know if the Undine can try it or not."

Serena stands right up against where the wolfsbane border ends. She forces herself to remain still as his hand comes closer, but her grip tightens around her trident.

His fingertips brush the scales at her shoulder. They both freeze, sucking in a breath.

"Is that okay?" he asks, his voice at a whisper.

Serena's eyes go wide. She presses her lips tight together, then nods. Her toe is now throbbing.

Liam's entire palm rests on her shoulder. It is cool relief, shielding her scales from the blazing light of the sun. He stares at her arm. The pad of his thumb traces one of the scales.

Slowly, Serena retracts it.

He pulls his hand away.

"It's okay," says Serena.

He glances at her, then puts his hand back on her shoulder. His lips part, and Serena can almost feel his breath against her face.

She retracts another scale, a little faster this time. The one after that disappears quickly. Small trickles of blood are left in the wake as each scale sinks into skin. Serena tenses, embarrassed for herself. She isn't sure why such a small amount of blood is humiliating.

Liam wipes it away with his palm. "Does it hurt?"

"Only for second," says Serena.

Finally, all of the scales along her shoulder are gone, and he is touching her, skin to skin.

"This is weird," says Liam. His hand drops to his side. "Sorry, I didn't mean to say that out loud."

"It's fine," says Serena, taking a step back and readjusting the quiver straps on her shoulders. "I was just thinking the same thing." She turns, holding her shoulder out of his sight while she re-scales her skin.

She glances down at her toe. It is swelling. "Okay, I really have to go now."

"Yeah, yeah," says Liam, looking back into the forest. "I have...things to do, too."

"Hey," Serena calls out.

"Yeah?" Liam is quick to turn around, eyebrows up in a hopeful arch.

"Thank you for the gift, Liam of Clan Werich," Serena glances to the cape stuffed up by her quiver.

He smiles, then performs a bow worthy of the king's court. "Happy birthday, Serena Moon-Shadow, Werewolf Liaison of the Undine Kingdom."

Chapter Twenty-Seven

The healer's cave is one of the closest to the Great Hall. Only Nerin's quarters separate them from the king's court. Serena pushes her way past beaded curtains, stepping inside. The cave is set on higher ground so that the tide never enters. Serena walks up a set of stairs carved into the incline. Moss that covers the stairs ceases to grow right where high tide stops.

Hailey Sage-Brush stands bent over a table, jarring dried herbs. In comparison to the drab colors of the plants in The Dry, and of the healer's cavern in general, Hailey's scales are a bright blue-green. It is exotic—the color of a tropical ocean.

The sheer amount of clutter in the cavern makes the space appear smaller, though it is five times the size of Serena's cave. There are lotions, salves, and more herbs covering every space. Thick stacks of books tower Serena. Even if the tide doesn't reach past the steps, the cave isn't nearly as damp-free as the archives, and the brittle pages of the books have long since yellowed and curled.

Deeper into the cave, a handful of assistants clean. Simone is easy to spot—her scales are some of the brightest red Society has ever seen.

"Serena...now this is a surprise," Hailey chirps. "I don't think you have ever set foot in my clinic." Hailey looks past Serena, as if she is expecting someone else. When no one appears, she stands, closing the lids on her jars at the table.

"Sit down, sit down," says Hailey. She motions to a cot set up on one side of the room and rolls a cart full of more jars to it. "Now, what seems to be the problem?"

Serena sits down, leans her trident against the cot, and crosses her arms. "It's my—"

"No, no—don't tell me. Let's see if I can guess." Hailey flutters around Serena, poking and prodding with sharp, beak-like fingers. "Short of breath?" Hailey bends Serena's neck so one side of gills are exposed. "Kelp indigestion?" Hailey pushes hard on Serena's gut.

Serena wheezes out.

"Hmm," says Hailey. "Maybe it is the breath."

"No, no," Serena stops Hailey's hands before they can bend her neck in the other direction. "It's just my toe."

"Oh," Hailey pauses, shoulders sagging. "Well, let's have a look then." She bends her knees to see. "What happened?"

"Wolfsbane," says Serena.

Hailey stands, taking a step back. "Wolfsbane?" She takes another step back, bumping into the cart of jars. "How did that happen?" Deeper into the cave, the assistants have all gone still, now straining their necks to see.

Serena furrows her eyebrows. "I'm the Werewolf Liaison."

"So?"

"So I have to protect myself somehow." Serena motions to her trident, leaning against the cot. "I use them on my weapon, and on the tree where I stay in The Dry."

Hailey's hands move back and jars clink together. "Can you just…get that thing out of here? All my patients have to sit there."

Serena sighs. Surely the swim here with the trident completely submerged in salty, cold ocean water, would have washed it clean of poison. "Listen, if you don't want me here…"

Hailey clicks her tongue. "No patient is turned away," she recites the healers motto, though it looks as though she wishes she could make an exception. She turns her head, snapping her fingers. The three assistants scurry forward. One sets a stool down in front of Serena, and Simone helps Hailey into a pair of gloves while the other approaches Serena's trident with a pair of clamps.

"Now then," Hailey begins pointing out jars with gloved fingers. "We'll need some Jimson weed, just a pinch of charcoal powder—a bit less, Simone, we don't want to kill the girl—yes that is it. And…" Hailey scans the jar labels with her eyes. "Some aloe for the burn. We'll treat the affliction inside and out," Hailey smiles down at Serena.

Serena swallows hard, staring at the charcoal being mixed in with a steaming mug of tea. The tea is passed to Hailey, who adds honey. She winks at Serena. "So it goes down easier." A quick stir, and Hailey holds out the cup.

Serena takes it, glancing from the healer to each one of her assistants. They are all watching.

"Cheers." Serena throws her head back, finishing the entire cup in one gulp.

The assistants all lean forward with wide eyes.

"Okay, you three—you've done quite enough. Back to work." Hailey shoos them away. "Sorry about that," she tells Serena, taking the cup from her. "They are a quick study when it comes to books, but have much to learn about bedside manners."

Hailey bends to study Serena's swollen toe, though she keeps her distance. "I'll just put some Aloe vera oil over the wound. We'll let it breathe tonight and tomorrow morning the swelling should be down enough to wrap it."

"Will everything go back to normal?" asks Serena.

"You've already transformed into fins and back without problem?"

"Yes," answers Serena.

"Good, good," says Hailey. She uses a sponge to apply the oil. "You'll no longer be able to grow scales there, of course."

"Wait—no scales? Do you mean, like, for the rest of my life?" Serena pulls her toe away from the oiled sponge.

"It's just on the tip of your toe, dear. Hardly something to be concerned about." Hailey stands, discarding the sponge and her gloves in a small bag, and double knotting the bag's opening.

"It is when I'm running around with wolves," Serena grumbles, getting up from the cot. "I need every bit of armor I can get."

Hailey's eyes go soft, as does her voice. "You really are doing this, aren't you?"

Serena looks at her. She wasn't aware there was ever any doubt. Serena is not a good liar.

Hailey lays a hand on Serena's shoulder, right where Liam did. It is surprisingly warm. "Scales are not the greatest defense against fangs or claws, dear."

"How do you know?" asks Serena, glancing over Hailey's bright teal scales.

Hailey shrugs. "Look at the king. I've been treating him every day since the Maiden's Massacre."

Hailey lets her hand drop. "He's had a rough go of it, but he can at least swim normally now."

Hailey sits down on the old cot, and motions for Serena to do the same. "I was supposed to be selected for mating that night, too."

Serena nods. "You were in my mom's caste."

Hailey smiles, her eyes wandering to the cave floor in front of them.

"Why weren't you selected?"

Hailey looks down at her hands. There is at least two rings on each finger. She twists one of the rings around her knuckle.

"I was only an Assistant Healer at the time—you wouldn't remember the Healer. She died shortly after that massacre. A lot of Undine did in the battles that took place after the fact. Once there were hardly any males to send, the maidens—even the elderly maidens—took up arms. Anyway, I remember she kept warning me about the dangers of mating. You know—the pregnancy, the birth. And everyone knew the werewolves had been on edge about their role in our lives."

Serena looks down at her own fingers. They have plenty of scratches, but are bare of jewels.

Hailey continues, "She scared me too much. When time came for the mating selection, I avoided eye contact and made it clear I did not want to go. The male Undine left me alone." Hailey smiles, her gaze drifting off and her eyes glazing over. "It's funny, it still stung that I wasn't chosen. Even after the Maiden's Massacre. I am grateful, of course, but I've always been disappointed that I wasn't whisked off by Murphy, head of the King's Guard." Hailey looks at Serena out of the corner of her eye, and clears her throat. "A daydream common to most of us."

"Is that so?" Nerin's voice rings throughout the cluttered cave.

One of the assistants drops a bucket. It clatters across the floor. All three scramble to get it up, shushing each other as they do.

"Yes," says Hailey, standing and clearing her throat. "At least back then. Greetings, Nerin."

Nerin nods in return without a smile to her face.

Hailey flutters her hands. "Well, I must get back to my concoctions. The king needs his medicine."

"Thank you, Hailey," Serena says, shifting on the cot at the sudden tension in the room. "The king is lucky to have you."

"He is lucky to have physical wounds that can be tended to," says Hailey. She glances at Nerin. "It's the emotional suffering that is most difficult to treat."

"Indeed," agrees Nerin, her voice softening. She looks at Serena. "It takes a strong person to rule this kingdom, inside and out."

"Of course," Serena attempts to stand.

"No need to get up," Nerin crosses to the cot and sits. The heat Hailey left behind, warming Serena's side, retreats.

In a way, Serena finds the cold comforting. It reminds her of her cave, and the deeper, secluded parts of the ocean.

"You are doing well with your punishments, Serena. I don't want you to think that it goes unnoticed by the king."

Glancing at Nerin, Serena wonders how much Nerin will divulge when the king isn't by her side. "The punishments seem...harsh. I mean, I'm grateful you declined the death penalty, of course," Serena says quickly. "It's just..." Serena rubs the edge of the cot with her fingers.

"What?" Nerin snaps.

"Am I the sacrifice the wolves want?" Serena blurts out the question that has been on her mind ever since she witnessed the meeting between her king and Alaric.

Nerin sucks in a breath, staring straight ahead. "What do you know about it?"

"I saw King Merrick and Alaric talking," says Serena. "The entire guard was there. It can't be that big of a secret, except to me," she mumbles the last few words. "He was concerned about whether King Merrick would follow through on a promise he made. The deadline is apparently coming up soon."

Nerin's eyes drop to the floor, and her shoulders sag. "Yes, yes the deadline is coming. One full moon cycle, to be exact." Nerin looks at Serena, eyebrows raised. "Can you think of something else that will occur during the full moon after next?"

Serena purses her lips, the only future her mind is on is her next punishment.

"Some kind of big...anniversary," prods Nerin.

"Oh, the Maiden's Massacre," says Serena.

Nerin nods her head. "The anniversary of the Maiden's Massacre, and your birthday."

"Right, but I don't—" Serena cuts off, her eyes going wide. "What does it have to do with me?"

Nerin stands, folding her hands in front of her and pacing the room. "The night of the massacre, a few choices had to be made, none of which suited the Undine species, but we weren't exactly in a position to bargain, either. When the king came ashore, you were the only infant left alive—he begged the wolves to spare you."

Serena stares at Nerin, transfixed.

Nerin stops pacing to face Serena still sitting on the cot. "The wolves agreed to let you leave with the king—on one condition." Nerin holds up her finger. "That you be returned to the pack on your eighteenth birthday."

"Why?" blanches Serena.

"I don't know. It is between the king and the wolves, and the reason has never been shared with me. Once you are delivered, the wolves say they will allow the maidens ashore again. Chasing us back to The Deep for eighteen long years is their insurance that the king will follow through with his promise."

"So will he?" Serena stands, stepping toward Nerin.

"Will he allow his own kingdom to die out just to save one girl?" Nerin arches her eyebrow at Serena.

Serena stays silent, the consequences of either decision settling hard in her stomach like an iron anchor hitting the seafloor.

Nerin's face softens, the hard lines around the corners of her lips disappear. She walks over to Serena, placing a hand on her shoulder. "I honestly don't think he knows yet."

Chapter Twenty-Eight

Rubbing her temples, Serena begins pacing the room. Would Society allow the Undine population to taper away, just to save one girl? Or would they willingly give Serena to the wolves? As an orphan, Serena is connected to very few.

What would Society do for me? If it were Sasha from the beloved Sunbeam family, no doubt the rest of the maidens would willingly give up their lineage for her. But maybe not for an orphan that few like—good Werewolf Liaison or no.

Still pacing, Serena glances at Nerin who stares at the ground in front of her, hands clasped together so tight they are turning white. Right now, Nerin is not the regal King's Second Serena has always known her to be.

What would she choose to do? Serena wonders. *What would I choose to do? I could take the decision out of all their hands, sacrificing myself to the wolves and allow the Undine to prosper.* Serena smiles. *I could give Cordelia her calfling.*

Swallowing hard, Serena wiggles her toes. The wolfsbane wound is bright pink now. Suddenly, Serena's head snaps up. "Nerin, what if we attempted mating again? Before the deadline? Not you and me, obviously." Serena's face goes hot with embarrassment. "I mean, just...Undine in general."

"We've tried since that night, although I suppose you wouldn't know it. The details of such practices were never taught in your classes." Nerin unclenches her hands and brushes them across her hair and back, securing a few loose strands in the bun at the nape of her neck.

Serena can remember only once when the mating and birthing cycle was discussed openly with the Temporal Caste. Evandre was invited in while Zayla took uncharacteristic leave from her front podium to the back of the caste room. For the most part, Evandre spoke of lunar rhythms in frogs, crabs, and the marine worm, and how reproductive systems react to external stimuli, the most influential being the light of the moon. The Temporal Caste followed the lecture scratching their heads and scrunching their eyebrows together. It wasn't until the very end that Evandre referred to the maiden body as being connected to the moon by blood, hormones, and soul.

After caste lessons concluded that day, Serena headed straight for the archives. There she found detailed explanations. Just as the moon creates tides on Earth, it interacts with the electromagnetic fields of a maiden's body, creating the ebb and flow of internal tides that trigger fertile physiological processes.

"Only the light of a full moon allows the fertile cycle in a maiden to emerge, as well as initiates Undine labor—which is a very stressful event for mother and child," Nerin says, continuing to unfold and refold her hands in her lap while she speaks. "We've tried traveling to other islands, but mothers, even in the early stages of labor, have had a difficult time handling the changes in the water, temperature, salinity, and acidity, among others. No child survived it, and sometimes, not even the mother. It is the same reason we cannot, or do not, migrate."

Serena moves her hair back away from her face. "Our caste lessons weren't very specific about birthing events."

Nerin nods. "We tried water births at the surface, on the ceremonial whale rock, and of course—more attempts on the beach. None of it worked. Even if werewolves weren't present, the mother was simply too stressed for a successful labor. It became evident that Undine react too strongly to emotion, such as anxiety, fear, or worry."

"Just like our sensitivity to herbs from The Dry," Serena mumbles.

Nerin's lips go tight. "Not only is the maiden's massacre still fresh in everyone's minds, but so are all the battles that occurred after."

"Not for the Temporal Caste," Serena says, her voice just a whisper. Something clicks, and Serena turns to look at Nerin, mouth open. "You've kept the details from us on purpose. You don't want us to know…."

Nerin lays a hand on Serena's arm. "The Temporal Caste is our last chance. The council voted to keep the details a secret, and the subject became taboo for the rest of Society to mention, especially to you and your caste mates. The less you know, the less there is for you to worry about."

Serena stands from the cot, crosses her arms, and begins pacing. "How long were you going to wait? Before announcing a pairing of the Temporal Caste to the King's Guard?" There isn't as much bite in Serena's voice as she intended. She stops pacing, finally understanding. "You were waiting until the king follows through with his promise by giving me to the werewolves, and they allow us to mate."

Walking toward Nerin, Serena sits down again, bouncing up Nerin's side of the cot. "I've been told that werewolves wouldn't bother us in the next full moon—they are otherwise occupied." Serena spits it out before she can change her mind.

"And you believe it?" Nerin asks.

Serena nods, all too aware that any hesitation might cost her. "We have one more full moon before the deadline is up. If we are successful…"

Nerin stands. "Then the king won't have to relinquish our youngest maiden." It is her turn to pace the room now. "Very well." She stops, turning to Serena. "I will consult with the king. In the meantime, let Hailey finish with your wound, then Kai can take you to another training session after. I will send for him."

Nerin nods to Hailey as she takes her leave from the healer's cave.

Pushing her large, metal cart toward the cot, Hailey watches Nerin disappear down the stairs then turns back to Serena. "Well, that was awkward." She kneels in front of her Serena, pulling the damage foot to rest on her knee. "She doesn't like it when maidens talk about Murphy, especially not in reference to mating partners."

"Why not?" asks Serena.

"Because," says Hailey. "Murphy is her son."

"I never knew that," Serena says, her mouth dropping open. She has trouble placing the large-boned Murphy in the same family as thin, uptight Nerin, and wonders what other family bonds she hasn't connected.

"All this time," Hailey clucks, "and never paired. It's a shame. But Kai shows promise for a good pairing. Not that I—"

"Can we hurry this along?" interrupts Serena.

Hailey looks up, her forehead creased in question.

"I'd rather not receive the entire kingdom sitting on this cot."

"Maidens," Kai enters the cave, taking the steps up two at a time.

"Too late," Serena mumbles.

"Must've been hanging close by," Hailey winks at Serena.

"I couldn't help but notice your trident is out of arm's reach," Kai says, sitting down on the cot beside Serena and leaning back against the wall.

"Hailey banished it to the corner," Serena gestures to her weapon. "Not supposed to touch it until it is sterilized."

"Why?" Kai asks.

"Because," Hailey shoos Kai toward the end of the cot, away from Serena, "the thing was wrapped with wolfsbane and she had already managed to get some on herself." Hailey lifts up Serena's foot, displaying Serena's momentary lapse of judgment right in front of Kai.

Embarrassed, Serena lets her hair fall to cover her face again as Hailey begins cleaning her toe with a stringent-smelling rag.

Kai leans forward. "Could be worse, considering your occupation."

Serena shifts in her seat, trying to pull her foot back.

Hailey doesn't give, keeping a death grip on Serena's ankle. "Be still."

Kai hops up from the cot and walks to the trident. He taps his chin, studying it. "Wolfsbane, huh?" He holds out a finger toward one of the tips.

"Kai Forest!" Hailey's shrill voice causes Kai to jump back. "Don't you go poisoning yourself. I'm low on charcoal as it is."

Kai crosses his arms. "I wasn't gonna—"

"Excuse me," Simone interrupts. She stands behind him with a bucket of steaming hot water and several rags.

"Oh, by all means." He gestures with a grand swing of his arm toward the trident.

She blushes and he steps back to watch her clean the trident.

"Ow!" Serena's attention is brought back to her toe.

"Hush. The sting will go away in a moment. This salve will help to harden the skin on your toe. We don't want it to be as soft as an Ungainly belly."

Serena risks a glance at Kai, but he appears not to have heard. Simone giggles at one of his jokes while bending to clean the bottom of the trident—hardly appropriate with Kai standing right behind her.

"Oh, for Poseidon's sake, Simone!" Hailey straightens, waving a toxic rag in the air as she scolds Simone. "No need to scrub the tarnish right off the thing. That is enough—thank you."

Simone sticks out her bottom lip, pouting. It is bright red, matching her scales. She gives Kai a smile and a wave before collecting her bucket and walking away.

Serena rolls her eyes but frowns when Kai wiggles his fingers in quick succession—a flirtatious wave.

"Well, that's all I can do for now. I suppose you'll refuse to allow me to wrap it again?" Hailey asks.

Serena nods.

"It'll at least heal faster, that way," Hailey shrugs. "Come see me once every other day—and don't make me hunt you down."

Kai clears his throat, and both maidens look over at him. He gestures to the trident, asking permission to touch.

Hailey gives a flippant wave of her hand.

Not hesitating to grasp it by the stem, Kai picks it up and spins it. The pointed tips make wide arcs, flashing against the glint of candles throughout the healer's cave. Even Hailey stops to watch. To his credit, he somehow manages to avoid both floor and ceiling, not to mention the rows of jars and books that surround him.

Finally, he stops, approaching Serena. He helps her up with one hand and places her trident in her other hand.

"Wolfsbane. Smart," he says with a smile.

Right now, Serena isn't sure if she'd rather have Kai's compliment or his flirtatious wave.

"Ready for another round?" he asks.

"About as ready as I am for all the other surprises in my life," says Serena, limping after Kai.

He hesitates, looking at Serena from the corner of his eye. Then his face splits open in a wide grin and his laughter follows them down the steps. Serena hopes Simone can hear it.

Chapter Twenty-Nine

Even before they leave the corridors that connect the main networks of Society, Serena and Kai hear that a new mating is to take place on the next full moon. The news spreads like an oil slick—a pairing between the Temporal Caste and the King's Guard.

Serena follows Kai, well aware that they will each take part in The Selection—the actual ceremony where couples are paired. A small group of maidens huddled together grow quiet when Serena and Kai pass, but when she steals a glance, Serena can see small jewels passed amongst the group. They are actually betting on The Selection.

Serena and Kai reach the archives and dress in robes, their back to one another, saying nothing. Mariam meets them at the entrance.

"More training?" Her lips are pressed tight together.

"As you say," Kai says, slipping past her.

"Excuse me," Mariam turns, following him in. "But I very well do not say. I never agreed to it."

Kai heads for the training tridents, picking one up and testing the balance in the palm of his hand.

"I apologize, Serena dear," Mariam says.

Serena shrugs, attempting a smile—very little of what transpires these days are in her control.

Mariam turns back to Kai. "Perhaps you can train in the Great Hall, or one of the guards training rooms..."

Her voice becomes background noise as Serena steps up to the table by the catalogues, still piled with werewolf books. One lies open, to the picture of the dead maiden with the wolf standing over her. Though her first reaction is to slam the book shut, Serena forces herself to look. She brushes her fingertips over the pool of the maiden's blood, remembering her dream and remembering the decision the king will have to make.

The pages are thick with deep red.

Serena feels Mariam's hand on her shoulder and she realizes the arguing pair have long since grown quiet. The Records Keeper leans around Serena, looking down at the picture. Kai approaches on the other side.

"I need a place to train, Mariam," Serena says softly. For now, she will do all she can to protect herself from the wolves.

Mariam's hand tightens on Serena's shoulder. "I'm sorry, Serena—of course. You are welcome here anytime."

Serena nods, taking a deep breath. She turns to Kai, meeting his steady gaze. "I am ready."

He nods, turning back to the tridents.

Behind them, Mariam begins to close the book.

"Leave it," says Serena.

Mariam pauses, looking up at her.

"It is a good reminder," Serena explains.

Mariam opens her mouth, as if she is about to say something, but then thinks better of it and moves to the catalogues to keep busy.

The training session is rough, and growing more so by the moment. They seem to be feeding off each other's intensity. Each time it grows to be too hard, Serena puts her hand to her shoulder, right where Liam's hand rested. She doesn't know if it is to remind her there are worse things out there, or better. Either way, she can't stop doing it.

After several hours of physical work, Kai tries teaching Serena how to come out of a roll with a wolf. Each time, she manages to get her feet tucked in, placing them right at his abdomen for the kick.

"Higher up on my chest," Kai instructs, picking himself up off the ground, trying to catch the breath Serena knocked out of him. "Otherwise fangs can still reach you."

Serena nods. "Again."

Kai lunges into her and they both go to the ground, rolling. This time, she manages to do it right.

"Good," says Kai, breathing hard.

Serena pushes herself to her feet. Her legs are trembling with exhaustion, so she leans against the cave wall for support. "Again," she says.

Kai picks himself up too, shaking his head. "No—the session is over. You need rest for The Selection tonight."

Serena almost snorts. "The Selection? I stand in line—how hard could that be?" She asks this despite the fact she is having trouble standing right now.

"I wasn't referring the actual ceremony, I was referring to after."

"Oh," Serena's cheeks go hot. She is trying not to think about what will happen after, if she is selected.

She looks over at Kai. His robe has become somewhat dislodged at his chest and the smooth skin underneath gleams with sweat. Green eyes under thick brows stare back at her. Serena bites her lip. Though most of the middle-aged maidens might look to Murphy as the prime matching partner, Serena knows the eyes of the Temporal Caste are all on Kai.

Soon, Kai will be on the beach with another maiden. Serena has trouble imaging the moment as magical. More than likely, they will be staring at the forest line, watching for werewolves, rather than getting lost in each other's eyes. They are going to need protection.

"No rest," says Serena, pushing herself away from the wall. "I need to go to The Dry."

Kai's eyes snap to hers. "Okay," he says. "I'll escort you."

Serena recalls what happened with Ervin. "I don't think that is a good idea."

He crosses his arms, staring her down.

Mariam has disappeared among the shelves. The silence in the archives becomes apparent, as if the books themselves are holding their breath.

Finally, the corners of Kai's mouth turn up in a smile. "I'm not sure the Werewolf Liaison has the authority to dictate where the King's Guard does and doesn't go." He straightens his robe, untying and retying the sash that holds it closed. "So if I happen to be in The Dry the same time and place as you, you can't stop me."

Resigning, Serena looks at the floor. "Fine—but can you at least wait in the breakers?"

He nods. "I'll stay until you call for me."

* * *

When Kai and Serena reach the surface, the sun hasn't gone down and the beach is well lit. She hasn't often scouted during the day, not unless she needed to procure an instrument or material from a wandering Ungainly. Poking her head above the surface far enough out so she won't be spotted, Serena observes the beach. Kai does the same beside her as they wait while one couple finishes their picnic. Serena keeps turning around to check the position of the sun. She can already feel the pull of the moon, anxious for its counterpart to relinquish the sky.

The couple on the beach kiss, and Serena is suddenly aware of how close Kai treads water next to her. She no longer looks behind her at the sun, not wanting to risk locking eyes with Kai. She stares straight ahead at the couple on the beach. The male's hands are curious, snaking up the female's shirt, and moving down her thighs. She pushes them away, giggling. It reminds Serena of Simone's laughter when she is with Kai. Her fists tighten because one night from now, it might be Kai and Simone on the beach. Except Simone won't be wearing a shirt.

Serena dips below water, cooling off. She doesn't know if she is warm from embarrassment or anger. Maybe both. Her hair glows. She waits until she has her bioluminescence under control, then reemerges. Kai glances at her but doesn't say anything.

The couple is packing up. They leave shortly after, arms wrapped around one another's waist. Even they know this forest is not friendly after dark. Serena puts her hand to her shoulder, turning to Kai. She doesn't speak, but her raised eyebrow says it all—*stay*. She raises her other eyebrow, so they are both arched as high as they can go. *Please?*

He nods.

Serena turns to the seagulls above who move in to scour the deserted beach. Serena can finally go forward. She swims under the shadow of the gulls. Their movement is predictable, zigzagging toward shore, closer and closer, ensuring the coast is clear. If there are any Ungainly eyes still watching the seas, they won't be able to discern Serena's darkened form just under the water from the seagull's long shadow.

Serena rides the next wave in, allowing her face and arms to brush the air. Her legs transform, and she brings just enough scales on her body to mimic an Ungainly bikini. It is enough so she looks the part of this world, unless someone gets close enough to see her webbed feet, or the gills at her neck. The heat of the sun disappears from her back.

Time to get to work. She enters the tree line, calling forth scales to cover her body as she does. Her first stop is her tree, where she can collect strands of wolfsbane flowers already strung together.

Once there, Serena pulls a braided rope from the tree, coiling it into tight circles. Before she can place it in her basket, Serena notices a small slip of paper tucked into the bottom weaves of wicker. She drops the wolfsbane and pulls out the note, unfolding it.

The scrawl is messy and tilts heavily to the right.

The beaches are yours.

A small, wolfsbane flower is drawn below. Serena smiles. A peace offering—Liam's way of letting Serena know it will be safe.

She tucks the note back into the basket and throws the wolfsbane rope over it. The beaches will be clear the night of the full moon. The Undine have a chance, thanks to Liam.

Serena spends the first half of the night preparing Forest Beach for the upcoming event, working to build a barrier between Undine and the rest of the Dry. Serena pauses multiple times to glance at the breakers, wondering if Kai still watches her, or if a group of maidens has come along to steal him away.

Back and forth she trudges, from her tree to the wolfsbane flower patch, and back to the beach. A lacy veil of poison flowers forms, hanging just beyond the tree line, enough that hopefully any Ungainlies on the beach won't notice.

As soon as it is finished, Serena says her goodbyes to the moon and returns to the water where Kai still waits for her. She approaches, exhausted and ready for sleep.

"Are you okay?" asks Kai.

Serena turns to look at the beach. "I'm tired," she admits.

They bob in the water, pushed back and forth by the waves.

"The Undine thank you for your protection," Kai whispers.

He says it so low, Serena scoots in closer, looking at him.

"Thank you," she whispers back.

Kai turns to her. "Do you know how much it kills me to have to stay here while you risk your life in The Dry?"

Is he jealous? "It's just my job," she says, nose scrunched up.

He smiles. "Meanwhile the King's Guard is relegated to waiting in the breakers."

"Kai," Serena lets herself drift even closer to him. A mischievous smile spreads across her face. "You did a really good job of waiting, tonight."

With her attempt at lightening the mood, Serena expects another playful smile from him, but it does not come. Instead, he closes the rest of the distance between them. "Some things are worth waiting for."

Serena bites her lip.

He moves even closer. "*You* are worth waiting for."

Under the surface, their hands bump together. Intertwining his fingers with hers, he brings their interlocked hands above the water.

Though surprised at the intimate contact, Serena's slender fingers fall into place between each of his, with his palm wrapped protectively around her knuckles.

Serena looks back into his eyes. They are swirls of deep green and pinpoints of gold, fringed with dark lashes. He lowers himself the short distance necessary so they are face to face. He leans in, lips parting.

Serena tenses, finally understanding what is happening.

No, yes, no, yes, no.

"Wait," she says, pulling her hand out of his and placing it on his chest, a buffer between their bodies.

This is happening too fast. He is too old for me.

Serena bites her lip. "I'm sorry." She looks down, preferring the safe, murky depths of the ocean to the wild in his eyes.

Raising his fingertips to just under her chin, Kai tilts her face up so she is forced to look at him. "Don't look down, Serena. It's okay if you are not ready. I will wait for you until my last breath."

Her lips part as he runs the pad of his thumb the length of her cheek.

Serena wants to respond. She feels she must. Just as she opens her mouth, a buzzing from below interrupts. Her lips press tight together as she watches

Kai dip one ear in the water to listen. He sighs, then straightens.

"The king's call," he says. "Time for The Selection."

Chapter Thirty

After Kai, Serena is one of the last to enter the Great Hall. She tries slipping to her old place in the back where she is shadowed by the overhanging cliff, but Nerin doesn't let that happen and motions Serena to her side. Serena hesitates.

Nerin glares, then starts to bend down to the king, as if she will have him call Serena out.

Serena sighs, then steps forward. This time, she has to push her way through the crowd. They are not expecting her.

She hears confused whispers. "Will the final punishment come today?"

Once she reaches the mid-platform, Serena offers a curtsey to the king, then looks at Nerin for further instruction. Nerin nods, allowing her to step up to the high platform. There are more confused whispers.

Serena takes her place besides Nerin, much closer to the king than they were before.

"Serena Moon-Shadow stands with king and council as holder of the title Werewolf Liaison," the king's voice booms throughout the Great Hall. It puts a stop to the whispers. "After consulting with my council, as you all know, we have decided to hold a pairing—the first in thousands of moons."

A jitter of bioluminescent lights and Undine popping up on their tiptoes runs through the crowd. Even the council, who now stand in front of the table of evidence instead of behind it, shift on their feet.

"Our Werewolf Liaison," the king gestures to Serena, "has deemed it safe. As such," the king continues. "She will take part in The Selection."

All eyes rest on Serena. Stiffening, she sucks in a sharp breath. She works to keep her face smooth, but her lips, pressed tight together, twitch.

"Go take your place," whispers Nerin. She puts her hand in the small of Serena's back, nudging Serena forward. The simultaneous pat is probably supposed to offer reassurance.

When Serena steps down to the mid-platform, she turns to curtsey. It is far less grand than when she first came in. She glares at the king, but keeps it short.

"Those that will accompany her are..." the king pauses. Serena can almost see him counting to three under his breath. "The remainder of the Temporal Caste."

There is a series of murmurs from the crowd, along with some shocked gasps, which filter away into disappointed whines. Aside from the Temporal Caste, they all knew this was coming—they've known for years now. Apparently, it all came too soon anyway.

No one moves forward, so the king begins calling them by name.

"Sasha Sunbeam."

More whispers. There was nothing when Serena's name was called.

"Simone Rosebush."

Serena risks a glance at Hailey, standing next to Zayla, shades of intense gold and dark teal running down their scales. Serena did not think about the effect this would have on Zayla, watching all of her students take such a risk. Or is she happy for them?

The final few Temporal Caste mates are called. Cordelia is the last. She takes her place at the end of the line. They stand before all of Society, just as they did a week ago during The Choosing.

"Murphy?' calls the king.

Murphy, standing with the rest of the King's Guard across from the council, calls the guard to attention. He gives leave to Ervin, the youngest member of the King's Guard.

Ervin steps forward. He moves toward one end of the line. He passes each Undine in the Temporal Caste, taking his time. Serena can't look, and when Ervin moves in front of her, her eyes shoot to the ground. He doesn't pause long before moving on. Heat creeps up her cheeks, and her ears ring.

Finally, at the end of the line, Ervin stops and extends his hand. The rest of the Undine in line lean out to see who he has chosen. Serena does not; she already knows. Cordelia.

Out of the corner of her eye, Serena can see Cordelia's hand move to join Ervin's, her bracelets clinking together. The union is accepted by both parties. They will mate tonight.

A noticeable hum of disappointment emanates from the guard. Murphy shoots his men a look, admonishing them.

Better be careful, thinks Serena. *Or they'll get buzzed.*

The next guard member steps forward, and makes his way down the line. He takes even longer than Ervin did. Of course, the decision is more difficult now. Cordelia was the prize catch. He passes Serena, and she shifts from one foot to another, refusing to meet his gaze. Just as Ervin did, he moves on.

Is this the way they used to do it? wonders Serena. *It is absolute torture. I'd rather be stoking fires in the armory.* Her thoughts move to how Ronan and Rayne were matched and her cheeks grow hot again as she tries to keep from delving further into the relationship of her mother and father figures.

The guard member has made a choice. It is the new Scientist Assistant, Evandre's apprentice. Serena busies herself with retracting and bringing forth scales along her arms. Five more members of the King's Guard walk by. Scales in, scales out. It is the same routine Serena used to pass time when she finished with a test or a project before the rest of her caste.

Finally, it is Kai's turn. He falls almost directly in the middle of the guard, as far as age goes. It is odd he is Murphy's second, with several guard members as his elders. Six; the number comes to her. He is six castes ahead of her.

Maybe he isn't too old for me. What would it matter anyway, once we reach Ronan and Rayne's ages?

Serena is distracted by his footsteps toward the Temporal Caste. He moves faster than the others did, passing the first few Undine maidens without hesitation. Serena is still looking down when Kai's feet reach her own.

He has stopped directly in front of her.

Serena's breath catches in her throat as his hand extends out.

No, yes, no, yes, no. The alternating words race through her mind.

But his hand does not stop. It moves up, touching the bottom of her chin, forcing it higher.

"Do not look down, Serena."

She meets Kai's eyes. The rest of the words of his sentence come to her, though they remain unspoken. *I will wait for you until my last breath.*

Kai winks at her, then moves on. Serena lets out her own breath. She is sure this time it is a mix of disappointment *and* relief.

Two maidens down from Serena, Kai stops. Simone. She accepts, her face breaking open into a wide smile.

Serena's mouth drops open. When Simone glances at Serena, the corners of Simone's lips pull up even farther. Snapping her mouth shut, Serena glares at Simone, then at Kai.

It won't happen, she tells herself. *He will wait for me.*

Several more guard members make their pick, all passing Serena, until only Murphy is left.

"Murphy XXX," the king calls the Head of the Guard to his throne. Murphy obliges, bowing before he ascends the steps to the throne. Murphy and Nerin bend their heads toward the King in discussion. Looking at the pair stand together, Serena can now spot subtle similarities between Nerin and her son—slightly hooked noses and high cheekbones. Her eyes falls to the king. *Maybe he mated with Nerin even before his wife died? Is Murphy his son?* But no, the king's face is much too square. Serena squints. *Is that a birthmark on his cheek?*

The three maidens left standing in line with Serena, including orange-colored Sasha, and they all fidget as the discussion grows heated. Nerin's hushed words are clipped and her hand gestures are aggressive in an uncharacteristic display of disagreement with the king.

Finally, the conversation ends. Murphy descends the stairs, his steps echoing in the silent cavern. Somewhere behind her, Serena can hear a maiden suck in her breath. Perhaps some of them are still under the illusion Murphy will pull them out of the crowd and whisk them away to The Pairing.

His hulking form draws closer and closer to the four remaining maidens. Beside her, Serena is aware that the others have ducked their heads, staring at the ground.

But her gaze remains on Nerin, who is glaring at Serena with narrowed eyes. Confusion freezes Serena in place, until Murphy's wide-shoulders replace Nerin's glowering scrutiny. Standing directly in front of Serena, he extends his hand. Serena's mouth drops open. Heat blazes up her neck, licking at her cheeks and drying out her mouth. She can't speak. Her eyes dart from Murphy to the king on his throne then toward Kai. Kai's face is blurred as grey creeps in from the corners of her vision. All Serena can see his hand, fingers intertwined with Simone's.

Focusing in on the pang of jealousy in her chest, Serena finds the strength to reach out and accept Murphy's hand. The union is accepted by both parties, and Serena feels sick to her stomach.

Chapter Thirty-One

The matched couples separate, each party expected to get sufficient rest before the event. Serena waits at the front of the Great Hall, allowing most of Society to leave with high tide before she does.

She wants to approach the king and speak to him directly regarding his decision about the sacrifice he has to make, but Nerin and Murphy stand on either side of him, their heads bent down and each speaking in lowered whispers.

"Kai Forest," the king's voice booms out.

Kai's head snaps up and the king beckons him to join the group at the throne. Taking his leave from Simone, Kai dips his head slightly toward her. That bottom red lips sticks out before she turns to head to her own cave.

As Kai passes Serena, on his way to the throne, he pauses. Turning toward her, he begins to speak. "Serena...I—"

"Kai!" Murphy hisses, annoyed at the delay in responding to the king's request.

Kai's shoulders sag. He glances one last time at Serena, then turns to approach the throne.

Serena turns herself, she can't watch him anymore. He is gone—paired with another. Apparently his ability to wait isn't too well honed.

Dragging herself from the Great Hall, Serena takes the long way to the orphanage, passing most of the residential caves as she goes—many of which she has never even seen before. Those belonging to the Temporal Caste that were chosen in The Selection are inundated with well-wishers, visitors with advice, and even those bearing their condolences, as if another Maiden's Massacre has already occurred.

The Swallow-Tail family cavern is especially full of Undine. With Cordelia chosen for the pairing, everyone wants to make an appearance there. As Serena passes by the opening, she glances in. Her eyes scan past the myriad of colorful maidens, searching for Cordelia's telltale burgundy. Finally, Serena spots her, sitting in a corner with Ervin. Their shoulders touch in the small space they have. Ervin leans into Cordelia, whispering something. Cordelia laughs. Her fingers brush his, and they both pause, looking down.

Faces start to look out from the room at Serena, so she moves on.

Although most of these caves are much larger than Serena's, they are packed with not only Undine, but with bins of food, shelves of tiny figurines and even a cage or jar with pets from The Deep. There are paintings and carvings etched into walls adorned with bright colors. One cave has a large assortment of musical instruments, and the Sunbeam cave even has a rug sprawled across the floor. The waters don't reach this high up in the mountain.

Compared to these, her own cavern is bleak, homely, and isolated. Just like Serena herself. She doesn't belong to this Society and she doesn't belong to Kai; she never did.

Maybe the wolves are a better choice after all, no matter what they intend to do with me.

Making her way to the orphanage, Serena retreats to the nanny's sleeping cove. Rayne is off studying up on recipes appropriate for pregnant Undine, and Serena hasn't seen Ronan in many moons. She assumes he is busy making replacement tridents for Murphy, Kai, and Ervin.

A few hours of sleep, and Rayne is shaking Serena's shoulder. "It's time, Serenita."

Serena stretches, then lifts herself to a sitting position in the cove.

Rayne watches her, smiling. "You are practically a grown maiden now. I suppose I ought to stop calling you that."

Shaking her head, Serena smiles back at Rayne. "Not yet, Mother Rayne." Serena hops down, taking Rayne's arm. "Do you want to escort me to the beach?"

"Of course," says Rayne, running her fingertips through Serena's hair. "Right after you eat something."

"Of course," mumbles Serena.

The meal passes with only a few arguments over the amount of food on Serena's plate, and before long, she is giving Rayne a quick hug. Serena swims in between a line of maidens, waiting just under the surface with bows and arrows should the pairing couples need help.

Serena is the last to arrive on the beach. Behind her, the nickel-shaded moon is full and large, dominating the entire sky. It pulls Serena from the ocean, water cascading down her scales as she sheds herself of the salty sea.

The matched couples are there, along with Murphy in front of them, all staring into the tree line. The only one to turn and watch as Serena emerges from the water is Kai, but she can't bear to return the glance. Simone is hanging on his arm like a suckerfish. Serena keeps her eyes on Murphy, until she takes her place beside him.

Serena looks behind her at Cordelia and Ervin. Cordelia's hands tremble, and she hides behind Ervin's back. At least this time, she has left all her jewelry behind. Nothing rattles.

Ervin wears a deep frown.

Serena's lips turn down, matching his. How is he supposed to proceed, with his partner scared out of her mind?

Leaving Murphy's side, Serena steps into the forest to retrieve something then comes back to Ervin and Cordelia. Serena no longer sees the most popular caste member, or the spoiled beauty. She doesn't even see the girl who is about to pair with Serena's best friend. Right now she sees the maiden who swaddled and rocked a doll like an Undine calfling. At this moment, Serena sees her species only chance for survival.

Serena extends her hand toward Cordelia. Ervin steps aside, raising his eyebrow. Serena swallows, and gives a friendly smile.

Cordelia glances once at Ervin, then toward the dark cliffs that loom on one side of the beach, and finally moves to Serena. The maidens lock hands, and Serena pulls Cordelia closer to the cliffs.

"The night of The Choosing, right after I was named Werewolf Liaison, I was sent out there on my own." Serena nods to the forest. "I saw a wolf, the very next night. And then twice after."

Cordelia's hand squeezes Serena's. "Did he try to kill you?"

Serena looks at Cordelia. She wants—she needs Cordelia to see the truth in her eyes. "No."

"Why not?" Cordelia asks.

Serena thinks of her jellyfish tree and smiles. "Because I brought something with me."

"Your trident?' Cordelia makes a pointed glance at Ervin's empty hand.

"No." Serena shakes her head. "I brought a little something from home, and..." Serena holds up a yellow flower, "this."

"Wolfsbane?" Cordelia steps back, throwing her hands up in front of her face.

Serena rolls her eyes, shooing Ervin as he steps forward. "It won't hurt you if you hold it at the stem."

Cordelia edges back, keeping her eyes on the flower.

"Go on, take it," encourages Serena.

Finally, Cordelia reaches out. Her hand is even shakier than before.

"I decorated an entire tree, and the ground around it with these. Sort of like a circle of protection."

Cordelia's bright blue eyes go wide as Serena speaks.

"The wolf would patrol the border, but has never crossed into the flowers."

Serena watches scales emerge along Cordelia's arm, then fingers, as she plucks the stem from Serena's hand.

Cordelia twirls it, as Serena does when studying the magical flower. The yellow petals are highlighted against Cordelia's deep burgundy scales.

"So this will protect me? If I hold this tiny little thing, I won't be killed?" she asks.

"Not exactly," says Serena. "But I've been busy. Look." Serena points into the darkened forest.

Cordelia steps forward, squinting. The rest of the Undine, Temporal Caste and guards alike, look too. They've been following the conversation, closer than Serena realized.

"I don't see anything," says Cordelia, whispering now.

"Keep looking," Serena addresses everybody. "Your eyes will adjust in a moment."

There are a few seconds of quiet, with crickets chirping in front of them and waves crashing behind them. The wind picks up, blowing out of the forest, toward the Undine maidens. A braided rope of yellow swings out. When it falls back among the trees, its color brings attention to all of the other hanging ropes and the line of flowers on the ground.

Cordelia breathes. "Oh."

"It follows the entire tree line to the cliffs and then north, where the ocean meets the forest."

All at once, Cordelia has stopped shaking. Her hand goes to her midsection, and she licks her lips. "It will hold them all back?"

"I think so," says Serena. But tonight is a full moon—a night where anything goes.

"Okay," says Cordelia. She looks at Ervin, holding out her hand. "Okay," she says again.

Cordelia buries the stem into the ground, so the rest of the wolfsbane flower stands straight up. The pair join hands, their eyes locked.

Suddenly the odd one out again, Serena turns away, heat creeping up her cheeks. A low murmur drifts out from the rest of the Undine.

"Thank you," Cordelia's voice cuts through the whispers.

Serena turns.

"Just for…everything." Cordelia finishes, her hand going to her stomach again.

The thanks comes too soon—the night has just begun. Serena nods, nonetheless, and turns back to the forest. Murphy steps up to her side.

"Ready?" he asks.

Serena smiles. This isn't her first trip to The Dry. "Are you?"

Murphy looks down, holding up his empty hand. "Here," he says. With that hand, the one that usually holds the trident, he reaches for her own hand and clasps them together.

Serena stiffens. "Murphy—I can't do this."

"We most definitely will not be doing anything but patrolling."

Serena whips her head around to Murphy. "What?"

"But let them see us walking into the forest together." Murphy takes a deep breath, his hand squeezing hers as he stares forward into the darkened forest. "The king wanted this. He believes the impression of our union will offer you further protection and support."

Serena tries pulling her hand away. "If the king wants to protect me, he knows what decision to make."

"Hush," Murphy whispers. "I told you we aren't actually going to do anything. I'm old enough to be your father."

Gross, thinks Serena. She risks a glance back at Kai. He is staring at Murphy and Serena's interlocked hands. She relaxes, no longer struggling in Murphy's tight grasp. She remembers how Kai made her leave the dummy head on the floor while training in the archives. In a kingdom filled with the buzz of rumors, impressions are everything. Maybe if Society thinks she is paired with the Head of the Guard, they'll be less likely to offer her up to the wolves.

Besides, it serves Kai right. He shouldn't have chosen another.

"You don't have any of that wolfsbane nectar poison on this, do you?" he asks, glancing down at her hand.

One side of Serena's mouth curls up in a smile. "No." Stepping forward when Murphy does, she follows his lead into the tree line.

As soon as Murphy and Serena are hidden among the trees, he releases her hand. Though she was almost positive his intentions were not to take advantage of the full moon, she breathes a sigh of relief.

"You weren't lying," he says. "You've been busy." He leans to the side as an especially long strand of wolfsbane floats toward him.

"Stay fully scaled," Serena reminds him. "It won't be as bad if the wolfsbane touches you."

"I wasn't planning otherwise," Murphy says, looking out in the forest. "Do you think your werewolf is here?"

Serena sniffs the air. The wind has died down so scents won't travel far. "I don't know. I could always call for him, if you think that is wise."

"No, we don't want to draw attention to what we are doing tonight." Murphy glances at the beach. It has gone quiet. He turns back around quickly. "Even still…"

"It'd be better to know exactly where he is," Serena finishes the thought for Murphy. She takes a deep breath. "I think I'll go scout a bit."

"Then I'm coming with you," Murphy says.

"No." It comes out fast and clipped. "I mean—you have to stay here. If something happens, they'll need you." She thinks of the untrained maidens, holding crudely constructed arrows and bows, waiting just below the breakers. The Temporal Caste will definitely need Murphy, should anything happen.

She looks at the trident in her hand, then thrusts it toward Murphy.

He clicks his tongue, shaking his head. "Have you learned nothing Serena Moon-Shadow? Never give up your trident." He pushes it back at her.

"Well," she smiles, "you aren't exactly setting any examples there."

"Too right." He smiles back. "Now, go." He puts his large hand on her shoulder. "Be quick and be safe. It won't take them long, and they'll each return to the water as soon as they finish. I'll patrol here until the last couple leaves. But they need to see us enter the water together, too."

They part, and Serena turns, hopping through the line of flowers before she has a chance to change her mind. She uses her trident to push aside the last rope of wolfsbane, and then she is on the other side of the border from her kinsmen, alone—or so she hopes.

Serena makes her way through the forest, first checking her tree. There are no new footprint borders around her circle, and no wolf either. She sniffs the air but the wind has gone silent. She can't remember the last time the night was as still as this.

She pauses, considering calling for Liam. Not knowing feels worse—she'd rather have him by her side, where she can keep an eye on him.

But what if more than just Liam come? It is a full moon, after all.

Serena considers returning to the beach. Standing in the forest with Murphy, though, trying not to imagine what is taking place on the beach, would be an awkward sort of torture. Instead, she continues to walk, keeping a parallel path to the beach.

Serena thinks of the three other maidens alongside her that were not chosen as mates. Like herself, they are not nearly as developed as the rest. They didn't have the full curves of Cordelia. They also kept their eyes downcast as each of the guard members went down the line. The guards only chose those that were ready and willing. Her curiosity of the events unfolding at the beach piques.

Before long, Serena is traveling uphill, using the stem of a trident to help propel her up a steep mountainside. It is territory she has never explored, and it is a stupid decision, especially on a night like this. But she needs to get away—away from Murphy and his impressions, forced upon her by the king himself. She needs to get away from Simone and her cherry red lips that are all over Kai by now.

With each step uphill, gravity pulls harder. Serena crashes through the unfamiliar landscape, angry with herself, and with her people. She quickly becomes clumsy with exhaustion, all too aware of how much farther she is from the ocean. Breath coming only in short, hard bursts, her gills flare, desperate for the comforting slide of oxygenated water. A thorn bush latches on to her scaled legs, and Serena pulls away from it.

"Let go!" She digs in her heels and gives another tug. It releases her, and Serena stumbles into a clearing.

The area is only a few spans wide, surrounded by harsh, barbed plants and a dry, cracked ground. The land is lit by the moon, bright and full, and closer to Serena than it's ever been. Serena isn't entranced by the moon, as much as she should be. She is looking at the sliver of a shadow that blocks it.

The form turns, a silhouette with wide shoulders. Serena steps to the side, the figure rotating with her. Finally, the moonlight ceases to shine directly in her eyes, instead falling on Liam's face.

"Careful," Liam says, gesturing to the cliffs that overlook Forest Beach and the ocean beyond it. "Another step and you'll be reunited with your friends sooner than you want."

Serena looks down. Her webbed feet toe the line of a drop-off. Keeping her heels planted, she peeks over the ledge at the mating Undine hundreds of yards below. Some have sought out secluded areas. Others...not so much.

Her cheeks heat, and Serena finds herself searching for Simone's bright red coloring. Simone and Kai are either no longer there, or Simone is covered in sand, obscuring her scales. Either is possible.

Serena peels her eyes away from the beach.

Liam is still staring at the mating Undine, lips pursed.

Anxious for a distraction, Serena notices the cracked ground is covered in light footprints. Liam's footprints. His scent is also much stronger in the little area.

"You spend a lot of time here," Serena says.

Liam nods. Serena looks out over the water, imagining her and Kai splashing each other at the surface, far out of reach of the land. She remembers the howl from this very cliff that cut through their laughter.

"For the view of the moon or the view of the ocean?" she asks.

Liam smiles. "A little of both, I suppose."

Their eyes fall to the Undine on the beach below them. One pair is already retreating into the water. Serena breathes a small sigh of relief for them—and for herself.

"You weren't invited?" Liam gestures down at the beach. "To the party?"

"I'm not all that popular with Society," says Serena.

"Could've fooled me," says Liam. "When I saw you enter the forest with the big one..."

Serena frowns. "Just how good is your eyesight?"

He has a half smile now. "It's better during the full moon."

They both glance at the luminous, perfect circle suspended in the sky, beautiful and ominous at the same time.

"You haven't transformed yet. Will you be able to keep your human form all night?" she asks.

"Not all night."

Serena takes a step back, hoping he can keep it together until she departs. But she's not sure he wants to. Far below her, another pair finishes and enters the ocean, hand in hand.

"What about the other patrols?" she asks, trying to keep him talking.

"I sent them home. They won't be botherin' you. Not tonight." He finally takes his eyes away from the beach, resting them on her. "Alaric is growing more desperate and the mating tonight will be one to remember." He says it casually, like he is mentioning what he had for dinner.

Swearing she can see flashes of his red in his brown-eyed gaze, she takes another step back, toward the cliff. "They won't be suspicious that you aren't there?"

He smiles, all white teeth. The little wrinkles around his eyes appear again. "They were just all relieved they didn't have to patrol themselves."

Serena finds herself staring at his teeth. *Do they look pointier than usual?*

She takes another step back. Her foot does not hit ground, there is only air.

"Serena!" Liam tries to grab for her.

Afraid of finding herself in his arms, Serena retracts from his hands. The extra momentum causes her to lean farther away and sends her right over the edge of the cliff.

Breath catching in her throat, she gasps. Her entire body is in free fall. It lasts only a second, but to her, it is a lifetime. Her scaled fingers grab hold of the ledge.

She hears scraping below. Against her better judgment, she looks down. Her trident is falling, the three prongs scraping the rocky cliff. It lands with a soft thud in the sand. From this height, it looks like a toothpick. The trident, along with the rest of the world, starts spinning. Vertigo kicks in as she dangles from the ledge.

"Don't scream, don't scream," she whispers to herself. Serena clamps her mouth shut. She cannot attract any attention from below. Poseidon be graced, no one noticed the trident. But if the Undine couples were to look up, there would be no finishing for them.

"Serena—grab my hand!" Liam yells.

"Please be quiet," Serena hisses up at him. The small ledge she hangs from crumbles under her grasp. She falls a little farther, catching another rocky outcrop with her other hand. Adrenaline rushes through her head. Black spots dot her vision.

"Serena, if you slip again, you will be out of my reach." His voice is stern, but not panicked. "Grab. My. Hand. And do it now."

Serena focuses on the fingertips, centimeters from her own. It is at least steady, when the rest of the world is spinning in her peripherals.

A few more rocks crumble underneath her grasp, and Serena can see spiky brown hairs begin to emerge from Liam's skin. His nails grow longer and…yellower.

"Liam?"

"Serena…" his eyes are squeezed shut, a grimace on his face. He reaches a little farther. Not because of a stretch. Bones in his fingers pop as they become disjointed, then meld back together. His limbs grow longer, and his hand is in full fur mode. One sharp claw scrapes along the scales on her finger, sending chills up and down her body. The talon is pale yellow against her midnight blue scales—like the reflection of the moon cast upon the ocean.

"Serena!" he says again. His voice is strained as he flings his eyes open. They are bright red. There is no denying it—he is a different wolf under the full moon.

Her heart jumps up into her throat. Her arm begins to shake, and she whimpers with indecision. *Risk the fall or risk the wolf?* Serena does not miss the irony—it is a similar decision King Merrick will make for her.

She looks down again. She might actually survive the fall—maybe she can push out and hit water. Surviving the wolf is...debatable.

One deep breath, and she swings her free arm up. Serena grabs him at the wrist, figuring his paws are useless without opposable thumbs. As she squeezes tight, both hands holding on now, he pulls. It is one, quick jerk—so strong she flies up and over him.

His shoulders begin popping out of their joints. Had she waited one second longer, she might have pulled them both over.

Hitting the ground hard and face down, the breath is knocked from her lungs. Her mouth opens and closes in tandem with her gills, both desperately reaching for oxygen. Liam's popping and groaning become muted as Serena fights for air.

Finally, her lungs expand. She breathes, panic ebbing and pain setting in. Pushing herself up onto her knees she spots Liam in a heap, head ducked under paws. His clothes are ripping and fur pokes through. He is transforming right before her.

Serena scrambles backward in a crab walk. In a blind panic, she can't seem to get on her feet.

"Serena..." Liam is still trying to talk, but the name he calls ends in a growl. He is hunched over, with the moon glaring behind him, like he carries the burden of Earth's satellite on his back.

While her hands slide on loose pebbles, Liam leaps, covering her with his own body. Fear slithers around Serena like a sea snake, constricting her chest and squeezing her throat.

She stares as his snout grows long, wrinkling when he pulls his lips back in a snarl. The teeth that made up his previously perfect and gleaming smile are nowhere to be found. Dagger-like fangs cut through his gums, dropping blood and saliva across Serena's chest, neck, and face.

She brings a shaky hand to her cheek, wiping it away.

"Liam!" Serena yells.

Roaring drowns out her screams with raw power that resonates straight to her bones.

She pushes up on her elbows, forcing herself to stare into his red eyes. He is fully transformed, breathing hard with the effort.

Latching on to the color in his eyes, Serena embraces it. She pulls energy into herself, feeling heat burn behind her own eyes. *I refuse to be a part of this*, she tells herself. *No more victims, no more sacrifices.*

Serena will fight for her life, and she will help the Undine fight for their beaches. Leaning forward, one side of her lip imitates the snarl in front of her.

"I quit," she breathes right back into him. They continue to stare each other down. "Now—get off!" She draws her knees in, then pushes her legs out straight into his chest, like Kai showed her. Liam flies off, falling to the side. His head hits a boulder, hard. Momentum rolls his body farther away, into the bushes.

Serena gets to her feet, reaching for her trident before she realizes it is long gone. Eyes scanning the shrubbery beyond the clearing, she spots the wolf in a heap, not moving. His hide is covered in thorns, but it rises and falls in slow, steady breaths.

Serena turns and runs away.

Chapter Thirty-Two

"Are they all gone?" Serena asks, stomping through the forest. She is only slightly less clumsy through the border of wolfsbane flowers.

"Yes—" Murphy cuts off when he turns to look at her. "What happened to your face? And your arms?" He gingerly lifts one of her arms. It is covered in scratches from her fingertips to her shoulders. Several scales are missing.

The cliff held strong for Serena, but at a price.

Murphy's forehead is creased with worry. Until he makes a show about looking at both her hands, and behind her back. His lips turn down in a full frown. "Where in the hell is your trident?"

Serena's arms drop to her sides. "Over there, come on."

"Over there?" He holds his hands in the air. "Over there?"

Serena emerges from the tree line, walking out onto the sand with Murphy on her heels, chastising her.

"Was Kai not clear about keeping your weapon with you, at all times?" His eyes are already scanning ahead, spotting a gleam of gold in the otherwise beige sand. "Agh!" His throat makes a guttural, choking sound. "Unbelievable."

Serena stops to survey her arms as Murphy picks up the trident, blowing sand off.

"Here." He pushes the trident out to her so aggressively Serena has to take a step back.

"Thanks," she mumbles, taking it.

Murphy rubs his temples.

"I'm sorry," says Serena.

"What happened?" he asks.

"Well..." Serena trails off, looking up at the cliffs. She doesn't really want to tell Murphy. Not until she has had time to process it herself. "Um, I tripped?"

"You tripped?" he crosses his arms, and raises an eyebrow. His look all but tells her she can do better. "You know what?" he sighs, lowering his arms. "That doesn't really matter right now."

Serena grunts. *I almost just died and it 'doesn't really matter right now'. Story of my life.*

"We have to go back home. People will be watching us, believing we have a connection now. We have to play the part."

"I don't exactly look like I've been rolling around in the sand," Serena says, holding her arms up.

"No," says Murphy, looking at her. "But maybe the woods?"

"Yeah, maybe." Serena smiles. The joke is his way of apologizing, but an uncomfortable silence follows.

Serena takes a deep breath. Tonight was a success—for the Undine, anyway. She really couldn't have asked for it to go better, fangs and fur aside.

Murphy clears his throat. "Shall we?" Murphy holds up his arm, bent at the elbow.

Serena glances up at the cliffs, worried about Liam. But she certainly can't go back now and risk facing the beast if he is awake.

She takes Murphy's arm, her hand nestled in the crook of his elbow. The pair walk into the waves, with only silence at their backs.

* * *

Their entrance into the Great Hall is similar. Hand in arm, they walk in with synchronized steps. The paired couples each stand together, in front of the king and Nerin. A few others have gathered, mostly family and friends of the Undine maidens and guards.

Nerin! Serena glances at the King's second, thinking about how uptight she appeared even when Hailey was just talking about Murphy as a previous potential mate. Nerin's lips are pursed, eyes narrowed. Serena leans into Murphy. "Was your mom upset about the king's idea?"

Murphy glances at Nerin, then Serena. "The king wanted us paired for real. She refused, and they finally came to an agreement that only the impression would be upheld."

Murphy and Serena's coordinated steps echo in the cavern. All eyes snap to them. For once, Serena is relieved to be in the Great Hall, even if she is the center of attention.

They pass the small crowd that has gathered. Serena can feel their eyes travel down the scratches on her arm and she hopes she managed to wipe most of the wolf blood from her face.

"I knew he'd be rough," Serena hears one of the elderly Undine whisper to her friend. The couples that returned before them must have reported Serena and Murphy disappearing into the woods together.

"Of course he would," the friend whispers back. "He didn't get to be head of the King's Guard by being gentle."

Serena's cheeks flush. *As if this wasn't already awkward enough.*

Murphy's stony face and sure steps do not falter. He leads Serena right up to the mid-platform, forcing his way in between two couples who have to back up to give them room. Disconnecting, Murphy and Serena's arms drops to their sides. He clicks his heels together, and bows—quick and purposeful. Serena curtsies. It is more graceful and slightly slower, but she is aware their separate movements complement each other.

This is weird, she thinks.

King Merrick looks at Serena. His gaze moves to her arms. His eyebrows grow together with his frown, and he shoots a glance at Murphy.

Standing beside the king, Nerin clears her throat. "Your king and Society thank you for your protection." Nerin is good at putting a stop to awkward moments.

Serena leans back, looking behind Murphy's shoulder to steal a glance at Ervin and Cordelia. They look…happy. Her eyes flit to Kai and his partner. Simone's lower lip sticks out, pouting. Kai is glaring at Murphy.

He's jealous? After he chose another mate? How is that fair?

Serena squeezes her eyes shut. *First the cliff, then Liam—no*, Serena tells herself, *then the werewolf.* After all that, Murphy yelling about her losing her trident. *He's lucky he didn't get a trident shoved right up his—*

"Serena!"

Serena's eyes snap to Nerin.

"The king wishes to know the details of the event. Do not ignore him."

Serena looks at the king; his downturned mouth tells her he is not happy.

"Details?" ask Serena.

King Merrick and Nerin both nod.

What kind of details could they possibly want? All I saw was Undine rolling around in the sand. Unless...does he want details about me and Murphy? Did everyone else give details before we walked in?

Serena shoots a glance at Murphy. He notices.

"Your majesty, I don't think—"

"Grace Poseidon, man," King Merrick interrupts Murphy. "All I need to know is if there were any werewolves!"

Murphy looks at Serena, eyes narrowed, as if it were her fault he defended her in front of the king.

Serena rubs one palm across the scratches on her arm, all too aware of the words she told Liam not an hour ago; *I quit.* Somehow, it is much harder to say standing here in front of the king, Nerin, Murphy, and Kai who spent hours to help train her, and in front of her Temporal Caste—once the last of their race, now hoping that on this night they conceived the next generation of Undine.

Serena mumbles under her breath.

The king leans forward. "What was that?"

Serena's eyes snap up, and she takes several steps holding her trident diagonally across her body.

She can hear Murphy scramble behind her. "Serena!" he hisses.

"Serena..." Nerin does the same.

She ignores them, eyes locked on the king.

She takes the first step up to his throne, pushing aside his massive tail with the stem of her trident.

The king's eyes widen in shock.

Three more steps, and their eyes are level. She stops and leans forward.

"There were no werewolves tonight. Your people are safe." All she can think of when she says this is bloody fangs, inches from her neck.

The king does not return her glare, at least not with the same ferocity. "I think you mean to say our people are safe."

Serena blinks. *Dang it. I definitely can't quit now.*

She eases off the king, backing down the steps. Murphy waits for her, he must have followed almost all the way to the throne.

"If there isn't anything else—" the king begins.

"There is something else," interrupts Serena, her back to him.

"What now?" growls the king.

Serena glances at Ervin, then Kai. "I request permission to access the king's library."

"Why?" asks the king. His voice is loud, nearly at a shout.

Serena turns, squaring her shoulders to King Merrick. "So I can protect our people, damn you!" She slams the stem of her trident into the cave floor. The crack echoes across the cavern; same as when the king demands the attention of his people.

The room goes silent, except for Serena's hard breathing. Her eyes are full of fury, and she could care less that she just damned her own king.

King Merrick leans back in his throne, mouth twitching. "Permission granted."

Chapter Thirty-Three

Serena turns to leave, a quick bob of her head sufficing for a departing curtsey to the king.

"Wait!" Murphy calls after her. "I will escort you there!"

"Any escort will need to get their own damn permission," she yells over her shoulder, not stopping.

There is a flurry of Undine talking over one another—Kai and Murphy, among others. As she exits the Great Hall, all she can hear is the king saying, "permission denied."

Serena smiles as she turns the corner.

She is to the archives in record time. She runs into the cavern of books, dripping wet with her robe in one hand and slippers in the other. "Mariam!"

Mariam is not at the catalogues. Serena runs to the first of the shelves, circling them.

"Mariam!"

She is stumbling into her slippers when Mariam emerges from the orca section, three books balanced in one arm and an open book in another. "What is it, child?"

"He gave me permission." Serena is red-faced, and out of breath. She doesn't actually have proof, finally wondering if she should have waited for a scroll or something. Surely Mariam knows Serena would not lie to her, least of all about the King's Library. If Mariam allowed unauthorized entry, she would lose her job.

Mariam makes a pointed glance at the robe, still draped over Serena's arm.

"Oh," Serena mumbles, slipping on the robe.

Mariam is still staring at her.

Serena's eyes jump from Mariam to the darkened entry of the King's Library, and back.

Mariam sighs. "Are you sure you want to do this?"

"Yes!" It is all she can do to keep herself from shoving Mariam toward the section. Shifting from one foot to another, Serena is practically hopping by the time Mariam walks to one of the walls.

Mariam unravels a cord strung around a nail, then pulls. A metal sheet slides open above the restricted area, filling it with light. The dust is so thick, you can see speckles floating in the air.

Serena pauses by the sign that reads 'restricted'. Running her finger over the three holes made by her trident when she was with Kai, Serena looks in the room again. Her hand drops to her side and she takes a tentative step forward amidst the settling dust. Although the restricted section is lined with shelves, the books are sparse. Serena could make her way through them in a month, tops.

"I thought it'd be bigger than this," Serena says, laying her hand upon one of the larger, hardback books. It is the Ancestral Book of the Undine, listing family lineages all the way back to the very first Undine, Atargatis, the Lady Goddess of the Sea.

Mom, Serena thinks. *I could find out more…*

Mariam sighs and walks into the room, pulling Serena from her thoughts. She pushes against the back wall on one side. It moves, slowly. A hidden door scrapes against cave floor. Mariam reaches inside, and tugs on another cord. Light protrudes from the room behind the half open door. Coughing at the plume of dust that floats out, Mariam turns back to Serena.

"This section was added after the Maiden's Massacre. The king selected one single book to be moved to his library, but wanted it hidden better."

Serena nods. This was the first door she's ever seen in Society.

Mariam exits, holding one arm out. Serena is clear to enter.

Serena moves her hand off the Ancestral Book, and steps forward. She knows exactly where she needs to start.

She walks past the rest of the shelves, and squeezes through the small space in the open door.

The dust in here hasn't had time to settle yet, and Serena coughs. Light filters down from the forest floor above illuminating a table in the middle of the room. On it lies one thick book. There is no title, nor cover pictures or markings that tell her the subject matter.

Serena opens the book. The first few pages are blank. No table of contents, author's note, or forward. But on the next page is a simple drawing of the wolfsbane flower. All at once, Serena remembers why she is here. Her fate did not lead her down the path of Archives Assistant—she is the Werewolf Liaison, and nothing will change that. Not even Liam, pinning her down and shifting into a werewolf directly over her.

The book begins with a verse directly under the flower:

A simple beginning
a life-altering change
fins and scales
to fur and fangs

Serena freezes, mouth dropping open. She closes the book, picks it up, and brings it with her. Outside the King's Library, Mariam is standing by the catalogues.

"That didn't take long," Mariam says, setting down a book at the table.

"Of course not," says Serena. "It's right here on the first page, under the flower. Werewolves are made from Undine?"

Mariam takes a few steps closer. "Those words should never be spoken, and this book should never come out of the King's Library." Mariam turns Serena around by her shoulders, and pushes her forward.

Serena digs in her heels, resisting the forced momentum. "Did we make the werewolves?"

Mariam stops.

"I mean, I knew we made them, but not from our own kind."

The mentor sighs, shoulders drooping. She is not shocked by the news. She has read the book. Serena wonders who else has.

"Where do you think all of our males go?" Mariam asks.

"I thought they all died in the battles fought after the Maiden's Massacre."

"Those old enough went to battle. But there were very few male Undine to begin with, which has been the case for a while now. Before the massacre, we only kept the biggest ones."

Serena's mouth drops open even more.

"Well, go on then. Might as well ask me any questions you have. It'd be faster than plugging through that thing." Mariam motions to the book.

"Fins and scales to fur and fangs," Serena repeats. "No wonder they rose up against us. We abandoned them as babies."

Mariam places her finger to her lips, then glances over her shoulder, as if someone would choose now of all times to enter the largely unoccupied archives.

"Male Undine calflings very often didn't survive three moons past their birth. They were weak, and so small. The female Undine showed ill effects as well, like their webbing..." Mariam gestures to Serena's feet. "But the majority made it. Whatever was changing us didn't seem to affect females as badly."

Serena sits down at the same table Ervin fell asleep on, inebriated with jasmine and chamomile tea. She wishes she had some now.

Mariam continues, "Times became desperate. Most of the elderly called it 'Poseidon's Curse'. Said we didn't respect the old gods like Society used to. All available maidens went through The Selection— we didn't have a choice. I, myself, lost three calflings."

Serena glances up. Mariam ran the palm of one hand up and down her arm, her eyes on the floor.

Mariam shook her head, squeezing her eyes shut. "It was too much. We were all under stress. The Ungainly began to get closer. Some tour company wanted to set up shop. We needed protection—and time. Hailey's predecessor came up with the potion. It didn't work, at first, but it was tweaked. The details are in that book, there."

Serena looks down at the closed book underneath her hands.

"It changed them to something that could survive outside the water, though transformations still took place. Different...transformations."

Serena shudders, remembering just how different their transformations are.

"Our first was handed to an Ungainly we trusted. Owns a dive shop near the shore. He kept his divers away from us, and has been chasing away other dive shops for years."

"You mean, a maiden just gave up her baby to some Ungainly?"

Mariam looks at Serena with a hard stare. "You can watch only so many of your own babies die before you decide to do something drastic." Mariam grasps Serena's arm. "The calfling would've died if we hadn't. But with the Ungainly—and the transformations—the calfling survived. And what's more, he grew big, and fast. He turned only on the full moons and seemed drawn to the water, but would never enter."

Serena swallows, finally ready to ask a question. "How did they come to be our guards?"

Mariam smiles. "That was his Undine mother's doing. It was a solution to unite with our sons at least once during every moon cycle, and it became considered good luck to have their blessing for more healthy sons."

"So why did the werewolves decide to revolt?"

Mariam sits next to Serena at the table, her pinky brushing the spine of the book. "There are several theories. I don't think anyone knows for sure."

"What do you think?" Serena prodded.

Mariam starts slowly, "The only thing our desperate times did was add more and more babies to their clan. Even the dive shop owner could not keep them all. When the first few grew old enough, they moved out and started the camp you saw. More and more babies were sent directly to the camp for raising. The clan grew strong. They organized, and adjusted well to Ungainly life—we did not." She takes a deep breath.

"I think they felt held back by their obligations to us. And you have to remember, there were a lot of emotions involved. Families were separated; grudges held. It isn't easy to lose a child, nor is it easy to learn you've been abandoned. But you have to understand—we couldn't have done it any other way." Mariam looks at Serena, resting half her palm over Serena's and half on the book. "They would've died, otherwise."

"Don't they know that? Why would it have gone so far as to lead to the Maiden's Massacre?" Serena's forehead creases in wrinkles.

Mariam pushes back from the table and stands. "That is something only the wolves can answer." She turns to walk to the catalogues, pausing halfway. "The wolves...and perhaps the king."

Chapter Thirty-Four

Serena spends the rest of the tide in the archives reading the book. By the time the light dies down, plunging the library into a predictable darkness, Serena folds the hardback closed, finished with the last page. Without a word to Mariam, she replaces the book in the hidden room and pulls on ropes, closing the light sources to both coves.

Serena goes directly to The Dry. There is a decision to be made, and Serena doesn't want the king to make it for her. As soon as her Ungainly legs hit soft sand on the beach, she sends out a call, loud and reckless, for Liam.

The ocean crawls forward, licking at her ankles, then retreats. One, two, three. On the fourth frothy wave, the forest in front of her moves in the wind. One braided rope, tinged with yellow, swings out. Serena knows her border of wolfsbane is still there.

The wind dies down and behind her there is a lull between the waves.

A voice howls from the forest. "About a month too early, girl—but if you are that anxious..."

It isn't Liam.

Serena's neck prickles with chills. "I am not here to submit," she says, her voice sounds small against the forest.

Laughter reaches out, playing tricks with her ears. It seems to come from everywhere. Serena looks between the trees, squinting. She can only smell one wolf, yet she feels surrounded. She brings her trident closer, holding it with both hands diagonally in front of her.

There is another lull in waves, as if the ocean herself waits to see what will happen next. The wind compensates for the quiet sea. Heavy gusts of air blow several strands of wolfsbane ropes out from between the trees. When they part like a curtain, Serena tries to focus beyond them. A blackened shadow leaps forward, taking the form of a werewolf. Its fur is as dark as the night, and its fangs are as yellow as the wolfsbane flower.

Serena raises her trident, and the wolf stops just short, snarling. He doesn't stare at the golden tips threatening to pierce his eyes—he stares at her.

"Alaric?" Serena recognizes him as the same werewolf that chased her the night of the excursion and as the one she watched confer with the king. The scars he left on her leg begin to burn.

Alaric pushes off his front paws, so he stands on two legs, towering above her. He is almost twice her size. He points one claw at her, the rest curling in. "I am the betrayed." His voice is gravelly and thick. The forest seems to lean forward with him, bearing down on Serena and her ocean. He sucks in a breath and seems to grow even taller. He roars, throwing spit against her hair as his growl thunders through her.

Serena uses a surge of adrenaline and lunges forward, aiming her trident at his midsection. He bats the weapon aside and Serena rolls with it so she doesn't lose her grip.

The werewolf follows. Serena gets to her feet, bringing the stem of her trident up to catch him under his chin. His jaw snaps shut as his head is thrown back. A quick spin, and she slams the stem of her weapon just behind his knees. His enormous body pounds against sand.

Beyond him, a plume of smoke drifts up from the trees. Serena sniffs the air. The scent of singed wolfsbane comes to her.

"No!"

They are burning the wolfsbane patch.

She starts forward, holding her trident at the ready. Still on the ground, Alaric reaches for Serena's foot. His claws dig in, ripping through the webbing between her toes.

Serena falls face first into the sand, knocking the wind out of her chest. She forces herself to move, rolling over. Her gills strain, searching for the air that won't come through her mouth. Instead, they suck in a steady stream of sand.

Alaric leaps, landing on top of Serena and pinning down her arms and legs.

Serena coughs, sputtering out granules that work their way from gill to mouth. The werewolf gets an eyeful of wet sand. He blinks furiously, releasing one of Serena's arms to paw at his face. Serena still grips her trident, so she thrusts it toward the wolf. It smashes into his snout with enough momentum to throw him off balance. Serena kicks out with her feet.

Just as on the night of the Temporal Caste excursion, Alaric flies, end over end, into the waves. This time, before he even splashes into the water, Serena is on one knee nocking an arrow already drawn from her quiver. She takes aim, the wolf's eye set in her sights.

Someone pushes her bow down. The arrow shoots harmlessly into the sand.

"Please don't," Liam's words tumble out of him between heaving breaths. He looms over Serena in his Ungainly form. "Not yet. I have to make sure the majority of the pack would back us first, and not just seek revenge for him." His eyes plead with her, his mouth downturned, showing just a touch of the gleaming white teeth behind his lips. No sign of fangs, fur, or claws.

Serena glances out at the werewolf, dripping with cold seawater, as she stands.

"Careful, Serena," says Liam. "You don't want to start a war."

"Sorry," Serena says with bite to her voice. She retrieves the arrow stuck in the sand and puts it in her quiver. "But the war was started eighteen years ago. I'm going to finish it."

My life depends on it, she thinks.

Now at the breaker line, the wolf shakes his whole body, ridding his fur of the salty water.

Liam takes a step toward him. "Alaric—the wolfsbane patch is enough for tonight. Leave her alone."

The wolf shakes his head, but Serena cannot tell if it is because he is still wet or because he is saying no to Liam.

Alaric stalks around Liam and Serena. Serena can't help but notice the way Liam slowly inches his way in between the dueling pair. When Alaric's back is to the forest, he dips his head and shakes his fur again. This time drops of water do not fly off, but hair does. He sheds his fur, showing bright pink skin underneath. Bones crackle and pop, Serena can see their distortion beneath his skin.

Liam produces a cape from a bag that hangs around his waist on a string. When she looks back up, Alaric is in Ungainly form. It is a frighteningly fast transformation. Serena stares at his naked body until Liam throws the cape at Alaric.

Alaric smirks as he unfolds the cape, and wraps it around him.

Serena tightens her grip on the trident.

"I mean it, Alaric—leave her alone," says Liam.

Alaric glances at Liam. "I have left her alone, for almost eighteen years now." He ties his cape closed and lowers his gaze at Serena. Black, wispy hair falls around his face in wet strands. "Her time is running out."

Alaric steps to the side, forcing Serena to counter. They make a slow, wide circle, with Liam in the middle. Something tickles Serena's feet. She looks down to find she is standing in Alaric's shed hair.

Gross, she frowns, looking down. Moving her toes around, she makes a small pile of the hair. "If I choose to go with you, on the next full moon—what will become of me?" Serena asks, keeping his eyes on her face and not what she is doing in the sand.

Alaric lifts his chin, looking down his nose at Serena. "So your king will be giving you the choice?" The wind picks up, whipping his cape just below his knees.

Behind Alaric the tide is receding.

He is right, my time is running out.

Serena steps out from around Liam. "Why do you want me?"

Liam glances at Serena. "So you *are* the sacrifice he was talking about?"

Serena nods, and they both wait for Alaric's answer.

He huffs, crossing his arms. "Ungainly women have trouble yielding pups—only one has managed so far. We believe we need a maiden."

Serena's mouth drops open and beside her, she can see Liam do the same.

The tide is nowhere near Serena, but her ears ring with the sound of rushing water. Panic blooms in her gut, twisting its way up her chest like a sharpened knife.

Liam is the first to speak. "You never said that was part of the plan."

"What's the problem?" Alaric holds his arms to the side. "We get our pups—they get their little baby…fishies, or whatever. Everyone is happy."

"Not her," Liam shakes his head, fists clenched. "Find another if you must!" he screams, shoulders hunched and rounded.

"No." Alaric's tone is firm. "It has to be her. We need her bloodline."

Smoke tendrils from the wolfsbane patch slink across the sky, reaching out over the ocean from the forest. Soon, it will dissipate into the ocean, just like Ungainly CO_2, over time. Whatever happens in The Dry eventually creeps into the ocean, and the creatures of The Deep pay the price. The Undine must have their beaches back, or they will never survive what is to come.

Alaric follows Serena's gaze to the smoke. "You hide behind the flower too much," Alaric's snarl turns up into a cruel, twisted smile. "There won't be any hiding after the next full moon."

"Serena," Liam turns toward her, but he keeps his gaze steady on Alaric. "Run."

She hesitates, considering both men. Liam's fingers are curled into his palms, and she can see the veins in his forearms turning a deep blue. Alaric stands with his feet shoulder-width apart, one slightly behind the other.

But there is nowhere to run. Two werewolves stand between her and the ocean, and behind her the wolfsbane patch is gone.

Alaric bows his head so he is staring at Serena through lowered lids.

"Serena..." Liam says. "Run—now!"

Serena bends for a quick second, laying her hand on the ground. Alaric lunges. She can see the action in his eyes before he does it. Serena dodges to the opposite side of Liam, opening her stride and aiming for the waves.

They are so far—the receding tide is wholly unnatural.

Out of the corner of her eye, she sees Alaric twist. It is a canine-like move, yet he is still in Ungainly form. Footsteps pound the sand behind her, approaching quickly. Just as Alaric is about to slam into her, Liam collides with him mid-air. They both fly over Serena as she sprints.

She can hear them hit the sand behind her and she prays they don't transform until she is submerged. The scales along her legs, responding to the fear coursing through her body, begin to fuse. Icy salt water splashes against her ankles as she reaches the farthest stretch of water. It encourages the remaining scales to emerge, forcing her legs together. The webbing between her toes grows into fins and Serena reaches full transformation before she is deep enough to swim.

She looks over her shoulder and sees Alaric throw Liam into the trees. He turns, running for Serena before Liam even hits the ground. Serena doesn't flounder in the knee-deep water. Like an invertebrate staring at the glowing extension of the deep sea dragon fish, she is mesmerized, unable to react to the danger. Instead, she opens her mouth, letting her voice flow freely. She steadies her heaving breaths by opening her gills, allowing both organs to work simultaneously.

The ocean responds, and before Alaric can reach Serena, he is backpedaling in the sand. Serena looks to the water. A huge wave, at least twenty feet high, barrels toward them. Serena pushes up on her arms. Her fins flap once in anticipation.

The wave engulfs her and she is gone by the time it recedes. Scales extend around her closed fist, protecting the handful of Alaric's fur she holds.

Chapter Thirty-Five

Serena sputters on granules of sand stuck in her gills, mouth, and throat. Her heartbeat flutters as quickly as her fins, and she is still calling out, purely out of fear. It has morphed into her echolocation whistle, but it is as loud as ever. Her world materializes before her as the sound comes back to her.

Serena slows. There is a mass of forms in front of her, several dozen of her size, if not larger. She inches closer, and they come into view. Undine—and lots of them. Almost all of Society, Serena imagines.

Her eyes go wide. It was her call—the call that can't be resisted, except this time the king did not counter with his own.

Murphy and Kai approach, their eyebrows furrowed as they scrutinize Serena. Murphy swims around her, leaving her staring into Kai's eyes. They blaze with fury and his jawline is tight.

Serena turns her attention back to Murphy, who is peering closely at her torn webbing. When he moves back in front of her, his eyes match the fury Kai's have already shown. Murphy turns, facing Society alongside Serena. Opening his mouth, he releases his own sound. Compared to Serena's soft, caramel harmony, Murphy's is a bone-shaking boom.

Those in the first few rows are pushed back, shocked by the sound that is normally reserved for reprimanding the guard. Another movement comes from within the group. The King's Guard makes their way forward, organizing themselves in a V-formation in front of Society. Murphy takes his place at the apex, then motions for Serena to join him.

It is a battle formation, and Serena can't help but think just how unready they truly are. Three guards don't even have tridents.

Serena approaches Murphy, taking her place by his side, and raising her trident in the air. It signals the entire guard formation to move forward, something Serena has seen Murphy do hundreds of times.

She leads them in a sharp curve, practically cutting through the mass of Society gathered behind them. Shoulders back and chin high, Serena doesn't look back to make sure they follow her instead of moving toward The Dry. Once she reaches the caves, she transforms and heads straight for the Great Hall. She can hear the sounds of several Undine emerging from the water behind her, and lets out a sigh of relief.

When she enters the Great Hall, Murphy is by her side, and the King's Guard is in a column behind them. The rest of Society enters in groups, quietly filling the room. King Merrick and Nerin are at the throne. As the council members come in, they take their place at the mid-platform.

Serena doesn't know when the last of the Undine filter in to the Great Hall, but the king nods, signaling her to speak.

"They are burning the wolfsbane patch," Serena says.

Sarafina, the Head Gardener, gasps. "All of it?"

Serena glances at her. She can't help but notice Sarafina's scales are the same shade as wolfsbane.

She probably takes the burning as a personal insult. Serena looks back to the king. "Yes, all of it."

"And how do you interpret this action, Werewolf Liaison?" the king asks.

"I think it is retribution, for the pairing," Serena says. "Somehow, he knows what happened."

The king nods, looking at Serena with sad eyes. "It was successful, the pairing. But it is unlikely they would continue to be so, especially with the wolfsbane gone."

Serena gets his meaning. It was a nice try, but there still must be a sacrifice—Serena in exchange for a new generation of Undine. He is aware that Serena knows of the deadline.

She glances at the king. "Do you know what they plan on doing with me?"

The king's spine goes rigid. "I..." he glances at Nerin. "I have never asked."

Serena nods, biting the inside of her cheek. There is a large lump in her throat, but tears do not come. She is too exhausted for tears, emotionally and physically. *Would it help, if I told him?*

The king slumps down in his chair, as if energy and life is slowly emitting from him. "What would you have me do, were you in my position?" he asks Serena, refusing to look at her.

Serena turns, surveying the crowd of Undine behind her. She sees Rayne and Mariam, leaning into each other for support. Cordelia is near the front, shooting nervous glances at Ervin, then back to Serena. Simone stands with the other Healer Assistants, all three staring openly at Serena.

She could make Kai happy, Serena thinks. *At least she seems willing enough.*

Serena turns back around to the king, lowering her voice. "I'd give me up, too."

"And that is your recommendation?" asks the king.

Folding her arms across her midsection, fingertips cradling her elbows, Serena stares at the three gashes her trident made in the cave floor. "Yes."

"Then it is settled," says the king, sitting up straight in his throne and bringing his trident to stand at his side. He raises his voice, so it permeates the Great Hall. "We go ashore in two days, and we will take our beaches back." He looks down at Serena, eyes blazing. In a softer voice, he tells her. "We will fight for our painted maiden."

Both relief and guilt flood her system, and Serena sags at the knees. Her hand goes to her mouth, and she has to doubt her king.

Is this the right call?

The king continues to speak to the crowd. "The council will convene in two hours to discuss the battle plan. And," the king looks at Serena, "the Werewolf Liaison's presence is requested."

Once the assembly is dismissed, Serena sinks even lower, her knees almost touching the floor.

"Serena," Kai is by her side, pulling her up. "Are you okay?"

"Yes…no." Serena shakes her head, trying to clear it of adrenaline. "I'm not sure." She looks up at him, remembering her anger at the pairing. But when Serena glances at Simone, she is turning away.

"What happened to you out there tonight?" asks Kai. "Your call was so desperate. Are you hurt? Were there wolves?"

Serena looks at him, eyes wide. He has no idea what just transpired at court.

"Liam was there—the one I normally see," says Serena. "And Alaric."

"Alaric?" Kai's mouth drops open and his eyes go wide. "Oh…"

"What?" asks Serena.

"Alaric was the first werewolf."

Chapter Thirty-Six

Being the first Undine calfling abandoned, Alaric's hatred burns deeper than most. In a way, Serena feels bad for him. She knows what it feels like to be left behind.

"And now the first wants his revenge on the last of our species," Serena says at a whisper, absently touching her mother's charm, embedded into the high center of her breastplate.

Serena feels Kai's warm hands move up her cold arms. He glances at the king.

"I think I understand what is going on." Kai looks back at Serena. "Alaric will never have you if I can help it," he tells her. She meets his sea-green eyes, boring into her. "Not if anyone of us can help it."

Taking a step back, Serena forces her gaze away. It is almost as difficult as resisting the pull of the moon. She can't let herself be caught up pining over Kai. The king has just ordered all of Society to war because of Serena. If she has to, she'll sacrifice herself, with or without the king's blessing—but she can't have Kai standing in her way or threatening to pull her back.

She focuses on the cold of the cave floor, imagining it seeping into her feet and up her legs, straight to her stomach where she feels the tingling sensation every time she looks at Kai. Dropping her hands to her sides, Serena glares at him.

"You said you'd wait for me…and then The Selection came, and you chose Simone." Serena swallows, determined to keep her voice steady. She fails as her next sentence comes out broken. "You chose Simone, the one Undine that is most unlike me."

Kai glances at the king, then at what jurors are still left in the Great Hall. He leans into Serena. "We can't do this here."

"Where, then?" she asks, almost yelling.

Nerin looks up from consulting with the king. Serena doesn't care. She needs to cut ties—if the battle goes badly, she doesn't plan on returning. How could she? Her surrender is the one thing that would leave the Undine race in peace.

"Come on," says Kai, taking her by the arm.

Serena allows herself to be led away from the Great Hall and down the corridor. The Undine bustle in and out of caves, charged with energy and calling out to each other. As Serena passes her kinsmen, under Kai's tight grasp, they look at her with curious, raised eyebrows. What has this girl done to warrant another full-scale attack on the wolves? There hasn't been one for a decade, now.

Serena shakes her head, keeping her eyes downcast. *If only they knew how much easier this could be.*

The smell of wood smoke could guide Serena to the armory blindfolded. There is a long line waiting outside the entrance. Maidens are volunteering to either enter The Dry as a second wave of reinforcements to the guard, or to wait in the breakers to execute their marksmanship skills. Crude bow and arrow sets are distributed, as are knives.

Kai stops at the end of the line and frowns. "I thought this would be a good place to talk."

Serena rolls her eyes. "It would be, anytime other than right before a battle." She twists her wrist out of Kai's grasp, and then grabs his. "Come on."

Moving toward the front of the line, pulling Kai behind her, Serena wedges her way in between bodies crowded in the packed hallway. Those being moved aside protest, until they see her. Then they grow quiet, just the way Serena likes it.

At the front of the line, Sasha Sunbeam is pleading with Ronan. "I want to fight."

Ronan shakes his head, and behind him, Murphy does this same. "The king's orders were clear, no one in the Temporal Caste goes to The Dry."

"But I wasn't even at the pairing," Sasha insists, a flash of red running through her bright orange scales. "I'm not with calfling—there is no reason to keep me back."

Serena turns, looking at Kai.

No one in the Temporal Caste? Surely they can't mean me, too.

"Sorry, Sasha. Please move aside," says Murphy.

Sasha turns away, almost running into Serena.

"Oh, sorry," mumbles Sasha.

Serena studies her closer—the maiden doesn't slouch with defeat, she is distracted and determined. When Sasha pauses, looking up at Serena, her whole face lightens, as though she's had another idea.

"You," Ronan calls out.

Serena turns as Sasha slinks away.

He bends the crook of his finger, motioning for her to enter the armory. Kai and Serena squeeze past Murphy—it isn't crowded at all inside next to the fires.

Ronan turns his gaze to Serena's trident. "It's been used."

Serena looks at her weapon. She wipes smudges off one of the tips. "That is what it was made for, right?"

Ronan grunts. "Let me at least sharpen it up for you."

Serena hands it over and the sound of metal touching a whirring stone drowns out all chance of talk. Kai and Serena cast nervous glances at each other, but neither holds the gaze.

Once Ronan finishes, he hands Serena back her weapon. "I have something else for you," he says. He retrieves an object at his workbench, then turns her around to place it in her quiver. "More arrows. These are stronger."

"Thanks, Ronan."

He moves in front of her, still holding one single arrow. It is smaller than the rest, and is made of a different material. It doesn't have as much give, and seems heavier.

"It'll pierce deeper," says Ronan, handing it to her. "Can get up to halfway into werewolf hide."

"Oh." Serena glances at Ronan. She reminds herself of all the battles fought ashore after the Maiden's Massacre, where they lost most of their male population. The expert with weapons that he is, Ronan must've been sent and it is a testament to his battle skills that he still with the Undine now.

She begins to put the arrow in the quiver but he stops her.

"Here," he says, pointing to a tab on the side of her breastplate. Farther down, there is another tab.

She unsnaps them, placing the arrow inside. When she presses the tabs back down, they hold the arrow securely.

"For emergencies," says Ronan, winking at her.

"Thank you."

Ronan grunts again and turns away. "The tridents will be finished by the time you go to The Dry," he tells Kai over his shoulder.

Serena smiles as Ronan rejoins Murphy at the cave entrance. That is all the well-wishing she will get from Ronan—a wink, a grunt, and several sharp weapons.

Turning her attention to Kai, she pulls him around the fire pit to the other side. Flames hide them from curious eyes peering in from the entrance to the armory.

Kai turns to Serena. "Simone and I—"

"Please, spare me the details," Serena interrupts, closing her eyes. She doesn't think she is strong enough to get rejected again—not by him. But when Serena opens her eyes, Kai is still in front of her waiting.

"You will hear me out," Kai says, his voice turning to steel. "You have to know this before we all go to battle. Simone and I didn't complete the pairing."

"What?" The statement catches her off guard. "Why not?"

"I told her I wasn't ready. We didn't do anything, except leave. She was not happy about it."

"Oh," Serena pulls her eyes from Kai and stares at the dying fire. She clutches a handful of Ronan's black powder and throws it over the pit. The blaze bursts out licking at Serena's scaled arms, then settles into a fierce burn.

"She only agreed not to make a fuss if we carried the illusion that we paired," continues Kai. "I think she is worried about her reputation among her peers."

Serena takes a deep breath, steeling herself for that penetrating gaze and turns back to Kai.

"You really are waiting…for *me*?"

"I said I would, didn't I?" Kai looks down, his voice going softer, and reaches for her hands.

Without thinking Serena steps back. Her eyes hop from the fire, to Kai, and back to the fire again. Jittery fingers tap against the scales on her thighs; they need something to do. She throws another fistful of black powder on the fire. Flames lick the ceiling of the cavern. Out of distractions, Serena reaches back and pulls an arrow from her quiver. She runs the pad of her thumb over the sharp point. It is comforting to have something solid and real between her and Kai. He is pushing Serena into emotions she hasn't before come into.

"Stop," says Kai, taking the arrow from her. "Stop acting as if you aren't a part of us. You have a place here. You have a place with me."

He steps forward, wrapping his arm around Serena and pulling her close. Their breastplates crush against each other. Serena's heart is pounding so hard in her chest she is sure Kai can feel it through all of the armor.

He slides her arrow back in her quiver, her body jolting as the arrow is sheathed. But Kai doesn't step away. Serena goes still, anchored within his arms. She tilts her chin up, and his eyes are on her.

He waits…and I am ready.

Rising up onto her tiptoes, her lips find his. She presses closer, wrapping one hand around the back of his neck. Fire spreads in her stomach, moving up to her chest, and it burns hotter than fire beside them. It burns better than the sun.

Kai tastes of smoke and salt. Serena parts her lips, wanting more. He responds, wrapping his free hand around her waist, pressing her into him.

Serena rises farther on her toes, drifting away like the smoke from the armory fire dissipating through cracks into the ceiling, past The Dry and up into the heavens. Kai places his hand on her cheek, embracing Serena and softly bringing her back to The Deep. She opens her eyes and smiles while their lips still touch.

When they pull apart, Kai smiles back. "Worth it?" he asks.

She blushes, biting her lip. It still tastes of him. "Undeniably," she answers.

"Come on, we'd better get back to the Great Hall before they plan everything without us," Kai pulls her around the fire and pushes his way through the crowded entrance with Serena in tow.

As they walk, Serena touches her lips with the tips of her fingers.

Chapter Thirty-Seven

For the first time in many tides, there is no Assembly in the Great Hall. Only King Merrick, Nerin, Serena, and the king's council are invited to the closed session.

A table sits in the center of the mid-platform. Motioning from his seat at the center of the table, the king beckons for Kai and Serena to sit. They do, nodding to each of the other occupants. One chair remains empty.

An awkward silence follows, as everyone stares at their hands. King Merrick glances at Serena under his bushy eyebrows. Serena folds her hands in front of her, trying to pull off the look of a Werewolf Liaison. *Whatever that is.*

Moments pass, and she wiggles in her seat. It feels weird to sit in the same type of chair as the king. She looks again to make sure she saw correctly that his doesn't have any extra adornments, and that it isn't taller than the rest—even by an inch. It isn't.

Still, the king towers over everyone else at the table. His shoulders are so wide, they extend past either edge of the chair. Beside him, Nerin is the complete opposite. She sits rigid, her back straight, but she still only comes up to the Kings shoulders. Serena wonders if he really isn't that tall. Maybe the chair has special lifts.

Serena leans back in her chair slowly and tries to appear casual as she glances under the table.

How did he get from the throne to the chair, without the high tide?

Serena's thoughts are interrupted by footsteps entering the Great Hall. Zayla strolls in, chin high, eyes locked on the empty chair. Serena straightens, glancing at the king. He appears not to have noticed her looking under the table at him. Nerin, of course, is frowning at Serena.

Zayla walks the long way around the table. Serena catches the scent of seasoned seaweed as she passes by. No sooner than she sits down does the king speak. "Let's begin. First, we'll need to know how many Undine will be going ashore."

"All that can fight, I imagine," says Evandre.

"No. I won't risk every last Undine to this threat," the king says.

"You don't have to risk anyone, save one," Serena mumbles.

The king slams his fist down. The entire table jolts and everyone flinches away from it like a school of herring scattering to avoid a shark. Only Nerin remains unfazed, her back so rigid she is as far as she can get from the table.

"I've made my decision," the king glowers as Serena, "and you will respect that. There will be no more talk of it."

Serena meets the king's eyes, her heart pumping like she's been racing up and down the beach all day. "As you say," she says, steady and even. The more the king refuses to take the right course of action, the more Serena wants to.

"The King's Guard will be the first wave ashore," Murphy begins slowly, breaking the silence and bringing everyone back to the task at hand. "We've accepted volunteer maidens to stand by as a second wave, though hopefully we won't need them. The third echelon will remain past the breakers, ready with their arrows. I have some of my guards conducting training right now."

The king nods. "Good. Many of the maidens have some experience, though maybe not the youngest generations."

"No Temporal Caste were accepted on the rosters, as you requested," Murphy says.

"Except me of course," Serena interrupts, glancing at the Head of the Guard.

Murphy pauses, looking at Serena then at the king. The rest of the table goes silent.

From the other end of the table, Zayla pushes back her chair and stands. "Your majesty, if you please, I'd like to announce my ruling on Serena's third and final punishment."

Now? Serena's eyes go wide. *She wouldn't...*

King Merrick nods his consent.

"I sentence Serena to prison. The amount of time to be determined by myself, or the king, when we have deemed she has learned her lesson."

"Prison," Serena repeats, blinking twice. "Prison!" She stares at Zayla, then turns to the king. "But I know our beaches. I know what can protect us in The Dry, and I know the capabilities of the wolves."

"Excellent. You can brief Murphy before you go below," says the king.

"And I thank you for your contribution," Murphy nods to Serena, as if that is the end of it.

Chair squeaking back as she stands, Serena raises her voice. "I am the Werewolf Liaison. You need me out there!"

"Serena..." Kai begins, leaning toward her. Serena turns, squaring her shoulders with Kai and fixing him with the fiercest glower she can muster.

He quiets, holding his hands up and leans back as far as his seat will allow.

Finally, the king turns to Serena. "You will not be going ashore. You will instead be carrying out your third and final punishment."

Serena glances at Murphy then the king, bringing her hand to the side of her breastplate, touching the special arrow Ronan gave her. "I am ready for this," she says, beseeching them to understand.

The king leans forward, clasping his hands together. "Regardless, Zayla's punishment stands. Besides, I will not risk the very maiden we go ashore to protect." He looks at Serena, eyes soft. "I will not risk my daughter."

The entire council goes still. A chill, colder than any werewolf can give Serena, runs up her spine. Next to the king, Nerin slouches in her seat. It is not disappointment. Rather, relief from the release of a burden carried too long.

"Daughter..." Evandre gives a nervous laugh next to the king. "What—?" She stops when the king turns toward her. Evandre glances at Nerin, then back at the king, and her smile drops from her face. "Daughter?" she says louder, staring at Serena.

Serena's mind races, trying to connect the dots. But there are no dots to connect. Her parents were killed by werewolves, and she has been alone ever since.

King Murphy picks up his trident and turns one side of it toward Serena. Right where the three prongs are melded together at their base by a crescent moon, rests a jewel. Midnight blue, with dark gray and black swirls throughout. Serena's fingertips move to the charm at her breastplate. The amulets match perfectly.

"Do you know how many times I've had to turn my trident to keep the jewel from prying eyes? I dare say most of Society isn't even aware a jewel was there to begin with," the king spins the entire trident slowly in circles, rolling it between his fingers. Evandre stares up at it, mouth open.

Serena snaps her own mouth shut, anger heating her face.

"You carry the family stone," he says. "You are heir to the throne, Serena. Worthy of the same shaded scales as the very first Undine, passed down through our lineage. Of course," the kings stops spinning his trident, glancing at Serena, "I've had all proof of that relegated to the King's Library."

"But...why?" Kai asks. "Why was the king's daughter raised as an orphan?"

Serena sinks into her chair, glad someone can speak for her. Hard lumps rise up from her stomach to her throat, making it hard to breath, much less speak. Zayla won't look at Serena.

She knew, possibly all along.

"My wife and son departed the night of the Maiden's Massacre, that much is true," says the king, voice hallow as he talks. "Those wolves tore through Undine bodies so badly, we could barely distinguish what parts belonged to each maiden and child. Had we not known how many went ashore, we'd have no idea how many casualties there were. Only one remained whole amidst the bloodshed by the time I got there." The king glances up. "Serena." He swallows, hard. "My wife was with twins. We kept it a secret throughout the pregnancy, though she was so large it was hard to hide it. We didn't announce it because, well—we just didn't want to jinx anything." The king lets out a strangled laugh that threatens to turn into a sob.

Nerin lays her hand on the king's arm.

He takes a deep breath, composing himself, and continues. "The wolves had an advantage— they could have torn into you just as easily. But they agreed to let me take you home, on one condition." The king looks at Serena. "That I return you to them on your eighteenth birthday."

Kai is the only one moving at the table. He keeps glancing in between Serena and the king, his fists clenching and unclenching.

"Why play such games?" demands Kai. "If they wanted her, why didn't they just keep her?"

"Alaric," the king sneers. He takes another deep breath. "Alaric is very cruel. He never forgave us for his abandonment, and he wanted something that would hurt me deeper. To give up a child after watching her grow..." he looks at Serena again. "Watch her graduate from her first caste, watch her swimming with her caste mates, watch her enter The Choosing and even watch her endure The Selection, with her chin held high..." The king shakes his head.

"He knew the distraction would drive me desperate. And I did desperate things in those first days. I sent wave after wave of Undine ashore to stop the threat, to protect my daughter. They were all slaughtered. Alaric was coaxing us out—and we lost more than half our species, almost all of our remaining males because of it."

Serena's hands lay flat on the table, shaking. Nerin places her own hands over them. "Serena—the idea to put you in the orphanage was my own."

Refusing to meet any eyes at the table, Serena keeps her gaze down in her lap.

"We didn't know how events were to play out, but I thought if the king ever did have to give you up, that it might be better to keep the two of you disconnected," says Nerin, squeezing Serena's hand.

The king nods his head. "While I was looking out for your best interests, Nerin was looking out for Society's best interests."

Tears spill over Serena's cheeks. Kai moves toward her, but Serena holds up a hand, warding him away. He sits back down, hesitantly.

"I became attached to you anyway, from a distance. Especially as I watched you grow into a young maiden," the king tries to smile, but it ends up looking like a lopsided frown. "I thought maybe if I named you Werewolf Liaison—you would conjure a miracle, since the whole matter has long since been out of my hands. I thought you would grow to love them, find a place there."

At this, Serena can see Kai tense out of the corner of her eye.

"I thought—what a relief this would be, if Serena might find happiness out of it, some way." He buries his head in his hands. "At the same time, I beat myself up over the decision. I also wanted to keep you here, and make you my heir. But I knew I had some making up to do, which is why I kept putting you in the spotlight. I thought if only the rest of Society could see how wonderful you are. How hard you work to protect our way of life, how smart and brave you are, and the magic your voice holds when you sing—like your mother. Then maybe they would embrace you as their queen."

"Enough," Serena says, voice cracking. She pulls her hands away from Nerin and wipes her cheeks dry. "I don't want to hear anymore."

The king, Nerin, and the rest of the table look at Serena, waiting. She squares her shoulders with the king and swallows hard. "I think that you've made some really poor decisions, and not just for me, but for the entire kingdom."

The king doesn't deny it, but nor does he nod. He stares at his hands, the shadows of the cavern creeping into the deep lines that etch his face.

"And I think," continues Serena, "that you are about to make another poor decision." She squeezes her hands into fists. "Instead of sentencing me to prison, give me to the wolves. Make peace with them. We are helpless to stop the decline of our ecosystem—we might be forced to the beaches soon enough. And if we haven't resolved our differences with the wolves, there will be none of us left, anyway."

"No—I won't do it," says the king.

"It's one for the whole of Society," says Serena, on the verge of shouting. "Why can't you see reason?"

He looks up at her. "I haven't seen reason since the day you were born, Serenita."

She sits back in her chair, tears threatening to spill over again at the diminutive Rayne so often called her, though now it comes from the king himself.

Serena shrugs. "I can't—I can't sit back watching the entire kingdom risk their lives for me." It doesn't seem right, no matter how much of an outcast they all made her feel she was.

The king smiles and blinks slowly.

"I figured as much." He raises his head, shouting out to the guards at the entrance of the Great Hall. "Take her to the pit."

Two guards come alongside her, thick hands closing around her arms. They lift her from her chair, turning her away.

"Be careful, please," says the king. "She is my daughter."

Pain spears up to her heart. Serena hunches over, grasping at her chest with her hands. It is difficult to breathe.

The king turns away, refusing to look at her.

Collapsing in on herself, Serena's feet drag. She is pulled the length of the Great Hall purely by the strength of the guards that hold her.

As they leave the room, the king resumes speaking to his council, his voice laced with steel. "We go to The Dry at dawn tomorrow. There are many preparations yet to attend to, and we will need every Undine's assistance. We will go ashore strong and proud, and we will fight for our right to extend the Undine legacy into the next generation."

His words fade as Serena and the guards move down the corridor.

Only silence emanates from the maidens they pass. Most are too busy to even notice. They are busy with preparations—determined chins raised high, set jawlines, and jittery fingers—anxious to finally wield the weapons that Ronan is working round the clock to construct. The colors of the painted maidens shine bright under the glittering minerals of the cavern hallways. They are bold colors—deep reds and blues, and brilliant greens and purples. There are hues of gold and yellow, and of course one bright spot of orange.

Turning a corner, the floor spirals as it drops into a sharp decline.

Serena doesn't talk. Her tongue is numb, her brain is numb, and her heart is numb.

The light dripping from above winks out, and Serena and her guards plummet into darkness. Beside her, strands of bioluminescence in the guards' hair flickers to life, providing enough light to navigate the uneven ground.

After what seems like an eternity walking down into the Earth, Serena lifts her chin just in time to see a spacious cavern open up above them, painted with colorful images of ancient sea deities. Poseidon is in the center, standing erect with one arm raised. His beard hangs past his chiseled chest, and a tunic hangs loose around his waist, obscuring an answer to the age-old debate—if Poseidon himself has scales and fins.

Serena is so engrossed in the paintings, she doesn't see the small, circular hole in the middle of the floor. Her foot hits nothing but air and she lurches forward. The guards' grip around her arms tighten and pull her back.

Almost thanking them, Serena snaps her mouth shut, remembering what they are about to do to her. She peers into the hole, it is pitch black. Realizing what exactly an Undine prison looks like, her heart starts racing all over again. She glances at one of the guards, but can't remember his name.

The other takes away her trident, and undoes the ties holding her breastplate on.

"Don't—just…I'll do it," Serena steps back, out of his reach. Shrugging out of her armor, she places it upright against the wall, right next to her trident. "It stays here," she says, staring them both in the eye.

They glance at each other, then nod. Serena walks back to the hole. "How far of a drop is it?" she asks.

One of them looks at her out of the corner of his eye. "If you really are the heir to the throne, I'm sorry about this. Please remember we are just following the king's orders."

"What—?"

Serena cuts off at her own gasp when they push her forward, right over the hole. She falls, her breath hitching in her throat and her stomach rising into her chest. She tucks her legs, expecting to hit hard ground any second. Instead, she hits water and it feels just as solid as the tree branches she so often crashed into in The Dry.

Plunging under, she automatically closes her mouth and her gills open. She waits until the stinging sensation on her legs subsides, then she opens her eyes. Pitch black. The water tastes stale.

She forms fins, then flutters her tail until she rises to the surface. The hole above is outlined by the receding glow of the guards' hair.

"Wait!" Serena calls. "How long are you keeping me here?"

The glow continues to withdraw. "What if I escape?" Serena says to herself, voice at a whisper.

"You won't," another voice answers her.

Serena turns sharply, peering into the darkness. "Who is that?"

The voice laughs. "Just…wait one more moment, and you will see."

"What?" Serena still turns, treading water.

Above, the glow has disappeared entirely. Serena keeps her eyes up, desperate for some sort of light source other than her own hair. It doesn't help illuminate anything past her fingertips.

The ceiling of the cavern above the hole begins to blink. Minerals glimmer like a spray of moonlight scattered across the surface of the sea. Poseidon himself lights up, his face and body illuminated with radiant specks of stone.

Ripples in the water softly bump into Serena and she tears her eyes away from the sea god. The crest on each ripple is highlighted with color. Serena follows them to their origin, where a dark shape is moving slowly toward her. The maiden brings her own hair to light, and the features of her face are illuminated. High cheekbones and pointed nose create a gaunt, almost haunting, appearance.

"Arista," says the maiden, introducing herself.

Serena nods and lights some of her own strands so the maiden can look upon her face, but she doesn't have to state her name.

"Serena Moon-Shadow," the maiden states for her.

Leaning back slightly, Serena narrows her eyes. "How do you know?"

"The King's Library," Arista says. "Your lineage is the first in the ancestral book. You are the heir to the throne."

Serena remembers having her hand on the book, about to open it until the other room appeared, catching her attention. If only she'd taken the time to read the ancestral book, certain secrets would have been revealed sooner and she would have a chance to sacrifice herself before she ended up in prison. "You had permission to enter The King's Library?" asks Serena.

"No," Arista emits a high-pitched laugh. "Which is why I'm here." Arista circles Serena, slowly. "Well, that and absconding." She makes a full circle around Serena, then stops in front of her.

Serena sighs. "So I've been told. Look, I have to go. Is there any way at all I can get out of here?"

"Sure," Arista shrugs. "If you can manage to smooth-talk one of the guards. Though obviously that hasn't done me any good—and I've had *a lot* of practice."

Serena forces a polite smile. "How often do they come?"

"So far, they've been here 7,310 times." Arista gestures to one side of the cave. Serena squints, but still can't see anything.

Arista sighs, and swims toward the wall, allowing more of her hair to light up. Just above the surface of the water are tick marks. The highest are within arm's reach. Serena swims closer to study them. The tick marks have different slants to them, and they are various heights. One is a squiggly line, appearing over and over again, almost in pattern.

"The tide doesn't come into the mountain this far," Arista explains. "And there is no moonlight. The only medium I have to judge the passing of time is the guard visits. They follow a pretty frequent pattern," Arista traces the etchings with her fingertips as she talks. "Each type of line represents a different guard."

"Who is that one?" Serena points to the squiggly line.

"Serena?" a distant voice shouts out, moving down the spiral corridors.

Swimming out to just under the hole in the ceiling, Serena waits. Arista floats alongside Serena on her back, her arms stretched out to the side like a lazy stingray. "Here he comes now..."

Serena doesn't look at Arista. Instead, she keeps her gaze on the constellation of Poseidon, staring down at Serena with judgmental eyes.

The reflection of Undine hair against the wall starts small in a corner, growing as the voice gets louder.

"Serena!" Kai's call rings down.

"Kai!" Serena yells back. "Get me out of here!"

Poseidon disappears completely, replaced by Kai's sea-green eyes. "Are you okay?" he yells, fingers curling over the edges of the opening.

Serena allows her own hair to illuminate so Kai can see her. "Yes, I'm fine. Please, just get me out of here."

"I'm sorry," he shakes his head. "I can't do that."

Serena grits her teeth, squeezing her hands into fists. Arista swims by on the other side, propelling herself with her fins. "Told you..." she sings to Serena.

"Why?" asks Serena, trying to ignore Arista.

"Because you'll go straight for The Dry, you'll sacrifice yourself—you've said as much."

"Kai—I need to be there. Please trust me on this."

"Well this is more entertainment than I've had in a long time," says Arista.

Kai looks down with a wry smile. "Hi, Arista."

Arista responds by diving under, then out again with a showy double summersault. She doesn't reach the ceiling by even one quarter of the distance. Serena could never make that jump, not even with a triple pike.

Serena turns away from the splash, then looks up at Kai, her shoulders sagging. "Is this how you imagine me waiting for you? In a prison?"

"I'll come for you, Serena. But we need to finish this first. I'm sorry..." his face disappears from view.

"Kai?" Serena shouts. "Kai, don't walk away!"

But the glow recedes, quicker than it did with the other guards, and the image of Poseidon returns. Serena hangs her head, then swims to a small ledge just under the surface of the water. Pulling herself onto it, she keeps her fins but curls her tail into her chest, wrapping her arms around herself.

There is no tide here, no moon, and no sun. Only the sea god himself to keep watch over the prisoners. Serena thinks of the sun, slowly disappearing on the other side of the globe. The next time it makes its appearance, the Undine will be at war.

Chapter Thirty-Eight

"Serena—Serena wake up!"

Someone is pulling at Serena's fins. Serena blinks, rubbing her hands over scratchy eyes. For a moment, she expects the smell of seaweed soup to drift in from the kitchen, and mother Rayne to poke her head in Serena's sleeping cove.

Serena opens her eyes to find Arista swimming back and forth in front of the ledge, agitated. Reality sets in, pressing down on Serena, weighing more than a thousand scrutinizing eyes.

"The guards haven't been back yet," says Arista. "I mean, I can't say they are late, because I don't know. But it's been a long time, and it just feels wrong."

"I know," says Serena, sitting up and swinging her legs into the water. "They are going to battle."

Arista stops swimming, turning to stare. "With who?"

"The werewolves," says Serena, glancing up at the only escape to the abyss. Poseidon is still there, standing guard.

"That," says Arista. "Is a very bad idea."

Serena snorts. "Tell me about it." She scoots off the ledge, dipping under the water then up again, fully awake. "Is there anything to eat in here?"

"Cave sponges," says Arista. "They grow along the bottom of the pool."

Serena's mouth turns down in distaste.

Arista shrugs. "It's no salted kelp, but you get used to them. Besides, every now and then you get lucky and find one infested with worms."

Serena puts the back of her hand to her mouth. Filleted salmon is starting to sound very good right about now.

"You know what?" Arista says. "I'm going to find you a sponge right now. It'll be like a welcoming present."

Serena nods, just so Arista won't mention the worms again. Once she dives under, Serena brings her hands to her temples.

I have to get out of here.

"Psst, Serena!" A voice calls down from the hole.

Serena doesn't hesitate to swim over and look up. Light blonde hair hangs down from the hole, framing a familiar face.

"Cordelia? What are you doing here?"

"I brought her," Sasha appears in the hole next to Cordelia, her bright orange scales casting a sickly glow on Poseidon's expression. Sasha throws over a long strand of material strung together. Tassels hanging from the bottom skim the surface of the water.

"The rug from your cave!" Serena exclaims, elation hitting her voice.

"I know—mom is going to be so upset. Come on, can you climb up?"

Serena grabs hold of the rug, then slips off.

"Try again," encourages Cordelia.

A second attempt is no more successful.

"It's too slippery," says Serena.

"Wrap it around your leg and we'll pull you up," hisses Sasha. She is getting impatient. They lower more of the makeshift rope into the abyss.

Serena goes under, transforms from fins to legs and begins looping the rope around her leg in a spiral from thigh to ankle. She glances around the darkened water. Arista is nowhere to be found.

Resurfacing, Serena shouts up. "Ready!"

Cordelia nods, then their faces disappear momentarily. Serena puts one foot on top of the other, keeping pressure on the rope in between them. She is heaved up in one big jolt, then again. The smile on her face grows wider as the hole gets bigger.

Suddenly, Serena is pulled back down. Her feet dip into the water. Glancing beneath her, she sees Arista latching onto the rope.

"I'm going with you," Arista says.

Serena shakes her head. "I don't think—"

Arista pulls again, and Serena is face to face with her.

Her eyes burn into Serena. "I go or no one goes."

"Serena?" Sasha yells down. "What happened?" Faces peer out over the ledge. "Who is that?"

Cordelia whispers to Sasha, and recognition dawns on her face. "Oh."

"She's coming, too," Serena decides. "Can you pull us both up?"

"I don't think that is such a good idea," says Cordelia.

"She's in here for a crime similar to mine—and she's been down here," Serena glances at the tick marks on the wall, "a very long time. If I am afforded the opportunity to leave—she goes too."

Arista meets Serena's eyes. *Thank you*, she mouths.

Serena nods and looks back up. "We are running out of time!"

The rope moves again, pulling both of them up. Water drips from their bodies as they are yanked higher and higher. Serena releases the rope with one of her hands, and grabs the ledge, pulling the rest of the way through on her own strength. Arista snakes out of the hold on the opposite side of the circle.

Cordelia and Simone release the rope, breathing hard.

"Thank you," says Serena. Looking from one to another. "But why are you helping me?"

"I want to fight, too," says Sasha. "And I figure if I show up with the next heir—they can't deny me again."

"I don't know," says Serena. "If something were to happen to you…"

"Please?" asks Sasha. "Do this one thing for me. We can call it my Choosing gift."

Understanding lights Serena's eyes. Sasha is calling in the favor she gave to Serena in the archives, when Sasha was willing to cover for her leaving under Ervin's guard.

Not to mention she did just break me out of prison.

"As you say," Serena sighs. She walks to the side of the cavern to pick up her armor and trident. She shrugs her armor back on, looking at Cordelia. "Will you be joining us, too?"

"No," Cordelia shakes her head, glancing down at her feet, then at Sasha.

Sasha gestures toward Serena. "Go on, tell her."

"Tell me what?" Serena asks, tightening the straps on her breastplate and ensuring the special arrow Ronan gave her is still there.

"I'm pregnant," blurts out Cordelia.

Serena's mouth drops open. "Oh…"

Cordelia blushes, her cheeks going the color of her scales. She rubs her elbow with one hand, looking away.

"I mean." Serena licks her lips. "Congratulations?"

"Thanks," Cordelia mumbles.

Serena thinks of Cordelia singing to a swaddled doll.

"How do you know that you are? I mean, isn't it too early to know?" Serena glances at Cordelia's midsection.

"Hailey tested me. I'm the only one that tested positive." Cordelia gives a nervous laugh. "I think some of the other girls are relieved."

Serena glances at Cordelia's midsection again. The deep burgundy color looks shinier than usual. She wonders if the calfling will don Cordelia's burgundy or Ervin's pale brown. Maybe it is bad luck to think of things like that.

"This is what you wanted, right?" Serena asks.

"All my life," says Cordelia. She smiles briefly and looks at the floor. "But…"

Serena prods Cordelia. "But what?"

Cordelia shrugs. "It's just…what if I can't give birth, because of the wolves?"

The cavern goes quiet. Even Arista, who has so far been exploring the walls with her hands, stops to look at Cordelia, then Serena.

"I need the beaches," says Cordelia. "I need my baby to be safe. And I think you have a better chance than any to make it happen." Cordelia tentatively steps forward, wraps her arms around Serena and squeezes tight.

Serena stiffens in the hug, unsure of what to do. She would've never expected this display of affection from Cordelia, much less toward the outcast of Society. A second pair of arms wrap around Serena and Cordelia, and Serena looks up to find Arista joining in, a wide grin on her face.

Clearing her throat, Serena shifts on her feet. The two maidens take the hint and release Serena.

"Well, have fun with your battle," Arista tips her head at Serena. She looks at Cordelia, her eyes drifting down to her midsection. "And the baby."

Cordelia put her hands over her stomach.

"And thanks for the release. I'll see you maidens later." Arista heads toward the sloped spiral leading out. Her bioluminescent tresses are the only ones still glowing, highlighting paintings that watch as she leaves.

"Should we stop her?" asks Sasha.

Serena shakes her head. "No time for that. We need to get to the surface." The urgency to get to the battle overcomes an uneasy sense of foreboding.

The last of the light disappears down the corridor, and the cavern goes dark. Poseidon's glowing eyes return, and Serena can swear he is frowning this time.

"Oh, stop judging," she hisses at him.

Chapter Thirty-Nine

After leaving Cordelia behind in the Great Hall, Serena and Sasha swim to the surface. A large group of maidens wait in the deep water with their bows and arrows before the waves crest and break onto Cliff beach. Half of them don't even have quivers, the arrows are tied to their hips with torn fabric.

Serena looks at Sasha, then gestures to the archers.

Sasha shakes her head. She holds out her arms and turns around, showing she has no bow. Instead, Sasha digs into the satchel tied around her waist, and pulls out a short, rusty knife.

Serena's shoulders sag. Sasha wants to be with the reinforcements, and judging from the fire in her eyes, there will be no convincing her otherwise. They swim wide around the archers, approaching the breakers where the second wave stands in wait. Serena turns to Sasha, pointing with her finger. *Stay here.*

Sasha nods, looking at the rows of maidens with their backs to her. If she stays in the rear, hopefully they won't notice until it is too late to send her away. Sasha tightens her grip on the stunted knife and swallows so hard Serena can see a lump move down her throat.

Edging closer, Serena puts her hand on Sasha's shoulder, imitating Murphy's warrior salute. Serena smiles, and mouths the words, *be careful.*

Sasha blinks, passing the knife to her other hand in order to return the salute. *Always am*, she mouths back.

Nodding, Serena releases the salute and backs away. She has to force herself to turn away, resisting the urge to drag Sasha all the way back to the lower caves to dump the innocent maiden in the abyss, just to protect her. Serena blinks, finally seeing some reason to Zayla's punishment and even Kai's refusal to help.

Serena tilts her chin down, streamlining to swim faster. Time to fight her first battle of the day, earning a position alongside the King's Guard. Hopefully they'll have no option but to let her stay. She finds the first wave of fighters huddled behind boulders at the next beach over— Forest Beach. They take turns poking their heads out from behind the large rocks to scout the shoreline, where at least a dozen werewolves patrol.

The pink sky tells Serena the sun is rising, but at the opposite end of the Earth. For now, the beach and forest are shrouded in shadows.

Seagulls call out, announcing the coming of the sun. They glide over the shoreline, searching for breakfast. Serena is in luck, this flock is full of black-legged kittiwake seagulls—one of the few seagulls that dive. On cue, rays of light creep forward, warming the ocean as the sun rises over the treetops.

It is time. Serena faces The Dry, withdrawing an arrow from the quiver on her back. Then she turns the case around so it is aerodynamic as she swims. She only gets the one arrow for now. It needs to be on target.

She turns and swims forward under the shadow of a seagull. Following the crisscross pattern as the gull slowly angles toward the shore, Serena keeps a close watch on the bird, trying to anticipate its movements.

The wolves that patrol on the sand won't be able to see her coming closer, at least not yet.

When the earth below begins to angle up, Serena pulls a fish from her pouch. She holds it in front of her as she swims, just below the surface of the water. The gull cocks his head, peering at the bait. Wings tuck in, preparing to dive.

Below, Serena streamlines her fins, preparing to jump. It happens so quickly, you wouldn't see it unless you were staring right at the bird. It dives for the bait, and Serena lifts herself from the water. For a split second, as the bird dives under, it's form is replaced with Serena's silhouette, elbows out mimicking wings. She pulls back on her bow and releases the arrow before she falls back under.

By now, the King's Guard will have noticed her. But the other wolves will have also noticed their fallen comrade. Serena stops to turn her quiver over for another arrow, then waits for the next bird. It doesn't take long, more of the flock moves closer at the promising prospect for food. She finds another shadow and when she is close enough, she holds out her bait, leaps up and releases another arrow. This time, Serena sees the guards creeping toward the shore, hidden in their own shadows.

Serena smiles. Murphy is taking advantage of the opportunity. The wolves on the beach are busy scanning the breakers for the threat, whining and anxious over an enemy they cannot see.

One more bird, thinks Serena, scanning the skies. She finds her fowl, and follows under its shadow. Her third wolf falls with an arrow to the neck. Serena doesn't hide back under the surface. She floats at the top, watching the guards close in on the rest of the pack. Kai and Murphy lead the charge. Against the enemy, they are quick, strong, and are surprisingly good countering werewolf claws and teeth. Serena reminds herself this isn't the first time the guard has fought the wolves.

Her eyes flit to Ervin, who was just sent sprawling across the sand with claw marks raked across his chest.

Well, maybe his first time.

Several guards come to Ervin's rescue, spearing his attacker through with their tridents. By the time the wolf has wheezed out his last breath, Serena's feet hit the sand as she walks out of the surf, shedding the salty seawater from her scales.

Kai walks toward her, and she braces herself for a fight. His breastplate is splattered in werewolf blood. Serena follows the drops down his arm to his hand that holds the three arrows she fired, already pulled from her victim's bodies.

Her eyes shoot back to his. He stalks toward her with long strides, shoulders heaving slightly forward in coordination with the opposite leg.

"What are you doing? How did you get out?" Kai hisses, scanning the surf as if the answer lies there.

Serena narrows her eyes. "You're welcome."

"You need to go back," he grabs her at the arm. "You can't be here. If Alaric finds you—"

Twisting her arm out of Kai's grasp, she glares up at him. "Are you going to throw me in the pit yourself, this time?"

"Now? We are going to do this now?" Kai looks at her from underneath thick eyebrows.

"As you say," Serena hisses through gritted teeth.

Kai growls. "We don't have time for this."

Serena waits as Kai starts to pace the beach, looking from his guards recovering from the fight, to the shadows retreating farther into the tree line as the sun rises.

Murphy steps in front of Kai, forcing him to halt his agitated pacing. "You are right—we don't have time for this. We don't know if one of them warned others, and we'll never win a fight on this open beach. We have to draw them over to Cliff Beach where we can control their entry, and where our reinforcements wait." Murphy turns to Serena. "Besides, I have a feeling she is going to do this anyway. She is as stubborn as the king." He winks at her, then turns back to Kai. "She'll be safer with us."

"Fine," Kai sighs, turning toward Serena. He reaches up, her arrows in his hand, and Serena braces herself for his arms to envelope her in order to place the weapons in her quiver, like he did in the armory.

Instead, Kai grabs her at the shoulders and turns her. Serena almost topples over at the rough movement. He shoves the arrows in her quiver and turns her back around before she has had a chance to catch her balance.

He leans in, fiery eyes pinning her to the spot. "You stay close to me and Murphy—but I want you in the trees."

A sharp, ear-piercing howl rings through the forest, cutting straight through Serena's heated core, leaving only ice in its wake. All Undine heads turn toward the sound.

"All right," says Murphy, turning toward Serena. "We may be facing more than fur and fangs alone. The wolves are integrated into Ungainly life, more so than us, anyway, and they may have Ungainly weapons."

Kai is tightening the straps around Serena's armor. "They pack a powerful punch. And have a farther range than arrows, but they can't penetrate our incandescent scales—only their fangs are thin enough to do that."

"That's comforting," mumbles Serena. She glances from Kai, to Murphy, then to Ervin joining the group brushing sand from the scrapes across his chest.

"You got new tridents," she notices. The weapons aren't nearly as intricate as Serena's, but they look sturdy enough. She hopes they've had time to practice with them. The one dozen bodies on the beach tell her they have. Her eyes pause on Ervin.

Has Cordelia told him she's with child? Would it make him fight harder, or would he be distracted?

Serena can't think of that now. Hopefully, Cordelia knows him well enough to make the right choice between telling him or not.

Serena looks at Kai, heat from their argument dissolving as he inspects the rest of her gear for faults. Already the large, uncomfortable breastplate feels more secure. "Are we really about to do this?" she whispers to him.

He turns, squaring his body with hers, and nods. "We'll be okay. And when this is all over, you can enlighten me on how to properly court a maiden of the throne," he winks at Serena.

Serena smiles back. "Your guess is as good as mine—or better, probably."

They both turn to Murphy. He gestures to the trees. "Alright warriors of the guard, and...Serena. Let's go."

The column, spread out in one, staggered line, moves forward. Serena calls forth more of her natural armor. Midnight-blue, diamond-shaped plates crawl up as far as her neck, extending to her chin and trickling out over her cheekbones until they look like permanent splashes of water across her expression. Besides her head and the exposed parts of her face, the only unprotected spot is her toe, where wolfsbane poison has left its mark.

Serena grimaces, longing for the yellow-petal shield she is so used to hiding behind. There will be no wolfsbane in this battle, the wolves made sure of that. Her grip tightens on her trident. Forged in the spiritual fires of the armory and blended with Undine ancestors flesh and bone, the weapon is more than a sufficient replacement to the poisonous flower.

Her feet take long strides across Forest Beach and she finds herself scanning the lot of dead bodies for the crescent moon-shaped birthmark, but doesn't find one. Liam isn't here.

By the time the next breaker hits the shore, the first wave of Undine have disappeared into the trees.

Chapter Forty

Serena runs with the King's Guard. There is no more formation. Here they must stick to the shadows and avoid any altercations until they get deep enough into the forest to draw the entire pack out. There is the occasional werewolf that must be brought down, but casualties are minimal and their bodies are hauled to the trees, hopefully to remain concealed.

Serena spots a low branch. She hands Murphy her trident, and leaps, pulling herself up. Kai and Murphy pause to watch. They cannot follow her, their extra weight too much for the thinner branches to handle.

Murphy tosses her trident up to her and the trio continue to move forward. Serena glides through the trees like a soundless bird, with Murphy and Kai clinging to her shadow below. Ahead, she spots a cluster of men. Some are in Ungainly form, some in wolf form.

More groups of werewolves are spread throughout the area. They have made their own barrier. Any farther and the Undine might reach Ungainly roads and settlements. This is where they will make their stand. She makes a low click in her throat, giving warning to Murphy and Kai.

Serena leaps higher into the next tree and finds a solid crook where branch meets trunk. She removes each arrow from her quiver, laying them in a row in front of her. Up high, leaves obscure some of the view, but her skill with the bow has improved quickly—even more so than her skill with the trident.

The forest goes quiet in the cold, early hours of the morning. Huddled around fires, even the wolves settle into silence. Their backs face the threat and tired eyes stare at flames, but Serena can see ears flatten against their heads, listening. It is the calm before the storm.

Serena takes a deep breath, and lets it out slowly. She has to force her arms to relax, pushing all thoughts of the king and the prison out of her head. She thinks of Cordelia and her hymn. Serena imagines Cordelia singing not to a doll, but to an actual swaddled Undine calfling, the first in eighteen years.

To her left, the sound of a twig snapping in two breaks the silence. All heads turn toward Ervin, werewolf and Undine alike. Through the twisted branches, littered with leaves, Serena can see his eyes go wide. He probably misjudged his steps. If he hasn't self-corrected his awkward gait in the water by now, it would only be exaggerated in The Dry.

There is a brief pause and then a sudden flurry of action. Many werewolves begin their transformation, the sound of bones popping out of joints resonating throughout the forest like the echo of the snapping twig. Those already in wolf form sprint toward Ervin.

An arrow whistles from treetop to ground, burying its pointed tip deep into the wolf's brain through his ear. The lead wolf is dead before his head hits the ground. He skids to a stop at Ervin's feet.

Serena lowers her bow, nocking the next arrow.

Another wolf nudges his dead comrade with his snout. There is a whine that morphs into a growl. More wolves join in with their own growl and half the pack turns toward Serena's tree.

The enemy divides, giving Serena the chance to loose one more arrow and help Ervin. When it, too, hits its mark, she tries not to think which maiden's son it is. At the base of her tree, Kai and Murphy flourish their tridents, revealing their presence in order to force the wolf pack to split even further. Serena moves out on her limb so she can keep both guards in her view.

Closer to Ervin, she can spot two more guards jumping into the trees. They begin felling werewolves around Ervin with their arrows even before their feet hit the solidity of the branch. A growl draws her attention back to Kai. Two wolves are closing in on him. As they leap, Kai hits one square in the jaw with the stem of his trident. There is no time to defend against the other wolf and its claws dig into Kai's chest, knocking him back. They both roll—fur, scales, fur, scales—moving out of Serena's sight.

"Kai!" Breath catching in her throat, Serena follows, leaping to a lower branch. Out of the corner of her eye she can see Murphy dealing with two more himself.

Murphy can handle it, she tells herself. *He has to. Kai needs my help.*

Kai and his wolf are still rolling. Serena nocks an arrow. Behind her, Murphy throws a wolf off him, directly into the trunk of her tree. The tree shakes right as Serena looses an arrow toward Kai's wolf. Her aim is thrown off and the arrow shoots harmlessly into the ground next to the dueling pair.

Damn it, thinks Serena. She has to make every arrow count.

One more roll and Kai is on the bottom. His hand reaches out, grabbing the arrow Serena shot. The wolf rears up, gaining momentum for a thrust straight at

Kai's throat. Serena freezes, all too aware of how it feels to be pinned beneath a werewolf.

Kai jams the arrowhead straight into the side of the wolf's neck. The dog goes limp. Arms shaking, Serena jumps down from the tree. She helps pull at the beast, rolling it off Kai.

Serena glances at the dead wolf's snout—no crescent moon.

"What are you doing?" Kai asks, his eyes skipping around the forest.

"You're welcome—again," says Serena.

He shakes his head, pulling the arrow from the wolf's neck and handing it back to her. "This isn't a competition," he says.

"Right, but if it was—I'd win," Serena takes the arrow from Kai and replaces it in her quiver.

A small smile lifts the corners of his mouth. He steps toward Serena, pulling a leaf from her hair. "Just stay close, okay?"

She nods but before she can say anything a lone howl echoes through the forest. Most of the fighting stops as the wolves turn. Many of the Undine cover their ears. It is bone-rattling, reminding Serena of Murphy's signal underwater. But this one sends shivers down her spine, and she knows it is Alaric.

The howl stops and the wolves turn back to their enemy. They stand taller and move slower, with more confidence.

"What was that all about?" whispers Kai. His hand goes to Serena's arm like a leash.

"A call," says Serena, remembering Alaric's howl when she was spying on the camp, "for reinforcements."

Chapter Forty-One

"Move!" shouts Kai, pushing Serena toward Cliff Beach.

He is insistent, practically wrapping himself around her as she runs. She has just enough time to turn and shout. "Murphy!"

Murphy thrusts his trident into the chest of a wolf. He looks up and nods. Whistling, first to his left then his right, he signals the other guards to move toward the beach.

Feet pound against the ground in sync, the rhythm growing louder when Murphy joins in. They settle into a pace, Serena slightly ahead while Murphy and Kai flank her. She looks at Kai. His eyes ablaze with determination but his forehead is creased with worry. He still thinks she might give herself up.

And I will, Serena tells herself. *If we can't fight our way out of it together.*

Serena's toes sink into soft, moss-covered ground, then catch on tangled weeds. She trips, falling forward fast. Her outstretched hands catch her before her face hits rock. A whoosh of heavy air goes straight above her head. She looks up and the long hairs of a werewolf's underside brush her nose.

Murphy and Kai turn to face their own attacking wolves. The trio are surrounded by a group of five. Serena gets to her feet, grasping her trident, holding it in front of her. Glancing to her left and right, she tries to mimic the powerful, confident stance of the King's Guard. Feet wide, shoulders squared, and trident at an angle. With a strong posture, her confidence grows.

Kai and Murphy side step, shifting so they each face two wolves, leaving her with only one. Serena looks at her opponent. He is bigger than Liam in his wolf form, and his eyes keep flitting to the wolves on either side of him. He is following their lead and isn't nearly as confident.

The dance begins. Kai bends, sending one wolf over the entire group with the stem of his trident. Murphy leaps forward, clashing with his opponent in midair. When they hit the ground, they are already tangled together in a ball of scales and fur.

Serena has more time. Her wolf starts forward, as if he is about to lunge, but then pauses, circling her. She continues to wait, keeping on the balls of her feet. Out of the corner of her eye, she can see Murphy wrap his thick arms around one wolf's neck, using his trident as more leverage.

Serena's wolf uses the distraction to his advantage. He leaps toward her, claws extended. His growl seems to stick in his throat, as if he doesn't really mean it. Serena lunges, spinning just out of reach of his paw. She puts all her momentum behind her trident, flattening out the tips and slamming down on the wolf's head as they pass each other. His jaw absorbs the impact of the ground, and his body follows. Disoriented and vulnerable, he struggles to get to his feet.

Serena cannot bring herself to deliver another blow. She steps away, breathing hard, allowing the wolf the same hesitation he gave her. As she brings her trident to her side, another trident pierces through the back of her wolf's neck, pinning him to the earth.

Serena bites down on her fist to keep from screaming, or gagging, or both. She looks up into Murphy's cold eyes.

"He'd of done the same to you as soon as he had the chance," Murphy says.

Serena shakes her head. "He did have the chance."

Murphy isn't paying attention. He is already looking to the ocean. They are almost there, but the wolves are descending again. Murphy pulls an arrow from his quiver and nocks his bow.

Serena puts a hand on his arm to stop him. "You aren't calling for reinforcements are you?" Her forehead crinkles with worry. If the King's Guard can't survive this, neither can the reinforcements.

Murphy gestures to the blue ribbons hanging off the end of the arrow. "Just looking for some interference to give us an edge."

He shoots, and the arrow flies out from the forest. There is nothing for the span of a breaker, and then a different kind of sound rips through the air. Serena steps back as a fish whizzes between the pair of them. She smiles up at Murphy.

"Come on," he says.

Before they can run again, another pair of wolves move to either side of the trio. Kai and Murphy lunge forward, Serena staggers back, frightened by the Undine's ferocity. The flurry of metal, prongs, fur, and fangs gives Serena no opportunity to step in and help.

"Serena!"

She freezes, then turns toward the familiar voice.

Chapter Forty-Two

Liam is one of the few of the clan Werich in his human form. Serena does not let that fool her—he is still just as dangerous. Kai and Murphy fight for their lives, and it looks as though they are being drawn away.

Narrowing her eyes in distrust, Serena turns to Liam.

"I didn't want this," Liam says. He is breathing hard, his clothes covered in dirt. Serena scrutinizes his bruised face and bleeding lip.

"Yet you've been fighting anyway," she says.

His fists clench shut, then open again.

"Are you about to change?" Serena asks, taking a step back. She glances at Kai.

He is too far away.

"Our transformation happens whenever the Undine fear level spikes, whether there is a full moon or not. Some have better control over others—"

"Those with certain bloodlines, like you?" asks Serena.

"Yes, but the wolf is always difficult to suppress. That is why I changed whenever you almost fell off the cliff." Liam falls to his knees, hunched over, then takes a deep breath and stands again, like he is battling an inner demon.

Tightening her grip around the stem of her trident, her palms squeak against the metal. She looks around, the King's Guard is hopelessly outnumbered.

Serena shakes her head, narrowing her gaze at Liam. "Why did you burn the wolfsbane?"

"It was Alaric; I couldn't stop him." Liam runs his hand through his hair.

Serena can see his fingernails extend out into sharp points, then go back to normal.

He continues, "I wasn't supposed to be talking to you. I thought I could change things...but Alaric sees a different path for our species."

Teeth elongate past his lips and Serena remembers them practically scraping at her neck the night of the cliffs. She shivers. "I don't trust you."

"You should. I am going to fix this."

"So am I," says Serena.

Liam shakes his head. "Alaric won't leave the Undine in peace, if you surrender. Even if you don't trust me—you can't trust him."

Another wolf approaches, ears flattened back, teeth bared at Serena. Liam turns, growling at him. The wolf's ears perk, then he tucks his tail between his legs and slinks around them.

Serena watches him go, then turns back to Liam. "We were the same species, once," she says. Her voice is low, almost a whisper.

Liam takes a step closer. "Listen—"

Serena lowers her trident, pointing it directly at his chest.

His eyes go wide. "Please, I need to tell you something."

Serena glances at Kai out of the corner of her eye. He is moving closer to her now. If she lets Liam close the distance, Kai might get distracted. She can't risk that. "You can tell me from there."

He swallows. "The night of the Maiden's Massacre—you don't know everything about it."

"What don't I know?" Serena presses forward so Liam has to step back.

He grips her trident just below the crescent moon that holds the three prongs and leans in until the tips puncture his bare chest. A small trickle of blood snakes its way down his exposed abdomen. "You weren't the only Undine to survive the Maiden's Massacre." Liam lowers his voice again. "One still lives."

Serena freezes, but her hesitation only lasts a second. She grits her teeth, and pushes her trident forward. Liam gives resistance, now gripping the weapon for leverage as he loses balance.

"Where?" Serena demands. The thought of one of her people in the clutches of Alaric is more maddening than watching the wolfsbane patch burn.

Liam shakes his head.

Serena grits her teeth. Drawing a small circle with the tip of the trident, she twists it out of his grasp. She swings it wide, rotating her hips. The stem connects with his temple. He stumbles back, barely keeping his footing as he falls against a tree. He puts his hand to his head. As soon as he pushes himself away from the tree, Serena throws her trident.

The three points spin in the air, but the stem follows a straight path, parallel to the ground. The center prong stabs through Liam's shoulder, burying itself in the tree behind him. Liam is pinned. Another prong rests on top of his shoulder, and the third just outside of his bicep.

He opens his mouth, wide enough to scream, but he only manages to emit a strangled whine.

Serena stalks toward him, her stride long and quick. Her chin is tilted down, her glare so intense it could've pinned him better than the trident.

One side of her lip curls up in a snarl. "Where?"

"Serena—" Liam's mouth opens and closes, the shock of his wound cutting off his voice. "I am trying to help you!"

"Where. Is. She?" Serena asks again, each word rumbles in her throat. She grasps her trident and rotates it.

The few centimeters of give it has is enough, and Liam cries out. "Not a she!"

Serena steps away from the trident. "Who then?"

"It was me—I survived. I was one of the infants." He grunts in pain, sweat dripping down his pale face. "I am told that I had a twin," he looks at her, eyes pleading before they squint closed in agony again.

Serena's gaze drop to the crescent moon mark on the side of his face, remembering the birthmark on the king's nose. "I suppose you have an affinity with the moon, too?" she whispers.

"What?" his chest is heaving with shallow breaths.

Serena looks at him. Behind the blood, sweat, tense muscles, and deep lines in his face as he grimaces, is a touch of innocence. He doesn't know that Serena is his sister.

"Serena!"

She barely has time to register Kai's voice when she is knocked aside. She hits the ground hard, ribs slamming into a large rock.

Her breath catches in her throat and pain explodes down her side and around her back. Her gills spread open and she can feel her stomach spasm. Serena watches the wolf that slammed into her get back on his feet and she realizes she can't move her legs.

"Liam…" Serena manages to croak out, sitting up. She doesn't take her eyes off the wolf stalking toward her. She can only hope Liam is still conscious and can hear her. "I'm so sorry."

The wolf bares his teeth, lowering his head. Serena wiggles her fingers, keeping her breathing shallow to minimize the pain.

"Me, too." Liam's voice is raspy and distant.

The wolf leaps, his mouth opening. He covers the distance quickly and slams into Serena's chest, knocking her down. She feels his hot breath push against her exposed neck.

This is it, Serena thinks. *Nothing will matter after this. Not the king, not Liam, not even Kai's kisses.* She stretches her neck long, hoping it will be quick.

Before fangs tear into her, there is the sharp zing of metal against teeth.

Looking up through the spaced prongs of a trident, and long, matted hair on the wolf, Serena sees Kai. She blinks, her lips forming the words *thank you*. In the next second, another blur of fur slams into Kai, and he is gone.

Chapter Forty-Three

"Kai!" Her scream is shrill and desperate. She thrashes on the ground under the wolf pinning her down. Her muscles give in to pure exhaustion, and Serena goes limp as she stares up into wild, red eyes. The wolf grabs Kai's trident with his teeth and tosses it aside before turning back to Serena.

She can move now, but has no weapon. She hears Liam struggling against the tree, but her trident holds strong. With her arrows trapped in between the ground and her back, she is out of options. Saliva drips from the wolf's mouth, pinging as it hits her breastplate.

Serena remembers her secret weapon; the miniature arrow fastened to her front. Before the next drop of saliva falls from the wolf's fangs, she grabs the arrow. Her hand is at an awkward angle, but she can't risk losing the chance. She jams the flint directly into the wolf's throat and blood splatters her face and the ground around her.

She sits up, pushing on the wolf with one hand and pulling on her treasured last weapon with the other. She has just enough time to turn the arrow for a better grasp and thrust it out in front of her, killing another wolf that attacks. It falls to the other side of her.

Screams ricochet across the forest when one of the guards fall under a small pack of frenzied wolves. And yet, more wolves are coming.

Serena gets to her feet, walks to Liam, and wraps her hands around her trident. One hard and quick pull, and the trident slides out of Liam's shoulder. He falls to his knees, clutching the wound.

"Liam!" she shakes him. His eyes roll to the back of his head, and he slumps to the ground, unconscious.

The blood isn't seeping as bad, and his breathing is becoming steadier.

His pack will take care of him, right?

Serena turns, searching for Kai. A wolf stands over him, shaking his head violently back and forth.

"Not him!" she yells, running toward Kai and grabbing his trident left stranded in the shrubbery. She approaches the mass of fur standing over him, her eyes tearing up before she can reach him. Her system has gone into pure panic.

Straddling over the wolf, she drops Kai's trident, and grasps her own with two hands. She raises it up, then thrusts down. The center prong skips off the spine. The wolf yelps, bucking his hind legs out. Serena keeps him pinned in place and thrusts her trident down again. All three spikes spear flesh. The wolf goes still with shallow, wheezing breaths. Serena pulls her trident out, blood matting the fur around the puncture wounds. Another thrust punches through more flesh, and the wolf stops breathing.

She swings one leg off, pivots, and kicks out. The wolf falls to the side, and Kai is splayed out on the ground, blood covering his torso.

Serena kneels next to him. "Kai!"

Her hands feel useless. There is so much red, she doesn't even know where to apply pressure. Kai is gurgling, and a small stream of blood trickles out of his mouth.

"No, no." Serena shakes her head. "You said you'd wait for me. Don't go!"

He lifts up his head. "Until my last breath."

"It won't come this night, Kai Forest." Tears run down her cheeks. "It won't."

"Oh, no," Murphy says, kneeling on the other side of Kai.

Recalling a quick explanation from Murphy during a training session on colored arrows and their codes, Serena reaches into his quiver and pulls out the arrow with red ribbons attached.

"No...don't!" Murphy shouts.

She nocks, aims toward the beach, and releases the arrow.

"Shit." Murphy watches the arrow disappear out over the ocean. It's distinct buzzing sound and the red, flapping ribbons will call in reinforcements.

She kneels back down next to Kai, looking at Murphy. "I had to."

It is not so much the reinforcements that Serena longs for than it is Hailey, the healer, and her assistants.

She looks down at Kai. "He needs them."

There is another howl, spurring Serena to her feet. "Just how many reinforcements do *they* have?"

If any more waves move in, this day could very well see off the last of the Undine.

"We need to get him to the beach," Murphy says, hooking one of his arms underneath Kai.

Serena nods, doing the same on the other side.

They half-run, half-walk to Cliff Beach, dragging Kai through the forest then into the narrow passageway, hard rock scraping at both their shoulders. Serena's webbed feet finally hit sand as they emerge from the trail. She looks at the breakers. The first Undine reinforcements are also coming onto the beach. Serena searches for Hailey's blue-green scales.

All she sees are scared, wide eyes. They look to Serena and Murphy for instruction, but there is no time for orders. Right behind them, werewolves emerge from the passageway.

Serena and Murphy drop Kai. Murphy moves forward, ready to intercept as many wolves as he can. Serena stands over Kai, planting her trident into the sand, deep enough so it stands on its own. She draws from her quiver and drops two werewolves coming her way.

But more filter out of the passageway, leaping over their dead brethren. Scattering across the beach, the wolves turn their full fury on the innocent maidens.

Serena watches in horror as the first of the wolves slams into a maiden with orange scales—Sasha.

The wolf tears into her soft middle. Orange scales dot the sand around her like blood splatter. All Undine seem to pause on the beach, equally unable to process and react to the scene. Sasha's screams don't last long. They die out as a wave reaches up, lightly touching the splayed out strands of her hair. Then the tide recedes, taking her soul with it.

The wolf turns to a group of stunned maidens.

Serena is finally able to nock an arrow and take aim. Beside her, Murphy continues to ward off attack after attack, keeping the wolves at bay, away from Serena and Kai. She tries to block out the growls and grunts occurring a few feet from her. As she is about to let loose her arrow, Murphy stumbles back and crashes into Serena.

She ducks as the rest of his bulky body summersaults over her, then she stands, releasing her arrow at the attacking wolf instead. The carcass slumps to the ground at her feet.

Serena looks back at the maidens, who stare at the wolf in front of them. The creature is aiming for another maiden—Lilly, the garden apprentice.

No, Serena thinks, stepping forward side by side with Murphy, who has regained his footing. An advancing trio of wolves distract them. Out of arrows, Serena drops her bow and picks up her trident. She and Murphy stand back to back, surrounded by werewolves once again. The enemy attacks. Murphy and Serena alternate turns parrying, thrusting, ducking, and blocking fangs and claws.

Serena risks a glance at Lilly, who kicks a clump of sand at the wolf. Her webbed feet scoop up plenty of granules. The wolf backs away, pawing at his eyes. This emboldens the rest of the maidens, and they inch forward, holding up their knives.

A flash of sea-green on sand catches Serena's eye. "Hailey!" she calls, waving her arms, then pointing to Kai lying on the ground.

"Can you stand guard?" Hailey asks as soon as she reaches Kai, already pulling vials from the pouch around her waist.

Serena nods. She faces her enemy with a new vigor alongside Murphy, yet more werewolves emerge from the passageway. Their ranks are as steady and plentiful as the waves. A lump rises in Serena's throat.

We need more help.

Together, Serena and Murphy thrust their tridents into another werewolf. Serena hits the midsection, twisting her weapon and ripping at his soft belly. His insides spill out onto the sand; revenge for the Sunbeam family and their fallen painted maiden. Murphy steps hard on the wolf's limp body so they can both remove their tridents.

Behind them, Serena hears Kai cough. She turns. When he opens his eyes, they skip around—wild in panic. Finally, they rest on her. He breathes, then lays his head back down.

"We need to get you back," Hailey says.

Kai shakes his head. "No, I'm staying."

"Kai, please—return to the waves," Serena pleads through heavy breaths.

Kai pushes himself up, looking at Hailey. "Can you wrap my wounds?"

Hailey glances at Serena once, then nods at Kai. "Of course." She begins digging in her pouch again.

Serena swallows hard, turning to face Kai. "Go back. That is an order."

Kai raises one eyebrow, along with his arms so Hailey can spin gauze around his midsection. "Last time I checked, the Werewolf Liaison doesn't outrank the Second in Command."

"Maybe not," says Serena. "But the Maiden Heir to the throne does."

"Serena…" Murphy's voice is strained.

She turns to find him holding his trident parallel to the ground. Two large wolves shove their full weight against it. When Murphy lifts it up, their chests are exposed. Serena thrusts her weapon into one of them. Murphy pushes forward, able to throw them both back.

Once she steadies herself, Serena turns, facing Kai. "Like I said, this night will not take your last breath from me. Go!"

"No." Kai takes his trident from Murphy. Her eyes scrutinize two sets of puncture holes across his body. One curves over his shoulder, the other spans his chest.

"Please?" she asks, voice soft.

He takes a step closer. "Can you guarantee you will return to me?"

Serena looks at the slow trickle of blood running down her trident, then out at the battle.

"No," she says.

Kai nods. "Then I'll have to stay to make sure of it." He takes position next to Serena, nodding to Murphy on the other side of her. Behind them, Hailey ties off Kai's wraps and slips away to help another fallen Undine.

Down the beach, Lilly and five other maidens withdraw their weapons from the hide of a downed wolf.

Just as the tides begin to turn, a fresh group of wolves arrive—led by Alaric. Serena grits her teeth at the howl he emits. But Alaric's call is answered by another. It is a deep rumble, moving in from the ocean. All eyes turn toward the water, Undine and wolf alike.

King Merrick sits on top of the whale rock, summoning the water. The sea obliges, rising up at his command.

Chapter Forty-Four

The king looms above the water. His multicolored scales glisten in the sunlight, lighting up the rock and the water that surrounds it like a rainbow. The king rides the arched kaleidoscope of colors like he has done it his entire life. Undine and werewolves alike stand transfixed. The wolves are prey to the first tidal waves that wash over the beach.

When it moves out, few of the wolves manage to escape. Many are drawn into deep water, where the second wave awaits. The water turns white with a frenzied panic as Undine attempt to drown the werewolves.

What is left of the wolf pack on the beach stare out, whining. They are powerless to do anything about it. Entering the water would just create more casualties. They all look to Alaric for direction. Another tidal wave comes, and Alaric himself backs away from it.

Murphy shouts, renewing the charge against the wolves. For the first time, numbers are almost in favor of the Undine. A few more waves might cinch their victory. On cue, the king sends another one. Serena launches herself toward a wolf, wrapping her arms around his neck. The wave washes over them both. They tumble over one another, and her arms unlock in the turmoil. She is determined to hang on to him. She reaches out with her legs, squeezing again around his neck. She transforms. Scales grow over her intertwined legs, and over his neck, helping to tighten the vise grip.

Her fins flutter and she drags him out to sea in a state of half-transformation, delivering the wolf to her people. As she comes back to shore she passes Ervin doing the same to another werewolf.

The temporary reprieve from the glaring sun, and the short jaunt in her own element reenergizes Serena. She uncrosses her limbs, and her feet hit sand. She rushes up to help Murphy and Kai.

Serena picks up her trident and knocks down a wolf before he can take Kai from the side. She keeps a wary eye out for Alaric, and Liam has yet to make another appearance.

The fighting grows more desperate from both sides, and more wolves continue to emerge from the forest.

Serena looks back at the king, frowning. What else can he do? He needs to get out of there. Already, the wolves that still survive in the water are paddling toward him. Hopefully the Undine in the water will help protect him.

A sharp crack echoes down the beach. Serena looks at Kai, eyes wide.

"Gun," he says. "Ungainly weapons—not good."

She looks to where she thinks the noise came from, but Kai is pointing in the other direction, directly at Ervin.

Bent over, Ervin holds his chest, seeming almost out of breath.

Serena starts toward him, but is blocked by another group of wolves.

Where are the waves when you need them?

Between exchanging blows with the wolves, she sees Ervin. When he takes his hand away, there is no blood. There is, however, a significant dent in his brown scales. The man holding the Ungainly weapon looks confused. He looks down, fiddling with the gun, then takes aim at Ervin again.

Serena fights harder to get through the wolves. Kai attempts to help her, but his trident is too easily knocked aside and his breathing is labored.

There is another crack. Ervin's shoulder is punched back and a few of his scales fly off. He stumbles in the sand and falls to his knees. As more Ungainly wolves are drawn to the weakened prey, two are spared to restrain Ervin. They hold on tight to his arms, and step on his legs, pinning them down.

The man narrows his eyes, stepping forward and raising the gun—this time directly against Ervin's forehead.

"Ervin!" Serena screams. She kicks out, using the same tactic Lilly did in desperation.

The wolves fighting Serena, temporarily blinded by sand, duck their heads. It doesn't help. Serena lunges to the side with her trident. The golden weapon slices through falling sand. Once, then twice, she stabs straight through the wolves' chests. Kai does the same with the third, though it isn't quite as precise. He leaves the wolf only wounded, not dead.

Before the last of the grain has fallen, Serena is through the maelstrom.

Crack.

Half of Ervin's face implodes. He falls forward, limp. Serena swings her trident in a wide arc over her head, gaining momentum. Her stem smashes into the side of one man's face, his temple cracking under the blow. Another man closes his fist and punches out. She catches his arm in between the intertwining double stem of her trident. She rotates her entire weapon, forcing his body to follow his arm. As he falls, Serena retracts her weapon, grasping the stem with two hands. She thrusts down, straight into his neck, driving him the rest of the way to the ground.

A searing pain punches into her gut. She bends over, and looks up—straight into the barrel of the black, Ungainly weapon. It reminds her of the tunnel leading to the archives.

This is it, she thinks. *My path to the afterlife.* She can only hope it will be as heavenly as the archives.

Serena refuses to look away. She'll face her death head-on.

Chapter Forty-Five

Behind the barrel, Serena can see the man's knuckles go tight as he squeezes the trigger. Suddenly, the tunnel disappears as it is pushed down by a trident; Kai has caught up with Serena. The crack still comes. Only now, it is aimed at her toes.

The hit is a lucky one. It is the exact spot where wolfsbane once touched, no longer protected by her hardened scales. Her foot explodes in pain, quickly surpassing the ache in her belly. She falls to her knees, next to Ervin's body.

Over her head, she hears the whoosh of Kai's trident. It finishes the job for her, and the third man is dead.

Serena glances down, ignoring the pain in her foot. Running her palm over Ervin's outstretched hand, she shivers. His body is already growing cold.

I'm on the wrong side, she thinks. *I always swim on his left.*

She moves closer to him to kneel in the sand, facing out to the water.

Serena squeezes her eyes shut and opens her mouth, but a scream does not form. Instead, a song does. It is a low, guttural moan—a note for Ervin. She mourns the loss of her best friend, the loss of Cordelia's mate, and the loss of a father to his unborn calfling who will never know him.

Heads turn in Serena's direction.

She raises her pitch and adds a slow beat to her tempo. This note is for Sasha Sunbeam and her orange-scaled family. A maiden daughter lies dead, torn to pieces on the beach. The next note is for the rest of the carnage that greets Serena's eyes. Two more of the King's Guard also lie dead, one overwhelmed by a flurry of fang and claw, and one a victim of another Ungainly weapon. The colorful bodies of several more maidens pepper the beach. Bright yellow, coral pink, and deep rose sparkle in the sunlight. Serena sings for them, slowly standing, balancing most of her weight on her good foot.

She turns to the ocean, opening her mouth further. She sucks air in through her gills and pushes it out of her mouth. Her lips round, adding a soft whistle to her harmony. This note promises retribution. She calls to the Undine still in the ocean and heads emerge from the deep blue water, answering her call.

The wolves on the beach stop, surveying their enemy. More Undine appear—even those that weren't enlisted for the battle.

Serena turns to the king, singing louder, encouraging the water to carry her voice all the way over to him. She works her throat, introducing new chords. The multiple shades that emerge pay homage to the rainbow of colors the king emits. All of the hues of the Undine painted maidens. He is the one true representative of their community, and Serena calls to him to stop this bloodshed.

He raises his massive trident in the air, acknowledging her call. Serena allows the last notes to leave her lips, then closes her mouth.

She can see the king work to manipulate the water once again.

This is it, she thinks. *He can save us all.*

Another tidal wave does not form. Instead, the water is pulled from the beach, and stays away.

The king continues to work. Serena squints, but can't understand what he is doing.

There is a growl down the beach—Alaric. Still in wolf form, he pushes three other wolves toward the water and they break into a run.

"Look at that," says Kai. He moves to stand next to Serena, breathing hard. "They think they can walk on water now?"

Serena's eyes go wide. "Oh, no."

"What?" asks Kai.

Serena's heart skips a beat in horror. Water splits, clearing a path straight to the whale rock, and the king.

"To the King!" Serena shouts, picking up Ervin's remaining arrows and jamming them into her own quiver.

The rest of Society catches on. Heads dip back below water as Undine swim to protect their monarch. Maidens closest to him jump out of the water at the wolves, running down the path of the parting ocean. There are several misses, but they manage to bring one down. The first wolf makes it to the whale rock. The king grips his trident; he will not make it easy for them.

He waits for the wolf to scramble up the steep, wet boulder. King Merrick lunges, trident aimed out. The wolf dodges, but slips. One quick flick of his trident and the king tosses the wolf into the water. The maidens below are no longer fearful. They take the wolf by each limb, and swim in opposite directions, tearing him to pieces.

Alaric and another wolf, the largest of the pack, have reached the boulder. They leap toward the king in unison. He can't defend against them both.

Ahead, Murphy is already running. Those in the pack that still remain on the beach turn to intercept the charging Undine.

First Kai, then Serena, run to lend backup to Murphy and the other guards. In V-formation, like birds flocking to nesting grounds, the group plow their way through the werewolf obstacles. Slower with their injuries, Kai and Serena bring up the rear. Serena tucks her trident under her arm and draws an arrow.

She takes aim at the wolves who fight on the rock with the king and shoots. Her arrows hits water, a hundred feet too short. Kai tries. His lands closer, but still hits nothing but water.

They continue to run, each step sending a searing pain up Serena's leg. She leans more on her good foot, refusing to look down at the injury.

The king's movements slow, his long tail a hindrance on dry land. He can't turn and twist to fend off the attacks like he needs to.

It is like watching the king and Alaric through the shrubs all over again. Only this time, they are exchanging deadly blows instead of mere threats. She remembers something Alaric said.

Only one other sacrifice will satisfy the debt.

"No..." says Serena, lips rounded.

The king is sacrificing himself. He knows they won't win the battle, so he is taking the initiative before Serena does.

Serena runs harder, pushing Kai in front of her. He pushes those in front of him, and soon the entire formation speeds up.

It won't help, Serena tries to channel reason into the king. *He won't offer peace upon your death—he still needs a maiden.*

Serena tries her hand at another arrow. This one hits the base of the rock.

Just a little closer, she thinks, looking up at the king.

He has one wolf pinned to the rock in between the prongs of his trident. Behind him, Alaric circles.

All of Society can see it coming. There is a collective gasp. It should be enough to warn the king, but he doesn't turn. Instead, he looks up directly at Serena. He holds one hand in the air toward her—his final farewell.

Behind him, Alaric jumps, opening his mouth wide. He clamps down over the king's shoulder. His front most fangs puncture the soft spot just above the king's sternum. Serena clutches her own chest, pain ringing through her body.

She skids to a stop, pulling Ervin's last arrow from her quiver. She nocks it and takes aim. Exhaling, Serena releases her arrow between mouthfuls of air. She keeps her bow in position, watching her arrow head directly for the mark—the space between Alaric's eyes. She knows her shot is right on target even before the arrow crosses the short span of ocean to the whale rock.

Just before the arrow hits, it is caught. The king lowers his hand, squeezing. The arrow snaps in two. It clatters against the rock, sliding harmlessly into the ocean. The half-smile on Serena's face freezes.

As if given a blessing, Alaric clenches his jaw. His fangs pierce the rest of the way, just below the king's neck. King Merrick slumps, the life going from his eyes before his head hits hard rock.

Alaric shakes his head back and forth, tearing at the king. Then he stands, one paw up on his victim's dead body, and howls.

Wolves answer the howl with their own, whether they are in wolf or Ungainly form. The magic suspended, even after death, Alaric races back to shore. A small, rainbow colored piece flops outside of his mouth like a lolling tongue.

The Undine maidens watch helpless, and in shock. Their king has died, in front of all of Society. Beside Serena, one of the guardsmen bends, throwing up. Serena has no more arrows, no more energy. She watches because there isn't much more she can do.

With a sacrifice made, the wolves retreat into the woods. Serena raises her hand, returning her farewell to her father, the king.

Chapter Forty-Six

After the last of the wolves' tails disappear amidst the shadow of the trees, Undine maidens come onto shore. They help the wounded back into the water. They collect Undine arrows and the few pieces of broken bows. Colored scales and dark blood, the only evidence left behind by battle will be washed away at high tide.

Serena returns to Kai, and burgundy scales, brilliant against the pale sand catches her eye. Cordelia emerges from the water, racing toward Ervin. Before anyone can stop her, she reaches him and turns him over. She leans back, gasping at the sight of his disfigured face. She is dragged back into the water, crying and screaming as someone picks up Ervin's trident. Others wait until Cordelia has gone under, then begin the task of wrapping his body, preparing to transport him home in the most gracious way they can.

Kai moves next to Serena and they lean into each other, wrapping their arms around each other's shoulders. Serena still limps and Kai clutches his chest wound. They stumble into the waves, allowing the maidens to escort them back to their kingdom alongside the dead.

* * *

Hailey's cave is packed with the wounded. Serena and Kai receive treatment in the hallway, where Simone applies various oils and creams, wrapping injuries with deft, expert fingers. Kai doesn't let go of

Serena's hand the entire time and quite possibly, Simone is too busy to notice.

Nerin walks the halls, speaking softly to the survivors. Serena does not remember seeing her on the beach, but Nerin has to know by now what has happened.

Nerin bends next to Serena. "Are you all right?"

"I'm fine," says Serena. "But others…Sasha—" her voice chokes up. She cannot finish the sentence.

"I know," Nerin pats Serena's hand. "I know."

My own selfish pride brought her to the battle, one from which she won't return.

Serena lays her head back against hard rock. "I suppose you will want to send me back to the lower caves?" Serena is under no illusions that the punishment will be forgotten, even after the king's death.

Nerin takes a deep breath, sending a quick glance at Kai. Kai squeezes Serena's hand.

"In light of the situation, Zayla has already declared your punishment fulfilled. The king himself recorded your pardon from serving punishments for the crime in the scrolls before the battle. I will announce it as soon as Society is well enough to assemble in the Great Hall," says Nerin, standing. "But Serena," she glances at Kai and Serena's interlocked hands once again. "Please, we must maintain appearances."

Murphy passes through the hallway in front of them, frowning down at Kai. Even after all that has happened, Murphy and Serena must hold up pretenses of a couple. And they can't do that when it is Kai's hand Serena holds.

"I'm don't—" Serena says.

She is cut off by a sharp squeeze of Kai's hand. "It's okay," he says, whispering. "It can wait." He releases her and stands to head to the Great Hall, holding his side as he goes.

After each injured Undine receives treatment from a healer, they follow Kai to the Great Hall. No one can bear to return to their caves. The holes left empty by those that have passed on are too obvious. Undine trickle into the Great Hall without being summoned and stand in tight groups, lending or receiving support, both physical and emotional.

Only the few that are tending to the bodies laid out in the armory, being prepared for the fires, are not there. Serena enters the Great Hall with Kai. Mariam and Rayne spot the pair before anyone else. They rush forward, placing a gentle hand on Kai's cheek before hugging Serena. There are no words. What can be said? Nothing will make what happened better.

"Serena?" Nerin's voice is soft, but it carries throughout the cavern.

Serena looks up at the high-platform. Nerin stands next to the throne. In the king's place is a large, hardback book and a tightly-wrapped scroll, cinched closed with the king's mark.

Serena walks forward with Kai, Rayne, and Mariam close behind her. The Great Hall falls silent. The only sound is Serena's tread, her pace awkward and imbalanced because of her limp. She automatically thinks of Ervin and has to stop to take a deep breath, fighting back tears.

She feels a supportive, warm hand on the small of her back. Drawing strength from the bloom of heat, Serena walks the rest of the way to the front of the room and steps up to the mid-platform, turning to face Society.

Behind her, Nerin picks up the scroll from the throne. There is a tear of paper as she breaks the seal and unrolls the scroll. Nerin clears her throat and speaks. "Serena Moon-Shadow," Nerin glances at Serena, then back down at the scroll. "You are hereby absolved of all charges for the crime of absconding."

The formalities seem trivial after the battle, and Serena feels guilty Society has to sit through it right now.

"The king's seal and signature accompany the scroll." Nerin holds up the parchment to the council members for their verification. Each nod their agreement. "The account is settled," Nerin glances at Society. "Serena Moon-Shadow is cleared of all charges."

There is no clapping, and no cheers—just a small murmur of agreement from the crowd.

"The king ends the scroll by a passage of reference in the Ancestral Book." Nerin leans over the throne to pick up the large hardback book.

More murmurs come from Society as they look upon a book normally kept in the King's Library. Many have never even laid eyes on the restricted literature.

Nerin balances it on her forearms as she flips through the pages. "Ah, here it is," she says, glancing at Serena. "Lineage of the First Undine. The story begins 200,000 years ago with Atargatis, the Lady Goddess of the Sea."

Heads bow in reverence at the mention of the first mermaid.

"But it didn't end with the Maiden's Massacre," Nerin continues. "Nor did the royal bloodline end with tonight's battle."

As the true story of the Maiden's Massacre and Serena's birthright progresses, Serena thinks how she will have to alter it to include the fact that Liam, the king's son and Serena's twin, also survived the slaughter.

As Nerin continues to read, Serena looks over at the council. She sees friends, but she also sees corruption, greed, jealousy, and anger. To her right is the King's Guard formation. They are strong, willing, and devoted—she can see that even now. But they are too few.

Next, her eyes scan all of Society standing before her. Maidens, young and old, each painted in the bold colors of the court. They all look to Serena with open mouths, faces finally enlightened with the truth.

Like scattered ripples on the ocean's surface, the cascade of colors reminds Serena of the king's own scales. He lives and breathes right in front of her, through the shades of his people.

"The king has made a new entry within the Ancestral Book." Nerin clears her throat and reads, "I hereby decree that Serena Moon-Shadow, my one true daughter and the last surviving maiden of the first Undine bloodline, take the throne as Queen."

Undine eyes flit over from Nerin to Serena.

Serena looks out at them, blood pounding in her ears.

In the crowd, Serena sees Rayne's hands go to her mouth and a small but prideful gasp escapes her lips.

"Your majesty," Nerin speaks up, gesturing to the throne.

Serena turns and floats forward, as if caught in a current. She steps up, taking Nerin's hand for much needed support, and sits down on the large throne.

Murphy and Kai leave the line of council members and come to attention in front of Serena. Behind them, the crowd shifts as the rest of the King's Guard makes their way forward.

Once the entire guard stands in front of the crowd, Murphy bows. Kai does the same, and the rest of the guard follows.

Serena looks behind her. Nerin curtsies. Evandre, Zayla, and the rest of the council are next.

Nerin steps forward, facing out to Society. "All hail our new queen." The words ring out in the cavern.

There is an echo, and it does not belong to Nerin. It belongs to the whole of Society. "Long live the Queen."

About the Author

Terra is author of the eco-fantasy novels in the Akasha Series, 'Water', 'Air', 'Fire' and 'Earth', as well as the Painted Maidens Trilogy. Born and raised in Colorado, Terra has since lived in California, Texas, Utah, North Carolina, and Virginia. Terra has served a 5½ year enlistment in the Marine Corp, has earned her bachelor's and master's degree and presently runs the language services division of a small business.

Terra currently lives in a suburb of Washington, DC with her husband of fourteen years and three children.

Connect with Terra:

E-mail: terra.harmony11@gmail.com
Facebook: http://facebook.com/terraharmony
Blog: http://harmonylit.wordpress.com
Twitter: https://twitter.com/#!/harmonygirlit

Discover other titles by Terra:

The Akasha Series

Elemental powers in the palm of her hand, and it won't be enough to save her. When Kaitlyn Alder is involuntarily introduced to a life of magic, she becomes part of an organization hell-bent on saving the Earth. Follow the saga as one of the most terrifying men the human race has to offer stands between Kaitlyn and Earth's survival.

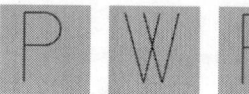

lottery that randomly selects families to conceive children as natural means hasn't existed in generations. Following her eighteenth birthday, Olivia Parker accepts her requirement to marry her childhood best friend, Joshua Warren, and is eager to start her work assignment and new life when it all comes abruptly to an end as she's arrested and thrown in prison. The only crime committed, her existence.

Olivia is unlike the rest of the world born not from "The Day of the Chosen." The truth haunts the government and puts her life in grave danger as one simple fact would destroy the perfect system. With Joshua's help, Olivia breaks free of prison and is forced on the run. Together they set out to find the promised rebel town in search of a new home and new life together. Their situation seems less than promising as they reach the town of Haven. New rules and customs must be adhered to in order to stay. Leaving would mean most certain death in the large expanse of the Gravelands. Time is running out as the government mounts an attack to destroy Olivia and bury her secret with her. Thrown into a world unlike their own, they must quickly adapt to survive.

Aberrant Excerpt:

Joshua and I both headed out of the council hall with Jacqueline leading the way. The line of young men had barely dwindled. I avoided their stare, their curiosity as they slowly proceeded forward, giving the attendant their name. I wondered how they knew about me and more importantly what they knew. Jacqueline walked a few feet ahead of us, giving us privacy to talk. I silently thanked her for still respecting us and our wishes. She was probably the only one in Haven who liked us. I didn't know if I should be relieved or angered by the recent news. I could feel the whispers, like tingles against bare skin as we walked further from council hall and rounded the corner. I was grateful to be out of sight from all those curious stares. "I guess we should consider ourselves lucky," I remarked. I didn't feel lucky. I tried to sound upbeat, but everything was quickly falling apart around us.

Joshua scoffed at the idea. "Lucky? I wouldn't go *that* far," he emphasized. "This is how it starts. Eventually, they'll make it a crime for us to see one another." He sounded disgusted.

"They sort of already are," I remarked, trying to understand the council's decision. "I think they just want to make sure I'm protected." Though I didn't quite understand how setting me up to meet multiple bachelors was any form of protection. It seemed as if they only wanted to keep Joshua away from me. The one person I could trust, implicitly. I knew the rules were different because I was different. They didn't seem particularly bothered by Joshua having a girl in his room. It didn't seem fair.

"Seems like they don't really care what we think at all," Joshua retorted as we headed into our building. "Were you okay last night? I worried when Landon escorted you out of the dormitory."

I walked slowly up the stairs, Jacqueline just a few feet ahead of us. "Aside from being locked in a room with no windows." I sighed. "At least they're giving me freedom from the tech center and a real bed. I should be grateful," I mocked. I didn't feel grateful, but I knew his mother at least tried to make it easier for me. As soon as we crested the top stair, I froze in place. The building shook with an alarming intensity as the first drone flew low overhead. The downstairs chandelier swayed and I held onto Joshua's arm and my eyes widened in terror. "What do you think is going on?" I asked watching the movement grow stronger as vibrations echoed through the dormitory. A nearby painting affixed to the wall crashed to the floor, the glass breaking. I could feel the ground quake beneath my feet as Joshua grabbed my hand, refusing to let go.

"We're being attacked." It wasn't a question. Together, we jogged briskly down the hall toward our rooms. I didn't know how much time we had. All I knew was the government was here, and they were searching for me!

What book bloggers are saying:

"If *Anthem*, "The Lottery," *The Hunger Games,* and *Divergent* had a child it would most definitely be *Aberrant*. Ruth Silver creates a world so shocking that the reader will not be able to put *Aberrant* down. The plot was exciting, fast paced, and full of new surprises." -*My Dear Bibliophage*

It was heart wrenching and fast paced, well written and yet kept me wanting more." - *By the Bookful*, Bethany

"The pacing and plot are phenomenal… at no point during this book did I feel like I could put it down. I read it in one sitting and am still crying for more! It's incredibly fast paced, and that starts from the moment you open to the first page." – *Lose Time Reading*

See more at: http://writeawaybliss.com

Reviews for 'The Rising':

"It was a great ride. I devoured every page and loved the whole thing through." *by* <u>*Ariel Avalon, Book Blogger*</u>

"This is a wonderfully unique story." and "I recommend this if you enjoy mermaids or werewolves with some great action, mystery and a bit of romance." *by* <u>*Darker Passions Book Blog*</u>

"The book is fast paced filled with action that keeps you on the edge of your seat till the very end, add in a little romance and mystery for the perfect balance. The author has written a beautiful story that sparks the imagination. I loved everything about the story and can't wait for the next one to see what happens to both Serena and Liam as their stories unfold." *by* <u>*The Reading Diaries Book Blog*</u>

32419782R00224

Made in the USA
Charleston, SC
18 August 2014